MISHOPSHNO

MISHOPSHNO

A Novel of the Early Chumash

KATY MEIGS

SHADY LANE PRESS
Ojai, California

Printed in the United States of America

First Edition, 2013

ISBN: 978-0-9893094-0-0

Shady Lane Press
E-mail: katymeigs@sbcglobal.net

Cover painting: Gordon North Grant
Back cover painting: Richard Applegate
Interior part drawings: Gordon North Grant
Book cover and interior design: Gregory Fields, fieldsgraphics.com

To the memory of my father, Stewart Meigs
and my uncle, Peveril Meigs III

The world is god

—what the old people used to
tell Fernando Librado (Kitsepawit)

CONTENTS

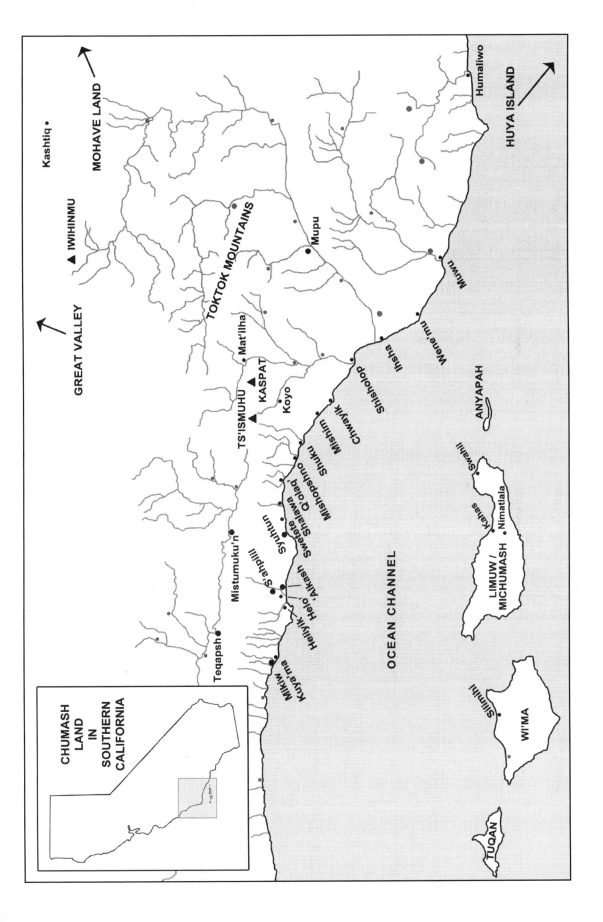

FOREWORD

The Chumash world was located in the present day coastal counties of Santa Barbara, Ventura, and San Luis Obispo in Southern California. The area has been inhabited for up to thirteen thousand years by the Chumash and their predecessors. At the time Europeans arrived the Chumash population was very dense, around twenty thousand.

The environment is rich and diverse, including the waters of the Santa Barbara Channel, the Channel Islands, coastal and interior valleys, salt marshes, creeks and small rivers, hills and mountains up to a height of nine thousand feet at Mt. Pinos (Iwihinmu, the Mountain at the Center of the World). In general summers are dry and warm, foggy along the coast, and winters are cool with regular but not heavy rain (snow on the higher mountains, other areas that never freeze). The waters of the channel can be quite calm at times, rough at others. There was formerly great richness of marine mammals, fish, and kelp life. In addition there were numerous mollusks and birds on the shore and around the marshes.

Diversity of plants and animals on the land made the Chumash self-sufficient and able to store a surplus. They did not need to plant or irrigate in order to have enough. The sea was the major hunting ground for the coastal people. Trade was continuous among Chumash within their territory, which ranged from the western Channel Islands with their fur seals and ironwood to the piñon pine-covered mountains in the east, and with other tribes on the periphery. Travel was by foot (running or trekking barefoot) or boat (planked canoe, dugout, or balsa raft) on well-established routes. Trade was conducted using shell money that was manufactured on the Channel Islands. The money supply was kept from expanding too greatly (inflating) by destroying quantities of beads during burials.

Because of the abundance of basic supplies and long-established towns and villages there was leisure, leading to the development of a complex social structure, specialized trades, refined craftsmanship, and elaborate religious cosmologies and ceremonies. The cosmos was made up of three worlds: the Sky World, including the Land of the Dead; the Earth World, including the Undersea World; and the Lower World, where monsters lived. There was memory of an ancient period when the First People, who were animals, lived and talked with one another. A feast of tales told of their doings. But history was seen as entropic, with power gradually weakening.

Social organization was anarchistic. There were people born to leadership in certain families, but others followed their "advice" based on their credibility. Social mores and taxes were upheld through tradition, pep talks, and vague threats of poisoning. Mistrust and suspicion were generally focused on people outside one's own village, however. Because the Chumash population was so dense, a shortfall in a crop one year could lead to hunger and poaching or raiding from those in a neighboring village. Yet people of several villages would frequently gather in the larger towns to celebrate important religious events that included general feasting and mingling. The purpose was to keep the three worlds in balance and the weather and food supply under control. These religious festivals involved sophisticated astronomical observations and cave painting. Members of the elite religious society ingested hallucinogenic datura root in order to have visions where they would meet "dream helpers" who would protect them and help the larger society.

All in all the Chumash were blessed with a wealthy, populous, and sophisticated social environment in a mild and beautiful physical setting.

INTRODUCTION

Although all the characters and incidents in the ethnographic novel
Mishopshno are imagined, there once was a real Chumash village of
Mishopshno (pop. ca. 300) in what is now southern Santa Barbara County
on California's South Coast. Syuhtun (pop. ca. 600), the biggest town where
they spoke the same language as they did in Mishopshno, is nowadays an
archeological site in the city of Santa Barbara.

The story takes place sometime before 1492. Europeans do not figure in it.
The action of the narrative begins on the winter solstice, the beginning of the
Chumash year. It covers a year in the life of villagers, mostly members of the
one-quarter of the population who were of the class of artisan professionals,
administrative leaders, and members of the religious organization known
as antap. It is not my desire to be elitist, but because of their status these
people had more interesting, if not more important, lives than most.

I was born and raised—and spent much of my adult life—in the
Carpinteria Valley, the location of Mishopshno's village and gathering
camps. The early Chumash are known as hunters and gatherers. However,
they did live in settled villages and migrated seasonally to established
campgrounds in the hills, much as nineteenth-century Carpinterians did.
Food was abundant so there was no necessity to be enslaved to the work of
planting and cultivating crops. In some ways life was edenic: one could pluck
or catch one's dinner and there was no need for laws or jails. In other ways
life was very rough: a broken limb meant probable death, teeth wore down
and could not be repaired, a small cut could lead to fatal tetanus, hence the
ever present possibility of "poisoning." And there were many dangerous
creatures, including grizzly bears, mountain lions, and rattlesnakes, not to
mention supernatural beings.

Despite the difference in way of life between the fifteenth and twentieth
centuries, growing up in the hills and on the beaches of Carpinteria, I felt the

presence and possible histories of forerunners. Their material evidence was everywhere I walked on trails and in fields: arrowheads, grinding bowls, pestles. The most desirable neighborhood of the town of Carpinteria was known as Concha Loma—shell hill. It was the exact site of the village of Mishopshno and achieved its height from a buildup of shell garbage residue over the millennia. The area now preserved as the Carpinteria Bluffs was a nearby hunting and gathering field for the village.

As a child I sometimes played "living off the land" with my country friends. I wondered how it was really done in former days. At last, in 1980, when I was a new mother, I made time to creatively reimagine that timeless time before "intruders" changed the traditional ways forever.

At first it seemed all I would need to do was review archeological reports and the historical accounts of early travelers to the area and then combine this limited information with my own experience and imaginings. It soon became apparent that there was a wealth of ethnographic information, however—most particularly that gathered by the tireless linguist John Peabody Harrington (graduate of Santa Barbara High School and Stanford University) and his Chumash consultants, most prominently Fernando Librado, Kitsepawat, philosopher and raconteur. This material was in the process of being digested and published by contemporary anthropologists and linguists when I began my own research. There was, however, no general ethnology of the Chumash. I made it my goal to create a fictionalized ethnology.

With that in mind I read everything I could find in Eugene Anderson's *Chumash Bibliography* (Ballena Press, 1978) and as well began keeping a daily journal of weather, flora and fauna, celestial events, and my own trips to the channel islands and backcountry as well as experiments in preparing acorns, venison, and other Chumash foods, that is, immersing myself in the life of the land over a period of several years.

After a few years of this work, I shyly went to the Santa Barbara Museum of Natural History and introduced myself, finding a warm and understanding welcome from Travis Hudson and Jan Timbrook in the Anthropology Department. Thus began a series of exciting and rewarding conversations with modern day anthropologists, archeologists, and linguists, most extensively with Travis Hudson, Richard Applegate, and Campbell Grant. Some of their work had been recently published and some was in progress, and I sat entranced for long hours in the Anthro office and the museum library reading unpublished manuscripts.

I finally wrote *Mishopshno* from 1983 to 1985. It could not compete with the trilling exploits of Aztecs and Neanderthal cave clans however, and it remained in manuscript form, occasionally read by an interested friend. In 2012, after several people expressed interest in learning more about daily life of the early Chumash, I decided to publish the book myself. I have copy-edited it and made one important change in accordance with new evidence brought to light by Santa Barbara Museum of Natural History anthropology curator John Johnson: the Chumash were matrilocal and matrilineal. Other than that the story is as I originally wrote it.

I beg the understanding forgiveness of Chumash people and linguists for my having eliminated markings for glottal stops and other diacritical symbols in the text. This is for ease of visual reading. I have used "Barbareño" words (the language spoken in Mishopshno) as much as possible. At times when I could not find the word I substituted a Ventureño word. For example, the names of the months used as chapter titles are in Ventureño.

I wish to thank the many people who helped me in the re-creation of Mishopshno village. Naturally, they are not responsible for errors of fact or interpretation. Sadly, too many of the people who were most helpful in the 1980s when I wrote the book are no longer living. I include them here along with the currently living.

Campbell Grant, friend, neighbor, scholar, and artist gave me my first inkling that something was going on back in the old, old days. His conversation and careful reading are much appreciated. Travis Hudson, Curator of Anthropology at the Santa Barbara Museum of Natural History, was very generous with his time, ideas, and then-unpublished volumes of *Chumash Material Culture*. He inspired me to imagine, to work hard, and to persevere. Jan Timbrook, Associate Curator, shared valuable information, especially concerning native flora. Linguist Richard Applegate patiently responded to persistent queries on all aspects of Chumash culture and shared his tapes and unpublished manuscripts. He has generously allowed me to use his painting of the Chumash cosmos on the back cover. Kenneth W. Whistler kindly allowed me to use his unpublished *Interim Barbareño Dictionary* and answered numerous linguistic questions. John Johnson took time to read the manuscript and made valuable contributions. Delee Marshall of the Ventura County Historical Museum shared her knowledge of basketry. I am deeply grateful to those who read and commented on the manuscript over the years, both those mentioned above and, in addition, especially Roxanne Grant Lapidus, Gerald Rouff, Patrick Finnerty, Ranell Hansen, Katy Peake, David Allen, and Arturo Tello, and members of my family.

I am indebted to Clifton Smith and Shirley Morrison, librarians at the Santa Barbara Museum of Natural History, for assistance in locating manuscripts; to the presidents of the Santa Barbara Writers' Consortium for encouragement; to the curators and docents of the Carpinteria Valley Historical Society; to Joan and Tony Priolo; and to Gayle Clay.

I benefited greatly from the encouragement, close reading, and suggestions of John Raymond. Roxie Grant Lapidus provided skilled copy-editing and proofreading. I'm grateful to Gordon Grant for his original illustrations and beautiful cover. I thank Gregory Fields for his tasteful design work.

I particularly want to thank my family for their support: Dorothy N. Meigs, David Meigs, Gaia Meigs-Friend, and above all Anthony Friend, who steadfastly encouraged me and made himself useful in every phase of this work.

Carpinteria, California, 1980-85
Ojai, California, 2013

PART I

CHAPTER I

MONTH WHEN THE SUN'S BRILLIANCE BEGINS
hesiq momoy an hushunuma kakunupmawa

It happened one time that the people of Mishopshno were leaving their village and heading northwest to the big town to join the celebration of Sun's return. As the people traveled, he, too, ran his daily circuit. But his power was weak, and his torch drooped over the ocean channel. Human beings had to move swiftly against the darkness.

Families of ducks and flocks of geese flew up out of the tall grasses of the salty Mishopshno lagoon when the people of the twelve families passed by, following the trail that skirted its long fringe.

Aleqwel, observing the flight of the birds and noting the heavy brown heads on the cattails under which the birds had been sleeping, thought to himself, "How good life is in itself. Even in winter, in the weak time of Sun and Earth, of Grandfather Kakunupmawa and Grandmother Shup, there is always something left to nourish the people." But thinking of the starchy cattail roots and the fat-dripping flesh of roast goose made his stomach grumble. Like others, he had been eating sparingly for several months. No one knew yet what crops the new year would bring. His belly looked forward to the coming feast at Syuhtun.

Aleqwel thought about the year that was ending. It had been a good year for the village, a year with rain. Some years within old people's memory were dry and fruitless. They belonged to the Sun. The people had been forced to scrounge like locusts on every blade of grass, every fowl, every shore creature, even on locusts. Even so, many died. That's how it was with the hand game. The balance was always kept. Some years the team of the people of the Earth Team—led by Thunder, Fog, and Sky Coyote—won

11

and there would be big crops. Other years the Sun Team—headed by Sky Eagle—would win the gambling match, and then times would be harsh. Corpses would litter Shup's surface and Kakunupmawa would run round and round collecting his prize: dinners of human flesh.

Aleqwel did not object to the pattern. Balance was the natural order. Not until the Winter Solstice Festival would he learn the results of this year's gambling, of the weather and crops to come. Just because the people's team had won two years in a row did not mean it was going to lose now. He had done the part required of human beings. He had played hand game all year long, gambling whenever he could. He fought hard for the Earth Team. It was enough.

The chiefs, who were the highest spiritual doctors—the wot, the paqwot, and the other powerful achanas—would determine the victor of the cosmic guessing game. They could not change the outcome, but they would make adjustments. He might wonder how they did it, but he would surely never know.

Even though it had been a good year for Mishopshno and the Earth Team overall, the year had gone badly for him. His storehouse was poorly stocked. Watching the black and white geese rise and fly south reminded Aleqwel that he did have some capabilities, however. Through the meager winter he had hunted geese and ducks and other fowl. The roasts had fed the hunger of his grandmother, his mother and her sister, and his own sister and little brother—the family of the late paint maker—through the cold short days of the officially favorable year.

Aleqwel tried to concentrate on his successes. He saw no use in doing otherwise. But the memories were beginning to return. They always returned. There was the funeral. Even with wealthy relatives, even with his mother's income as a curing doctor, the funeral expenses had strained the family. He thought of the exorbitant cost of the redwood grave marker.

Even now, many months later, Aleqwel could not see a way to pull them out of encroaching poverty. His late father had been a master craftsman. His skill as a paint maker far exceeded his own. He had had connections, contacts, and could turn out quality products rapidly. He had also been a good deer hunter. He had not been easily distracted like his elder son.

Aleqwel had often thought, "If only I could find a rich husband for my sister. She is a good enhweq: home-centered, hard working. I suppose she is attractive…" He looked ahead at his sister as she walked silently, meekly. Her basket hat was bent against the weight of the carrying strap, which supported the net holding the heavy burden basket. Ponoya had worked so hard these months making extra baskets, hoping to sell them at the Winter Solstice Festival. She must be tired. Too tired to think of marriage.

Aleqwel thought, "She is young," as he watched her silent steps rearranging the dust in the path before him. Was she too young to marry? He was older by several years, but he could not conceive of marrying. He scarcely dared to look at women. But then he was a man and men ripened in a later season.

Something about this explanation did not convince him. It was his friend, Alow, the fisherman. Alow who had sped ahead to Syuhtun in his father's swift canoe. Alow was of his own age group. They had drunk momoy, tea made from the datura root, the same winter. Yet Alow was notorious for looking at women—and doing more than looking. Aleqwel sometimes felt his friend's enthusiasm was excessive.

Ponoya's elder brother glanced at her ragged, cropped hair. Its shining darkness barely touched her shoulders. He recalled how long and thick and glossy her hair had once been—before the mourning period. Would any suitor find her attractive now? If the Mourning Ceremony for all those who had died that year in Mishopshno had not fallen only a few months after their late father's death, she—and he and all of the family—would still be blackening their faces and staying clear of any thought of marriage. Aleqwel began to think of his father. He found it difficult to remember to append "late" or "former" to his father's name, for in thought as much as in speech, it was dangerous to name a deceased person, now a ghost. It could do as much damage as calling out a living person's true name, although with different results. He returned to his thought: if the former paint maker had been killed just a few months later, the family's mourning might have lasted nearly a year, until the ceremony was held. But if it had been just a few months later, the bears would have been hibernating and the former person would still be alive.

The line of travelers came at last to the end of the rushy banks of the great dark lagoon and headed north across a sooty plain. Here and there enduring oaks spread their evergreen boughs over the field. Their fire-blackened trunks blended with the color of charred soil. There were few green shoots in the fields, for, as yet, there had been little rain.

It is better, thought Aleqwel, to travel when there are green sprouts and to feel the coming life in them. There is little pleasure in walking across barren land. Yet he, like most who followed the northward path to Syuhtun, knew patience. The rainy season had scarcely begun. There was still time, enough time. Didn't his grandmother, his Nene, always say, "Late rain means more seeds"? Nevertheless, doubts would arise among the people. It was good to have spiritual doctors, achanas, to take care of it.

The travelers, their food and bedding on their backs, kept up a good pace while trying to be considerate of both young and old. At last they came to a medium-sized village on the ocean bluffs. A creek known to be bitter ran through it. The rush-thatched dome houses were little different from theirs at home, at Mishopshno. The village resembled Mishopshno in its size and situation. It, too, was partly deserted. Only the very young and old, the ill and the poor remained. The others had already departed by boat or foot for the Festival of Kakunupmawa at Syuhtun.

Aleqwel found it comforting to be near the yellow houses and blue smoke of settlement. In such places, villages where achanas worked, he could sense man's power at its strongest. On the trail, in the woods and hills, where he sometimes liked to wander, there were no true doctors to keep order. Out there was wildness, uncontrol. Dangerous creatures roamed abroad, ferocious killers like Grizzly Bear and insidious stalkers like Rattlesnake. There were power-mad doctors who had chosen, or been driven, to live apart from society. In the wild such outcasts played with their charms and their poison and their were-beast and were-people creations. And then there were the nunashish, monsters from the Lower World: the yowoyow, who snatches children and throws them in his basket of boiling tar; the giant haphap, who inhales as food everything in his path; the holhol, a condor-like witch of a bird who devours a person's insides. Aleqwel could not name them all. How would he, a craftsman, a novice among the initiates and not a doctor, possibly remember how to behave if he encountered one of these monsters? Instinctively, he felt for his atishwin, the talisman given by his dream helper, tied round his neck. Whenever he went out of the village he could do little but rely on his dream helper, Lizard. So far he had protected him.

The pilgrims rested there, at Qoloq village, as Sun rested in the hole of the sand dollar. Qoloq was a friendly ally just then. They squatted on their heels near the trail and poured water from tar-lined baskets into their drinking cups. They ate what they had brought and what they were offered.

Aleqwel and his sister and their mother's younger sister sat together and shared a cake of cold acorn mush. They chatted quietly. They did not have a lot to say; it was a somber time of year. Like the others they were anxious for Sun to return, for rain to fall.

Though the sky shone blue overhead, Sun's rays fell thin and cold. Winter life was diminished and lean. And for Aleqwel, Ponoya, and their little brother, Anakawin, and Aunt Kanit and Anihwoy there was an added loss, the loss of the former paint maker. They had no uncle to take them on, other than their great-uncle. They had spent that winter working hard, harder than ever before.

Most of the travelers, subdued as they were, sounded festive and animated in their conversation. Aleqwel could hear them talking about food, and dances and distant relatives and suitors whom they hoped to see at Syuhtun. Such talk was an antidote—like medicinal tobacco or cure-root—to the gloom of the season and the uncertain spring ahead.

Ponoya talked to her brother modestly. Her tone was so empty it made him want to cry. How he hated that bear! That gross, mindless death dealer had caused this change in his once-lively sister. Whenever he thought of the bear he longed to scream and throw dirt into the sky. He felt as he had on the first day, that day in summer at the gathering camp. He had flailed then and raged as was proper. It had not satisfied his grief. He had thought of other actions he could take, but he was weak. Even with his spirit helper, his atishwin, he was weak compared to the bear. It angered Aleqwel further to face this weakness—and it frightened him. The family would still have to go to the hills to gather seeds and fruit.

Ponoya interrupted his thoughts. "Brother, you will carry the shrine pole into Syuhtun this year. It heartens me when I think of you painting it. In the year to come, when I see it standing atop our hill, whenever I pass by or come to it with an offering or request, I will be reminded not only of our peoples' strength but of our family, our Coyote Family's courage and endurance."

Her words gave him energy. Perhaps his sister was not dispirited, only tired. "Yes, sister," he replied, "it is an honor to attend the shrine pole, but there are many members of the antap. Sometimes you talk as if I made the feathered pole all on my own. I am only a novice."

"You were an apprentice paint maker last year, too," she reminded him. "And now you are a guildsman."

Ponoya succeeded in lifting her brother's spirits. Despite their recent loss and diminished wealth, their leader, the wot, had selected Aleqwel to work on the sacred object. To assist in such a project, to use his new trade, to make a contribution. Aleqwel sat back on his heels.

Shy Aunt Kanit was just opening her mouth to speak when two boys came running up. One was saying—too loudly—"Older brother, older brother, aunt, older sister!"

"What is it you want, nephew?" Kanit replied. "What are you doing? Have you been staying out of trouble?"

Aleqwel and Ponoya's younger brother stopped shouting and glowered sullenly at his aunt as if to say, "You know I never get into trouble."

"Do you want some food, little one?" asked Ponoya kindly. "Has our mother given you any? We have plenty."

"Sure, sure," said her little brother. He took a big piece of mush and gobbled it up in two bites. "I already ate with my cousin. Isn't there more ilepesh or hutash?" he asked. "I'm tired of acorns."

For a moment, Aleqwel felt like growling at his greedy little brother for asking for more valuable golden chia or redmaids seed cakes. But he knew how children were. They still needed lots of instruction. They could not help acting as they did any more than he could help make the rain. He said, "What have you been up to?"

"We are scouts," replied Anakawin, proudly. "We are finding the trail. Some places it is overgrown and rocky. We are clearing it away."

The route they traveled was a major trail, unlikely to be overgrown, but Aleqwel said, "That is useful work."

The boy, encouraged, continued, "We go up ahead. We look north and south trying to find the path and we tell the leaders where it is. We track, too."

"Run up ahead then and show us the way," said Aleqwel. "We don't want to lose the path."

But Aunt Kanit warned, "Be careful! Don't go too far! Keep clear of the tracks of dangerous animals!"

The two boys listened politely to the advice from their elders and ran off again—to follow or to ignore it.

The elder three, seeing the movement of Sun and the preparations of others around them, rose and readjusted their baskets in their carrying nets. They set the carrying straps against brow or basket hat and leaned forward. A thin white cloud like a sea monster swam in front of Sun. Slowly, slowly the thin line of travelers began to move westward.

Beyond the village of Qoloq, where they had rested, the way unfolded as before. There were fields of black stubble where the people had burned. There were scattered green oaks. To their north deep blue mountains ascended jaggedly into the sky. To their south the gray-blue ocean channel rippled in thin sunlight. The people's course went straight, up the broad coastal valley.

After a while, the people began to climb a large hill. The grassy fields gave way to oak forest untouched by deliberate fire.

Here, on the hillside, darkness enclosed them. A green-leafed canopy shut them apart from the sky. The gray oaks twisted. Their gnarled old limbs turned so that the world around Aleqwel seemed to be moving. It was changing, constantly changing, and charged with living beings. Everything wound and curved, and what thin light found its way into the forest was as broken as the sparks that dance on the surface of the ocean.

But, while the high-roofed grove was sinuous and confusing, it was also roomy. There was space along with the shattered light. There was space for many kinds of beings to move and to breathe.

Gray sandstone boulders lay scattered here and there beside the trail. Their curved surfaces were pocked green, red, and yellow with lichens that sometimes looked like barnacle scars on whales' backs. The scent of bay filled the close air. Bracken and berries and poison oak tangled underfoot. Owls slept in the trees. If it hadn't been for the large number of people traveling together through the wood, it might have been a frightening place.

The party was nearing the top of the hill. It was a shrine hill for the villagers on the farther side, and, for canoemen at sea, a landmark. Aleqwel was thinking of the red shrine pole atop the hill when he felt something grip him tightly around the legs.

"Anakawin," was all he could say, "Little Coyote!" He prayed that his spirit helper had not been frightened away by the shock of the attack on his knees.

"Older brother! Older brother!" cried Anakawin frantically, clinging like a mussel to a rock.

"What is it?" Aleqwel finally cried.

Anakawin stuttered. The words came out thickly, like Coyote words. "A bear! There's a bear! Right up ahead. Right there. I tracked him. I came close." Anakawin shook. "This close." He showed how close. "I smelled him."

Aleqwel could see that his younger brother had been attacked by fear. He had seen something. But a grizzly bear? "Little brother," he said with the artificial calm of elders around frightened children, "I know you have seen something. But how can it be a bear? It is cold, the heart of winter. All the bears are sleeping in the mountains." Anakawin had been the one to discover their late father's remains. No wonder the boy twitched at every strange shape in the forest.

"I wasn't afraid," cried Anakawin, trembling. "You know I wasn't, older brother. But I wanted to kill him and I could not. What do I have? Only a child's bow. I have no atishwin," he sobbed in despair.

"Don't worry, little brother. Even a man's bow would be little use against him. As for a protector, surely you have one or more, even if you haven't dreamed them yet. You must have or you wouldn't still be alive after all the trouble you get into. But the bear, are you sure it was a bear?"

Anakawin was insistent. "It was sort of a strange bear, though."

"How so?" Aleqwel knew his brother had never come near a grizzly bear. The closest he had been was when he had discovered their late father's entrails strung out atop sage and sumac in the foothills.

"It was a strange bear because it didn't eat me. It didn't charge at me. It looked more like a hunter stalking. It crept close, then fell back, then followed, then waited behind trees. I was stalking him, too."

"Keti!" exclaimed Aleqwel. "Why?"

But his brother couldn't explain why he had done it. "When I came right up to him"—the boy was beginning to catch his breath, even to enjoy the story—"it was near a big rock, a slab. He was a bear, a real bear, but he just stood there. And then he ran away."

Real grizzlies did not behave like that, stalking and running away. They attacked, as Anakawin said. A lesser bear might behave that way. But in winter? Anakawin was too upset to be questioned further. "Show me where it happened," said Aleqwel.

When they got to the place near the top of the hill, ahead of the line of travelers, Anakawin pointed out the spot where he had first seen the bear hiding.

"Shadows," whispered Aleqwel to Ponoya reassuringly when they returned.

"It might have been some other kind of nunashish," she whispered back, not entirely reassured. "A were-beast."

They said nothing to Anakawin. There were no tracks. At the dark boulder pile where their brother said he had stood in the breath of the bear, they looked and saw lichen-splattered rocks mounded up in shadowed heaps. The rocks had shapes like turtles and mud hens, stinkbugs and badgers. They had forms like First People.

"Little brother, don't be afraid," said Ponoya gently. "I could see a bear here myself. But it can't be. Our older brother is right. They are sleeping now. Perhaps you saw something else."

"No! No! No!" cried Anakawin, offended that his sister thought him afraid. "Se! It was big and brown and had an ugly face like a sycamore eating dish." But the boy was beginning to grow calmer with his family beside him. Whatever he had seen was clearly gone now.

Suddenly, the boy turned around and saw that they were near the old shrine pole. They were halfway to Syuhtun. His young mind began to race ahead to their goal. He thought of the food and games, the opportunities to explore. He forgot to be angry and afraid. "Have you seen mother?" he asked, changing his mood abruptly as children do. "Why don't we go down and find her? Maybe she would like our company."

The great achanas of Kakunupmawa—the paqwot and the wots of the twelve villages, along with their assistants, astronomers, and weather experts—convened at Syuhtun to settle the year's debts, to resolve disputes that had arisen between individuals, and to penalize transgressors against the community. After some discussion, they also agreed on the festival tax: how much seeds and money each village would be expected to contribute to the festival organizers. Then they withdrew from the big town and went up into the hills. There, they awaited and assisted the return of Sun.

When the celebrants from Mishopshno arrived at Syuhtun in the evening they found the highest antap officers, the elite spiritual leaders, already departed and the less-exalted initiates working hard, preparing the ceremonial ground.

Next day, the antap workers were still building the structures that would be used in the Solstice Ceremony. Some were helping build the walls of the big enclosure. Others were thatching the great house that would be the dwelling of the paqwot on his return. On the mysterious night of solar renewal the Sun's highest officer—the paqwot—would receive offerings from each celebrant, and each would have the opportunity to dance his own personal dance. The special house they were building was already the largest house in the big town. Here, by the sacred ground, the antap saw to its final thatching.

Women of antap, wives of the paqwot, wives of the village wots, and women doctors or apprentices or venerable heads of great families assembled from every village of the land near Syuhtun. They came from Heliyik on the western shore of the Great Salt Lagoon and as far to the southeast as the salt marsh at Mishopshno. They were busy organizing, preparing, and cooking food for the feast that would follow the ceremony.

Aleqwel, the elder son of the late paint maker of Mishopshno, enjoyed watching his mother working with the other women. She was still strong, stronger even than a young woman. Though most antap women were wealthy and could afford to spend much of their time in the fine art of basket making, they worked hard whenever there was a festival. Aleqwel saw them as the foundation, like the foundation coil of a basket, which gave form and strength to the edifice of the antap society.

Though her face and breast were painted as red as the other women's, the widow Anihwoy stood out from most of the others because of her cropped hair. Aleqwel watched her as she carried heavy baskets of seeds and water, working just as women usually do. He admired her. Her mourning must still have been living in her, but she did not cry out. She worked for the people.

As he ground red stones—the color of blood and of joy—into fine powder, as he mixed the powder and diluted it into a stain for the fence posts of the ceremonial ground, Aleqwel took comfort in his mother's presence. His mother was a daughter of the powerful Coyote Family of Mishopshno. Her uncle was the alchuklash. And his father's family was from the Owl Family of Heliyik north of Shuytun. If the power of their family had declined with the death of the paint maker, it had not yet been extinguished.

Working in the sacred enclosure near his mother he felt surprisingly refreshed by hearing the archaic sounds of the antap language. He laughed when he heard the peculiar insults that the initiates hurled at one another in a way that defied the decorum of the outside world.

"Hey you, Turdeater! Get your hairy balls over here!" a house builder called to a venerable old carpenter, both initiates.

Aleqwel in the past had not felt comfortable with the insiders and their esoteric lore. It was his sister, he believed, who had inherited a doctor's abilities. She should have been initiated. But the family had only been able to afford the joining fee for one child, and he was the eldest. It was his mother who had paid. As a boy he had studied with his antap teachers, but it was the craftsman's world that brought him most pleasure. For the first time, this winter, in the sacred place under construction, with cane mats being rolled out into walls and feather banners set to fly in the wind, with the coarse calls of the thatchers and the "pepepepe" of the chattering women, he felt at home. For once, the sensation of being in Coyote's world—that strange world that stands on its head, where truth, amazingly, overwhelms etiquette—gave him comfort and security. In this place he could exercise the paint-making trade he was coming to know, which he had inherited. At the same time he could serve the sacred community. It did not matter that he had never mastered the ancient grammar.

Reflecting on his failure at words and his lack of knowledge of the pathways of the lesser Sky People sent Aleqwel's mind roaming to the doctors and the hills. The spiritual doctors, the achanas, went to the sacred caves, the forbidden places. He guessed that. From there, they would travel to the Sky World. They would learn what others could not learn. They would uncover the results of the celestial hand game. The achanas had ways of knowing what would come to the people. They could see whether the Earth Team of moisture or the Sun Team of drought was the victor. Not only did they know, but they could fix things a bit, save a few lives, maybe rescue a whole crop. Even though he had been trained in antap lore, in languages and ritual and the secret meaning of history, even though he had drunk momoy tea and met Lizard, his dream helper, Aleqwel had no idea how the achanas did these things. It was a mystery still.

He looked into the well of paint in the stone mortar in front of him and at the red fence growing around the sacred enclosure. He gazed down at the new village shrine pole by his side with its vermillion trunk, its shiny black feathers of condor and crow, its white shell beads and seagull down. He could not help but think of all the paint the achanas took with them when they went to the hills. He suspected that the doctors re-created the First People, there in the caves. With his own pigments, he believed, they conjured the Sky People and insects and dangerous beasts. He had never been inside one of their caves, but he had heard stories. Paint makers, when they meet in their brotherhood, talk just as canoemen or basket makers do.

As he crouched there stirring wild cucumber seed oil into his red powder, slapping the sides of the mortar with his fiber brush, Aleqwel envisioned what it would be like to create animals, people, gods. What would it be like to stir things to life? To press his hand—like Lizard had at the beginning of human life—on a rock and see it become man's? The things he had sometimes made with his brush—a formless shape on a beach stone, a copy of a basket pattern or a body design he had seen in a foreign village— had filled him with excitement. But they had never evoked a living being. Suppose he were to paint his atishwin, the way people danced the dances their atishwin taught them....

Just then, he heard noisy shouts coming from the area near the north exit of the sacred ground. The shouted words, though in the antap tongue, had a different quality than the scurrilous insults of the workers. Aleqwel looked up from his red paint and his dreams.

A strange man came loping into the sacred area under construction. He was small and spindly, but his voice was a deep growl and something about him evoked fear.

The insults he was calling to the antap were no Coyote insults. They had no truth in them. They were accusations, threats. "Poacher!" he barked. "Thief!" "Trespasser!" Each member of the sacred circle was thrown his or her own epithet as the intruder gesticulated and dashed wildly around.

He came close to Aleqwel, who was still dizzy with his artistic imaginings. The man was dressed in bearskin like a wot. His eyes were dark and round. Saliva dribbled from one side of his mouth. "Who is this man?" Aleqwel shuddered inside himself. "He speaks the antap tongue, but he is not one of us. He looks crazy, kilamu. He carries no weapon, though. So why should I be afraid?" But he was.

The little man with wide eyes and bad words halted in front of Aleqwel, who remained frozen on his heels beside his paints and mortar.

"Paint maker!" the foreigner roared at him as if uttering the worst insult in all the Earth World.

Aleqwel forced himself to keep the man's stare. He felt sick in his stomach. He said nothing.

The intruder's eyes could not hold. They roved around the young man as if searching for a lost treasure. They pounced, at last, on the shrine pole beside its creator and protector. He began heaping piles of loud insults on Aleqwel, mounding them up like coyote droppings, cursing and calling him "Poacher!" "Trespasser!" "Thief!" He knew the private names, the secret true names even, of all of Aleqwel's dead relatives. The last thing Aleqwel remembered hearing was the intruder calling out his own father's secret name as he lunged toward the shrine pole, grabbing for its feathers. The young man, caught between wanting to hide and to strike out, found himself throwing his body in front of the sacred object. A rage thick as congealing tar blurred his awareness of the rest of the world.

In a flash the dance manager appeared. The intruder, still uttering curses, was firmly escorted out of the ceremony ground. The dance manager addressed the uninvited visitor quietly, but with disdain, "Who do you think you are, the master of ceremonies? The paqwot? Ha. Ha. Get out of here, you little squirt! You stinkbug! You are not one of us. Go back to your own people, if you have any. This is not your place." And in less time than it takes to break a flea's back the intruder was ejected from the sacred ring and escorted out of town.

A shudder of revulsion like a subtle earth tremor ran through the antap. Prayers were said to restore the sanctity of the place. Spring water mixed with coastal sagebrush was sprinkled in all quarters. A doctor blew purifying tobacco smoke through a dark green tube to the four winds. Only when they were satisfied that all was clean again did the people go back to work. Everything continued as it had before.

The dance manager returned to Aleqwel. The shrine pole lay serenely intact on its matted resting place. There had been no damage done. Aleqwel could hardly speak: "Who was that wokoch, that intruder. Why did he call me a thief?"

The dance manager was still trembling, "I've heard of him. He has some reputation. He's an antap, alright, but from another country. From Shuku village, I believe. But they say he is unpopular and lives apart, stirs up trouble. The words he shouts are bad, but try to have courage. He is gone now."

Shuku! It was difficult for Aleqwel to have courage when his father's ghost had just been summoned by a hostile stranger. He had never before experienced such a sinister insult. The reason was beyond imagining. Yet the secret name had been spoken and the balance of the worlds had been skewed. Nothing for him could continue as before. Shuku!

Aleqwel looked over at his mother. The other women had resumed their work after the purification. But Anihwoy stood as she had been standing when the intruder first entered the arena. She clasped a large basket of acorns tightly in front of her as if it were a young child squirming to get down.

"Mother!" he cried.

And suddenly seeing where she was, the woman set the basket down on the firm earth and ran to her son.

"Shuku!" he cried. "The wokoch comes from Shuku. And he has called up father's ghost."

"I know," she said. "I know." Though immobilized, she had not been deaf.

Shuku village was Mishopshno's southern neighbor and sometime enemy. The ghost of a dead soul brought death wherever it visited.

Alow, the young fisherman from Mishopshno, was enjoying his first day at the Festival of Kakunupmawa. He had heard nothing of the disruption at the ceremonial grounds for he had spent all morning on the hockey playing field. He was sweaty and feeling elated. Qoloq village, usually weak, had put up a surprisingly strong defense. More than once he had come shoulder to shoulder and playing stick to playing stick with his cousin, Kulaa, on the opposing team. But his side had prevailed in the end. Alow felt good now as he climbed the hill to the top of Syuhtun. He felt ready for the sweathouse.

At the top of the hill, not far from the ceremony grounds and closer still to the red-staved cemetery, he paused a moment to experience the cool breeze blowing on his warm body. People leaving the tournament pressed around and past him. He was thrilled to see so many new faces. He was surrounded by fine athletes and skillful cheaters, by toothless women and young flowers. Here and there he was struck by the sight of a man-woman, one of those women who had been born a man but who from an early age had dedicated her life, her body, to the service of sacred power. When he saw such a woman, even an aging one, Alow was overcome with awe and admiration. But it was the fresh flowers he longed to gather.

On the other side of the hill the houses of Syuhtun fell away in orderly lanes to the sand and sea below. The big town was like Mishopshno grown up into an adult. Alow tried to count the houses, but there were too many. The homes of the rich sat high on the hill away from flood and tide, while those of the commoners were set below on riskier sites. They looked like so many basket hats to him, some plain, some finely figured, laid out by a giant basket maker to sell at the festival trading fair. House and hat were made of similar materials, plucked from the same mud of stream and marsh. It was not such a wild imagining. But at other times the young fisherman had seen the houses of the people as being no different from the dwellings of field mice and wood rats. Indeed, rodents and other animals had once, long ago, before the Great Flood, been people. So it was natural that their habitations might be similar.

Alow passed the ceremonial enclosure with only a quick look. He was not antap and had no business in there at this time. He did not mind the exclusion. Soon he would be meeting with the canoe guild, and though he was not yet a member of that elite body, he had kinsmen—uncles, his father, his grandfather—who were. With them he would participate in the real work. He had made a plan and here, at Syuhtun, he could begin to put it into effect.

The dry penetrating heat of the sweathouse purified the young man and the short bath in the cold stream cleansed and braced him for the evening's meeting.

The brothers of the tomol guild met in the house of one of the wealthy Syuhtun canoe owners. He was an older man and wore a bearskin vest like the one Alow's grandfather, the leader of the Pelican Family, wore back home. Alow would have liked to have seen his old grandfather there at the gathering, but Silkiset was nearly doubled over with arthritis now, and he had to remain at home with his ailing wife.

Others of his family were out in strength: his uncle and cousins from home, kinsmen from Qoloq and Shalawa and more distant villages. Even his father was in attendance, sitting quietly by the door watching some other men playing stick dice. The men's counters stuck in the sand like fences round the sacred ground.

When Alow arrived most of the men were still gambling. He threw himself right in. It was a good way to broaden his contacts. He felt strong: his team had just won the field hockey match. From the small pouch in the carrying net at his waist he took out his rolling bone. Alow belonged to the Earth Team, whose celestial wot was Two Thunders. Everyone was descended from either the Earth or Sky, and these two groups played against each other and married each other. He found a man from the Sky Team who agreed to contest with him. He disentangled a length of shell money from his upswept hair and laid down his bet. Then he took his turn with the bone. He laid it on the back of his hand and with a flick twisted his wrist. The bone landed between his first two fingers. He drew two marks on the dirt in front of him.

After a while, as Sun drew close to his ocean destination, the gambling dropped off and men began to talk. At first, the talk was formal, full of guild business, and then they began to exchange stories. Alow kept his ears open when some men from Helo and Heliyik spoke of a boating accident that had happened way up in the western land beyond Kuyamu and Mikiw. A rainstorm—not a big one, there had been no big ones yet—had caught a boatload of fishermen unprepared as they worked just beyond the kelp bed. In the clouds and the rain the men had lost their bearings. They drifted until they finally crashed on some rocks. It was some way down the coast. Their tomol broke apart.

Alow listened to the guildsmen's tales of disastrous attempts to land at night. He heard of sea monsters, of men who murdered their wives by capsizing their boats and swimming ashore alone. And he listened to tales of rich trading voyages to the islands across the channel and to the island beyond the islands. He paid close attention to the recital of goods that were traded and the prices they brought. Alow was a fisherman and, though young, he owned his own boats. He owned a dugout for the lagoon and a raft made of bundles of bulrushes, or tules, for the bay. He fished in the kelp and in the channel with his father in his father's plank canoe and he thought himself a good tomolman. As a fisherman he already made a good living. If he wanted to he could marry. But his grandfather, the head of the Pelican Family, the man who wore the bearskin vest, was a wealthy tomol owner. Alow knew the old man planned to build yet another tomol that winter, and he had implied that Alow might use it in exchange for a certain percentage of the fish he caught. Alow expected to be paddling this canoe by summer and had already recruited a crew—a cousin for a mate, and a bailer.

Although fish might bring a good income, it was trade that brought wealth—and island trade brought the most wealth. Ocean travel meant hardship and danger, but that did not deter him. He would go to the islands in his grandfather's soon-to-be built plank canoe.

The days were drawing near the one when Sun would be renewed and people would learn the results of that heavenly game that foretold their destiny. In respect for Sun's weakness the men of the tomol guild spoke more quietly, more seriously, than they sometimes did. They did not want to upset anything. Anticipation and uncertainty, hope tinged with fear, excitement about the upcoming festivities possessed them. They talked earnestly of trade and boats and fish. They spoke of how many fish there were and where, about the big ones they had caught and the bigger one that got away.

The old-time stories unfolded of the days when humans and animals were one people, when Pelican and Cormorant and Duck Hawk were fishermen. The ancient tales were full of useful knowledge, too. They taught as much as the stories of last month's disaster. At the meeting Alow found what he had hoped to find. Besides getting information, he was able to initiate arrangements with seasoned merchants. He would begin his trading career with forays up the northwest coast. He would rely on the constant market for woqo, the pure tar adhesive, which Mishopshno possessed in abundance.

Later, the sky began to darken. Star crystals began to gleam in the western sky, indicating important places on the way to the Land of the Dead in the Sky World. The protective girdle of the Downy Path lighted the way. Alow took his leave from the helpful guildsmen. He wanted to return to the small encampment of his fellow villagers before it grew much later. His father had already gone. Perhaps he would be at home when Alow arrived.

With the coming of dusk most of the people had retired indoors. It was dangerous to be out much after sunset. Even in a large village like Syuhtun there was much to fear. As he approached the camp Alow spied a figure moving about from house to house. Drawing nearer, he saw that it was a woman, the younger sister of his friend, the apprentice paint maker.

"Little brother, little brother," he could hear her calling. She sang gently to the night as if hoping that the youngster would recognize her voice and spare her from having to shout his name. Even calling out his nickname might embarrass him.

Alow came up to stand beside the girl. She jumped as if she had just encountered a dangerous beast.

"Oh, it's only you," she sighed. "Where have you come from? Did you see my little brother? He's been disappearing all day long. He's as slippery as a piece of wet seaweed. I can't keep track of him anymore. Not since our . . . our late father went West. The boy is just wild."

"Have courage. Alishtahan," said Alow, grasping for something reassuring to say. "He is just getting older. Boys are like that. Don't you remember the things I used to do?"

"Like swooping down out of the oaks on us girls when we went to the creek for water? We thought you were mountain lions. Or holhol birds. I said I would never forgive you," she laughed. But the laughter faded like the day. It was getting darker and colder. Her worry returned. "He does such odd things, stupid things. He gets more dim-witted every day. Next thing I know he'll be carting our acorns down to some damp sea cave."

"Cheer up. I'm sure he is alright, wherever he is. But if you'd like I'll go out and look for him for you."

Before the young woman could answer, another figure stepped out from the shadowy oaks that sheltered the little Mishopshno campground. The stranger made no greeting, no gesture of friendship. He stepped right up and with a hiss warned Alow: "Drop the feathers! Quit poaching!"

The demand made no sense. They were fierce words growled in a foreign accent, "Stay off my land!" Then the stranger seemed to realize that Alow was not the man he expected to find. He began to falter. He stuttered. He swung toward Ponoya. "Your father!" he shouted at her. His face was in her face. "Your father! Paint maker!" He called a string of her father's names, his nicknames, his titles. He culminated by screaming out her late father's real true name, the one given him in secret by the soul doctor, the alchuklash, at his birth. It was the name that was himself. This stranger invoked the name he should not know. It was a name that invited destruction out of the Land of the Dead.

Ponoya crumpled under the stream of abuse. This strange man wished her harm. He was harming her. He had conjured her father's ghost. Why did he want to destroy her? She didn't even know him. People began to stick their heads out of their doors to see what the commotion was about.

Alow was furious. Yet he hesitated to strike or even touch the offender. The man might be carrying poison. He tried to place himself between the wounded girl and the stranger.

Before Alow could act further, maybe to move violently—and foolishly—against the intruder, a young man appeared at his side. It was Halashu, the wot's nephew. Halashu had been spending his day trying to keep order and to solve the problems of his fellow Mishopshnoans. He was determined to keep Alow from engaging in a fight. The village must be kept out of danger of reprisal by people from the stranger's village. Maintaining harmony was Halashu's vocation. His usual procedure was to intervene and try to talk individually with all parties. He could see that this occasion required more direct action. He and Alow bodily carried the intruder away from the camp.

Aleqwel found Ponoya lying on the ground where they had left her when he finally returned to camp from the ceremonial ground. The delinquent Anakawin was at his side.

Ponoya sat up. She was a strong girl and recovered quickly. She held Anakawin close. "Where have you been?" she cried. "Where were you?" But she was unable to speak about the intruder. All evening she was quiet.

The boy Anakwin lay on the ground on his camping mat that night trying to understand what had happened to his sister. She had been lying on the ground and crying but then she seemed to be better lying with Kanit beside her. The eeriness of his own evening's experience kept him awake much longer than usual.

Had black wings really covered Sun? He had been playing down in the hollow by the creek near the edge of the town. He was digging a bear trap and lining it with poison oak and berry thorns when a dark shape had fallen from the sky. Or had it? The thing seemed to him to resemble a crow or a raven, but it had been much larger. It was larger even than a buzzard or a condor. Could it have been like the bear he saw that they said was a rock? Had he seen an apparition, some achana's creation? Or a nunashish from the Lower World? If he had seen a real nunashish would he die? Should he ask his great-uncle, the alchuklash, to cure him? But the old man was still in the mountains with the other doctors, with the paqwot. Perhaps he should tell someone else. If he awoke in the morning before Aleqwel did, then . . .

Anakawin now found himself in a dark room lighted by the penetrating overhead gaze of one large star crystal. It glowed with a reddish fire that flashed rhythmically down at him. Its fiery sharp tooth of pain shot into a small spot just behind his eyes. Then he heard his sister's furry voice in the thick muffled dark. The voice was saying over and over, "Anakawin, Little Coyote, come home! Come home! Where have you been?"

B ut when Anakawin fully woke his elder brother had already left for the ceremonial ground. While Aleqwel and the other antap would be privileged to watch the dancers practicing for the next day's ritual and to welcome the returning doctors, even to participate in the ceremony of digging the hole for the Sunstick, he, Anakawin, would be cowering indoors with the noninitiates, fasting, not daring to set foot outside lest angry Sun gobble him up.

Anakawin felt as hungry as Grandfather Sun. Yet he wouldn't be allowed to eat until the next evening. His discomfort nearly obliterated his nightmares. He hated sitting still. He hated fasting. He knew he was supposed to reflect on the meaning of the winter solstice, on peoples' weakness, their abject reliance on the power of Sun and of Thunder and Fog for all things, and on the ways human beings could encourage the Sky People to beneficial action. He understood the meaning of it, but he was too young to make a difference. He knew he was supposed to contemplate death, the brevity of life here in the Earth World, to meditate on the road to the Land of the Dead and the eventual enjoyment of eternal life in Shimilaqsha, the town of the Land of the Dead. But he hated thinking. He didn't like to think of nunashish and death. He hoped his Nene's canoe would arrive soon and that she would have time to play cat's cradle with him.

The day dragged on, overcast, shadowless, cool. When Aleqwel returned home that evening to his family's campsite he was so tired that he could hardly speak. The others, sitting or lying by the central fire, were silent, too. Whether their muteness came from thoughtful reverence or from fatigue he could not tell. They might be waiting patiently for the former paint maker's ghost to roll through the door and finish them all off. He sank down by the fire. "Mother is coming soon," he said. Ponoya began to weep softly.

They had no evening food to cheer them, but they had one hope: tomorrow would be a new day, a new year. Tomorrow there would be dancing and feasting. Tomorrow they would learn the fate bestowed on them by the gambling of the Sky People—Sun and Sky Eagle (who was wot of the Sky World), Sky Coyote (who was the North Star), Fog, and Thunder. For better or for worse, the suspenseful waiting would be over. The next day the achanas would pull Sun back into the sky. And the people, the grown-up people, would donate their bodies to inspire the fertility of the fields.

Nene had been brought by tomol along with other elders. She arrived at the campground with Anihwoy and the darkness. It was time to begin the stories, the stories of the First People. All eyes were on her. All ears were open. All day long the family had been waiting for her stories, their only food. Though Nene often told about the ancient days, the time before the Great Flood, the tales tonight would have a special significance. Soon now their own mundane lives would intersect with those of the First People. On Solstice Night they would be so close to the Downy Path that they could nearly touch it. The way to the Sky World would be open before them, the heavens accessible. They would be in a position to affect their own fate, even if only slightly.

The first story was of the man who had followed his wife to Shimilaqsha town up there in the Land of the Dead. He was one of the few who had returned to the living to share his knowledge of the way there. "I know about this journey," she said, "because my grandmother heard it from her grandmother and she heard it from the young man, a wot's nephew, to whom it happened." Nene began: "It happened one time that there was a young man who loved his wife very much. But one day, when she was cleaning her ear with a stick, he slipped and bumped her. It killed her."

Aleqwel knew this story by heart. He tried to feel the comfort that comes from knowing that all those whom he had ever loved, who had died and gone on before him—most especially the man who had been his father— were having a good time in the Sky World. But when he pictured his late father he could not quite envision the festive life of Shimilaqsha. Instead, he saw guts strewn all over the mountain sagebrush; he saw the spindly little man denouncing and threatening his family. Was the late paint maker's ghost still playing happily and peacefully in Shimilaqsha? Or had it been torn away from its new home by the intruder's gross summoning? Had the ghost returned, unnaturally, to the Earth World? Aleqwel looked over at his sister across the glowing fire. She had a basket cup of water beside her. She seemed to be listening intently to Nene's narrative, as if hearing it for the first time.

The story of the wot's nephew's journey to the Land of the Dead and his return to his mother's house was a long story. Nene finally finished with the usual ending "And he went home and hung up his carrying net." She paused briefly to rest and drink some water. "Now," she said stalwartly, "I will tell you about the adventures of Thunder and Fog."

It was one of Aleqwel's favorite stories. Like the previous one it had a special meaning which, as an antap, he had learned to decode. He recognized the hidden references to landmarks on the road to Shimilaqsha.

As an initiate he might travel there himself one day. But he had loved the story ever since he was young, younger even than Anakawin. Even now he delighted to hear of Coyote's outrageous doings. It was not just because Coyote had been his remote ancestor. No, he loved tales of the improbable—of instinct winning out over well-bred manners. Keti! Such a wild idea.

Nene began: "It happened one time, in the days before the Great Flood, when animals were still people, that the granddaughter of Moon gave birth to twin boys. They were called Thunder and Fog, and they had different fathers. They lived with their grandmother, Moon, who was also called Grandmother Momoy.

"One day they decided to explore the world all by themselves. Fog, the younger, was careless, as younger brothers often are. But Thunder was cautious and insisted on bringing along his magic flute for companionship and protection.

"They made themselves a toy canoe and turned it into a real tomol. It carried them all the way down here to the town of Syuhtun, right here. Then the boys took off to travel around and see the world.

"Of course, they soon got into plenty of trouble, for Fog was mischievous and couldn't mind his own business. He teased an old woman who turned out to be a witch. She got even by rolling a burning basket at the boys. Thunder saved them by using his flute as a pole and vaulting over the hill to their Aunt Yucca's house. There, under her loving care, they recuperated."

Grandmother took a breath. Around the fire, pairs of dark eyes were fixed on her. The eyes, reflecting the fire, glowed like sparks of Kakunupmawa. After drinking water she continued her tale. She was glad she had paid attention to her grandmothers and learned to tell the stories well.

"Then the boys met their grandfather, Coyote, who could see the future. He offered to travel with them and be their guide, for he had been everywhere. So they went together. He gave them a downy cord for protection. But even far-seeing Coyote, the great doctor, ran into trouble. First, he had to save little Fog from a witch who had grabbed onto his wrist and wouldn't let go. Then, Grandfather Coyote poked his nose into an achana's cave and the next thing they knew he was shut inside. He was killed.

"The twins cried.

"But the stench of Coyote's carcass was so strong that the doctor finally threw it out of the cave. The sound of Thunder's flute revived the old man. He said, 'I was only sleeping.'

"And so they went on their way. One day they met the haphap. As you know, he is a terrible giant, a nunashish who sucks in trees and rocks and living beings whenever he breathes. He carried the boys back to his house to eat them. But Thunder and Fog used their flute atishwin and the downy cord that Coyote had given them and they managed an escape.

"Then, along came the yowoyow, another nunashish, and he tried to throw them into his basket of boiling tar. But Grandfather Coyote warned the boys, so they tricked the monster and got away."

"At last, Holhol, the condor impersonator, found them. That bird is far-seeing and one look or word or touch of his devours people. It managed to succeed in bewitching the boys. It killed them. Fortunately, Coyote came along and revived them, for in those days, before the Great Flood, such things could be readily done.

"They went on and on, and all along the way Thunder kept them entertained by playing his flute. Slowly, slowly, all the time they came nearer and nearer to the Land of the Dead."

Aleqwel listened to his grandmother's description of the way there. It was the same downy path taken by the man who went after his dead wife. Aleqwel was certain that he, too, could find the right landmarks if he had to. He even had a flute for companionship. And a lizard's foot besides. But finding the way was not the only difficulty. There were dangers and trials along the way. And then there was the problem of finding the way back. He had stopped listening. But the story had gone on. It was a long, long history.

"Soon, the three arrived at Shimilaqsha. It was a very big town, bigger even than Syuhtun. The people there were laughing and talking and singing and dancing. They were having a good time all the time. They never had to work. They played games and gambled and ate seed cakes. They ate cherry-nut balls and all the best food. The aroma made Coyote very hungry. But he found the food there was as illusory as the wind. It made him mad.

"So they left that place and Coyote took them off to Sun's house. It was huge and made all of crystal. Inside were the First People, the animal ancestors of human beings. Sun was out gathering human bodies from the Earth World, the surface of Shup. Fog asked for some water, for he was very thirsty. But the animals told him there was no water to be had in Sun's house. The boys wanted to leave.

"But Coyote had another idea. Sun had returned with a loud crash and Coyote had seen his torch and was intrigued with it. He thought it would be fun to carry that torch around the world, just for one day.

"So, that night he stole it and next morning, early, he went out. But he was clumsy. He didn't hold the torch right. It dipped too low and everything on Shup got burnt. Everyone, everywhere, was angry at Coyote. They were furious. Furious.

"He and the boys were thrown out of the sky. The fall killed them. But a wot gathered Coyote's scattered bones together and he revived. 'I was only sleeping,' he said.

"Then, Coyote restored the boys to life and they all went home, to their own homes, and, at last, they hung up their carrying nets."

She ended the story with the ritual conclusion in which everyone is home safe and the carrying net is hung by the door. Anakawin was lying sound asleep by the fire, his rabbit fur blanket pulled up to his chin. His head lay against his sister's thigh.

Though the smoke hole displayed neither Moon nor stars to help him with the hour, Aleqwel could tell that it had grown very late. And though that once young man, the friend of Nene's grandmother's grandmother, and Coyote and Fog and Thunder had all returned from Shimilaqsha, Aleqwel was wondering where his late father was. He wished so badly that he were still in the Earth World, though not as a ghost. The mourning period had been too short. He needed someone to talk to. There was no uncle for him, other than his great-uncle who was so powerful that he seemed unapproachable. His mother only had her sister. And his late father's family was all in Heliyik in the western lands. He hardly knew those kinsmen, though he had seen them, here, at the festival. But his father had been his closest adviser, his teacher.

Aleqwel thought: "I must advise myself now. I feel certain of one thing. If I am going to defend our family against this intruder and his threats—maybe against his poison, too—if I am going to defend against this, whether it originates only with this wild man or with the wot of Shuku himself, I will need more power. Lizard, my atishwin, has protected me since I first drank momoy tea. But I will need greater strength. I really must approach my mother's uncle, the alchuklash. He will know what steps I should take."

Aleqwel wanted only peacefully to carry on his late father's trade. He had hoped to find balance in seeking, grinding, and selling pigments for paint, in earning money to support the family. But this decision to fortify his power had been inescapable. Without power, all would be lost. His grandmother must have been watching him, for she said, "Have courage. Alishtahan! Tomorrow, light will begin to return."

Usually they were up before dawn, but this morning they slept late. It was dangerous for Sun to find them in their sleeping places. But the days of the Festival of Kakunupmawa were extraordinary. This day particularly so.

The many hundreds of people who had gathered in the already big town of Syuhtun moved quietly through the morning and with circumspection prepared for the evening's revelations. By midafternoon they began to wend their way to the newly built arena. Its fresh mat walls and fresh red paint welcomed and inspired them. Feathered banners, one from each village, streamed in the breeze. The people came inside through the southern gate. They arranged themselves facing east. East was the place of the master of ceremonies—the paqwot—and Kakunupmawa. The eastern section of the large ellipse also held a small enclosure that was the heart of the sanctuary. They called it the center.

From the center emanated sounds of mysterious beings. The participants recognized the roaring and whistling. They felt themselves in the early stage of leaving the Earth World. In spirit they were about to cross the trembling bridge to the Timeless Time.

Halashu was one person who moved easily into the Timeless Time. When he entered it, he did not leave his everyday wits behind. At this moment, though, he was peering around at the many ornamented and robed leaders and doctors who surrounded him. There seemed to be as many of them as there were commoners. While waiting, he began to count. It was difficult to do without his counting sticks. Everyone moved around so much. Eventually he had to give up. But he could see that there were hundreds and hundreds and hundreds of commoners and that he was still part of a minority of the elite.

The crystal hairsticks, the long bearskin robes, the heavy serpentine beads—these all set him apart from others on most days. But today he was surrounded by people in expensive furs and feathers of eagle, hawk, and condor blurred with red, black, and white paint. Quartz stones glinted in the mid-afternoon light, transducing solar radiance into the rainbow colors of Shup. It was a concentration of power. Halashu, with his admirable arrow-like posture, stood out no more than a single green bead on a serpentine necklace.

The master of ceremonies, attired in his awe-inspiring eagle robe, arrived. A hush fell over the crowd. The paqwot greeted the people. Then, he began to speak briefly and simply, so that all might understand, about the significance of the occasion. He bent their thoughts and hearts to the histories of Sun and the Sky World. He spoke of the Land of the Dead and its pathway to the Earth World. He invoked the Beginning and the End and the new Beginning in the West. He talked of Coyote and of Sky Coyote, of Grandmother Momoy and the teams of Sky Eagle and of Two Thunders and the nightly hand game they played above.

At the mention of the hand game the people became exceptionally quiet, scarcely daring to cough. They anticipated a word, a hint of their future.

Halashu spotted the carrying box of the Sunstick, finely crafted of rare cedarwood, with its open lid inlaid with white shells arranged in patterns of power. He felt sorry for the commoners, far back in the crowd, who could not see the implement as he could. But then, they might not appreciate its fine craftsmanship. Certainly they could not grasp its refined technological use.

At this important moment in the ceremony the wot's nephew suddenly had a temptation to turn around and look for the powerful women who attended the dead. They were standing together, not far back, women and women who had been born men, young and old, a stately and serene group. As intermediaries between Shimilaqsha in the Sky World and the Earth World, these women were as indispensable as he and the other wots in keeping Grandmother Shup and Grandfather Sun in balance. Intimately, they knew the Downy Path leading between the worlds. Intimately, they conversed with ghosts. It was they who tamed the Land of the Dead.

Halashu picked out his friend, the man-woman Konoyo, from among them. She and her companion apprentice stood by the chief caretaker of the dead like fledglings under an outstretched wing. Neither of the young women noticed Halashu. Both were devoutly observing the paqwot elevate the Sunstick from its cedar resting place.

Pure white egret down, blown from the tool's carrying box, scattered in the late afternoon breeze. The soft feathers carried prayers skyward. The leader was praying: "To the north and the south, to the east and the west, to the distant zenith and to maternal Shup beneath our feet. O ya ya ya ha." As he prayed he scattered feathers and seeds on the sacred ground. Then he breathed a pipeful of pure tobacco smoke to the four winds.

Halashu attended the prayer, but at the same time he kept an eye on the apparatus that would draw back Grandfather Sun. The Sunstick was probably the most wonderful object the people possessed, the tool that enabled the paqwot to pull languishing Kakunupmawa back into the northern sky. The shiny blue-green pole, raised from its dark keeping place, had come back to life. At its point there was a stone with a hole like the center of a sand dollar. It rested at its perfect angle. Crescent Moon was there on the stone. What power was greater than the power of balance? And the Sunstick had the capacity to become the impervious axis of the Three Worlds. Yet, it was an empty tool—he admitted with some pride—without the paqwot's infusion of human energy.

The master made some subtle adjustments. With ceremony he drove the blue-green stake into the soil of Shup. The people were now aligned with the center of the Three Worlds.

At last, he performed the operations. His men, all powerful achanas, stood as the twelve rays of Kakunupmawa. They circled the blue-green Sunstick and began scattering feathers from their hands. They cried, "It is raining! It is raining! You must go into the house!"

Tension fell away from the audience as when first drops fall after a long drought. The paqwot had succeeded in pulling Grandfather Sun back. Balance would return. Sunlight would come again. And rain and fog that made seeds spring from the fields. People breathed again. They coughed. Babies cried.

Halashu loved the Winter Solstice Ceremony. He might never in his life be called on to perform it, but it touched firmly on his own duties. Though still young, and delegated to keeping order and harmony among his people in camp, he knew that one day he would have the responsibility of going to the caves and traveling to the Sky World. He, too, would learn to uncover the wins and losses of the games played up above by the Earth and Sun teams. Now, he listened intently to the master of ceremonies, as he made another little speech. It came almost as an afterthought. But it was important. In a simple way the paqwot was explaining what he had learned in his recent celestial visit. He was forecasting their future.

What Halashu heard pleased him. He smiled at his mother's brother, the wot of Mishopshno and at his father, the assistant wot. But the tall men wore serious, impassive looks. They had gone to the mountains, too. No doubt, they were already intimately acquainted with the results. But Halashu, who had been in the village finding lost children and getting rid of troublesome intruders, was as surprised as any commoner.

Though the future sounded hopeful, the paqwot's words were cautious. He spoke carefully. Fortune is never a matter of perfection, he told them. Power is ever declining since the days before the Great Flood when people and animals were one; there is less and less that a doctor can do to intercede with the Sky World. It is always imperative to save seeds, no matter how plentiful. Then he gave specific instructions. He assessed how much of each crop needed to be stored up. Though the winter and spring would bring rain, enough rain for seeds to sprout, and though fish would come back to the ocean channel, the next year and the years beyond were still unknown. It was a conservative speech.

From the paqwot's words Halashu inferred one thing: the friends of man—Thunder, Fog, Sky Coyote, and all the Earth Team—had won the yearlong hand game once more. Things would—or could—go well for the people as long as nothing else upset the balance. But it was the third year in a row they had won. Someday things would change.

This time, when Halashu looked around to catch the eyes of his cousins and yes, even the young apprentice caretaker of the dead, he saw cheeks flushed red with joy as well as red paint. It was as if a threatening storm wave had broken and washed away as harmless foam.

But the good tidings necessarily brought to mind the bad years. Halashu had heard of drought years, of hunger, when the reserves in the caves had not been enough to feed everyone. Old people had died and mothers' milk had dried up. Everyone suffered. Especially, he'd heard of quarrels, talk of poisoning. Then there was the looting, the accusations of poaching and stealing by their southern neighbor, Shuku. There were raids of retribution. Storehouses were ransacked, burned. He'd heard tales of people with their hair on fire, people dying slowly from arrow wounds. Shuku was always a worry when there was drought.

All this had last happened before Halashu had been born, before he drank his first momoy tea. And though he disliked imagining those days, sometimes an image would come like a forgotten memory. Now, just as he smiled at those he loved, happy at the prospect of another fruitful year, an unpleasant picture presented itself to him.

He was about to turn his eyes to the east, to the master of ceremonies, when he recalled the little Shuku man who had broken into the arena with threats and curses. He had refused to go away and had crept back into the encampment like a dangerous beast at night. Even in a good year, such a thing could portend disaster. Shuku was a large and powerful village. The people there spoke in a different way. They were never friendly with their weaker neighbor. Unbalanced strength between neighbors could lead to war. A war could be started over anything. Thinking this, Halashu's countenance began to more resemble his uncle's and his father's.

The paqwot was concluding his address: "See how the destructive power of Grandfather Sun has penetrated Grandmother Shup, the source of life. Believe! We are in the center of opposites. From the two will come offspring, our nourishment. Have courage! Alishtahan! It has always been so. Participate! Show the children! Remember! Remember!"

The twelve rays of Kakunupmawa, each in his own unique attire, danced. Each danced the dance of his own season, of the season of Momoy, of Rattlesnake, of Bear, and the others. Each swayed to the songs and the music until the time when the sky began to grow dusky and the path to the Sky World opened before them over the ocean in the west. The way to Timeless Time was disclosed to the people.

Later, with night fully fallen, the people made their offerings of sacred gifts. One by one they approached the newly built great house where the paqwot sat surrounded by his rays, all of whom were seated on chairs made of whale vertebrae. These offerings were not the taxes that went to support the festival. They were paid already. These were devotional gifts from everyone. The people of the twelve villages formed a line like a snake. Each woman, each man, whether highborn or common, had a turn. Each person was needed. Slowly, slowly the snake moved.

When the people's giving was completed, the twelve rays danced again. One by one they danced. Then all the wots of the twelve villages danced. Then the other achanas. Then the men had their turn. When it was very late and very cold and they were all done, the feast began.

The feast went on all night. Everyone who had been edgy from fasting and tense with worry over the future now made up for it by gorging on delicious food.

The Coyote Family sat close together, silently enjoying their portion of acorn porridge, seed meal soup, fresh and dried fish, preserved greens, cherry-nut balls, brodiaea bulbs, and aphid sugar condiments. Everything they had craved all winter was before them in abundance.

Aleqwel shivered a little in the damp winter night. He tried not to appear gluttonous as he thrust his fingers in his mouth. He watched the wives of the paqwot, their faces red and sweating as they oversaw the huge operation. The cooking vessels were immense. The dark steatite pots from Huya Island and the plain stone ones looked very heavy. There were hundreds of baskets, huge ladles, and countless bowls. Aleqwel turned to his little brother who was eating greedily by his side. The boy was burrowing into his porridge with all four fingers. Aleqwel felt it his duty to correct him. But he was unable to work up a convincing tone. After all, the boy was hungry. He was only a child, a taniw.

Aleqwel's mind had begun to stray from his family, from his dinner, even. He thought ahead to the sacrifice still to come. He looked out toward the brush and the hills beyond the village sanctuary.From the corner of his eye, he saw his friend Halashu already heading off into the woods with a foreign and very common-looking girl. She had worn a grass skirt, not a soft deerskin one like the well-to-do girls wore. Aleqwel admired his friend for the determination with which he carried out his obligation.

Aleqwel understood the absolute necessity of encouraging rain to fertilize Shup. Even in a good year the new year's offering could not be neglected. He would play his part too, however he could. But paint making, his family, the shrine pole, the intruder, were easier for him to think about. He was not prepared for this night, and he was reluctant to go on. He wondered, "Why should I feel the need to prepare? Are women that difficult?" He had to concede that maybe they were. Even familiar women were unpredictable. And foreign women were.... He looked over at his sister as if seeking inspiration. But she was already being courted by an ardent singer. She had no choice but to go with him. That's how it had to be.

Aleqwel had been brooding so deeply that he was startled when he became aware that Ponoya's suitor was his own friend, Alow, the fisherman. Before he could find his tongue and object about possible impiety from sticking so close to home, the young couple had quietly abandoned him to his brother, aunt, and mother.

It was not right for him to stay with his family. He had to find a partner. He felt a surge of sadness for his aunt, Kanit. No one ever seemed to notice her, even though she was not homely. She was too shy to approach anyone herself. Would she ever marry, he wondered? With a small shock, he realized that this was a matter over which he now had considerable responsibility.

Aleqwel wandered away from the sanctuary. He retreated from the paqwot's house and the feasting, from the old and young men crooning like animals and making him feel crowded. As always, when he felt that way, he went down by the creek toward a grove of dark oaks. He had no torch to guide him. But the starry light of the Downy Path shone clear. Hard breathing and moaning in the sagebrush and sumac kept him aware that he was not alone.

Yet he felt alone. All the new happenings in his life, the responsibilities and dangers, made him feel more alone than he ever had before. He no longer felt as he had in the days and nights of his youth when going alone to the hills renewed his sense of protection, of being understood by the living world around him. Now, even with his family and closest friends, he could feel alone. And the woods could be sinister. He thought of Alow. Why did he go into the brush with his sister? Such an act violated the impersonality of nature they were supposed to be promoting. She was a friend. "It's the divine force we are trying to encourage," he grumbled to himself, "not matrimony. The fisherman treats the occasion as if it were a clambake." Aleqwel stumbled over a rock and nearly fell atop a copulating pair. He tried not to notice who they were or if any of the writhing couples around him might be his sister and her wooer.

Soon he found himself near the dark gurgling creek with its leafless sycamores and pungent bay trees. Here all was obscure. "Why have I come here?" he asked himself as his cold toes ached amid damp decomposing leaves. "I'll never find a partner here. Any seeds in this place have already been watered."

He turned his heavy feet back toward the village. Making his way through the streamside bracken he nearly tripped over Nacha, Halashu's noble cousin. She was sitting astride some anonymous old nobody, a grizzled man with bangs and stringy hair. Aleqwel wanted to run, but now he no longer thought he could take himself back to Syuhtun, to the feast and the women. He felt convinced that if he did, if he touched a woman, he would lose the small power he had cultivated through solitude. That it was Solstice Night made no difference.

He was about to set out—somewhere—when he felt eyes on him, and he turned and noticed a lone figure a short distance behind him on the trail. The woman was solid and low-breasted like someone who was no longer young. Yet she was not old. She was dressed in deerskin and heavy beads. She must have been one of the rulers. But something about her manner was coarse. Her dress was sloppy, dirty even, if night light revealed truth. Her hair was unkempt. In no way did this person resemble his well-kept sister, Ponoya, or even his dignified mother. In the dim starlight, with waxing Moon having already set, Aleqwel could barely make out what he thought was a reddish patch in the woman's tangled black hair. It disgusted him to see her body paint smeared. She had probably already been with someone. He was repelled by her, and drawn to her. He felt his excitement growing. It would be impious to resist that which was more powerful than he.

The strange woman spoke to him. As he expected, her deep voice brought words with a peculiar sound. But he understood them, insinuating as they were. In smooth accented syllables with a hard edge, she invited him to come into the fields with her.

Aleqwel had no choice but to go.

As early dawn spread pale and gray over the eastern range the young paint maker emerged from an oak grove by the side of the village stream. He began to make his tentative way toward his people's camp. The paths and brush around him were marked with little scraps of fur and broken beads, the remains of the night's sexual devotions. He stumbled over an occasional body of some spent, sleeping participant. It was the first day of the new year.

Aleqwel found his way to camp like a salmon finds his river, neither by thought nor by intention, but by instinct. He had no more thoughts. Even his body was numb. He did not feel refreshed, purged, as one was said to feel after the ritual. Instead, he was enervated, drained of energy, drained even of will. He had a sense of irritation almost like that caused by a bad case of poison oak. He wanted to sleep.

In circling the hill of the village Aleqwel skirted the banks of a small tule-filled lake. By the shores of the lake he saw two people squatting. He recognized his friend Halashu and the young caretaker of the dead, Konoyo. She was a fastidiously groomed young man-woman. The two looked serene in the early light, untroubled, as if wrapped in a soft fur blanket. Even though he had seen Halashu go off with a commoner in the early evening, Aleqwel thought enviously of this pair, "Their lives are easy; their status is secure." But what made him feel most badly was thinking, "They have each other."

He did not greet them or even try to attract their attention as he went on his solitary way. He felt like the Mishopshno salt marsh at low tide. He slogged heavily homeward toward his empty sleeping place.

It was midafternoon when Aleqwel awoke. The women in his family were moving about the campsite, brushing their hair, singeing their bangs with sticks from the fire. Their eyes showed nothing, neither of consumed pleasure nor of compassion bestowed. As he slowly woke and sat up, Aleqwel witnessed the motions of pious women.

"Hurry up! Hurry up!" cried Anakawin, shaking his elder brother by the arm. "You sleep too long. Who do you think you are, an alchuklash? It's almost time to leave for the dances."

Aleqwel felt unable to move. He could not think, either. Where had he been? How long had he slept? He couldn't remember. He no longer cared about the festivities, not even about erecting his revered shrine pole. He only wanted . . . he sank back into his nest of soft fur, all resolve lost.

"Hurry up, older brother!" urged the boy yet once more. "Maybe you will see that woman again when we go to the dances."

Slowly, Aleqwel began to remember, to know what he craved.

His sister handed him a basket of soup. "Are you happy or sad that the night is over?" she said lightly.

He scooped the warm broth into his mouth with a mussel shell spoon. He remembered.

He thought he had better go and bathe.

What did Anakawin know of the woman, anyway?

After the sweathouse and a dive in the ocean Aleqwel felt differently. He worked up an enthusiasm for the dances. They would be a pleasant change from the intensity of the previous night's ceremonies. He wondered, too—only out of curiosity, he told himself—if he might spy a woman there, one with a reddish tint at the crown of her dark hair. Perhaps this day she would look young and clean and tidy, well-kempt and ordinary.

The dances were delightful. They brought joy to the dancers and release to the spectators. The songs burst forth like the sighs of the mother of a newborn child. The words of the songs raised everyone's spirits as they brought to mind the paqwot's prediction. Life would prevail.

The people sang and danced until late afternoon. And they continued. Bonfires were lit as a winter mist began to creep into the ceremonial enclosure from the southern sea.

"Come out, Sun, come out!" sang the people, enticingly, at the very end of day. "Come out, so that you may see your grandfather." A faint red ray of setting sunlight shot through the gray skin of fog that shrouded them. It was a moment to be remembered, to be spoken of, later, at home, in the village or on the trail. It was a moment when the world had revealed her beauty to the people.

By the time the dances ended Aleqwel felt almost whole again. But secretly, hidden even from himself, he was a little disappointed. He had searched everywhere—prudently, of course—and had found no woman like the one he had known the night before. She probably looked too plain for him to recognize. Her reddish hair, no doubt, would be covered by an ordinary basket hat.

Still later, in the blackest night, the young man attended the widows' dance. His mother and sister, along with other women in a similarly sorrowful plight, danced in a ring around the fire. Aleqwel and the men encircled the grieving women, women whose husbands or fathers had been lost in the previous year.

In the south, by the sea, three venerable antap sang and shook their doleful deer-hoof rattles. The women moved slowly. And the wot's poisoner went among them shaking his bags of dirt, dancing with the women.

The songs were sad, grievously sad, and Aleqwel could see tears wetting the cheeks of his mother and sister. They lamented the man who had been husband and father. He had been a gentle man and a hard worker. He had shot many deer. That gentle man had sent his eldest child to go with the prestigious antap to learn things he himself could never know. The women sobbed for that hardworking harmless man, who was never a doctor or even a boat owner. That man had happened, one time in summer, to cross untimely paths with a hungry grizzly bear.

Patches of the Downy Path and crystals in the sky, winking through the coastal fog, informed the mourners of the passage of night. Everything was backwards at this time of year. People slept during the day and came out under the stars. Now, in the cold heart of the night, the women began to sing the renewal song of Grandfather Sun. With sorrow and hope women—and men with them—wept.

The participants heard the sound of the unending surf, dimmed, but not silenced, by fog. It crashed on the sand. It rolled in and out. It sucked itself seaward. Again and again and again. The ocean water hissed across cobble and breathed over the sand. It played its own ageless song. The mourners sang to the music of the sea:

> *"Listen, hear the sound!*
> *Listen, it's the sound of the world.*
> *It is everlasting. Always enduring. Eternal.*
> *Oh, why does it rumble so?*
> *Why does it roar?"*

Two men danced the seaweed dance, swaying with feathered wands.

The women sang and sang. They sang across the night.

Slowly, intangibly, Aleqwel began to feel as if some poison or foreign body which had been in him was being lured away. His mother's face, his sister's face, though glistening in the firelight, though red-streaked with paint and tears, had peaceful looks like the faces of patients who had been healed of an illness.

The leader sang: "Go down to the water and bathe your faces: we shall endure."

And the women of the round dance wound their way down to the shore and rinsed away their tears in the cold dark sea.

The next morning was gray and overcast. The paqwot called the people together in the ceremonial ground for the last time. "Sun is returning!" he proclaimed. "Things are well for the people. Sun is returning. Rain will fall. You can go to your homes now." And he and his twelve assistants undertook the ceremony in which the blue-green Sunstick was retired to its downy resting place.

And so the many hundreds of visitors, Syuhtun's guests, returned to their campgrounds. They were tired but rejuvenated, cautious yet hopeful. They began packing their belongings for their homeward journeys. Not much and everything had happened during the dead time and the renewal.

Burden baskets loaded with cookware and blankets were placed inside carrying nets. Mats were unfastened and rolled up, revealing the curved ribs of round camp houses. Relatives and old friends cried their farewells. Newfound friends and lovers did the same, but with stronger expectations. The campground was being abandoned.

Alow, the young fisherman, had persuaded his father, Mushu, to carry the family of the curing doctor home in his tomol, though Aleqwel would walk with the village antap. The women of the Coyote Family carried their burdens down to the gray seaside and set them to rest on the fine pale sand. The girls, Ponoya and Kanit, were excited to be going home by canoe. It was a luxury to travel sitting down—though not without hazards. "Suppose Alow were your husband," said Anakawin mischievously to his older sister, "suppose he was angry with you. He could tip the boat over and drown you. He could drown us all, while he and the old man swam for shore."

"Taniw, where do you get such ideas!" interceded his aunt Kanit. She saw that her niece and best friend was blushing, unable to find her tongue. "We've known Alow all his life. He is like our brother. He's practically lived with us since he lost his mother. You know he's not the sort of man to try to kill his friends."

"You protest so much, aunt. Do you wish to marry him? Anyway, I have heard of such things, of such murders."

"We're not saying it has never happened," Ponoya found her voice at last. "But Uncle Alow! Anyway, who ever said anything about marrying. Uncle Alow knows many girls. He probably already plans to marry someone from Kuyamu or Mupu. Don't let your words carry you away like a bad current, little brother, or soon you will be lost at sea."

While the young people, assembling their gear at the shore, squabbled with anticipation over the coming sea journey, Anihwoy, the widowed curing doctor, having been trained by the antap, joined her elder son in the final labors of the festival. Halashu's uncle, Tilinawit, would carry the new shrine pole to their home village. And Aleqwel would assist in removing the old one and erecting the new one.

This local observance was the one Aleqwel had been awaiting. He had painted the thick bright red branch and had offered feathers from his father's modest collection. It was the last project that father and son had worked on together. Later, keeping protective watch over it, keeping it safe from jostles and spills and the spells of intruders, Aleqwel had come to feel a deep commitment. Nothing was more important than giving the living access to the timeless. Nothing! For a person to have his prayers and offerings, made at the shrine pole, heard and received was essential. For an individual to be able to cross that bridge and break into the fabric of Timeless Time—if only for an instant—was the only worthy goal. Aleqwel cried and sang the song his atishwin gave him when he appeared in his dream. On the first day of the new year his enthusiasm had faltered—but only briefly. The widow's dance left him renewed.

Before leaving Syuhtun town, the antap gathered at the top of the hill. After a blessing from the paqwot each village separated to form its own parade. The wot of each community held high his vermillion stake with its fierce black feathers. The twenty antap of each village followed behind. Silently they walked, as they would walk silently all the way home to their far-flung villages.

Aleqwel wondered how he had let his personal reactions consume him. He did not even like that strange woman. How could she have seized his attention? And before, the intruder . . . He had let fear shake him from the balanced center he tried to maintain. But now he had recovered. Neither person could touch him.

On this morning, overcast though it was, Aleqwel felt clean. He was almost clear. His strength was returning as surely as if he had taken a salt water purge. He looked up ahead at his great-uncle, the alchuklash. The old man was draped in beads and atishwins. So important was his profession that he stepped near Tilinawit and the wot's poisoner at the head of the procession. Aleqwel renewed his decision to fortify his power. When the Festival of Kakunupmawa was over he would ask the alchuklash to prepare momoy tea for him. Soon.

The parade moved slowly at first because of the congestion. Later, on the trail, as people spread out, they established a brisk, dignified pace. They did not stop to rest. They had all day.

At first, the processions from the different villages traveled together: Mishopshno, Qoloq, Shalawa, Swetete. One by one, groups, carrying their shrine pole aloft, dropped away when they came to their own lands. At Swetete, a village on the beach not far from the big town, those who had farther to go turned inland. They skirted a large lagoon. Tules and cattails grew tall and thick. The dark surface of the water trembled with white gulls and black mud hens. When the parade passed by, gray whirring clouds of startled ducks and geese flew up into the air. The birds quickly disappeared into the gray sky. It was a cool day, halfway between fog and cloud—perfect weather for traveling.

The enforced silence did not bother Aleqwel. It was good to be quiet. Every now and then he could look over at his mother who walked by his side. Two antap in one family—and that did not include the alchuklash. They were not insignificant people. Bears and snakes were still sleeping. Aleqwel could drift in thought as he liked to. He considered the bridge between the worlds. The shrine pole was a bridge like the pole bridge on the Downy Path to Shimilaqsha in the Land of the Dead. The pole was a center. It was like the sacred tree atop the highest mountain, Iwihinmu, in the Center of the Earth World. Around the center the forces of the six directions could compete. But at the center all was still, in balance. For the first time in his life, with his father's gruesome death, he had experienced a severe upset. Everything was in disharmony. His world was broken; it had fallen apart. But poise returned. Or he hoped it had. He considered the need for balance beside the small part people could play in altering the balance. It was the power struggle of Sky and Earth, of the Sky World and the Earth World, their home. He knew that people had power, but sometimes he doubted how much. Maybe power had declined more than the doctors let on. No, he couldn't think like that. He must have courage… hope.

Aleqwel considered power in all three worlds. The trees and boulders had knowledge and will. Even the black stubble by the roadside had some small power of its own. There were animals and fierce nunashish, too. Then there were the mighty Sky People. They inhabited large crystal houses and held strong influence over every phase of life. Sky Eagle was their wot. Aleqwel gave up trying to enumerate all the power beings. Yet it was only by naming—and knowing—that they could be controlled. As an antap he had not learned the important things. And if the antap—who alone possessed complete knowledge—did not keep track of things, who would, or could? Aleqwel thought he ought to ask the soul doctor, his great-uncle, the alchuklash, and the other teachers to work with him more, to help make up his deficiencies. But the thought began to fade after a few miles on the trail. In truth, long memorizations, enumerations, lists, charts interested him as little now as they ever had. Though he felt more personally the fundamental need for balance and for restoring balance, it was only paint and living rock that moved him.

For the following miles, past the place where the Shalawa antap left to ascend their tall hill—called "Halfway to Syuhtun" by Mishopshno navigators—past the forest where Anakawin had been frightened by a bear-shaped boulder, past Qoloq and even to the first cattails and tules of the large lagoon Aleqwel concentrated on observing the life around him.

At the outskirts of home, the poor, the old, the lame, and the dogs came out to greet them. Prayers were said. Egret down and sagebrush water were sprinkled on the ground where they passed.

The antap paraded through the lanes of the town. Then they headed out along the sea bluffs to their village shrine hill. The low mound scarcely compared with pine-covered Iwihinmu, the mountain at the Center of the Earth World. Yet, in its mysterious way, it was a replica of that sacred peak.

The initiates paused to purify their steps by planting small bundles of sagebrush. Sun had already begun his retreat into the ocean. Only his bright orange cloak could be seen through the clouds. The ocean's roar, below, was constant, but muffled. It sounded like the roar of blood in the ears.

Aleqwel's heart beat fast. This day was the closest he had come to feeling part of the antap. His work on the shrine pole was his first act for the spiritual benefit of the entire village. Until this season his connection with the First People had been private, solitary. Now, in this moment of ascension, he looked proudly on the vermillion pole, the black condor feathers and the white of shell and down. He determined to serve the community in any way he could.

The old pole was retired, to be burned. The new one, installed. In the same way that the living are born, do their work and pass from the world while the new come along, the poles were exchanged. The antap all cried. The wot turned the long black feathers to point east and west, toward the beginning and the end. With his feet he tamped new dirt around the base of the shining pole. He buried the roots deep in the sandy soil. The pole was of good strong toyon. It would endure. Then,the wot piled rocks around its base. Sun was lying on the mirror of the ocean. In the dusk the village leader turned to the four directions. He addressed Grandfather Sky and Grandmother Shup with his prayers. His offerings were seeds and money beads. He prayed for rain and for food. He prayed for the dead.

Then the other antap joined in. Aleqwel prayed. And offered. He wondered how long it would be before the rains came.

Walking back to the village, Aleqwel found himself asking what he could he do for his community. He remembered how the people and the antap had helped his family with prayers and with food during the mourning time. He could still barely provide for his family. What talents did he have to share besides making paint and being an inferior student of the antap? His command of the antap language was rudimentary and his understanding of the Sky People limited. He had only his desire to serve. He turned and looked back at the new shrine pole on the cliff above the ocean. Its beauty, strong and bright, against the gray sky and mirroring sea struck him profoundly. The red trunk filled him with joy, the black feathers—the ones from his late father—with awe.

For a brief moment a different feeling stirred in Aleqwel. He could not name it. It was just a passing uneasiness that made his stomach hurt. No doubt he had been fasting too much. His mother could give him some medicinal tea. Or, if he went to his great-aunt's, he could get some good food. Even in winter she and the alchuklash were well supplied.

Sitting by the fire of his great-aunt and uncle's house, politely sipping a bowl of warm fish soup and chatting about the festival, Aleqwel shared some of his thoughts and memories. They discussed the anticipated rain and the time when the homecoming canoes might be expected to arrive. Alewqel recalled, but didn't speak of, the lewd stranger desecrating the ceremonial ground. He saw him threatening, cursing his father's ghost. He heard the words "poaching" and "valuable feathers." He remembered his sister lying crumpled on the ground. He would speak privately with his great-uncle soon.

"Tell me," he asked his great aunt, surprising her with his abruptness, "did my late father ever bring you feathers—condor, eagle, owl, egret—I don't know which ones, rare ones that he found in the hills?"

"Yes, of course," answered the old woman. "Your father had a good eye for trade. When he took his money to Matilha or some other place he traded for paint. But he didn't close his eyes to other bargains. You ought to know that. He often brought nice feathers for the alchuklash, even for the wot."

"But did he go hunting for them in nests? In the hills?" the youth insisted.

"Oh, I don't know anything about that," said the old woman, looking to the alchuklash for confirmation. "I don't think he had time for that sort of thing. He was a paint maker after all. Of course, if he was fortunate, he may have found something. Even I have some success in that," she smiled, proud of her power.

Shamefully Aleqwel returned to his soup, banishing all doubts about his late father's integrity.

The tomols did not depart Syuhtun on the day the shrine poles were raised. By the time all the cargo was assembled and then loaded into the planked canoes it was nearly midday. And by midday the onshore breeze began to chop at the smooth water. Then a westerly swell developed. The weather achanas decided it was too dangerous to embark.

There was little to do on that last day of waiting. Nene went for a walk outside of town, looking for herbs. Ponoya counted—again!—the money she had made from the sale of two basketry gambling trays she had woven. She tried, not very successfully, to keep an eye on Anakawin. She and Kanit went and sat near the beach so they could watch the broad-shouldered tomolmen at work. Such idleness was a luxury for them. At home they rarely had much leisure. Sometimes a young man would stop to chat—even joke—with them. But the tomol guild was having an informal meeting and Alow was mostly away.

That night, as she slept out near the shore, the crashing of the surf kept Ponoya awake. Always before she had found the monotonous sound soothing. It was so familiar that she scarcely heard it. But this night, for the first time, her imagination worked with the water. She imagined drowned fishermen, broken fragments of tomol rushing in on wild foam. No one in her family was a fisherman. She had never experienced that kind of waiting. Could she have the strength for it? No matter what people said, it might not be so dreadful to be an old maid, like Kanit. Keti! What was she thinking!

Ponoya fell asleep thinking about selling baskets to help reduce the family's financial worries. But she dreamed of the Swordfish, the wot of the Undersea World. He was the ruler of the underwater world where drowned seamen spent eternity. Drowned men never joined their loved ones in Shimilaqsha. The Swordfish wot—he had a long grey beard—spoke to her.

But she could not make out his foreign speech. The phrases seemed hollow, like bubbles full of empty sound. They were watery words.

After consulting the weather achanas, the fishermen decided to leave early before any large swell could develop. The skies appeared darker, the clouds, denser and higher than they had in the days before. The voyagers stood bare-legged in the cold winter ocean, making their prayers, asking for divine help. They threw seeds upon the water. The women of the Coyote Family climbed into their unsteady canoe. They awaited the calm spell. Then—with a rush—their brothers from the tomol guild pushed them out through the unformed wave. Alow and Mushu were wet to the waist when they pulled themselves aboard the outbound tomol.

The voyage home over gray water began smoothly. There was a steady swell growing, but the oarsmen kept the canoe well inside the kelp bed where it was calm. The day was young and cool. Nene reminded the young women to wrap up in their rabbit fur capes.

Mushu set the rhythm, calling the chant from the rear of the high-eared craft. His son responded. The double-bladed paddles rocked from side to side while Anakawin kept them bailed out with a small tar-lined basket. They skimmed over the surface of the ocean like flying fish.

Ponoya concentrated on the powerful movements of Alow's back as he sat in the bow of the tomol rocking from side to side. He was pulling, pulling. Seagulls screamed overhead, like Grandfather Coyote demanding a meal. Nene, who was too kind-hearted at times, fed the scavengers some cold acorn mush. Now they would never go away.

The gray beaches, the pale cliffs, the dark green woods, the blue smoke of villages flew past in a colorful blur. Ponoya could have been in a dream. Why had she never noticed the power of this landscape before? Or Alow's grace? She had known him all her life—he was like an older brother. He ate, even slept with them. Yet she had never noticed his beauty before. She had even teased him about girls. She hadn't appreciated his kindness. But he had been thoughtful. He had rescued her from the possibility of an insufferable stranger on Solstice Night. Now that she saw his kindness, and his beauty, she knew she would never stop seeing them. She didn't know what she would do, though.

The new vermillion shrine pole atop Halfway Mountain shone out through the grey. Its fresh black feathers guided them anew: east and west, to the origin and the destination. Their destination was southeastward—but only in common time. It would always be west in the end.

The second half of the trip went faster than the first, but with more suspense. The western sky was darkening. The breeze quickened. Thick clouds billowed over the high-peaked mountain range. But the swell was at their backs and the men paddled without resting. Throughout, Alow never spoke. They raced faster than flying fish.

As the danger of wind and rain became more threatening, the women cast seeds and shell money onto the water. They addressed the Swordfish wot.

Ponoya began to wonder if it might have been a sacrilege for her to have gone out on Solstice Night with someone she knew so well. She confessed to herself, as the white water lapped near—and over—the sides of the low tomol, that that night had not been quite as it should. Though Earth and Sky knew that she and the fisherman had never been together before, never even looked at each other, still, it had to come out—the love she gave that night had been personal, not arising from an outside power, or compassion. If anyone had been compassionate it was he. Keti! She trembled. It was so easy to make mistakes, fatal errors. Now, because of her, they would all drown. If only she had found an atishwin last winter.

Black mounds of hardened tar stood above the beach. They seemed to welcome them. "Haku, Haku!" they said. "Welcome back to Mishopshno. To your home."

The tomol skirted the rocky reef that was near the shore. It left the great sea lions reclining there to continue in peace.

The red tomol rode in on a wave that was large enough to make the girls shriek. Everyone got soaked with the foamy spray. But the canoe did not capsize.

They were met by many hands. The hands belonged to the guildsmen who had gone ahead, to Alow's cousin, Chaki, and to Chaki's father and to many other cousins.The seafarers climbed out into the water. Mushu carried the old woman, Nene, to the shore. She protested, but he, who had long been exposed to the cold wet sea, was deaf to her cries.

Guildsmen helped unload the canoe. The idly curious and the highest dignitaries, as well as their kinsmen and guild brothers, met them on the shore.

The passengers wobbled home on shaking legs. Toward the end Kanit had been seasick. At the time she had wanted only to jump overboard, to throw herself into the arms of Swordfish, wot of the Undersea World. Now, just a few minutes later, she was amazed to find that she wanted to live.

Everyone was tired. Anihwoy had made a fire. There was little fresh food for them to eat, but what they had they shared. Anakawin lay his head in his mother's lap and fell asleep. The others were in good spirits, though a little giddy. The men—Aleqwel, Mushu, Alow—passed around a mixture of powdered tobacco and ground mussel shells. They took turns chewing the wad until they felt queasy. Then they went outside to vomit. They came back inside and began again. They grew light-headed and silly.

"Do you think our friend Halashu, the next wot, will ever marry?" asked Alow.

"Oh, I suppose so," said Aleqwel as dizzy as his friend, but annoyed by the gossip. "He's a good man. He speaks well. He can shoot. Why not?"

"Oh, you know why not, as well as I do. He never goes with real women, only with women who were born men . . . and now, with only one."

"What of it? Many men—most even—find such women attractive," he said pointedly. "Anyway, what is there to prevent him from marrying? He'll have to do it eventually. But he's young, like we are… no hurry."

Ponoya, who had not even chewed tobacco, broke in impertinently, "Well, my friend who floats free like a white cloud, maybe you can offer your service as a real woman finder."

The fisherman shut his mouth and a silence fell on the group. Mushu looked at Ponoya as if noticing her for the first time. He laughed.

In the giddy silence they heard a sound. It was hard to say who heard it first. It was the sound of fat drops. Of fat drops falling far apart. It was the sound of first falling rain. It was a beautiful sound. The music of the year's first rain.

The villagers went to their sleeping places tired, tired and content. All was just as the paqwot had told them. The friends of the people had won once again. It would be a good year.

CHAPTER 2

MONTH OF DATURA

hesiq momoy momoy

The night was dark, dark. Grandmother Moon was dead. The menstruating women were off in the pit house. In the home of the curing doctor only males sat and one old grandmother, who was considered a former woman, since she no longer had menstrual periods. Nene moved slowly because of her arthritis. She ladled dark acorn mush into tightly woven baskets.

Aleqwel, Anakawin, and Alow sat cross-legged on the woven hearth mats, waiting to be served.

The gruel was thin, flecked with scraps of dried fish. There were a few cakes of cooked ilepesh, a few dried greens to share. They ate hungrily, slurping from their spoons. A yellow dog lay on the sandy floor by the low door.

Finally, Anakawin, his basket empty, burst out plaintively, "Why doesn't it rain anymore? Didn't the paqwot promise it?"

At first, no one responded. The paqwot knew more than they did. He didn't need any of them to explain or defend him.

Finally Nene took pity, "Be patient, taniw. The season is not yet over. Remember when rain fell after the Winter Solstice Festival? Late rain means more seeds."

"But Grandmother Moon is already dead and there has been no more moisture."

"Don't worry, little brother," soothed Aleqwel. "There will always be fish in the sea and birds in the air and squirrels below the earth. We will survive."

"I wish we had roast goose tonight. Or deer meat. Father..."

"The one who was our father," Aleqwel corrected. "You know not to speak carelessly of ghosts. Though it's hard, it's safer not even to think of those who are gone. Have courage! Soon our life will again be as it once was."

Anakawin looked doubtfully into his empty basket, hardly daring to ask for more.

Nene, as if by magic, took the bowl from him and refilled it from the stone pot. "I believe there might be some dried berries," she said. "Would you like a berry drink?"

In the dark, smoky room the boy brightened. Then he made a submissive remark to his grandmother like one yielding the bones in a hand game contest. "My cousin told me that Grandmother Moon died last week, before her time. I told her it couldn't be true. Is such a thing possible, Nene?"

"Your cousin is right this time, taniw. It does happen sometimes. I can't say why but Momoy's strength gets taken over by the wot of the Sky World. His wings cover her face."

"But she can be made to come back?" he asked anxiously.

"The doctors, like my alchuklash brother, understand the ways of power and the restoration of balance. You know they have influence with the Sky People."

Anakawin reflected. "The alchuklash is strong. But Grandmother Moon is dead again. Is her dying the reason there has been no rain? We are hungry and cannot hunt with the women away."

This time Alow answered. "Grandmother always has come back. The women will return. We will be able to hunt again. Our health will grow. There will be rain." He said it in such a way that the boy believed him.

Nene prepared the boy his drink of crushed manzanita berries and water. She said, "I must go out now to see how the women are." She wrapped herself in her dark otter cape and made a torch of rolled willow bark. She tilted the large tar-lined water basket from its wet stone and poured some into a smaller basket vessel. She lit the torch in the fire and went outdoors. The skinny yellow dog lifted his head and looked at her. Then it dropped its hungry eyes back down on crossed forepaws.

The old woman moved slowly in the night. Her joints ached. It was not far to the sunken pit house where the unclean women were staying. But the way was dark and the going slow. The conical storage house loomed up at her out of the dark like a nunashish from the Lower World.

In the moonless night, the thought of falling down and lying in pain on her back with, perhaps, no one noticing her absence made even the old woman just a little jumpy. A screech owl or a great-horned owl might fly over her, flapping with its wings. It might cry out suddenly. It might try to scare her to death. She would have to lie there with her pain and listen to the distant cries of coyotes. She would have to wait for one of them to approach her. And there would be the birds, the great dark birds. There would be buzzards, eagles, condors, crows. Crows would come to peck her eyes out. And they would not leave behind brilliant poppy petals or shimmering blue abalone to light her way to the Sky World. If she got to the sky, she would surely fall off the moving pole bridge and sink into the sea…

The mound of the family pit house rose before her—at last. Expertly, if slowly, she descended the pole ladder. The room was warm and smoky. The women were reclining lethargically, doing little but scratching themselves desultorily with curved abalone shells. They dared not contaminate themselves by using their own hands or fingernails. Two cousins were arguing in petulant tones.

The women were glad to see Nene, though she could only bring them water. She was a face from outside. Their isolation was great. They had been apart for several days. They insisted that she stay with them, that she share her gossip. They wanted her to tell some stories.

The men had moved close to the crackling fire in the womb-like house. Now they were beginning to grow drowsy. They sat silently, as men alone often do.

Finally Alow said, "You, who have unclean women, may not hunt, but in my house there are no women. I always thought it was a disadvantage. But perhaps it is none. I have learned to cook a pot of porridge. I come and go when I please. Lately, I've been following the wot's advice and taking my tule raft out to fish every morning. Don't ever despair, friends. There is always something swimming in the kelp. And I will share what I catch with you."

Aleqwel was touched by this show of friendship. He put his arm around Alow's shoulder. "It's true, we have very little money left," he said.

"Don't worry. Things will work out. Soon I will have a new tomol to use. The altomolich says he will begin work soon, and I can trade and make more money than I need."

Aleqwel laughed hoarsely, "I can see you have been scheming again. You only think of one thing—money, money, money."

Alow looked hurt.

"Oh, I beg your pardon," modified his friend.

"I forgot, you do have other interests. Young women, for example."

"What's wrong with money and girls?" complained Alow, drawing away like one wounded. "You might do well to turn your mind to such things yourself."

Anakawin was having a good time eavesdropping. His anxiety was falling away. But now his elder brother revived it by addressing him, "Say, taniw, don't you think Nene has been out for a long time? It's not a good night to be walking under the sky. Maybe she has fallen. Take a brand from the fire and run out to look for her, will you?"

Anakawin didn't want to go out into the cold and dark. He wanted to hear more about women and money. He said, "It's a bad night. My power is weak. What if I get attacked?"

"What would attack you? The dangerous animals are hibernating. Think of Nene and run on ahead."

"But there are still nunashish from the Lower World."

"They won't come into the village. Our doctors are too strong."

"Well," said Anakawin defiantly, "I don't know. I saw a nunashish right outside of Syuhtun. That's the strongest town there is. And don't think I am afraid, either."

"Keti! What a story! You probably wouldn't know a nunashish if you saw one. You wouldn't be here now if you did come up against one."

Anakawin looked as if he might cry. No one ever believed him.

Alow could see that the boy was sincere, whether or not he was telling the truth. "What sort of nunashish was it?" he asked calmly.

"It was a holhol," Anakawin said proudly.

"Not a crow or a buzzard?" inquired his brother, still disbelieving. "Are you sure?"

"No! And not a condor either. Though it was enormous and had white under its wings. Its head was even a little red. But it was a real being, not a bird. It had strange feathers that rustled like words."

"Keti!" exclaimed Alow. "Why didn't you tell us about it? Your condition is dangerous. You could die!"

"Well, I haven't died yet," sulked Anakawin. "But if you send me out there. I didn't think anyone would believe me." It was half a lie. All this had happened, but he had forgotten about the incident soon afterward.

"I'm still not sure I do believe you," said his elder brother. "But you must ask our uncle alchuklash to cure you, anyway. Tomorrow!" Aleqwel may have been uncertain of the story, but his heart was beating hard.

With the maddening inconsistency of children, Anakawin now snatched a glowing brand from the hearth fire, nudged the dog into awareness with his foot, and walked boldly into the night. He didn't even bother to throw a blanket around his thin shoulders.

After the boy had gone, Alow removed the cane plug from his pierced nose, opened it up and shook a little tobacco into his hand. He tossed it into his mouth, chewed it a while, spit it into his palm and offered the wad to Aleqwel. "Don't worry! Cheer up! The boy probably didn't see a monster at all. It must have been a condor—though it's rather odd so close to town. Your brother will be all right, though. He must certainly have an atishwin."

Aleqwel didn't say anything. He took the lump of tobacco and chewed. Then, he passed it back to his guest.

Alow was starting to become light-headed from the drug. He said, "Speaking of Solstice Night... I didn't see you. What did you do? Did you go with anyone? It's your duty to like women at least that much."

Aleqwel snapped, "Who said I don't like women? I can't help it if I'm not indiscriminate like you. You'd go with a wood rat if she invited you in. You went with my sister."

"She's no wood rat, let me tell you."

Aleqwel was angry. He sprang to his feet. He wobbled.

His young friend helped him out the door.

He vomited. In a few moments the two went back inside. Aleqwel declined more tobacco.

"You never told me who you went with," goaded Alow.

"I don't know," Aleqwel stated simply.

After a long pause, Aleqwel spoke again, "I'm going to be drinking momoy again soon. I need to strengthen myself. My uncle alchuklash says this is the best time of year. I will have to prepare by fasting again."

Alow said, "Do you remember the year of our initiation, when we drank it together? We were found by our dream helpers, our atishwins, but I felt so sick. I'm glad I'm not a doctor. Can you imagine having to drink that brew every year?" Then he added more seriously, "Is it because of that intruder?"

Aleqwel indicated yes.

"And your sister," Alow asked cautiously, "if I may mention her. I have heard that she is going to try again, too. Does she really need an atishwin? It isn't really necessary for an enhweq. Do you think it's safe?"

"She is in danger from the Wokoch, too," Aleqwel said. "He cursed her. She must take the chance. You know very well that the risk in gaining power is less than the risk of having none. Without a spirit helper she will be vulnerable to any attack, whether from bear or evil-wisher." He continued, "Friend, you know well that my mother's family are alatishwinich, with many spirit helpers; they are close to the First People. And they have good balance. Our late father, who was also my friend and teacher, was of the Earth Team like you."

Alow agreed that it was good for women to be strong in supernatural power as well as in musculature. Still, he looked worried.

Aleqwel said, "You have the concerned look of a father... or husband."

"More like a brother," insisted the fisherman. He disclosed nothing that Aleqwel could either brood about or rely on.

Aleqwel threw more oak wood on the fire. It was warm only near the fire.

Alow said, "I must be going home now." But he didn't move.

Aleqwel understood. It was cold out. And the moonless dark was troubling. A person felt weak going out alone. "Stay here," he urged. "Stay with us. We have room," he indicated Ponoya's empty sleeping place.

"No," said Alow. "No, I'd better be home tonight. My father may come in. It's better for him not to be alone. But, my friend, ichantik, when Grandmother Moon is reborn, come duck hunting with me. The lagoon is crowded with birds now."

Aleqwel sighed, "I'd love to go. I feel I'm letting my family down. They want meat, but I seem never to be able to hunt. If it isn't Moon in her darkness, then it's some necessary fast. When Moon is reborn, I will be preparing for my momoy taking."

"I'm sorry, ichantik, I forgot. Are you certain it's forbidden to hunt birds at that time? They're not really meat, after all. Anyway, why not come along and help out in some other way?"

Just then, Nene and Anakawin and the yellow dog burst into the little house, banging the doors.

"I was just leaving," said Alow. "The food was good, good."

"Well, hurry along then," said Nene. "It's a bad night to be alone. Come see us again when you can."

"Kiwanan, kiwanan," called Aleqwel and Anakawin softly in farewell to their friend.

The next morning, in the gray before dawn, Aleqwel woke up thinking hopefully, "The women should return today. Grandmother Moon will wax. Our health will grow."

Nene was already up, tending the fire.

Before leaving for the sweathouse, Aleqwel said, "Don't you ever sleep, Nene?"

"Old people were made not to sleep," she replied, "so they can keep the fire going at night."

Her grandson showed her his affection. "I wish I could bring you a bird, or even a rabbit," he said sadly. "But at least I can work."

"You are only doing what you must," she returned. "Have courage. You will succeed."

Aleqwel, wrapped in his rabbit fur blanket, laid his sweatstick over his shoulder. Nicely hewn from a long porpoise rib, it accompanied him like a friend.

The sweathouse lay near the ocean, beside the village creek. Unlike a house, it was not thatched with reeds, but was compacted of earth and sunk in the ground. It looked as if it could have been pushed up by a gopher or mole. Aleqwel ascended the roof to the entrance. He climbed down the pole ladder.

Inside, the dry heat was scorching. The large chamber was crowded. Old men lay impassively beside the greenwood bonfire. Young men squatted or stood around the walls. Aleqwel found a place to stand near a man he knew well—the woodworking artisan.

What conversation there was between men was quiet and rumbling like distant surf. Men came in and sweated and then ran out to the cold creek water. It was too hot to think.

The woodworker remarked tersely to Aleqwel, "I didn't see you here last night."

Aleqwel said nothing. His head was drooping. He had not yet begun to sweat, and the heat was at its most oppressive.

"The bard was here. He talked to us about Old Woman Momoy and her grandson," the woodworker continued.

"Sorry to have missed it," mumbled Aleqwel.

"In truth, Piyokol tells the story much better. This bard of ours is somewhat painful, don't you think? He stumbles and slurs. He even forgets," the woodworker confided. "It's a shame to be stuck with him. But what can we do? He's trained. He's antap." Then, perhaps realizing the young man he was talking to was also antap, the craftsman lapsed into silence.

Aleqwel began to sweat. He felt better. But the smoke was so thick it made his eyes burn. He kept them closed as he talked. "Where is Piyokol, anyway?" he asked.

"Haven't you heard? He had so much success at the Winter Solstice Festival that the paqwot and the wot of Syuhtun invited him to stay on for a while."

"For the whole winter?"

"Who knows? Mishopshno is small. We're distant from the a big center. We may feel we are wealthy and strong, but it is only true when compared to those weaker still."

Aleqwel began to scrape off his flowing sweat with the porpoise-bone scraper. The drops fell on the white sand floor, staining it. He felt ready to leave and moved toward the ladder.

"See you here tonight?" asked the older man.

"I'm afraid not, ichantik. The alchuklash is coming to cure my little brother." Immediately, he regretted saying it; now there would be questions, eavesdropping, gossip.

"I didn't know about your brother. Is he very ill?"

"No. No. It's just a formality," Aleqwel replied. "He may have seen a nunashish, that's all. He's fine. Fine, really."

"Ah, good. Good, I hope," replied his colleague, uncertainly. A nunashish!

Aleqwel ran to the creek. The eastern sky still breathed the iridescent sigh that comes before Sun appears. Aleqwel threw himself into a small cold pool. He submerged three times until his blood ran cool. No rattlesnake would be able to smell him when springtime came. He lathered with soap plant and washed his long hair and short beard. He climbed out feeling clean and good. Things might be about to become once more as they should be. He would spend the morning grinding paint.

He shivered a little inside his rabbit fur cloak as he walked home. Quietly to himself he sang the song his atishwin had taught him:

"Lizard, my protector
Impressing your hand on the rock
My hand"

It was a short song, but so beautiful. He could feel its power all through his limbs. He recalled his first vision. Lizard had come to him and shown him the rock on which he had imprinted his hand. It was the original rock. The imprint was the model for all human hands. Aleqwel had put his own hand on the print in the rock from before the Great Flood. It fit exactly. It was then Lizard offered to make Aleqwel excel in his craft. He offered to become his protector. "Use me!" he had said.

He taught Aleqwel the song.

Aleqwel touched the atishwin hanging at his neck. He had found the lizard's foot, his talisman, in his own right hand when he had awoken to the alchuklash's song. All these things happened. Back then, in that former month of Momoy.

Lizard had been a strong atishwin for him. Once, when Aleqwel had been caught swimming in a riptide, Lizard had saved him from drowning. And he had, indeed, given him skill in his craft. Now, more than ever, now that he was without his teacher, Aleqwel was grateful for this gift. He kept Lizard in his thoughts. He sang his song. And when he was entirely alone he danced his dance. He wondered what he might learn if they met again.

At home Aleqwel found the women cooking, eating, talking away. "Pepepe," they said. They were already dressed, groomed, painted.

Aleqwel went to his sleeping place and combed his hair. He tied it up in a flowing topknot and wound it with money beads. He dressed it with a small leather pouch and his flint knife. Then he trimmed his beard and put fresh tobacco in his nose plug. He adjusted his bone earrings. He wrapped his empty carrying net three times around his waist and hung strands of money around his neck. He was dressed and ready to join the women at their meal.

He himself had already begun to fast in preparation for his drinking the momoy root tea. While eating meatless porridge from his soup basket, he spied his brother, Anakawin, still lying at his sleeping place.

"Hey, taniw, hurry up! Don't you know that Sun is almost over the mountains? You'd better get washed or he'll see you and want to eat you."

"Yes, yes, I know," came a muffled reply. "And, if I don't wash, a rattlesnake will smell my warm blood and bite me when he comes out in spring."

"We say those things because they are true, you know," said Ponoya, sipping at her equally meatless acorn mush.

"Come on, lazybones," said Aleqwel. He set him upright on the sandy floor. "You can't afford to take any chances—especially not before you are cured."

In the morning they all worked. Everything was as usual. Because of the cool breeze they worked in the shelter of the windbreak. Aleqwel sat a little apart from the women and began to make up some black charcoal for body paint. The women sat together on their mats and prepared the day's food. They used the big baskets of dried acorns that they kept in the house. "Tap, tap, tap," they cracked the acorn shells. Then, with their tall pestles, they ground the nut meat into meal in deep stone bowls. They transferred the bitter meal into leaching baskets and poured fresh water over it until it was sweet. Each woman did her part. They laughed and chattered like birds and occasionally broke into song.

Aleqwel found the chatter slightly annoying, though he usually did not. He was a little envious today. Men couldn't—wouldn't—gab like that. They couldn't even laugh. But it felt good to be working again and to have everything once more as it formerly was. Even little brother was behaving as he usually did. He was hanging around, asking interminable, pointless questions. Now Aleqwel found himself saying as he had so often before, "Little brother, why don't you do something useful?"

"I can't think of anything. What should I do?"

"If I tell you, you will refuse. You need to think of something yourself."

"I can't. There's nothing to do."

"Why not help Nene gather some firewood?'

As Aleqwel had expected, the boy haughtily refused. "Woi! That's work for women and little babies."

"Well then," said his brother, "why not get out your small bow and go shoot a squirrel to eat?"

After a while, after Kanit and Ponoya had gone down to the creek with their dirty dishes and the water basket, Anakawin too sauntered away. He had his small bow and blunt arrows in hand.

"Where are you going?" asked his mother.

"Where do you think? Down to the brush by the bluffs."

"Well, don't stay all day. Don't forget your uncle alchuklash is coming tonight."

The boy ran off without answering.

Sun rose higher. The wind died down. It was less cold. Aleqwel worked well. He forgot himself. He was content.

The women were parching and grinding ilepesh seeds. Their shouts and laughter over the tricky work of parching in the basket tray made Aleqwel look up. They were having too much fun. He glanced down at the ocean to rest his eyes. It spread out flat and gray all the way to the islands. Today, it was slightly white-capped by the ocean breeze. A big cloud floated over the water. It cast a dark shadow on the sea. Aleqwel could barely make out the shapes of the red fishing canoes in the kelp bed. He raised his eyes to the islands beyond. It was almost time for Sun to rest in the hole of the sand dollar.

"I'm going to leave for a while," he told the women as he set off to relieve himself in the brush. He had not noticed until just that moment how his bowels were twisting. He hurried. In the oaks and sycamores birds called to him. "Pulakak, pulakak," a red-headed woodpecker screamed at him. Aleqwel answered as best he could.

When he got back home he found that a woman of the common people was speaking with his mother. The woman's manner was shy and respectful.

Aleqwel rested and eavesdropped. The woman was saying, "Yes, it has been hurting for some time now. At first he thought it would get better, but now he can't even eat."

Anihwoy was listening attentively.

"I heard you were a good curing doctor. I haven't much money."

Anihwoy indicated that such things as payment could be worked out later. She went into the house for her medicine kit.

"Which one is it?" Aleqwel heard her asking as the two women disappeared down the trail that led to the other side of town.

He was still lolling there, gazing out on the restful white gulls and plummeting brown pelicans, and thinking how fortunate it was that his mother had a useful, paying profession when he heard a familiar, "Haku, haku."

It was Alow.

But the fisherman was not calling to him. He was addressing the young women of his family who had returned from the creek and were lying down taking their rest too. They offered Alow some ilepesh loaves.

Ponoya said, "We watched you fishing. Your father's tomol looked deep in the water. Were there many fish?"

"Oh, it was just like summer," he claimed. The basket of dripping, flipping fish that he had set in front of Nene was indeed full. But the fish were cod and rockfish, not the big tunas that summer brought.

The old woman looked delighted with them, nonetheless. "You are a good boy," she said.

Everyone else laughed.

The fisherman joked with the girls. He seemed very cheerful. Finally, he noticed his friend. "Come with me, ichantik," he said. "I'm off to see the tomol builder."

Aleqwel was ready for a change of activity. "Can we stop by the woodworker's? I promised to drop off some wood stain?"

"Sure. Sure."

Aleqwel cleaned up his work and his work place, while his friend paced back and forth in front of the girls like one of the long-legged shore birds following the tide.

At last the two were on their way. "Grandfather has told me I can take the new tomol to the islands. Do you understand what this means, ichantik? This will be my first major trip. I will be wealthy. Wealthy!"

Aleqwel was pleased. It was good to have rich friends. Friends who might even become in-laws. But he had some doubt. "So the altomolich has really begun work on the canoe?"

"Well, not quite yet. Not just yet. But soon, soon."

They stopped by the woodworker's house. Both of the young men admired his bowls. One new bowl was of oak. Two were carved from sycamore. Each was round as a sea urchin's shell and as smoothly polished as an abalone. They wanted only red stain and shell inlay to be perfect.

Aleqwel supplied the paint. When the woodworking artist finished counting out the lengths of shell money, Aleqwel asked, "Who are the bowls for?"

"For the wealthy, of course," laughed the craftsman. "Two are for the wot, one for the wot's poisoner."

"Ah," sighed Aleqwel.

The altomolich was at the beach. The two friends found him at his usual work spot high on the sand up against the great rocks of black hardened tar. He was doing something to an inverted tomol. His boy apprentice was helping him with a pot of hot liquid tar.

"This one leaks badly," said the tomol builder. "I'm almost ashamed to admit I built it myself. But, then, I made it a long time ago, even before I mastered my craft."

"Well, you've certainly mastered it now," said the fisherman.

"Flattery will not make me work any faster. On the contrary, I will move more slowly. Just to be certain to keep up my reputation."

"But when will you start?" insisted Alow. "Before the rains begin?"

Aleqwel whispered to his friend, "Don't you think it might be better to be more respectful. After all, he is a master. And he is old. He has arthritis, too."

Aleqwel addressed the old tomol builder. They talked of caulking and tar and pine pitch sealants. They talked about paint. Aleqwel acknowledged that he had not enough paint on hand to cover a whole tomol as would be needed. But he expected to make a big purchase soon.

The altomolich said, "A tomol is not built quickly. There are many steps, and each one must be done perfectly. But there will be time, even for the impatient." He said this for Alow. Now he turned to him. "Don't be restless, grandson. If you are impatient, you will always have difficulty in life. One must always wait for the right moment for anything. It's like watching for the break between waves to push your boat out. When I am ready, I will begin your—your grandfather's—tomol."

Alow and Aleqwel soon made their farewells and headed rapidly down the beach. They walked south in the direction of Shuku land. The tide was low and they found it easy to slink around the rocky mussel-covered points of land. At high tide these places were covered by water and hard to negotiate.

Extracting a flint knife from his hair, Alow said suddenly, "Shall we tear off some mussels?" And when they came to a spot where they had several rocks to themselves, and where they were almost alone, they set to work.

The black mussels were tenacious, strong. They clung to their rocks even more persistently than moss or lichen to theirs. The men hacked with their knives. They sawed, twisted, pulled, and finally yanked the tough shellfish from their attachments. Slowly, slowly, their carrying nets filled. The two friends moved from rock to rock working their way down the beach. Soon they were entirely alone but for the black seal that swam, nose up, near their rocks.

Alow said, as he took a big tug at a stubborn mussel, "Have you decided? Shall I tell my cousin Chaki and our friend Halashu? Will we go duck hunting soon?"

"Not yet for me. Let's wait until after Ponoya and I have drunk our momoy. Or go without me."

"I'll do both if you wish," grunted Alow, wrenching off a mussel. "But I wish you weren't fasting. I'm in a mood for some stick dice right now. I can feel my power."

"Just as well for me, then, that I'm restricted," smiled Aleqwel. "What would I do for an opponent if we were both Sky People?"

"We'd probably both be losing everything we had to my cousin Kulaa over in Qoloq. I never do get to play him."

Their nets were nearly full. Aleqwel was thinking about the momoy that both he and his sister would drink. It was powerful. Dangerous. They could die. But if they lived they'd have its power.

"Look," said Alow. "We have accidentally crossed into Shuku land!"

"Keti!" cried Aleqwel, sprinting back over the invisible boundary. "Some of their mussel gatherers may have seen us!"

"Don't worry," smiled his friend. "See, they are way down there." He pointed with his whole arm. All his fingers were extended. "Look at them. They look just like us—but they're not. They're foreigners."

"I have heard that they really come from the islands, not even from the south lands."

"My father says that, too. They are traders. But he says I should remember that they are human beings, above all. You know, my mother was from Wima Island."

Aleqwel replied with vehemence, "It is hard to remember that they are human beings when they behave like such coyotes! They trespass and steal and attack our women. They even kill, and then they make war on us. All because their village is larger and richer than we are."

"But look at them," indicated Alow once more. "See how they gather mussels. See them bending forward, jerking back just as we do. They must eat just as we do. They probably even have intercourse the same…"

Aleqwel flushed at mention of the sex act. "You would know more about that than I. But it seems to me we'll have to learn to live with these people without fighting or we'll be the ones who are destroyed. They will have to be made to respect our power, though. I'm glad I wasn't born to be wot. What a job!"

At Alow's house they found his father squatting on a mat in the dark interior. His fishing gear was spread out in front of him and his tools, too. But he was not working.

"I brought some mussels," said Alow.

"Why bring them here? I'm not a woman. I don't cook. Take them to one of your cousins. Then she can invite us to eat with them."

Mussels were no delicacy.

Alow and Aleqwel hauled their nets to their cousin Chaki's house that he shared with his wife Pichiquich and their baby. The baby, Kelele, was asleep on her cradle board. It was propped against a wall of the house. Pichiquich's mother was helping with the cooking and grateful for the mussels. "I think my son-in-law is out hunting with his father," she said.

"Tell him, if he wants to hunt birds, I'd like to go with him," said Alow deferentially.

As they left, Alow said, "May I go to your house with you now, ichantik? Father seems to need to be alone."

"Is your father always unhappy?" asked Aleqwel. He surprised himself with his indiscretion. He truly wanted to know.

"As long as I can remember," replied Alow readily. "His power is diminished. Yet he continues to live. Fish still come to him, though he says it's me they give themselves up to. It's because of my late mother, of course. He wanted desperately to follow her to the Land of the Dead."

"And that's all that's wrong with him?" asked Aleqwel, choosing his words carefully. "He has not been… poisoned by anyone?"

"Isn't that enough! To be troubled by a ghost!" snapped the fisherman crossly.

-

The young women were sitting in front of the house dexterously thrusting their bone awls into new baskets they were coiling. They worked from left to right sharing a bowl of water between them. They dipped their fingers into it as they wrapped the dry mekhmey rushes of their baskets. The baskets were beginning to take shape as small porridge bowls.

The young men went inside to get some food. Their stomachs had begun to complain of hunger. "Mussels are no great treat," said Aleqwel, "but they're a blessing to someone who is fasting."

The young women promised to clean and cook the shellfish as soon as they could. "I'll prepare a meal for your father," said Ponoya to Alow when they happened to be alone for a moment just before he left. "Do you think he will mind?" she said sweetly.

Alow could not be sure about his father but he himself would be glad of her attention.

The alchuklash sent one of his apprentices to get Aleqwel. The old man's house was high on the hill. It was furnished very comfortably with chairs of whalebone and bearskin blankets and otter capes.

The old man spoke to his grand-nephew about the apparent success of Anakawin's recent cure. They discussed Aleqwel's preparations for taking momoy. The doctor also asked about Ponoya's health. She was in a dangerous condition. At her last drinking she lost the trail and nearly died in the wilderness. And now a strange doctor was calling an ill omen upon her. The alchuklash was interested in the intruder.

Aleqwel told him what little he could.

Then the old man said, "I am going out today to beg of Grandmother Momoy a small piece of her root. I will use it for the young peoples' visions. Will you come assist me?"

"But you have apprentices. And you have your interpreter, too. I have no skill in these things," protested Aleqwel.

"But you are antap, and you are my grand-nephew. I have always believed you have a talent for this work. Won't you try it?"

"Woi! I am no good at astronomy at all. And I'm not drawn to retrieving lost souls. I have my own work. But if you wish it, Grandfather, of course I will accompany you."

The two men—one gray-haired, earlobes elongated by heavy jewelry, neck encrusted with fearsome atishwin talismans—and the other, young, scraggly bearded with only a solitary lizard's foot hanging at his breast—set out. They seemed to wander haphazardly through the sagebrush on the southern bluffs. The old man veered off the trail. He headed first toward the sheer cliffs, then inland toward the soot-blackened valley. The younger one followed him. The pair moved slowly with their heads bent.

Aleqwel knew better than to make conversation. This was an important moment. It had to be an offering of just the right kind. But all the numerous momoy plants looked the same to him.

Aleqwel wondered whether he ought to tell the alchuklash about the dreams he had been having. At night, in the dead of winter, he would travel to Syuhtun. There, he would see the face of the intruder. It was an animal's face. He was never sure what animal. The lips would utter his dead father's name. They said it over and over. In his sleep, Aleqwel wanted to scream and throw dirt in the air. But there is always a hand at his throat. Sometimes it is a woman's hand. She whispers, but her voice is deep. She wants him to come with her. The thong of her buckskin skirt is untied. She offers him valuable feathers. Aleqwel pulls away. He gasps for air. He runs toward the empty chaparral, but she is after him. Her arms flap so that she goes faster. Her reddish-streaked hair flies. As he turns to look back at her he runs into other arms. Sometimes they are the long strong arms of Konoyo, the man-woman. She is the woman who talks to ghosts. The strong arms hold him. The caretaker of the dead laughs at him. He wakens with intense relief.

Last night was the third night he had the dream. The red-haired woman seemed to be getting closer and closer. Konoyo was growing more difficult to find. Could uncle alchuklash do something to strengthen him against the woman? What would happen if she were to get him?

He touched his protector atishwin on its cord of milkweed twine. He wondered if someone was trying to poison him. He played with the dried foot. "My protector, my protector," he whispered. Lizard had always been strong for him. But he had never had to fight poison, ayip. Aleqwel wondered why he had never thought much about poison. It was all around him, an inescapable fact of life. Maybe it was because he had never had an overwhelming desire to poison anyone himself.

He looked up. They were standing at the foot of the hill where the new shrine pole was erected. The black condor feathers pointed to the mountains and the sea. From the pouch in his hair Aleqwel extracted a few egret feathers and some seeds of golden chia and red maids, hutash and ilepesh. He cast them at the base of the pole and to the four winds. He prayed for balance, protection.

The alchuklash addressed prayers to a vigorous broad-leafed shrub at the pole's foot. In return the bush exuded a peculiar odor. The datura giver had found his perfect momoy plant.

Aleqwel handed over the special knife.

The doctor prayed for permission to remove a little piece of root. "Forgive me," he said.

Grandmother Momoy consented. Though her plant flourished all along the coast, no one but the alchuklash could touch her roots. Only he knew how to brew them to the right strength. He turned them into vision and healing.

Aleqwel thought of the ancient days, when power was stronger in the world. Anyone—women, children, commoners—could climb the pole ladder to the Sky World. A person could do it anytime without having to resort to the potion of Grandmother Momoy. He had heard that there were a few powerful achanas who could still do it. But he found it hard to believe. Had not power declined too much over the ages? And yet, sometimes, when he was walking alone in the hills, especially at evening time, he believed he just might bump into Grandfather Coyote at some turn in the trail. The old wizard might easily lead him away to see the world. They might even venture as far as the crystal houses in the sky. One could really never be sure.

When they returned to the doctor's house, the old man said to his young assistant, "I think you should drink your tea under the shrine sycamore. Sleep out. That way you may hear the voice of your late father speaking through the leaves. It would be good if you would communicate with your dead father."

Aleqwel, without being aware of it, had been hoping to receive this very suggestion. "Do you think," he stuttered, "something could have happened to my late father to make him die? Something other than his own omissions or deeds?"

"Poison, you mean?"

Gradually, the novice paint maker began to talk, to talk about everything, even his frightening dream.

That afternoon the datura giver had his final meeting with the six young people who would be taking momoy—four of them for the first time. He told them that, though it is invaluable to find a protector, an atishwin, there is always benefit to be gained from drinking momoy—even if no dream helper comes.

All six knew that two of them had tried before, without success, to find an atishwin. Ponoya, one of the two, had become so ill that she had died for several days before returning to consciousness. But the other one, a boy, had the opposite experience. Like Grandmother Momoy's amazing grandson he seemed to be immune to the potion. It had had no effect on him at all.

It was these two the alchuklash was watching especially carefully. They were the mysterious ones. He did not want anyone to die, particularly not his own kinswoman. The boy—he was a puzzle. Had he been fed momoy water as a baby? Probably there was little danger of his dying.

The alchuklash talked informally with the young people. He assessed their readiness for the act. He evaluated their purity, their courage, their strength. Then he led them to the sacred enclosure where he made his formal remarks. He told them that their twenty-one days of fasting had put them in a pure state that would make them accessible to visits from spirit beings. He told them that he, like Coyote, would give them a drink of the root of Grandmother Moon's flower, momoy. He knew they had heard all this before. But it never hurt young people to hear the truth again. He said,

"Momoy is powerful. Like everyone of great power she is also dangerous. She can be malevolent as well as benign. She is amoral. Be careful with her. Is there anything more dangerous than momoy? Yet, she can give you power, too."

The young people stood silently, listening as if for the first time.

"What is more dangerous than momoy?" he continued. "It is to live without power. Without power you are nothing. You are less than the lowest commoner. You are less than a baby."

No one was offended. None was a commoner. The ceremony was prohibitively expensive.

The old teacher reiterated how power brought success in gambling, in work, in sports. He told how it gave good health, defended against enemies, and, above all, how it brought protection from every danger on the last trail. It led souls safely along the path to the Land of the Dead. "Only your atishwin will get you across that trembling bridge! Soon you will drink from the sacred cup. You will shake. You will die. You will enter the Timeless Time. How will you get there? What will you see? How will you return?"

He sketched the way, the possibilities. He reviewed the pitfalls of travel along the time-worn road. He talked of flying. "How will you recognize your atishwin?" he asked again.

Ponoya knew the litany by heart. Your dream helper will come as one of the First People or as an animal. It will be Pelican, perhaps, or Hawk or Butterfly. He—or she—will say: "I am your atishwin." And he will teach you his song and give you his talisman. She had looked out for him the last time, but he had never come. Her momoy dream had been so confused. She remembered nothing. Now she would try again. She did not fear death any more. It might be easier for her in Shimilaqsha—if she managed to get there. Her father would surely be in that festive land.

The alchuklash was reminding the initiates who found atishwins in their dream to keep them happy. He told them to sing their song and dance their dance and to be sure to use them. He advised the young people to grasp onto them for strength. As the day grew old and waxing Moon rose out of the east, the alchuklash began to bring his speech to a close.

"Remember," he concluded, "gaining a dream helper is not everything. To drink momoy is what is important. Then you will see the true nature of things. And, if you see the true nature of things, then you will have proper values. You will live in a civilized way. This is more important even than finding an atishwin, than individual power."

"But if you do find a spirit helper, keep him happy. Never lose track of him. Don't boast about him. Be shy even to mention his existence.

Remember: never ignore him or lose the talisman he gives you. If you do, power will leave you, and you will surely die."

On this dire note, he dismissed his students. They were free to go home, to reflect on his words, and to fast. Soon he would come to them with his old friend, Grandmother Momoy.

Grandmother Moon was strong on the day of Ponoya's journey. But, like a pregnant woman, Moon in her fullness slept in the day and never showed her potent face until twilight.

The enhweq awoke early. She bathed and groomed herself as usual. Neatly, she painted her face and breasts with red ochre. As always Kanit served as her mirror, telling her how she looked. The others stayed out of her way. Aleqwel trembled more than his sister did.

When the alchuklash and his assistant arrived, the family left the girl alone with them in the house. They last saw her sitting on a sleeping mat not far from the fire. Her slender legs were tucked to one side and her soft red skirt with shells and beads dangling from the fringes was gracefully arranged over her knees. Her expression was impassive. Aleqwel took the look to mean: "Life in the Earth World is brief. Who am I to resist the ways of our makers?" Aleqwel left with sadness. And hope. His sister appeared strong, beautiful and strong.

The day was overcast and gray. Dew sparkled on the plants in his mother's garden that she had made by transplanting some healing herbs. But there were no puddles of rain. Aleqwel went to walk on the beach. Maybe he would find something useful there.

Inside the house the alchuklash prepared his potion. He mashed the root in its ceremonial mortar. His assistant poured spring water from a special basket. The alchuklash mixed the ingredients carefully. He had the art of precise dosage. He prayed. He handed Ponoya the drink.

She swallowed it without hesitation. In a short time she began to turn pale and to perspire. She began to tremble and sway. She fell over dead.

The alchuklash laid her out gently on the sleeping mat and covered her soulless body with a soft fur blanket. He sat down at her side and motioned for his assistant to leave them.

Aleqwel had gone out into the gray morning with only his gathering tools and a small portion of food for later in the day. They were in his carrying net tied around his waist. He thought he might collect some abalone or dig for some clams.

He crossed the mouth of the village creek and headed north along a broad curving of sand and high dunes. The beach was busy. Men were fishing in the surf, throwing out their long lines with many-barbed hooks. Women were digging for clams in the dark wet sand, while small children tore at the same wet sand in pursuit of disappearing sand crabs. They made a good fish bait, but, as often as not, the children tossed them at each other in tickly glee.

Other children raced each other on the dry sand. Several practiced their hockey game by kicking small round beach stones.

As usual, Aleqwel noticed every detail. Fear enhanced his attention. In particular, his eye was caught by one small boy—one of the common people—who was drawing patterns on a large beach stone using a chunk of a partially burned wood.

Aleqwel looked out over the channel. He could see half a dozen red tomols and low-lying tule rafts anchored in the kelp not far from shore.

After only a few miles of walking, Aleqwel came to the sandy point at the mouth of the lagoon. To approach it he had to walk up into the dark spreading estuary where the dunes were blanketed with short grasses and broken shells. Among the tall reeds of the salt marsh, the thatch grass and mekhmey basket rushes, he spied a few men in dugouts. They were fishing in the smooth water of the lagoon. Gray ducks and black-and-white geese, snowy egrets and blue herons were feeding peacefully in the red-brown water. A duck hawk and a bald eagle hovered overhead.

It was a rocky fertile place with many shellfish. The rocks were encrusted with mussels, barnacles, limpets, starfish, sea anemones, skittering crabs. And abalone. Aleqwel withdrew his whalebone pryer from his net. He began giving sharp blows to a large red abalone. It fell off onto the wet sand. He knocked off a few more. Then he came to a stubborn one. It wouldn't give. He used the bone tool to pry it off. When he had a fair-sized heap he packed up the shells into his carrying net.

With the same whalebone pryer, he then began to dig clams. Before long he had accumulated a good big pile of them.

Soon it came to be the time when Sun rests in the hole of the sand dollar. The gray clouds were beginning to break up and drift away. The outlines of the islands began to peek through on the far side of the ocean channel.

Aleqwel propped himself against a rock, making a chair in the high sand. He ate his little meal of ilepesh loaves and dried pohoh. He looked out at the fishermen in the kelp. He could distinguish the small dark bodies of seals and sea otters lounging in the red-brown seaweed. Everything looked clear to him.

Even the islands were becoming illuminated. The sunlight was shining on them in a special way, a way that highlighted distant hills and valleys so that a person could almost see the blue smoke and red tomols of the people who lived there. In fact, he thought he saw a little wisp of blue haze in the middle of the long island hanging right above Kahas Harbor. Kahas was the port of Michumash Island, the biggest island the four—maybe it really was smoke.

Aleqwel did not own a canoe, and he had never made the difficult journey to the islands. He realized that he probably never would. Yet a tomolman like his friend Alow could do it. If the new tomol got finished in time, Alow would certainly go the islands. If he survived, he would come back a rich man. Aleqwel wondered how that would affect them all. It was not as if Alow had said he wanted to marry his sister. Ponoya might even be dead at that very moment. Everything was uncertain. It was as indefinite as a wind rising out of the south.

Aleqwel ate and dreamed of far-off places. He did not regret not being a tomolman. Yet he longed to travel across the ocean channel the way the First People had. People like Coyote and Lizard just dived in the ocean and swam. They swam underwater the whole way. He also yearned to cross the mountains as they did. To leap from peak to peak like the fastest racer on the day of the harvest celebration, the Hutash Festival. Despite traveling to the Sky World in vision, the young paint maker had seen little of the Earth World. Heliyik village, north of Syuhtun on the Great Salt Lagoon where his father came from, was the farthest he had ever been. "If I am to realize my dreams I must go farther," he thought. "I must talk with knowledgeable people. I must get to know artists and foreigners. I must go to the mountains, to the mountain at the center of the Earth World. Maybe one day I will even go to the islands." Soon, he would make a trading trip to the mountains near Matilha to replenish his supply of paint stones. He itched to set foot on the trail.

It was time to lace up the carrying net and move on. Aleqwel thought of all the ducks he had seen in the lagoon, the mallards, pintail, teal. He wished he were going hunting. He wished he could feed his family better.

The young paint maker went to the home of the alchuklash's assistant. They gave him some dark acorn soup. At dusk the alchuklash arrrived. He said Ponoya was doing well. She was still sleeping. She was talking some and dreaming. Aleqwel slept soundly that night in the house of his kinsmen and suffered no dreams.

The next day dawned as cool as the day before. But it was clear with little moisture. After sweating and bathing Aleqwel found himself wandering down to the house that belonged to Alow's father.

Mushu said bluntly, "My son isn't here."

Aleqwel hadn't really expected him to be indoors on such a fine placid morning.

Mushu's house was dark. The fire was crumbling. The room was not very tidy either—nets and fishing implements were lying around in disorder. Aleqwel offered to help sort out torn nets from whole nets, good hooks from broken ones. It was something even he, a rock grinder, could do.

The older man allowed him to do it without actually giving permission.

Aleqwel wondered why the man had refused to move in with kin after his wife's death, why he had not remarried. It was sad to see a house without a woman. It was frightening to see a man with such obviously ebbing power. He began to speculate on what the man might have done wrong that such a thing had become of his life. He recalled what Alow had said, that his father often went without sleep, that he roamed the beach at night. It made him think of ghosts. Suddenly, he didn't want to stay there any longer. It made him think of poison.

He left both doors open behind him to let in the morning sunlight. But before he could get far away he was met by a pleasant, "Haku, haku." It was his friend Halashu. The wot's nephew was heading toward Mushu's house. He leaned in the doorway. Graciously, but urgently, he urged Mushu to get out and fish while there was still time. "Soon it will be raining," he said confidently. "It will be impossible to fish then. Work now, fisherman, while the sea is smooth and the fish are friendly. It's like summer out there. We need you now. What you catch feeds us all. You are a strong hunter."

Then he spoke to Aleqwel, standing outside the house. He inquired into his sister's health. He was pleased with Aleqwel's favorable reply. "My cousin Nacha will be journeying soon," he said. "Come, share some food with our family."

Aleqwel was far too polite to decline hospitality. He was actually happy to find such powerful companionship.

He joined Halashu on his morning round of exhortation. They went to the homes of wealthy and commoner alike—encouraging them. The future wot convinced them to work harder, to increase their productivity. It was important to keep up their spirits. People responded affirmatively to the gracious young man. But they could not conceal their doubt about the rain.

Would it really rain? What was the weather achana doing about it? Halashu sought to reassure them, to urge them on.

Aleqwel was impressed by his friend's skillful use of words. He did not have that skill. As the two were returning for something to eat at the assistant wot's house atop the hill, Aleqwel remarked, "How strange is the hierarchy of power in the Three Worlds! Surely, it is natural that every person—from antap to commoner—has his own place. Everyone has his own allotment of power." He was thinking of the common boy he had seen on the beach drawing with charcoal. "Why is it, then, that sometimes there is one—even among the common people—who has more power than others of his kind?"

Halashu replied, "Common people are like towhees. They have no guilds, no tools to make money. They cannot afford to join the antap or to drink momoy tea. And so most of them never find an atishwin to help them."

"Which makes it difficult for them to attain power in this world or enter the Land of the Dead," finished Aleqwel.

"Yes, that's how it is," said Halashu. "There are many towhees and only a few eagles soaring above. It's the natural way. But sometimes there is one who rises, who changes his feathers. Even this seeming unnatural event is natural, too, if you notice closely how things are. Some eagles are fiercer than others. I often think of our great storyteller, Piyokol, who came from the commoners."

"How can one change his feathers?"

"In his case, an atishwin came to him somehow. I don't know how. His skill grew. He found a powerful patron—my uncle."

"It's a marvel," said the young paint maker. "But how much easier it is to lose power than to gain it! How much easier to slide down than to soar to the majestic sky. To molt, you might say. How strange it all is!"

"Yes, yes," agreed the seemingly imperturbable Halashu.

It was nearly sunset when Aleqwel got back to his own home. He found his sister talking in a confused and sometimes unintelligible manner, but struggling to get her bearings. The alchuklash was helping her. The old man looked pleased.

With Aleqwel's help the momoy giver led teetering Ponoya down the short path to the sandy beach. Evening was a quiet time of day by the water's edge. Most of the fishing boats were pulled up on the shore under the shadow of hulking mounds of tar. The creek trickled meekly into the sea.

The doctor sang to the girl:

"You are here at Mishopshno
It is the beach at sunset
You are here. Here you are."

The girl tried to speak. She had difficulty focusing her tongue. Her experience was buried, hidden, untranslatable.

The alchuklash continued to sing while Aleqwel held his sister's hand. The doctor sang the song over and over. He had sung it to Aleqwel when he had come back with his atishwin. "You took momoy. Now wake up," he sang. Aleqwel remembered hearing the words from a far-off land.

Ponoya looked up at them. She became coherent.

Aleqwel turned to leave, but his great-uncle said, "Stay! Stay!"

The young woman opened her mouth and shared a fragment of her vision. Her experience was as clear as Sun at noon on the summer solstice. It was as rich as fiery Sun disappearing in front of them now.

She said she had walked and walked and walked for many days. The trail was mountainous and rocky. She was tired. But never lost.

Suddenly, a nunashish, a terrible grizzly bear, sprang out at her from behind a boulder. She was scared to death. Something buzzed in her ear. The buzzing grew and grew.

Ponoya's words began to fade. They seemed to be melting with Sun into the sea.

The alchuklash brought her back. He prompted her. "Who was buzzing?"

"The noise maker said, 'I am Hummingbird, your spirit helper. Use me!'"

"Iyi!" Aleqwel exclaimed.

The doctor suggested that it might be best for Aleqwel to return home and tell the family the results.

"What happened?" the alchuklash then asked Ponoya.

"I got light, light. I began to float up in the air. I was flying fast, very fast. The directions were confused. When I finally landed, Hummingbird was standing beside me. She sang in my ear. She said it was her summoning song."

"What is the song that she sang to you?" persisted the achana.

Ponoya remembered it. She sang it in a thin flutelike voice.

They rested for a while in the twilight shadows. They sat on a smooth rock of hardened tar. Ponoya felt blessed. Hummingbird was a powerful atishwin. Quail or Butterfly, the kind of dream helpers women found more often, were not as potent. As Sun drifted behind Tuqan Island, she wondered, "How many bodies has Sky Eagle picked up in his travels today? Why is mine not one of them?"

"Do you think I have a gift for power, Grandfather?" she asked.

The old man smiled and wrapped her in a warm fox robe. Ponoya huddled in her fur, perched on the shiny black ledge of tar. She was still shivering. The momoy had been very bright. Her hands protected her newborn ears from the harsh cry of gulls and she still squinted at the mild gray sea, as it slipped away into darkness.

"They say the ocean is the reflection of Sun and the place in which to see things clearly," she said. "I never understood that before."

"Yes," said the old man. "Yes, they say that."

He helped her to her feet and guided her along the gently rising path to her home.

She sang softly, softly:

> *"Hummingbird, my atishwin, come*
> *Fly to me like down*
> *From the four winds."*

When she discovered a cord with the dried remains of a small bird at her throat, she was not surprised. Yet she was amazed at seeing the evidence. She really had an atishwin!

It was nearly noon, another cold clear day. Anihwoy and her younger sister were sitting in front of the house shelling and grinding acorns and singing a song that made the work go faster.

Aleqwel sat pulverizing red stone. He was feeling cheerful, light-hearted. The women's singing pleased him. He thought that at midday he might go get his flute and play a bit. It would keep the voice in the instrument happy.

Alow arrived bearing an openwork basket full of silvery rockfish. The fish looked good to the family.

The fisherman squatted near the women. "How are you?" he asked.

Anihwoy answered, "We are well. All well. My daughter is inside lying down. She will be up soon."

Alow said, "I am glad things went well."

"Yes, they did. They did." The mother smiled without letting up on the constant churning of her long stone pestle.

Alow took the reply to mean that Ponoya had not only survived her ordeal but had found a helper in her momoy dream. He was happy for her, for her family. Beneath his thoughts he felt a lightness, a sort of springing sensation. It was something like the way he felt at the beginning of a footrace when the referee gives permission to let loose.

The paint maker looked cheerful, too. Now that strain had fled from his friend's face Alow was made aware how much Aleqwel had suffered since summer when he had lost his father. Alow had lived so long without a mother and with scarcely a father that he had forgotten how difficult it could be—in the beginning. He had forgotten how long it took to find one's own courage and to learn to take a meal of parental love in any hospitable home. Alow addressed his bright-eyed friend, "Ichantik, let's get some ducks tonight! I can tell our friends now."

Aleqwel protested: "You know I am fasting."

"Oh, you don't need to kill anything. Just come along. Be our carrier."

And Aleqwel, in his good mood, could see no harm in that. In any case, bird hunting wasn't real hunting, not like stalking deer. Birds couldn't smell so well. They weren't real meat, anyway. Hesitating only a little, Aleqwel consented.

In the evening Ponoya joined the family for food. She had a big appetite. Aleqwel was glad he had fresh fish to roast for her.

Just after sunset Alow stuck his head in. He smiled to see Ponoya sitting up. He said kind things to her, warm things.

He told Aleqwel, "My cousin Chaki and the wot's nephew will join us. Meet at the log bridge when Moon is low. Bring your trap."

Aleqwel agreed.

"Well, I'll be going then," called the fisherman as he retreated into the night.

Aleqwel went straight to his resting place after eating. Falling asleep he could hear Nene telling stories to the women about Grandmother Momoy in the ancient days.

He woke while it was still night. He took down his carrying net from its peg and tied it around his waist. He grabbed a bit of cold acorn mush. He wrapped up in his tan rabbit cape and scooped up the cumbersome duck maze and slipped out of the house.

The cold air was damp and biting. The star crystals glittered in the black. Over the western sea a diffused light glowed. Moon was nearly full. It was an auspicious time.

His friends, draped in fur, were standing by the creek. Alow and Chaki looked like beached sea animals, and Halashu appeared noble in bearskin. They had brought nets and traps, bows and arrows.

The friends crossed the log without giving a thought to their steps. The creek rushed under them with its reassuring clatter.

Soon they stood on the banks of a large lagoon. Halashu led them to the tall cattails where his dugout was tied. All four climbed in. Now, at high tide, the vast salt lagoon was easy to navigate. And Grandmother Moon lighted the way through the sinuous channels of the watery expanse. The brackish water glistened. Islands of red marsh weed rose and threatened to capsize them. Occasionally, a white-winged egret or a green heron would materialize on long legs, flying away on slow wings at their approach.

The men admired the birds in their flight. Their feathers were valuable. But they did not shoot at them. Though the muddy water was not deeper than their height, they had no wish to accidentally fall into the thick cold slime.

"Why has there been so little rain?" complained Alow softly.

"Will there be enough seeds?" worried Aleqwel.

"What do the achanas say?" pressed Chaki.

The questions everyone asked themselves were really for Halashu. What could he say? "There is still time. It will rain. Didn't the paqwot learn of it? Besides, even in a bad year, we can endure. Mother Earth, Shup, gives us many things to eat even if we don't relish them—shellfish, insects, grass. In the end, rain will always return."

Something troubled Aleqwel. "What if a foreign achana wanted to cause us harm, wanted to make a drought, could he do it?"

Halashu gave a small sigh. "It's always a danger. But what doctor would want to do such a thing? It would also bring drought to his own people. He would have to be very powerful—and very crazy, kilamu—to cause such universal harm. He'd have to be from the Sun Team and have Sky Eagle on his side."

They had come to a place halfway across the lagoon, a spot not far from the invisible boundary that separated their half of the salt marsh from their northern neighbor Qoloq's. They would not cross the line, even had they believed it profitable. Some wandering insomniac, some suspicious achana, someone wholly unlikely to be there or perhaps another duck hunter would undoubtedly spy them. They could be killed for poaching. It would be an incident. No one wanted to be marked for death or to be the instigator of war. Qoloq was a friendly neighbor, and not insignificantly small.

The ducks slept in the high grasses.

The four friends moved quietly, carefully, in the fading moonlight. On the soggy banks of the lagoon, where mekhmey rushes and cattails grew thick, where ducks and waterfowl slept, they set up their traps. They built mazes with the tule blinds.

At the very last drop of moonlight the young men grabbed a few mud hens sleeping under the grasses and set them in the hearts of the traps. Their call would lure the ducks into the remorseless circular mazes. The shores of the lagoon were thick with wintering water birds. In the first gray of the eastern mountains, the three hunters took up their small bows and wood-tipped arrows and went to shoot the birds that were beginning to awaken. Aleqwel collected the green-winged teal, the many-colored mallards, and the dark pintails that the other men shot. He loaded them into their carrying nets. When the nets were full, the men quit shooting. They exchanged their catches, hoping to keep their luck strong. It was only by sharing that they could keep it so.

Sun peeked out over the mountain tops.

The four friends began to pole their way back across the flat red-brown water.

A few days later the same four friends went back across the lagoon in their dugout to check their duck blinds.

Halashu poled through the murky water in the early light. He remarked on the size of the morning surf.

With characteristic optimism, Chaki said, "Rain will come soon." Then he mentioned how appreciative his family had been of the roast duck they had eaten after their last hunt.

Aleqwel said nothing, but remembered how grateful his family had been when he brought in and cooked the birds that he himself had not shot and that he could not eat. His violation—if it had been one—of the hunting prohibition tugged at his gut. But the smiles on everyone's faces—especially wan Ponoya's—made him determined to go out again—and to take his bow.

In the silver morning, all four men carried their small bows as well as their carrying nets. Now, Alow spied some of their duck blinds among the rushes by the bank. He leapt from the dugout and hurried to tie the line to a clump of cattails.

A muffled cry told the others that he had found their prey. Inside the spiral mazes they could hear mud hens and some squawking ducks. Silently, efficiently, the men slogged through the black mud and crept into the tall marsh grass. Many of the birds were already dead. Others quacked feebly.

The men twisted the necks of the survivors. They filled their nets and rolled up the bulky traps. They loaded the willow wood dugout.

Alow said, "Listen, I hear human beings. Others have got here first."

"It's because of the surf," said Halashu. "There's no fishing today. Everyone has decided to spend the day getting birds."

Aleqwel was still uncertain, torn between wanting the best results from his coming momoy quest and needing to help feed his family. He suggested that they return home and come back to hunt another day.

But Chaki—the eldest—declared authoritatively: "Birds are like fish. They are without number. They never run out. They give themselves in abundance to those with the skill to capture them." Aleqwel had to agree, there were enough birds for everyone. But, in a warning flash, he determined not to hunt this time. He would only assist the others as before.

The friends left their dugout behind in the tules and tramped onto higher ground, to the plain where the mud was hard. A duck hawk hovered overhead. A few black-and-white geese were in clear sight, feeding greedily on low-growing grasses. Others were undoubtedly sleeping in the thick cattail forest.

The young men came to a place that looked deserted. They heard distant voices but saw no people. They concealed themselves behind tall reeds and plucked out wood-tipped arrows, the short kind that fly fast and sure.

Halashu, an archery champion, drew first. At all the big celebrations, at the Hutash Festival, he competed in shooting. He excelled at distance and at accuracy. Every day he spent time practicing with his father, the assistant wot.

But his friends admired him less for his skill at striking leather targets than for his hunting ability. Halashu shot and killed animals gracefully, with seeming ease, with his horizontally held bow. His friends said that his strength was not so much in his eye and arm as in the way he could call animals to him. The way he could persuade them to give their lives.

The morning was overcast and the geese blended into the sky. Halashu's first arrow struck a fat goose just as it was about to lift off from the ground. Halashu shot geese until he finally missed.

Aleqwel ran to the empty field to retrieve the fallen birds. They bled darkly. But most of the birds the wot's nephew hit he killed. He was right on the mark. They were good big geese.

Chaki touched the mountain lion paw around his neck and then shot. He was strong, too, brawnier even than young Halashu. His shoulders were square and his body tapered like an arrow point to small square feet. His appearance was wholly admirable. Chaki's fame was in hunting big animals: sea lions, seals, swordfish, giant sea bass—anything from the sea. But he did all right on land, too, even with mountain lions. He had power. Force.

Aleqwel dashed out to retrieve Chaki's kill. The carrying nets were filling fast.

Alow shot. He had a few misses of birds in flight. They were difficult shots. But Alow was filled with enthusiasm. He wanted more tries. He sent the paint maker to pick up his fallen arrows.

Aleqwel complied. He too, was beginning to grow breathless with fervor. Envy was beginning to stir in him.

When Alow finally relinquished his turn, Aleqwel found himself reaching for his own bow. Chaki gave him a questioning look. But no one tried to stop him. Geese were only birds, not real hunting.

Aleqwel shot, and not very well. His hands trembled slightly and he was out of practice. After a few misses, he hit a nice fat goose. It was standing somewhat far afield, but still. Perhaps it was bewildered at being stirred from sleep. When the arrow hit it, it fell. It did not struggle to rise. The archer's other attempts were unsuccessful. They were embarrassing shots for someone whose inadequacy at deer hunting was said to be compensated for by a talent in fowling.

Aleqwel ran out into the damp gray field to retrieve his one bird. He thought: embarrassing or not, this one fat bird will make a fine meal. Then it struck him that his ill-luck might have come from his failure to follow the hunting prohibition. He bent down and hauled up the heavy gray-breasted bird that lay at his feet. As he rose, he prayed that his momoy drinking would not be affected by the infraction. He turned round on his heels.

A sharp pain like a fierce cramp shot through his right leg. He could not help but cry out. The scream that came out of him was like that made by the birds when they were hit.

His three friends ran to him. Halashu pulled the arrow out of his calf. He examined it without touching the point. He ran and threw it into the water of the salt marsh.

For a moment Aleqwel died and left the Earth World. When he returned, he vomited. He had seen the bloody arrow. It was not one of their own. It had a foreign look. It belonged to another party. But the other party—the invisible other party—why weren't they aiming better? Couldn't they see he was a man? No one would shoot that way, except maybe a child. But this arrow was no miniature blunt-tipped one.

"Woi! No good! No good!" Halashu cried. He set out to track down the other hunters.

Chaki stanched Aleqwel's blood with a handful of cattail fiber. He and his cousin carried their friend back to town. They left the birds and the dugout behind for Halashu, praying they were not abandoning him to enemies.

On the way home, Aleqwel, in his stunned state, demanded to walk.
"Se, se. No, no." his friends insisted.

Aleqwel's awareness turned gray and hazy like the hovering sky. Once, as they neared the footbridge, he said thickly, "I should have drunk it sooner. I knew I was weak. If I die, it's my own fault."

Alow reassured him that the wound was shallow. It would heal.

But all three knew that Aleqwel referred not to death from the severity of the wound but to the poison that might have been introduced on the point of the arrow.

Anihwoy took hold of her wounded son and helped him to lie down by the healing fire. She gave him a cup of water with tobacco and powdered shell in it. It would help ease his pain.She cauterized his wound with mugwort and sutured it.

Aleqwel had grown calmer when he saw his mother's house. Though he yelled at her and her burning and stitching, he felt calmer still when she touched him. Before drifting into sleep he thought, "If it were poison, I would be dead already." And he drifted off peacefully.

When he awoke, it was night. There was a terrible loud noise as if surf were crashing on his head. The fire was glowing in the darkened house. Everyone else must have been asleep. Rain was breaking over the roof. He could see little streams of water here and there where the thatch leaked. He went back to his dreams. When he next awoke, it was day. Through the open doors he could see the ocean rippling blue-gray with the breeze. The sky was blue.

Pain shot up out of Aleqwel's leg in waves. The pain seemed to him worse than on the day—which day?—when he had been hit. A small groan escaped from him.

His mother came with more tobacco tea. And he slept again.

Later, it was Ponoya with food: bowls of thin acorn soup.

His mother dressed the wound with an astringent poultice of oak bark. She brought more tea to kill the pain.

Next morning Nene went to visit the spring in the oak forest on the far side of the playing field. She took small offerings: money, tobacco, hutash seeds. She placed the offerings around the spring in the four directions. She faced the Center of the Earth World. She prayed "Yaha yaha ha." "U, u, u" and "a a a," she prayed as she turned to the four winds. Then, she placed herself—herself and the sacred spring—in the still center. She requested water from the spring. She said, "My grandson is a thirsty man. I ask of your water that he may drink."

The power of the spring gave permission.

Nene had brought a small wooden vessel for the healing water. She borrowed a small amount of the pure water.

All day the wounded paint maker woke and slept and woke and slept. But he was getting stronger. His grandmother gave him spring water to drink. Everything came together to heal him.

Toward evening he asked his mother, "Who shot me? It was not one of my friends."

"We don't know," replied Anihwoy. "None of the hunters admits to doing it."

"Yet there was no poison either," he mused, perplexed.

The next day Aleqwel was awake all day. But he was still unable to walk.

At midday his mother examined the wound and announced, "I believe that you are healing."

"Yes, I am healing," he said. "But why?"

Later on the alchuklash looked in. He, too, scrutinized the wound. "It's more important than ever for you to drink momoy. She is our greatest healer. We'll do it before the end of the month, while she still is at the height of her power."

Aleqwel was greatly relieved. The alchuklash had said nothing about the ducks and the geese and his hunting, about prohibitions. Momoy would strengthen him.

Anihwoy was proud to be able to cure her son herself. She was glad that he was strong enough that the injury had not touched his soul. Aleqwel told her she was the best curing doctor in the village, in all the surrounding land.

By the end of the week the young paint maker could stand up and limp around the house.

The alchuklash had asked the wot to commemorate the recovery. There had been no poison on the arrow, but the circumstances of the accident had been suspicious. Though his wound healed well, Aleqwel was not free from doubt.

The wot announced that a party would be held to honor the recuperating antap youth.

The night of the festivities, the young man walked out of his mother's house for the first time since his injury.

He was overwhelmed to find the whole village—hundreds of people—all gathered in the ceremonial enclosure to celebrate his revival. The people were cheerful and festive, even if a little cold and hungry. The music of flutes, whistles, and rattles seemed to warm and satisfy them.

Aleqwel had attended many such parties. Every individual was important to the community, and every life spared was an event to celebrate. But such a celebration never had been held for him. He had always been healthy. He had never known the people cared so much for him. In fact, he had somehow believed himself anonymous, almost invisible.

Now, his face shone in the firelight. Lizard's foot lay lightly on his chest. His former resolve to serve the community grew even firmer, like a plain bow backed with sinew. He wondered what he had wasted his lonely youth dreaming about as he wandered in the hills. The people were everything.

The alchuklash, master of this month of Momoy, of Coyote, the momoy giver, said the prayers. He blew the smoke and scattered the down. He made a little speech of gratitude at Aleqwel's recovery.

Aleqwel felt he was in one of his tobacco dreams. The occasion seemed so unearthly. It was so delicious.

The best dancers performed their most amusing dances. One of Aleqwel's own kinsmen came out daubed and bedraggled as Old Man Coyote himself. The young man was ready to laugh.

He could hear some of the women grumbling, as if shocked by the obscenities. Yet, the guest of honor was amused to see how few of these women left the enclosure. He was already laughing when the dance started. The men, of course, all remained.

Coyote, seedy and forlorn, crafty doctor in disguise, sang his cosmic lament:
>*"My power has left me.*
>*My power has left me.*
>*Bad. Bad. Bad.*
>*What will become of me now?*
>*I can only wait to die."*

He pawed the earth and sniffed and danced as coyotes do. It was all very sad.

But Coyote always makes a comeback. He gets even. The people were laughing when Coyote sang his complaint, "I've lost my power. I've lost my power," while waggling a limp penis in their faces. They laughed. Some called out insults at the Old Man. One cried, "What a fool you are to have your own penis for an atishwin!" Only an idiot would put his faith in the ephemeral. They teased him.

Coyote moaned, "I have nothing left. Nothing but my empty song."

How sad! How sad! His song was so melancholy that the villagers' hearts wept for him. They pitied the old impostor in spite of themselves. They forgave him everything.

Coyote began to drag his tail. He looked uncomfortable, pained. It was time for the squeamish to leave the arena.

No one got up and left.

With a sudden cry—"my bowels are twisting"—Coyote turned his back to the audience. He squatted on the sacred ground. He defecated.

"Iyi!" the men shouted.

Women whispered, "The old fart really did it!" He had piled excrement in the holiest place. The women now felt justified in fleeing in disgust. Fastidious Kanit was among them.

Aleqwel was laughing so that his sides hurt more than his leg.He was pleased that his mother and sister were sticking with him. Maybe they even appreciated the humor in Coyote's atrocities: the world turned upside down. Except for his pain and a little fatigue, Aleqwel had rarely been happier.

The dance ended. The revelers went outside and ate. It was a modest feast; it was still the heart of winter.

Aleqwel whispered to his sister, "What did you think of our kinsman?"

"Filthy!" she exclaimed.

He chuckled. "But it takes a lot of skill—practice—you know, to do Coyote's dance. Even if he drinks gallons of sea water beforehand to manage it."

"So that's how…" exclaimed Ponoya, revealing her true interest in the event.

Later, as they shared food with their neighbors, he asked his mother, "I've been trying to remember. When I was ill, did it rain?"

"Oh, yes," she replied. "It rained a lot. Every night for three nights."

"Keti!" laughed the honored guest. "So that's why the wot was so ready to give me a party."

"You know that's not the reason," said his mother.

"I'm not so sure," replied her son. "Tell me, whatever became of the ducks and geese I caught?"

"We ate them. Alow roasted them for us. They were delicious." She saw concern flood the face of one who has just recalled many forgotten things from the recent past. Aleqwel had remembered not only the rain, but their hunger and poverty and even the mystery veiling his own injury.

"Don't be afraid," Anihwoy said. "Alishtahan. Have confidence. You were only doing what you had to."

There was more rain. Night and day. Momoy's month was waning. When Aleqwel met with the datura giver he exposed his fears to him: his fear of the intruder who used his dead father as a curse, his fear of poverty, his fear of archerless arrows falling out of nowhere.

The old man listened and again suggested that it might be best for Aleqwel to try to meet his late father in the Timeless Time. It would mean sleeping out under the shrine sycamore.

Aleqwel longed to see his father, to hear his gentle voice. He agreed to try it.

On a damp blue morning late in the life of Grandmother Moon, the young paint maker with the youthful beard followed the white-haired achana up the creek trail. It led out of the village toward the hills. As he walked, Aleqwel noticed that his limp was much better.

A light wind blew white clouds that were round as puffball mushrooms across the pathways of the sky.

The trail was slippery with mud, but it was not steep.Aleqwel had come wrapped up in his rabbit fur blanket. His great-uncle pointed out the first signs of new growth: the tender grass shoots, the shiny new leaves on the oaks and the spikes of oak flowers, and the blue flowers of the brodiaea, or sihon, whose bulbs were such an important food.

Aleqwel would have to have been blind to have missed these signs, but he was used to receiving lessons in the obvious. He pointed out various fungi and indicated the fresh oily leaves that leered from poison oak bushes by the side of the trail. Lifting his eyes to the distant hills he saw a pale blue haze of chaparral flowers: sweet ceanothus.

The two men were like happy children awed with the new life born from the rain's power. They were delighted with the bright pairs of butterflies. There were monarchs, the color of artist's ochre, and mourning cloaks, in their black robes with yellow fringes. There were little white butterflies and little yellow ones. All seemed to speed like messengers. They announced the coming of flowers, of seeds.

The shrieks of jays were loud and delirious. Doves moaned in courtship. Fat black crows harped at one another. Other birds danced. The woodpecker and the white-crowned sparrow flashed through the trees.

The earth smelled warm and of thick vegetative life. Aleqwel filled his lungs with hope, even with joy.

At the shrine tree he made his bed of rush mats on a layer of fallen sycamore leaves.

The alchuklash had prepared the tea. He mashed the root in the ceremonial mortar and mixed it with water from the sacred spring.

They sat down together at the bottom of the tall, tall tree, whose branches touched the sky. The youth tucked his legs close against his thighs. He listened as the old achana imparted his last advice. They prayed for a successful journey. The doctor tied pieces of squirrel and rabbit fur to the skeletal limbs of the sky-reaching tree. His prayers were carried to the four winds.

The tall sycamore grew by the banks of the village creek. The intense odor of its rotting leaves was a good, stimulating smell. Its white mottled limbs were nearly bare except for clutches of dry leaves at its crown and a few leafy remains that shared the lower branches with knots of fluttering fur and strings of sacred down. The dry leaf fists rustled in the morning breeze. The winter creek gurgled through rocks and fallen leaves. A red-headed woodpecker flashed white wings as it flew from the tall sycamore to a sprawling oak. As it flew, it called its name: "pulakak, pulakak."

Aleqwel drank the pungent tea from the cup handed him by the datura giver. Before long he began to tremble. And then to shake. The doctor helped him to lie down.

While still awake, he lay on his back and watched yellow morning sunlight dripping down the dry leaves of the shrine tree. It caught now and then on a soft fluff of rabbit fur or lighter-than-air egret down. Prayers made; answers pending. The sunlight fluttered like green leaves, then turned liquid as drops of rain. The curled-up leaves captured the glowing rain the way cisterns clasp rain to arid rock. But these sunfires ignited the tree's leaves and soon the sycamore was gleaming with the radiance of campfires in the sacred enclosure at night. Then, the Earth World extinguished itself and only the eternal flames remained.

The old man sat down beside his patient and tried to keep him comfortable and calm. He listened to his delirious words and tried to make sense of them.

The day unfolded under the dry rustling leaves, the white mottled limbs, beside the gurgling creek.

The young man walked—and ran—all day long on a westward-leading path. Following Sun he had long since passed Syuhtun and even Heliyik village, where his father's people lived. Now, just when he had begun to feel utterly discouraged, lost and hopeless, he discovered these recognizable signposts of the westernmost land. It was the high road across the sea to Shimilaqsha in the Land of the Dead.

He removed his eyes and revisioned himself with golden poppies. With a trembling heart he pursued the path to the crystal house of the wot of the Land of the Dead. He felt as if he were being crushed under the stone weight of fear. Yet he managed to cross the wobbling bridge without any mishap. He reached the land of eternity and in no time was united with his beloved father.

His father appeared well. He greeted his son warmly. He assured him that his new life was a never-ending festival. There were games and dances and endless platters of food. ("Though, of course, we don't eat it; we only smell it," he confided with a hint of warning.)

Aleqwel asked about his grandfathers and his father's grandfathers. All were well. Their life was good. But…

Aleqwel's ears went up like a jackrabbit's. "But?"

His father's words were serious, worried: "I have heard a sound from the Earth World. I'm not sure what it was. It was only a whisper. But…"

"But?" whispered Aleqwel.

"But it sounded like it might have been my name. My own true name. If so, it means I will have to go back. And if I do, I will come as I now am—a ghost. I will haunt you and pester you—all our family— until you are as dead as I. It won't be the same as visiting me here in Shimilaqsha. Here you are the strange one, the dangerous one. Here, I am safe for you."

"I thought I heard the name spoken," confirmed the son. "That's why I came. The curse was called on us by some minor achana from Shuku, a small man. Do you know who I mean?"

The elder paint maker had taken his son far to the side, away from the playing field where a great hockey match was under way. "Look down there," he pointed to a far-distant Earth World. "Down there people sleep while we sport and play. Many things are backward between the different worlds. Many things are backward in the Earth World itself. They are not as they might be. Because of this discrepancy, there is poison."

Aleqwel waited, wanting, but not wanting, to learn what he would learn.

"Son, do you believe, with the others, that I was killed by a bear?" Then the tale began inevitably to unravel, like a worn-out basket.

His late father had been the victim of a bear doctor. Aleqwel listened to the gentle but inexorable words: "The women were under the trees gathering acorns. You were helping to guard them. I was alone, stalking deer. Inadvertently, I ran into a bear doctor. He was out practicing his vile tricks."

"In Mishopshno land?" interrupted the son.

Of course, of course in Mishopshno land. Would he have been so stupid as to trespass after deer? Did his own son believe him a poacher? No, naturally not.

"It was easy to see that the intruder was an achana and not a real bear because of the fastenings on his costume. Only a woman would have mistaken him for the real thing—though his eyes did have that vacant animal stare, lusting and afraid." The imposter had stood beneath the nest of a bald eagle. It was a nest that belonged to the wot of Mishopshno. The bear impersonator from Shuku clutched valuable eagle feathers in each paw.

Aleqwel's father had caught the intruder at his unspeakable thievery.

In that moment of shame, the bear impersonator had unfastened his disguise. Inside he carried strands and strands of shell money. He tried to purchase silence.

But the deer hunter had been outraged. He was fierce with indignation. He scoffed at the bribe, accused the achana of terrorizing women in the camp and of stealing. He demanded that the man vow to stop. He threatened to expose him.

Rejected, the bear achana reverted to his inhuman side, his brute ferocity. With a mighty cuff of one of those paws that grasped stolen feathers he knocked the deer hunter to earth. Then he mauled him.

The next thing Aleqwel's father knew it was night. He was wandering around the cemetery looking for a trail. It was the same westward trail, the wobbling bridge, that had led Aleqwel to this very town of Shimilaqsha.

With concentrated fury Aleqwel said, "Did you recognize this evil doctor? Who was he that I might find him and kill him?"

"Yes," said his late father. "I used to know him as a boy. I called him 'Taqaq' because he wobbled on his little legs like a quail. Others called him 'Choi.'"

"'Choi' means 'small.' Is he one of our own people, then?" Aleqwel was puzzled. He thought he had been beginning to understand things.

"He was, once, long ago. But his parents made bad magic. That's what was said. It was an inauspicious marriage. His mother was from here and of the Sun Team. She was angry that her husband, who was from Shuku, was not acccepted here. She painted rocks in the hills and brought on a parching drought. Then her husband caused an earthquake. They were banished. I don't know what happened to them."

"They fled to Shuku," guessed Aleqwel, "to our enemies."

"I heard that rumor," said his father. "But I never saw them again. I heard that even in Shuku, where there is much magic and poison, the family's ways were too secretive. They were unsocial. They moved outside the village precincts into the hills. I am not surprised the boy became a bear doctor. There is no question that they were a powerful family. But they were not well integrated into any community."

"As a bear doctor he could serve the people, whom he needs but would prefer to shun," Aleqwel said. "I know who this man is. He intruded into the ceremonial enclosure at Syuhtun. I thought he was insignificant because he was so small. It is he who summoned you. But why? Are you not dead enough?" Aleqwel began to cry. But when he reflexively reached down for clods of dirt to hurl, his father stopped him.

"Perhaps he believes the rest of our family knows about his poaching—and the killing—too. His crime makes him afraid you have found out. Perhaps he is trying to frighten you, to make sure you are silent, too."

"He has failed! I will do worse than just expose him!" cried Aleqwel. "Tell me, Father, what is the beast's true name?"

But his father did not know. "There are other ways of combating evil," he hinted vaguely.

Sadly, it was time to leave. Aleqwel sang Lizard's song and found his way back to the Earth World with less difficulty than he had feared. He had done nothing to tie himself to the dead, and he knew the trail markings by heart. He left behind his golden poppy eyes and returned to the Earth World.

By sunset, the young man, dreaming on his bed of leaves, appeared to grow less agitated. His waking fits of talking had given up their hold on him.

His old uncle covered him with a warm sea otter blanket and lay down beside him for the night.

In the morning, in the first gray light, the alchuklash began singing the momoy-waking song. Aleqwel woke. His gaze fixed on the withered sycamore leaves in the sky as if he were seeing precious crystals sparkling in every one. At last, he averted his eyes from the painful vision.

The momoy giver looked straight at him and sang. He was delighted to find the boy not at all kilamu, not acting crazy. The alchuklash interpreted the meaning of the returning voyager's contorted words. His father's killer was Shuku's bear doctor, the Wokoch at the Winter Solstice Festival. The killer was afraid of being found out, so afraid that he provoked attacks to ensure silence. Without question, he had caused the wound Aleqwel had received when he was out bird hunting.

"But there was no poison. Why doesn't he kill me?"

"He is afraid he would be recognized as the dual killer, I suppose. And he would be attacked in return by our village professionals." The alchuklash was referring to himself, the wot, and the wot's poisoner. "Like a rattlesnake that withholds his venom to send a living message, he wants to frighten your family away."

"With the wrong results. Now that I know who he is, I must destroy him!"

"Yes. He underestimates the strength you get from your atishwin. It's possible he will try to kill you, if he suspects you know."

"How shall I get rid of him?" demanded the young man, who was barely able to sit up on his reed bed, yet was resolute for action.

But the alchuklash, surprisingly, cooled his language. "We must discuss all this with the wot. His decision will be necessary."

By midday Aleqwel was able to walk, leaning on the doctor.

The signs of new life, of birds and butterflies and green shoots, were as intense as on the previous day. But the man who had drunk momoy for the second time in his life noticed only an undying red flame that seemed to grow in his eyes in the place where the bright poppies had lain. To an outsider he might have looked as if he suffered from pain. But he suffered more from anxiety. He was afraid that the flame might flare up and out of control at the slightest breath of wind, the way small sparks from the fall burning sometimes escape and ignite the hills and mountains in an all-consuming blaze. He was afraid this might happen if he was not given the permission he needed to avenge his father. And so he walked with caution and fear of his own vision. But he walked with determination. Life would unfold in its own way. He was only a participant.

His mother greeted him with happy tears. She made his bed by the fire. He slept and slept.

In late afternoon the ksen, the wot's messenger, came to the paint maker's house to invite him to a discussion with the wot.

Aleqwel wrapped himself in his rabbit fur robe. It was cool and growing dark outside. Thankfully, the way to the wot's house was not far. They had only to pass the red-fenced cemetery and the ceremonial grounds. After passing the wot's large granaries, they arrived at his double-sized house. The wot's house was dark and smoky and cavernous.

Aleqwel admired the room and its expensive furnishings. He knew the wot had to maintain a large house to provide for both of his wives and their local and out-of-town relatives. And he had to put up visiting dignitaries and their messengers and some of the poor and homeless as well. He admired the luxury without craving any of it for himself.

But this evening the families and guests were not at home. Only the wot, the alchuklash, the poisoner, and the bear and rattlesnake doctors were present. They sat on whale vertebrae stools by the fireside.

Aleqwel squatted on a mat on the sandy floor. Thunder growled over Syuhtun in the northwest.

"Our momoy giver, Coyote's heir, has spoken to me of your recent visit," the wot said. He rolled his bright eyes up toward the sky. He paused grandly.

Then he said simply: "I appreciate your just desire and your request. Yet precipitous action is always ill advised. It could even bring our village harm—disaster—if, for example, it were seen by our populous neighbor to the south as an attack on their village itself. In short, war with Shuku has never been to our benefit."

"It is winter," the leader continued. "We are weak. It's a bad season to go to war and to die. Battle is not the sport it was in ancient days."

Aleqwel was flooded with disappointment. He knew what was coming.

"So I ask you to wait on your request. Wait while I prepare the ground, while I attempt to bring the evildoer to an end through official means, through politics, through talk. To you, Aleqwel, I say, be strong, be patient. Build your power. Make yourself invulnerable. One day you will need to rely on it."

He continued: "This month you have made a great step. You have visited Shimilaqsha and spoken with the dead. This is not for everyone. And you have an atishwin to help you as well. Build on these things. You are antap. Increase your knowledge. With the guidance of the alchuklash you may find yourself another atishwin. Doctors, as you know, have three, four, even more spirit helpers. They are alatishwinich."

"But I am not..." interrupted Aleqwel.

"A layman may have more than one, also," conceded the wot. "In any event, this is the way for you to protect yourself and your family now, by building strength. At the same time, I will see what can be done to protect our village from this murderer who steals our feathers and endangers us all."

The wot's last vehemence placated Aleqwel. Reluctantly, he tried to assimilate the man's advice: have patience and drink more momoy. But he felt frustrated: frustration of his push for revenge, frustration of the longing to return to his former simple ways, frustration of his life's first big urge to action.

Thunder gave the house a decisive shake. "More lakes and hills under construction in the mountains," laughed the alchuklash. White light flashed over the smoke hole. The wot stepped outside to ask his messenger to put up the smoke hole cover before the rains came.

Aleqwel had previously cared little for grand action. He had treasured his life of social obscurity. He had been happy as an apprentice, providing good service and maintaining a small reputation as a loyal son and brother and a congenial friend, as one who is steady as a shrine pole. He had been an acceptable student of the antap. He had enjoyed his lonely walks in the hills and his dream of serving the village in some obscure way that would not draw attention to his own person. Now he felt forced to commit to action in defense of his life, his family's existence. Killing went against his nature, yet he thought he would have to do it. And now that very decision to act was being thwarted by those who were more powerful than he.

The wot returned from outdoors with the first splatters of rain on his bearskin robe. He stood beside Aleqwel, touching him as a father would a son.

"Remember," he said, as if already accepting the boy's acquiescence to the plan. "The path to power is a dangerous one. You must be careful, circumspect. Remember, life is social; don't let your new power set you apart like this evil one. Use your knowledge for the good of the people. Keep your balance."

Aleqwel simmered. Passivity and patience were his lot more than his choice. The wot's recommendations were orders to one as relatively powerless as himself. And—worse—the wot was right: war was indeed a possibility.

Aleqwel sprang away from the searing sensation of the older man's hand. "Yes. Yes, I will do it. Of course, I will do it."

He ran out into a world dark with heavy rain. He pulled his cape tight. He squished down the slippery hill path, his topknot bobbing as he went. The crash of surf below and the dying thunder in the south accompanied his homeward steps, while the dying glow of lightning over the southern islands illuminated his way.

CHAPTER 3

MONTH WHEN THINGS BEGIN TO GROW
hesiq momoy ihsha cpuun

The day when people anticipated the return of Grandmother Moon moved toward evening. At dusk they assembled in the ceremonial enclosure. The wot spoke to them. They mourned their absent protectoress. They cried and wailed. They kicked the dogs to make them howl. They were filled with grief and misery that their kindly grandmother was dead.

The day was dreary and overcast. The people had no way to scan the Sky World for a response to their lamentation. But when the achanas proclaimed a rebirth they believed in it. Tears of sorrow turned to joyous shouts and grateful prayers of welcome. The dreadful dark time was over. New life swelled up. "Welcome back, Grandmother Moon," they cried.

With nightfall came a light drizzle. The people who squeezed out of the gates of the enclosure were in a happy mood. They tripped over dogs they had recently kicked and called out good-nights to their friends. They were being given a wet winter after all. It was always best to have faith in the doctors.

As Alow, the fisherman, stumbled down the seaward path to his father's house he was caught up by a solidly built young man with a booming voice. "Cousin, Grandmother Moon never neglects us, does she?"

Alow stopped and turned toward Chaki. Alow was perhaps the only person in the village disappointed by the rain. "The master was going to begin work on the tomol tomorrow," he said.

"Don't worry. He will do it soon, soon." said Chaki. "Crops are more important. Be patient, cousin. We will make our voyage."

Chaki's young wife Pichiquich came up beside them, a cradleboard slung on her back, the strap pressed against her epsu basket hat. The baby was sleeping, but Alow crept up to her anyway. With his little finger, he shook some of the shell ornaments dangling from the cradle's hood. "Lucky little Kelele," he sang to her. "Uncle Alow is soaking wet, but you are wrapped with rabbit fur and snoozing under a roof." He stroked her cheek and murmured compliments on her beauty. He whispered endearments both tender and absurd.

"Cousin," said Chaki. "Permit the taniw to sleep. Can't you ever let the girls alone? Listen to me: I'm in the spirit for some hand game. Would you like to play?"

"Nothing I'd like more. Shall we include some others?"

Pichiquich spoke up. "I will play on your team. Do you think the paint maker—or his sister—would join in? They are of the Sun Team like my husband."

"Yes, yes. They are indeed. I'll go invite Aleqwel," offered Alow, who loved to gamble. Not only was gambling his duty, but it took his mind off the inactivity brought on by the rain. It gave him the opportunity to amass money that he could invest in trade goods to take to the islands. He would sell them for even more money. He would make his fortune. Alow had no objection to having a woman teammate. Women were excellent gamblers, often better than men, though better at shell dice than hand game.

The paint maker agreed eagerly to the game. He took seriously the wot's admonition to increase his power. He was prepared to accept any occasion to test and—he hoped—increase his strength.

The drizzle had turned into a real rain by the time Alow and Aleqwel arrived at Chaki's mother-in-law's house. They brought not only Aleqwel's money, his black and white playing bones and his cotton blanket, but his whole family to sing for him and to otherwise encourage his play.

The smoky house was already filled with family and neighbors of the participants. Pichiquich's mother offered food to her many guests. Alow was pleased to see that his cousin had invited the old tomol builder, Saqtele, to serve as scorekeeper. It was a prestigious position, and the altomolich was frequently sought out to fill it. It was believed that his pride—and irritability—made him incorruptible.

Rooters noisily boasted of the strength of their favorite players. The dogs restlessly walked around. Eventually, the teams seated themselves on either side of the fireplace. They got comfortable on the mats, adjusting their cotton blankets—which had come from the faraway Mohave—over their knees and laid out their bones in their laps.

The scorekeeper set the game in motion with the starting song. Rain began to drip around the edges of the closed doors. Smoke began to fill the room under a closed ventilation flap.

The two friends, Aleqwel and Alow, might have been strangers—or even enemies. Their looks were impersonal, calculating, meditative, tricky.

They placed their bets—a big pile of money beads—on the sand in front of the scorekeeper. Chaki and Aleqwel won the right to take the first turn. They took the black and white seal bones in their hands and hid them beneath their blankets. Before long they drew out closed fists. Chaki was chosen to be his team's killer. He touched the mountain lion paw on the braided string around his neck and sang his guessing song. "Ah, ah, ah, ah," he groaned, calling his atishwin. His supporters sang with him. Suddenly, he jerked his head toward one of his wife's hands.

She opened the hand. It held a white bone.

Chaki had made a wrong guess. A bad start. But women can be difficult to kill. Even wives.

Once more Chaki sang his song. The combined singing of all his many backers filled the house. He thrust his head toward Alow's right hand. The bone was black. It was a good kill.

The scorekeeper gave Chaki's team one tule counting stick for their one correct guess.

Then Chaki and Aleqwel hid the bones. Alow did the singing. His song was effective. He killed both black bones.

The scorekeeper awarded him two tule counters.

The teams were warming up. As yet the wins meant little as the game was just beginning.

The two sides continued to trade turns concealing the bones, singing, guessing, striving always to control the power of seeing through solid objects, of seeing into things. For the evening they aspired to be as strong as achanas.

The rain beating on the sealskin flap and on the thatch made a drone for the singing. At tense moments, one or another player would suddenly break into his power song, calling his atishwin to his side. No one wanted to lose. Yet the game remained friendly. The teams were nearly equal in strength. No one broke easily. The dogs settled down by the walls and fell asleep.

After a long, long time Chaki and Aleqwel's team began to take more and more counting sticks from their opponents and to have fewer and fewer taken from them. Eventually, they took all the counters. Then they collected all the money.

There was cheering, vociferous congratulating, more eating. None of the spectators went home because they knew the play would resume. This time even more money was piled up in front of the scorekeeper.

The tension was tighter, the winning side slower to emerge. Children fell asleep in grandparents' laps. Adults cheered out their praise. Chaki's wife had invited a good contingent of her Seal Family and other Earth Team members to sing for her. The rain was on their side. Pichiquich and Alow finally pulled ahead and hauled in all the shell money.

No one wanted to give up. Aleqwel and Chaki removed their nose ornaments and shared a plug of tobacco for stamina. A few people walked out.

The third game went back and forth with no side pulling ahead for a very long time. It was clear that neither team had significantly greater strength at this time. Still, no one would quit.

At last Pichiquich said, "I'm sorry. I must get some sleep. The baby will wake soon."

The men were tired, yet disappointed. The contest was so close that nothing much had been decided. Yes, Alow and Pichiquich had a little money to split, but there was no definite validation of superiority. Although his team had won, Alow was dissatisfied. He was certain that if the game had gone on he could have made more money to help finance his expedition. He managed to console himself with the knowledge that there would be other nights, more opportunities. Power was always in flux. He wondered how his cousin felt, losing to his own wife. Before leaving, Alow sought out the scorekeeper. He wanted not only to thank him but to talk with him about the new tomol. He wanted to offer to help with the work.

"Do you think your help will speed me up, fisherman?" the older man answered bluntly. "I have apprentices to help me. They do a good job after years of training. You are a pleasant young man and dedicated to your work; you should stick with it. Do I offer to come help you with your fishing lines? I would only tangle them, I'm afraid."

Alow was hurt but undaunted by the response. "I want to help so that I can learn at least the basics. It will make me a better navigator. I promise not to get in the way."

The tomol builder relented. "That is sensible," he said. "If you are sincere about it, come by my house on the next dry morning. We'll be making boards. I might be able to find something for you to do. But don't try to rush me. Do you understand? It will only end up slowing things down."

I t rained all night and the next morning, too. At midday the sky began to clear. There was no fishing, hunting, or tomol building that day.

Alow impatiently repaired his fishing gear. Impatiently, he strode down to the shore after the clouds had burned off and combed the beach for good pieces of driftwood. He was even impatient in the crowded sweathouse. The bard's story moved too slowly. The old antap stumbled along painfully and it was a long time before the protagonist hung up his carrying net, signifying the end.

When the bone worker—a man of the Sun Team—suggested they go to his house to gamble with bones, Alow agreed. He spent the rest of the long day rolling bones in front of the artisan's doorway. He was good at twisting his wrist and flipping the bones over the back of his hand. But the bone worker was better. More and more often he totaled the eight points necessary to win.

Alow unwound more and more money from his hair and from around his neck. He was getting discouraged. He loved to gamble and felt righteous in doing it. But he still hated to lose. It was not just the money.

The next day was clear, sunny, and cool. Instead of going out with his father or taking out his own tule raft to fish in the kelp beds, Alow, after bathing in the creek, went directly to the tomol builder's house.

The guildsman was already at work in the yard by his house. His greeting to Alow was instructional: "The first thing that needs to be done in building a tomol is to accumulate enough tok string to tie it all together. Then you can begin."

Alow admired the stack of logs, redwood and pine, that Saqtele had piled up under a shelter by his house. He knew the altomolich had been collecting them carefully and curing them slowly after hauling them off the beach or purchasing them, mostly from the islands.

"Look," said Saqtele, "no knots. Not one. I never take a log with any weakness. Your grandfather's tomol will have choice boards. Observe for yourself how dry they are." Then he led Alow to one side and uncovered a large split redwood log, already made up. "This will be the base board," he said like a proud parent.

Alow ran his fingers along the board, admiring its straightness and its strength. Saqtele said, "My boy got it on a trading trip to Wima Island several years ago. It cost many epsu baskets of acorns and ilepesh. I've been saving it for the right tomol."

The island was called Wima, or redwood, not because the tree grew there, but because so many washed up on its northern shore. Alow felt a stab, partly pain, partly longing. His mother had come from Wima and he had, in fact, been born there. They had left when he was a baby, and he could not recall the family home or his kin.

The apprentices were working with whalebone and antler wedges to split the seasoned logs into rough boards. They greeted Alow. He knew them well. One was the son of the bowl maker, the other the son of the tar worker. Both young men were of about his own age. Neither came from the wealthy canoe-owning families, but they were something more than poor commoners.

Saqtele did not let Alow split logs. Even the skilled apprentices sometimes ruined them. He was allowed to bring logs to the workers and carry away the rough split boards and stack them.

The four men worked until Sun took his rest in the sand dollar. They followed his example. The master builder's wife brought wooden bowls filled with thick porridge and dried tuna. Some of the men went to the brush to relieve themselves. Then they returned to their labor. Crudely hewn boards, some long, many shorter, piled up in the work yard. The altomolich toiled at the heavy pounding alongside his young apprentices.

At midday the four men took a second rest and ate again. The young apprentices talked about gambling. They complained that with people already beginning to go to the hills to harvest yucca it was difficult to find enough people to make up teams. The young tar worker said to Alow, "You are of the Earth Team, aren't you? How would you feel about some hand game tonight?"

Alow replied, "Since my cousin has gone to the hills now, and even my ichantik opponent, the paint maker, has gone, yes, hand game would be fine. I warn you, though, you'd better be strong. I am desperate for winning."

"Good, good," responded the tar worker, not the least put off by Alow's threat. After a while, he said, "Say, isn't the paint maker's sister your current girlfriend? I admit, I could be interested in her myself. The family's homecoming should be doubly sweet for you."

"How's that?" asked Alow innocently.

"They'll be bringing back yucca stalk with them. I've heard there's only one thing as sweet as baked yucca stalk…"

The bowl maker's son, shy and a little slow, burst in, "I know what that means. It's sex."

The interrupted apprentice laughed. "Yucca and sex. What could be better? You are fortunate to have such sweet things to look forward to." And he laughed so hard that Alow decided it would be pointless to say that he and the daughter of the late paint maker did not engage in casual sexual intercourse.

The men worked steadily all afternoon. Alow noticed some slender plumes of water in the channel. Migrating whales. Just before they were about to hang up their tools, when daylight was beginning to fade, the tomol master inexplicably consented to letting the fisherman try his hand at making a few boards. Alow was as strong as the others. No one disputed that he could strike the wedge with mighty blows from his cobble. But he lacked technique. He wasted a few boards. He was not ashamed of it. He knew that ultimately he would pay for the wasted boards.

The apprentices tried to recruit their master to serve as scorekeeper for the evening's hand game competition. "I see these boys all day, do I have to spend the evening with them, too?" he complained to his wife. But he agreed in the end. He insisted, however, that they let him out early so he could get to the sweathouse to hear the bard telling the old-time stories that they could only hear in winter time.

Alow also thought it might be pleasant to go down and listen to the old stories after the hand game. His luck had been mediocre, but tonight it might soar. The tomol building had begun at last. He was content. He even reflected happily on the possibility of sweetness in Ponoya's homecoming, succulent yucca and sex, or not.

To his great happiness Alow and his partner, the bowl maker's son, had a strong victory over their Sun Team opponents. He carried home a big basket full of shell money. His father was not in the house.

It was late by the time Alow managed to get to the sweathouse. Many men were asleep on the floor. He spotted his father crouched against a far wall. He walked over to sit by him and whisper about his night's winnings. Mushu seemed as pleased as he ever did to hear his son's news. He closed his eyes and leaned back. Perhaps he was listening to the bard.

The bard was in the midst of a long involved tale concerning Swordfish, wot of the Undersea World.

Duck Hawk, the nephew of Eagle, wot of the Sky World, had fallen into the ocean and sunk down to the Land of the Swordfish in the Undersea World. Coyote, the trickster, who had been sent to retrieve Duck Hawk, was hiding in the Swordfish wot's house. He had wrapped himself in whale skin. Now he trembled as he watched the uncouth swordfish tearing apart an entire whale for their dinner.

Alow told his father he had seen whale plumes that day.

"I saw them too," Mushu said. "The whales are going to their summer campgrounds. You should have come fishing with me. I saw tunas, too."

Alow hated to miss the first pohoh fish. But he did not regret his day. "Will the swordfish bring us a whale this year, Father? Some of the common people are looking a little thin."

"You heard the prayers of supplication at the greeting of reborn Moon," said his father stolidly. "One can never be certain what the swordfish will decide. Anyway, I've lived through drought and scorching heat, earthquake, war, and looting. Be glad we are in a good time now."

"But some of the common people may starve."

"A few of the common people always starve," said his father. Then, as an afterthought, Mushu said, "We cannot count on a great whale to offer itself every time people are hungry. We cannot depend on the swordfish to hunt for us. We must hunt sea animals. Shall we try for some sea otter, tomorrow?"

Alow agreed to go out.

His father said nothing. The bard was continuing with the story of clever Coyote pitting his wits against the fearsome Swordfish wot. Alow resumed attention. The swordfish were every fisherman's dread. If a tomol man were to capsize, to drown at sea, the swordfish people would strive to snatch his flesh and chew his bones. If Alow was captured by them he would never reach lovely Shimilaqsha and rejoin his mother and baby sister.

Alow prayed—not for the first time—that should he die at sea, a fate that had come to many fishermen, passengers, and traders, his body would wash ashore. That way he could escape the terrible watery wot who had teeth like awls. He could evade the Swordfish wot's murky submerged country that was so alien and unwelcoming to human beings. He recalled the brave men he had known who were now confined, forever, to the depths of the Undersea World. He also vowed not be led astray by ghosts. They would not torment him. He would not be like his father.

Father and son awoke early the next morning in the cold, smoldering ashes of the sweathouse. Alow was stiff jointed, but eager to move.

The two bathed thoroughly in the village creek. They groomed themselves, Alow plucking his beard hairs with clamshell tweezers. Then they loaded up Mushu's tomol. Instead of lines and nets they threw in big bows and bone-toothed arrows and harpoons of island ironwood.

The winter surf was strong. But in the early hour the swells were tamest. The worn red tomol slipped through without great difficulty. But the ocean water was cold. Alow was grateful for his old fur vest that kept his chest warm.

With quiet paddles they glided toward the dark kelp forest that was the home of the fish that fed the people. It was the temporary home of the big migrating pohoh that were the people's favorite food. And it was the permanent home of the humble bottom dwellers that kept them alive in winter. But today the men's thoughts were not directed toward the deep beneath the fleshy tangles of kelpweed, but to the surface. Though the early light was dim the two men easily picked out the forms of sleeping sea animals. They saw basking seals and sea otters lying on their backs on the thick red-brown leaves.

Alow prayed for an animal—maybe more—to give its life to them that day. He scattered golden ilepesh seeds and black hutash seeds on the kelpy sea and threw goose down to the four winds.

Father and son worked quickly and quietly. They ignored the large seals, which would not fit in their tomol and were easier to hunt on land, and paddled straight toward the otters. They did not need to worry about the soft-furred creatures catching their scent. Otters' noses were not keen like deer's. But they were sensitive to vibrations in the water.

Nevertheless, the hunters were able to bring their tomol close to a sleeping otter. Mushu strung his large sinew-backed bow, the one with the points that curved backward, the kind used against people in war.

Alow tied the anchor line to a clump of seaweed.

Mushu set his arrow, knelt forward, drew, aimed, and shot—all in one motion. He struck the sea otter right on the mark, just above the collar bone. The surprised otter squealed and yelped like a dog. Then it whimpered.

Alow and Mushu moved in closer with the tomol. Mushu clubbed the dying animal until it was entirely silent. They hauled it aboard.

The noise of the wounded otter alerted the other animals. They woke up and dived into the ocean.

Mushu and Alow paddled their tomol, whose dull red color blended with the kelp, westward through the floating forest. They came to the mouth of the estuary. To the northwest they could see the blue smoke of Qoloq village. Here, on the border with the other village, they found an otter lounging on its leafy bed. It held a spiny sea urchin against its chest and was pounding it with a rock. Sea otters ate more frequently even than people.

Alow took a turn at shooting. This time, the animal, already awake, moved before he was hit. He sank into the sea. But the arrow tooth had bitten him in the side. As he swam he left behind a trail of dark blood. He cried beseechingly.

The men in the tomol kept pace with him. They moved in behind him. Alow threw the harpoon. This time he found the mark. Alow hauled in the heavy line while Mushu paddled the tomol to the dead animal.

The two sacrificial animals nearly filled the tomol. Sun was not yet to midday. The men headed for home.

That afternoon on the beach they butchered the sea otters. They divided the meat to be shared with family and the poor and those to whom a favor was owed. Alow was surprised to find his father slicing a good piece of meat he said he was giving to Anihwoy, the curing doctor. Tersely, Mushu informed his son that she had lately been treating him to restore his vitality and to help him sleep. His father always surprised him. He informed his father that the Coyote Family had not yet returned from the hills.

Later in the afternoon, while he scraped the otter skins to prepare them for curing, Alow noticed some of his neighbors returning from a long trip. They, too, had been out in the hills harvesting fresh yucca stalks.

"How was it?" he shouted.

"Good, good," was the reply.

After Alow delivered seaweed-wrapped bundles of otter meat to several households in the village and saved some for the Coyote Family, there was none left for himself and his father. Someone else would feed them.

The last place he went was to the tomol builder's house. Saqtele showed him a heavy clam adze. He demonstrated how he and the apprentices had formed the rough-cut boards into finely shaped lightweight planks. The master craftsman told him, "Don't worry that you have missed any of this. You do us all more good when you are out hunting."

On the way out, when Alow's hand was already on the inner doors, the tomol builder said, "Soon I will begin my most important work, the shaping of the boat. It is very difficult. I must get the bow curve just right, and the proper symmetry. The thickness of the wood must be perfect, too. I'll need the captain's eye. Will you and your father and grandfather be ready to give advice?"

The new tomol, Alow's dream, was becoming a reality. "It is almost impossible for my grandfather to get around. He needs to be carried, even to the sweathouse. But I will tell him. He might like to come. My father seems to have his mind set on a sea lion hunt. But, for myself, I will do everything I can to be there at the framing."

Making his way home in the shadowy dusk Alow noticed that the outer door of Anihwoy's house was open. The family must have returned home. He decided to bring them their portion of otter meat even though the hour was late. Climbing the short rise to their house with his bundle Alow was suddenly struck by the seed of truth in the teasing apprentice's remark. He was looking forward to a sweet homecoming. He even wished it would be as fleshy as the apprentice imagined it. For the first time he realized how much he wished it. Real sex with Ponoya, not just ceremonial—was it even possible? He would have to be alert. When he saw her he would know.

The whole family was inside. Anihwoy was building up the fire. They had just arrived. They were dusty, tired. The curing doctor looked pleased, pleased with the meat. She inquired into Mushu's health.

"Very energetic," replied his son. He was trying to discern Ponoya's expression, but it was dark inside. He thought her face looked thin.

The talk was of the camp, the new shoots, the yucca harvest. The family was gratified that it had not rained on them. "Now that we are back, it can flood," laughed Anihwoy.

But Aleqwel protested: "Not while I'm roasting my stalk!"

Even Ponoya in the corner laughed at this. Alow thought he heard her make a flippant comment about men.He went outside to help Aleqwel with the roast. With rock-weighted digging sticks they excavated a good-sized hole. They called Anakawin to help collect rocks for the pit.

The boy moved slowly and stiffly, but he complied.

"Is something wrong with the taniw?" Alow asked his friend when they were alone beside the cooking pit with moonlight falling on them.

"He's fallen into some trouble again," Aleqwel sighed as he loaded logs and kindling into the trench.

Anakawin ran lamely into the house for an ember.

Alow continued, "He's a good boy when he has something worthwhile to do."

"Yes, that's true. But he won't do just any ordinary thing. It must be exciting."

"He has suffered a lot."

Anakawin returned, and they set the fire in the pit ablaze. It pleased them to throw the stones onto the fire. Then Aleqwel lay the long damp grass-bound yucca shoot on the hot rocks. All three took part in burying the roast in dirt. It was a funeral that promised an enticing resurrection.

They left the stalk alone to steam and smolder. In a few days they would have a sweet meal.

Inside, the women were preparing a sparse supper. The friends ate and talked. Then, old and young retired to their sleeping places. The four youths yawned, but stayed awake. They wanted to enjoy one another's company a while longer.

"What happened to the boy?" Alow asked with directness that bordered on the impolite.

Aleqwel answered, "On our first day at camp he walked right into an unburnt yucca plant. The spears cut him painfully. Mother treated him, but he had to remain in camp for the rest of the trip."

Alow was perplexed. "I don't understand. He's really no dim wit, not like the stupid boy in the stories. How could he do a thing like that?"

Ponoya broke in to defend—if such it was—her younger brother. "He says the yucca is his aunt, that she ought to let him into her house. I'm worried about him."

Aleqwel whispered to Alow, "You should know, ichantik, there is someone who wants to harm our family. Someone who killed my father. Someone who injured me. I know who he is. He will do anything. He will call up ghosts, create apparitions, send monsters. He stops at nothing."

Alow was stunned. Yet, he was impressed by Aleqwel's knowledge. Finally, he was able to say. "I know what it's like for a person to be beset by a ghost. Is it possible that Anakawin has that trouble? Or it may be that he did see a nunashish on Solstice Night. How can we know? Young boys, even without troubles, can be inattentive at times. They are often clumsy. That one is proud. Maybe he spoke of Aunt Yucca to hide his own carelessness in falling into the spears."

"Don't you think if Anakawin were being led by a ghost we would have seen it, too?" suggested Kanit, meekly.

Ignoring her remark, Alow said, "In spite of what you tell me, I think the boy is probably suffering because he has no father, no uncle, to look up to and guide him."

"He has me," said Aleqwel, hurt. "And the rest of the family."

"The rest of the family are women," said Alow. "And you, yes, he loves you. But your nature is so different from his. You always wander around thinking about... what? Your work? Who can tell? You are so quiet. So resigned. Like you, ichantik, that boy has power. Yes, I think so. But his talent leads a different way. He needs something else."

"He needs an uncle like you," laughed Aleqwel after he had gotten over the bite of the criticism—and the extravagance of the praise. His mother's family were alatishwinich. His father's family were craftsmen.

The tension began to draw away like a tide that has reached its high water mark. If Alow was stung by the joking reply it affected him only like an insect sting, setting him into heightened activity. He began to boast of his upcoming expedition. "What I pay for acorns and ilepesh here is not what I will charge on the island. In turn, what I pay there for furs and huya bowls and beads will be doubled at home—and tripled when I take it over the hills. I am being paid for my exertion, above all, for the risk." He did not look too troubled by the risk.

Ponoya said darkly, "You have never taken a canoe to the islands before. Is it wise to be so confident?"

"I have every reason for confidence. My cousin Chaki is going with me. And my cousin Kulaa too. They are both experienced in the channel. So are our cousins who will be our tomolmates."

"Then Chaki will be your leader?" asked Ponoya with a tone of relief.

"Yes, that is so," admitted Alow almost as if he were opening his hand to expose a black seal bone to an opponent. But if he was a little humbled he could see that the others were still impressed with him. He took the initiative again. He began to lecture them about the benefits of trade, just as he had heard Chaki do. He called it the real source of all wealth.

At this Aleqwel protested. "I have always believed that hunting and manufacturing were the sources of wealth."

"Money is manufactured only on the islands. They have the guild, the tools. You must travel—trade—to obtain it. Money is the measure of wealth, is it not? And venture procures it. Risk is everything. Not only risk of life, but financial risk. Wealth is but a manifestation of power, and power comes only with confronting danger."

Ponoya contradicted the fisherman, "I believe having a powerful atishwin is the greatest wealth of all."

The men had to agree. Aleqwel doubted that he, a craftsman, would ever become wealthy in money. But it was comforting to know that Alow would. He had faith in that. He imagined him wearing the bearskin vest of a tomol captain. He saw him old and arthritic, perhaps wot of the Pelican Family. It was too bad his sister did not like him, that she always teased him.

But when Alow eventually rose to leave, reciting the standard formula, "I'm going for a while," Ponoya called out, "Kiwanan! Come again when you're in the neighborhood!"

The tomol framing and the sea lion hunt were delayed by rain. It rained steadily for two and a half days. People camping in the hills hid out under the oaks. In the village men crowded the sweathouse, listening to the bard while they twisted tok cord and wove nets. The alchuklash was aware that the time when day and night are in balance had come. It was a harmonious, favorable moment. But the ceremony—which often marked the end of the rainy season—had to be postponed because of the rain.

At home women were keeping the fires going. They prepared meals of the vestiges of their stored food. They wove mats and coiled baskets. They played shell dice. A lot of money changed hands. The balance of the cosmos was maintained by this perpetual gambling.

Because of the scarcity of fresh food and because of the irritable tempers that were shedding dangerous sparks in the combustible village, the arrival of new yucca shoots was greeted with thanksgiving.

On the second afternoon of rain Aleqwel and Alow went out to check the pit where their own fat yucca stalk was roasting. At the first drop of rain Aleqwel had run out to cover the place with seal skin. Now the friends were relieved to find their subterranean delicacy dry and well-cooked. Aleqwel asked his younger brother to run to the wot's house, where their mother was playing shell dice with the wot's wives, to let her know the feast was ready.

They were a large gathering in a small house: Mushu and Alow, the Owl and Coyote families, Anihwoy's nieces and nephews. Rain fell steadily on the thatched roof.

The long red stalk was as sweet and succulent as they had dreamed. And there was otter meat. Nene had prepared some of the last grains of golden ilepesh, and there were a few balls of cherry-nut meal. They even had a taste of aphid sugar.

Ponoya asked her mother what Nacha, the wot's daughter, was doing. Was she gambling? With whom? What sort of basket was she working on?

Anihwoy described Nacha's basketry project in keen detail. She elaborated on the wives' projects, too. Then, she lowered her voice—one never knew when a spy might be outside the door. "The wot's first wife is well pleased with her daughter. This coming year she will drink momoy. She seems willing to marry, though she still cries at the thought of having it arranged for her. Lyamlawinat's wife is losing her desire to eat because of her son Halashu though."

"Why?" asked Alow in surprise. "He does everything so well. He shoots well. He speaks well. He is handsome. The people admire him. What could he possibly do to upset his mother?"

"I know," guessed Aleqwel. "It's because of Konoyo, the caretaker's apprentice, isn't it?"

"Yes," said his mother. "That's it. The wot's sister is frantic because Halashu seems to be only interested in the woman who was a man. He appears to have no interest in girls, in enhweq."

"Well," spoke up Ponoya, a friend of the apprentice, "I'm sure he won't have much choice in the enhweq he will marry. He might as well not form a strong attachment to someone else."

"True, true," agreed Anihwoy. "In fact, his mother told me there are only two or three girls in the whole world that they know of who might be appropriate wives for him. As a matter of fact—this is a secret—the ksen will soon be going over the mountains to investigate one of the enhweq they have heard about. The problem is that the young man's mother is afraid he may be thoroughly uninterested in women—in natural-born women. If he married he might neglect his wife, offend her. Not only would it bring personal disaster, it would endanger the friendship between villages formed by the marriage. Right now, the wot is feeling a particular need to strengthen his connections."

"Because of us and what happened," whispered Ponoya.

"Not only because of us. Our southern neighbors are a constant provocation. Whenever we are weak they take advantage of it."

"Mother," said Aleqwel in a serious tone, "I do not believe Halashu's mother should worry so much. When we were in the hills I also remarked on his attachment to the caretaker of the dead. He told me that in spite of his affection he was willing to marry; he could be happy living with a woman. But he said that Konoyo was the only woman he knew who didn't talk too much, who understood him, whom he admired totally."

"Did you tell him it would be completely unsuitable for him to marry a man-woman?" asked the upright Kanit, indignantly. "A wot might find such a person an asset—as a second wife—but…"

"Halashu understands better than any of us the necessity for building political alliances," said Aleqwel, grumbling. He liked Konoyo.

"Konoyo is very beautiful," said Ponoya. "We all know she attracts men from other women. Isn't that right?" she looked at Alow.

He was noncommittal about the woman's powers. He said, "I wouldn't want to marry a man-woman even if she was strong and beautiful. She still could not have children."

"That's right. And everyone knows they steal other women's babies," added Kanit.

"Konoyo wouldn't do that!" cried Ponoya. "She's your friend, too."

"Well, maybe she wouldn't… but you never know," muttered Kanit.

"Do you think then he would give her up?" asked Anihwoy of her elder son.

"I hope not," he replied.

"But you think I can assure his mother that he has no aversion to… marrying?"

"Yes, I think so."

Nene admonished, "That young man should take more interest in deciding his own future. He ought to take care to find out about the woman he will marry. Some wives are lazy and incompetent. Or they may be jealous. It will matter. It's important to learn a woman's ways and her character." Nene's was the last word that evening on Halashu's obligations.

Throughout this discussion Mushu had sat silently chewing his supper. He might have been listening to the rain or feeling the chill of the late winter evening. Surprisingly, he now spoke. He asked about the food situation at the wot's house. "The wot has been coming around exhorting us to hunt sea animals. Whales are passing by. I see their plumes every day. But the swordfish have not seen fit to drive any to us."

"I saw plenty of food at the wot's house. Though the wives complained about shortages. They insist that none of the common people has died of hunger yet."

"Will there be a shellfish party this year, do you think?" asked Alow.

"They talked about having one…" Anihwoy was interrupted by a loud noise. It was as if the whole house was being pelted with pebbles.

Aleqwel reached for his bow.

Ponoya grasped the atishwin around her neck.

Faces were alert, readied. Kanit whispered, "A raid!"

A child cried, "Is the ocean eating us?"

"I don't think so," whispered Mushu. Such things had happened.

"It's the haphap," stuttered another cousin. But they were not sucked out of their house.

Nothing shook.The snakes that held up Shup were not shifting around. They were not quaking the Earth World.

In a few minutes Mushu stood and went to the doors and stepped out.

He was bombarded by a steady fall of small—and larger—rocks of ice. They stung into his head and face and glanced off the flint knife in his topknot. Laughing, he caught some in his hand and brought it inside.

Anakawin stared at the handful of hail. "Are they pieces of lightning?" he asked. "Woi, you mustn't touch them!" He grew more and more agitated. "No, no. I know what they are. I can hear them. The star houses are breaking up. They're falling apart." He had worked up a real panic. The other children were now crying with him.

Nene tried to hold him. "Se, se. No, no." she insisted. She took a lump of hail in her hand and showed the boy how it melted. "See, it's not that kind of crystal; it's not quartz. It's made of water."

The boy had never seen such a thing. Relief spread over his face. Then active interest.

Nene talked to him about snow, the kind they sometimes saw on the top of the mountain range. "Snow is cold, cold," she said. "I have seen it at Iwihinmu, the mountain at the Center of the Earth World. We were gathering pine nuts. Snow is soft and white and deep as a house. Someday you will see it, too. But you will need your fur. What I have in my hand is a kind of snow. It's cold and wet. But this kind is hard, hard. Watch out for your head!"

The boys were already scrambling to their feet so they could run outside to play in the hard snow.

Anihwoy asked anxiously, "Mother, do you think the hail will damage our house?"

"No. There is a charm of the Three Worlds in the water basket. We are protected. But in the valley and the hills the fragile shoots and tender flowers—the mountain cherry blossoms—they will be in danger."

They sat and listened to the rattling of the hail on the thatch and to the shrieks of the children playing out in the cold. Before very long the noise stopped.

Mushu said, "Son, I think we had better leave while it is still safe."

"You're right, Father. We don't want our flint knives broken by water."

"Or your flint heads either," teased Ponoya.

On taking leave, Alow looked first at Anihwoy and then at her daughter. He said, "It has been a sweet, sweet feast. I could hardly wish for more."

"Come again soon," they said invitingly.

Rain fell all night. There were bouts of hail, of wind. By morning the storm had worn itself out.

The high mountains were blanketed with snow. The air in the village was biting and clean. The snow-capped mountain peaks looked soft and enticing, as gentle as alighted fog. Anakawin wanted to go right up there.

His sister told him it was too far. The mountain crest was days and days away. It was a desolate place. No one lived there but nunashish. Only the ksen, delivering important messages, ever went into the high mountains. And he had feet like wings.

For the time being, the boy consented to playing in the mud created by the rain and melted hail. He taunted the swiftly rushing creek and sifted through fascinating debris on the grey sand.

The whole village was wet. Men and women spent the day gambling.

The following day was equally clear and fresh. The air felt a little less cold. The mud was a little less liquid.

Eight men of the Pelican and Cormorant families came together for the hunt. Each one was equipped with a club and a lance and a bone saw in his carrying net. The hunters sweated and bathed in the cold, rushing creek. Then they met together down on the beach near the black malak spring. The soft tar oozed slowly, wrinkled, expanding in widening ripples. The spring was no good for anything. It produced tar that was always soft, that did not adhere well. Nevertheless, the gooey mass did manage to trap small bits of floating wood and broken shell. Visiting foreigners often marveled at it.

Mushu's late sister's husband took the lead. He was well ornamented in necklaces of shell and stonework and other things. There was even a braid made of seal whiskers. The leader offered prayers to Earth and Sea and to the four winds. He blew egret down and scattered seeds.

The hunting party set off southward down the beach. They rounded the point, passing the mussel-covered rocks. The tide was low; it was an easy walk. Soon they came within view of the southern border. They could see into the doings of mighty Shuku land. They saw no animal hunters.

The beach here spread out from the base of high eroded cliffs. The men could look up to their red shrine pole high above, where it pointed to the Sky World. Just ahead of them, toward Shuku, lay dark, inert masses, that looked like rocks without mussels: the sea lions were in their sleeping place.

The leader directed them with economical gestures. He pointed out two huge bulls sprawling on the sand.

The men positioned themselves between the animals—which were several times larger than they were—and the ocean. They were close enough to touch the giants. To be crushed by them.

Another signal and the men thrust their spears into the enormous creatures' breasts.

Awakened at last, and suddenly, the sea lions struggled to escape. They lumbered awkwardly. They were massive, but slow. Their injuries confused them. The sand hindered them.

The hunters beat on them with clubs, driving them higher and higher onto the sand. They drove them away from the saving water.

Deep anguished bellows rent the placid gray morning.

Alow and Mushu, Chaki and his father were all clubbing one giant. Nothing about the animal was particularly ferocious. But its bulk was deadly. The whole beach had become a flailing, heaving tumult.

A thrashing sea lion knocked Mushu off his feet. His family yanked him aside just before the crushing animal rolled over on top of him. He recovered his balance quickly.

Eventually, both bulls were clubbed into submission, while the other sea lions dragged themselves to a marine escape.

The hunters quickly killed the stunned bulls.

The men stopped to catch their breath and to touch their atishwins. They began to think about what they would make from the animals' hides, their claws, their bones. They stood about, panting, imagining the ways in which the great beings would assume immortality.

Sun was just showing over the eastern mountains.

The men set to work butchering the animals with their saws. They cut them into pieces that they could carry away. They wrapped the fatty flesh in seaweed and packed the bundles into their carrying nets. They had to make several trips back to the village before they were all done. Dark red stains painted the sand where they had worked.

The wot came out to praise the men. He spoke of how important their contribution was to the well-being of the people. Then the leaders went home to scrape clean the big sea lion hides. Alow and Mushu began to unpack their share of the meat. Mushu reached into his topknot for his flint knife.

It was not there.

He groped around in his disheveled hair. He couldn't have lost his knife. He needed it. He liked it. His fingers combed lengths of bead money. They encountered his gopher skin pouch. But there was no knife.

It was a good knife, an exceptional knife. He used it every day. Losing valuable things was not a good sign. His weakness would probably return. There was nothing for him to do but retrace his steps and find it.

Alow was left alone to divide the fresh meat of their kill.

Mushu felt some symptoms of age: deafness from years on the ocean, stiff joints, bad teeth. But his eyesight was still keen. He scanned the sand from the soft tar spring below the village to the site of their hunt on the border with Shuku. The tide was beginning to creep in. He saw the remnants of footprints, some blood. But there were no flint knives.

He went over it all again, unable to leave. He could not accept another defeat. Anihwoy's herbs were having an effect on him; he was beginning to care what happened.

There were rocks south of the place where the sea lions had slept the night, rocks on the border. Mushu sensed a living presence in the rocks. Some sort of animal was watching him. He looked up.

It was a woman stranger. She was crouching yet not trying to conceal herself. She held up a sharp-pointed well-hafted knife. "Yours?" she said with a foreign accent. The word choice was tentative but the action certain.

He was embarrassed, confused. This foreign woman was blatantly trespassing. Had she been stealing his knife? He would be justified in killing her. With what? His hands? A driftwood log? He might force himself on her. They were alone. It was his choice. He said, "Yes."

She slipped into the language of the islanders. "Come get it then. If you still want it."

He was very angry now. He advanced toward her fiercely.

When he got closer he saw what sort of woman she was: younger than he, but no enhweq. She was well dressed in soft buckskin. A cape of island fox covered one shoulder. She wore huya beads and earrings like miniature baskets. She was clearly not of the common people.

"What are you doing here?" he hissed, trying to sound as threatening as a snake. "It is very dangerous here. Is it because you are an islander that you do not know our boundaries?" He spoke haltingly, but clearly, in the island tongue.

She must have understood him. Her reply was proud, but touched with weariness. "I know the boundaries here... all of them. Too well. I am tired of boundaries." She crept down the rocks sideways like a crab. She offered him the knife by its wooden handle.

Mushu accepted it without any expression of gratitude. But his anger was subsiding.

She said, "How is it that you know the island speech? Are you a wot? No, just a fisherman, I imagine. The other men with you this morning, they are fishermen, too, aren't they? Where are they now?"

Mushu thought, this woman is not stupid. Not even kilamu. But something made her desperate, unquiet. She looked well cared for, well fed, nicely clothed. Why would she take this risk?

The woman saw him watching her. She removed her cape. Her breasts were shapely like those of an enhweq who has not borne children. She was painted red in the style of Shuku village.

As the fisherman stared she untied the thongs of her soft skirt.

The man grew frightened. He had tried to be disinterested. Her action was more than he could tolerate.

He thrust his knife back into his hair and reached out for the woman. He took her by the arm but not cruelly. In any event, she offered no resistance.

He led her across the sandy beach recently scarred by patterns of roiling sea lions, human feet, and dark blood. He took her to a low sea cave, one that before long would be filled with rising ocean water. It was damp and obscure in the cave. He grabbed her cape and flung it on the wet sand. Then he spread the woman out on top of the fur. She fell apart easily.

He did not force her.

In midafternoon in Mishopshno village things were quiet. Many were following the Sun's way and taking their rest.

Alow had finished cutting up the meat and had distributed most of it. He scarcely noticed his father's absence. Instead, he was talking to the tomol builder's wife. She told him that the master was down on the sand and that he had begun work on the tomol's framing.

Alow rushed down to the tar rocks. He found the three tomol builders beside the perfect base log, which was lying in a forked frame. He threw himself on the sand and silently watched them. They made careful measurements, measures of hands, fingers, sticks, strings, all recorded on the wood planks with yellow ochre.

The altomolich called to his apprentices, "Look! See! Here! Do it this way! This is the way it has always been done." Finally he spoke to Alow. "Come help me. Your father and grandfather have not come." He held up a bowed stick. "You have arrived in time for the shaping of the hull. It is the most important thing in building a wooden canoe, as I have told you. If the shape is not symmetrical…"

Alow knew how disastrous an off-center tomol could be. As in everything else balance was essential. He squinted and motioned with his hands and gave the best opinion he could venture on the curve of the bow.

It was nearly dark when the men finally returned to their homes. Alow did not find his father in.

The rainy season seemed to have come to an end. People who had been camping in the hills at the time of the hailstorm reported that some of the tender shoots were damaged. Even so, the spring ceremony was a joyful time. Flowers were coming. Seeds were on the way. The Sky World acted in supreme harmony. Sun neither dwindled nor scorched. Moisture was in Shup's soil. A fragile balance obtained.

At the ceremony whistles shrilled well into the night. The people fed their hope on yucca, fresh greens, the meat of sea animals.

And then, soon after the ceremony, it rained again. Some people began to grumble. They were itching to go gathering in the hills. They had grown kilamu from lack of activity. Their storehouses were emptying of seeds and fish and acorns. There were isolated reports of stealing. Some of the common people got into fights. The harmony of the Sky World was not always matched with harmony in the Earth World.

The bard stopped telling winter season stories because he was afraid the rattlesnakes might be coming out. The snakes got angry when they heard the old tales. He did not want to be bitten.

Hunting and fishing and boat building came to a halt. But Shup was drinking deep. Rain was more important than work.

The people continued their other winter occupations: weaving mats, coiling baskets, twining string, making nets. They had only gambling and dreams to keep away hunger. Mushu, the fisherman, went for long walks, even in the rain. But most people gossiped and told outrageous stories or muttered and rubbed their smoke-irritated eyes.

Then Sun came. Families hiked to the hills to harvest yucca and lily bulbs. Children ran around dizzily with small bows and miniature digging sticks. Hunters and fishers set out. The tomol builder began to steam planks and bend them to fit the new tomol. The people stretched their legs.

Still, they were hungry. Tilinawit, the wot, decided to cheer them by giving a shellfish party. Abalone, mussels, clams would be easy to gather at low tide. At this time of year they would still be safe to eat. He determined to announce the party soon. But first he wanted to take care of some other business. He sent for his ksen.

The ksen was tall with long thin legs. He was neither young nor old; he was of an age with the wot. Most important, he was the strongest distance runner in the village, and it was a village of good runners. He was quick as a mud hen: here one moment, somewhere else the next. He had other good qualities, too. He was very quiet. He could walk quietly and hear things without being seen. His ears were as sharp as a coyote's. People sharing a secret or a piece of gossip would first look around to see if the ksen was nearby. What he knew the wot knew. But the ksen had another kind of quietness. He was taciturn. No one but the wot knew what he knew. He was a strange man. Admired and feared, but unknown. He was a mysterious, lonely figure in his black and white paint.

The wot had been acquainted with his runner since their early childhood. Only he could be said to know the ksen well. And he trusted him completely. He had to. The ksen delivered and returned messages. He traveled everywhere. He reported vital information. He had always proved reliable.

Now his feet glided soundlessly along the damp path that led to the wot's house at the top of the hill. There was snow again on the purple-grey mountain peaks, on sacred Tsismuhu. The village creek rushed to the ocean. The ksen noticed these things and not idly. He was one of the few who was sometimes required to surmount desolate ranges and to ford high streams. He was one of the few who knew the villages, the people of other regions. He knew all the big towns.

He and the wot were alone. The wot said, "Sit down. Sit down." and "Eat. Eat."

Ksen was too careful ever to refuse food. If a Mohave offered him a live lizard he would eat it. But the wot had delicacies others could only dream of at this time of year. Cherry-nut balls. Fresh meat. Fowl.

The wot commenced, "You remember how happy we were when our friend, Piyokol, was invited to stay at Syuhtun?"

"Yes, it was an honor."

"Yes, an honor, a great honor. But we have missed him here. Especially in the sweathouse. He has been gone a whole season—the storytelling season."

Ksen said nothing.

The wot went on, "And now the rattlesnakes will be coming out. Why do you think he has stayed away so long? Have they bribed him? Or kept him there by force? Maybe he has been bewitched."

"Would you like to find out, wot?"

"That's a good idea. I'm worried about him. He's like my own nephew."

"Yes, wot."

"Keti!" exclaimed the wot as if only remembering at that moment. "Concerning my nephew… when you are traveling do you think you could stop by a village in the north? It's Mistumukun. You know it, don't you? Give my respects to the wot. He has a daughter who is of marriageable age and inclination. Inform me of her character and of the wot's. Are they well-to-do, polite, civilized, and so on?"

Mistumukun in the northern lands was much farther away than Syuhtun, where Piyokol had been invited to stay. It was, in fact, over the high snow-draped mountains.

Ksen replied, "I believe spring is here at last. Yes, I will climb the high range to the northern lands."

"Good. Good," said the wot. "May you fly fast."

But before the ksen could rise to leave, Tilinawit added, "There is one more place I'd like you to visit. Go there first. It's not far away; it's very near, actually. But you may find it the most inhospitable."

T he ksen missed the shellfish party. He was trotting down the southern path that runs along the bluffs to Shuku's creek when the first villagers began to set up their camps and build their fires on the beach. He did not much like mussels and abalone anyway. They always reminded him of bad times, days of poverty and hunger, of dry winters. Even so, he was sorry to miss the festivities. But his work required him to do so. He had a reward for having to miss so many parties. He was often able to attend festivals in far-off places, sometimes in the big towns. Everywhere he went he was well fed and sheltered. His life had variety.

The strong hunters—they would be warriors if there was a war—were out walking near the outskirts of Shuku village when they spied a strange man running toward them. They set their flint-tipped arrows on their recurved bows and knelt on the ground.

The ksen was hoping to be offered a good meal that afternoon—if he was not killed.

The archers must have noticed his black and white paint, his ksen's insignia. They lowered their arrows and unstrung their bows. They escorted him to the wot's house at the top of the hill.

On the beach at Mishopshno crowds were beginning to gather. Families clumped around fires. Women carried heavy huya pots—the kind that would not break when put in the fire—and water baskets and bowls of flour for soup. The wot had selected a day in the declining life of Grandmother Moon when the low tide—a winter-like tide—was expected to occur in midday.

The morning unfolded warm and blue. There was a strong wind coming down the mountain canyons. The day was as warm as some of the days in the last months of summer. But the people recognized it as an ephemeral kind of heat, brought on by a certain kind of nunashish. The villagers worried that the blue, purple, and red flowers in the hills and valley—which should turn into sihon bulbs, and ilepesh and hutash seeds—which had already been battered by hail, would now be whipped away in the wind or shriveled by heat.

White-and-gray seagulls floated on the wind currents over the people in their human camps. The scavenger birds rose up, were pushed backward and sideways, but never fought the wind. It inevitably carried them somewhere they found acceptable.

The ocean lay calm. It rippled faintly, shining like the inside of an abalone shell. The islands jutted out of the water sharp and clear. They could have been a reflection of the northern range. Despite the wind a certain stillness prevailed in the heart of things. Children were already splashing in the cold ocean waves.

The distant mountains hung over the village like a dark purple windbreak. They looked near. The warm brown sandstone boulders, the hidden caves within, looked close enough to touch. Certainly, it would be easy to stroll to them in an afternoon. Soft blue ceanothus, the erect stalks of yuccas, ornamented the naked hills. For once, the wild place appeared tame, even inviting. Something stirred in the people. Soon they would be walking toward the hills to their springtime camps. The cramped, smoky, hungry waiting would end.

This day, before going out, before the opening up, they celebrated the last moment of their poverty, the death of winter. Even clams and sea urchins—no one's favorite food—looked good to the people. With some soup and a morsel of roast yucca stalk.

The southeastern portion of the village of Mishopshno comes to an end in a cliff. It is a good place for spotting big fish in the channel and spying whale plumes. From the cliff a person can look directly down the beach to a point of land topped by a low hill. At the peak of the hill the feathered shrine pole stood. Anyone could imagine powerful swordfish driving a mighty whale to shore. It was always uplifting to stand or sit on the top of the cliff and admire the vermillion pole with its two black condor feathers and then to look out to sea and gaze on the rocks, the teeming kelp, the deep channel, the cheerful red tomols. Konoyo, the young caretaker's apprentice, stood on the cliff for a moment to nourish her spirit before descending the short path to the beach.

At the base of the cliff, at the bottom of the path, flowed two springs. One was a water spring that trickled out of the oak forest. The other was a black spring of rippling malak tar. It was near these springs on the dry gray sand that the Coyote Family had set up a day encampment. The esteemed caretaker of the dead had established herself nearby and she was soon joined by her apprentices. These two groups were almost entirely surrounded by common people. The commoners seemed to be serious about the party. Already, children were being instructed in digging technique and prying technique and were being given baskets and carrying nets to fill.

Konoyo came over to help her friends Kanit and Ponoya carry a heavy pot. She stayed to chat. From somewhere down the beach Alow and Halashu appeared. They sat down at the crackling fire. Alow immediately started talking about the new tomol, which he had just shown to his friend. Grandly, he invited everyone to come take a look at it. But, surprisingly—to him—only Ponoya accepted his invitation.

Before long, the wot, who had been working his way down the beach, stopping to talk at every campfire, approached the group that his nephew had joined. He spoke to them all like an uncle. His tone was dignified, positive. He explained the purpose of the shellfish party. He commiserated with those who had discomfort from hunger. He spoke of the sorrows of winter, the lack of a whale. Then he described another scene. He praised the coming beauty of new shoots, the colors of the flowers. He presented a picture of a transformed valley. He advised patience, courage. Sun's warmth would soon bring forth what was gestating in Shup. In addition he gave advice on the gathering. He told them which animals to take and how many. He warned them never to take mussels and clams when the summer fishes were visiting. In that forbidden time they turned into deadly nunashish. He mentioned the coming harvest, the traveling, the going of separate ways. He encouraged people to enjoy themselves together as one village before dispersing to the hills. He hoped they would take pleasure in the simple feast and remember one another. Then he was gone.

The wot's speech filled the listeners with confidence. If any had dim fears of someone working harmful magic against them, the fears were extinguished. The words were like a charm.

The unfinished tomol lay below the village's famous tar rocks, the vein of brittle woqo that the tar workers mined. The adhesive rocks were prized throughout all the enitre Earth World. Below these mines was the boat works. Families built their fires all around. People looked out on a rocky reef dotted with basking sea lions.

Alow led Ponoya through the lounging bodies of men, the purposeful bodies of women, and the active bodies of children to get to his grandfather's new tomol, the one commissioned for himself. The first round of planks was not even on yet. But finished boards were stacked up against the black tar rock. Alow explained how the boards were prepared, from the making of the first rough cuts—in which he had participated—to their steaming in a pit of boiling water. He demonstrated how they were bent to shape by being placed on a log and stood on. He seemed to know as much as a master builder.

Ponoya saw vividly the procedures he described, and more vividly she saw how much he cared about the canoe. Somehow that made her feel strongly for him. Then, she was truly curious about the method of construction. It was all a mystery. There were no women in the tomol guild. At the height of her interest Alow said, "Look, we have all our prying tools, our nets, with us. Why go back? Let's just keep walking. There are good rocks near the mouth of the lagoon where the dune grass grows. By the time we reach them the tide will be low. What do you say?"

Ponoya said, "Yes."

Mushu was walking alone along the beach. Shore birds, small ones in families and solitary bigger birds, ones with long drilling bills that curved outward or inward or extended straight as an awl ran in front of him. They chased the waves and probed for food. They turned and were chased back by the lapping water. The tide was going out. People here were crawling all over these rocks that fronted the village. Children were calling to each other and tugging on mussels. They whacked at abalones with small prying tools.

Mushu's nephew, Chaki, was among those tearing off handfuls of black mussels. His wife, Pichiquich, was nearby prying off small stubborn limpets from the oak-gray rocks. The baby was swaddled on her cradleboard, which was supported by her mother's forehead. Chaki said to his small daughter, who was wide-eyed and babbling in her snug container, "Now do you see why we call you Kelele like the little limpet? See how much work your mother has pulling it off!" He turned Pichiquich around to show the baby the tiny cone-shaped limpets. Pichiquich turned herself back and resumed her patient effort, saying, "How can she see me work when I am facing the other way!"

"What I am saying, Kelele, is: What is small can be powerful. Small, but powerful, that's what you are."

Mushu laughed gruffly. He had always been fond of his late sister's child. He wished he could do more for him. Fortunately he was a strong man on his own. Mushu even stopped to talk to the baby for a moment or two. Then his eyes clouded over. He became distant. He headed farther on down the beach.

Up at the mouth of the lagoon, just across from Qoloq land, it was not very crowded. There were a few adventurous parties. There were young people. Alow and Ponoya. The rocks were covered with mussels and abalones. They were crawling with crabs. Alow and Ponoya worked slowly and steadily. Once they both dived for the same skittering crab and ended up catching only each other. They laughed then. Another time a big crab pinched Alow's thumb and Ponoya pretended to cure him with a ball of sea lettuce tobacco. She chewed it first and then put it in his mouth. He pretended to become energized by the medicine. They both laughed hard.

In spite of their play the carrying nets filled quickly. Soon they were resting on the dunes above the rocks, staring out over the iridescent ocean. The islands in the south were sharp like teeth and there was not one cloud. It was very warm in spite of the wind.

Alow was trying to get the basket adjusted in his carrying net, while Ponoya stared out at the pale ocean and the dark kelp beds. The only fishing boats out were on the other side of the border. She could see the rocklike forms of seals and otters basking among the leaves of the kelp sea forest. She reflected on Alow's good qualities: he was not only fun but enterprising, and he was generous when he hunted.

Meanwhile, Mushu gathered abalones from the outermost rocks, the ones that even at low tide were waist deep in water. He worked his way southeast, beyond the shrine pole. He kept walking farther and farther down the beach in the direction of Shuku lands. There were fewer and fewer villagers where he was going.

Soon he was entirely alone. It was hot, hot. He sat down on a beach rock. It was time to rest anyway. Sun was hot, but resting in the sand dollar. Mushu wondered about the heat, what it would do. The wind wasn't too bad. He had experienced worse. He looked up into the wind. A white-headed eagle hovered above him. It was spying, hoping to gather a meal. The bird soared toward the cliffs. Mushu turned to follow its movements, its techniques.

Someone was squatting on the cliffs above him, watching.

Mushu was disturbed to see the woman he called "the Unquiet One," Wenla. He did not want to have to shout to her and possibly attract attention. There was nowhere really to hide. He ignored her and waited.

She must have run down the path, for she was instantly at his side. She chattered at him in that half-forgotten island language. She pointed toward a hollow in the cliff. She began to undress.

"Woi! Se, se!," he cried. "No, no!" He explained to her that the village was having a gathering party. People were everywhere. "See," he gestured to his bag of abalones. He indicated for her to go.

But she stayed and stood close by him.

"Go! Go!" he insisted. He whispered the imperative in island speech, then in the Shuku tongue.

She would not go.

In desperation Mushu took six fat abalones out of his carrying net and put them into hers.

The woman looked pleased. But she did not move.

Mushu jabbered about death, about killing. He made motions of shooting with a bow, then of clubbing. He had, for the moment, forgotten her indifference to such things. Finally, he pointed at Sun and then to the western horizon. He promised to return after dark.

Apparently satisfied, she turned and ran off.

In a few minutes a party of shellfish gatherers joined the fisherman in his foraging.

He wondered again who the woman's husband was.

Alow and Ponoya, bearing the weight of their coming feast on their foreheads, walked slowly in the direction of their family fires. They sucked their own saliva to slake a growing thirst and talked about the gratifying meal that lay ahead.

The way back was not far. But they had barely covered a small part of it when Alow complained of fatigue. He said he needed to rest in the grassy dunes before going on.

Ponoya laughed again. She pointed out that part of him, at least, was not at all in a restful condition.

"All the more reason to lie down," he replied.

Alow gathered some green-hair grass at the water's edge. They climbed to the top of the white dunes where the sand formed a shallow dish and lay down on the grass. Ponoya made no effort to move away as Alow turned toward her. Their bodies were touching.

"Would you go with me to pick poppies someday soon?" he asked. He stroked her with his free hand. His fingers wove among the fringes of her skirt. They played with the thong ties.

She laughed bravely. "I have been warned about such invitations."

He laughed back. "I'm sure you have… And will you come with me?"

After their rest Ponoya and Alow were tired. They were disheveled and tired. They had difficulty standing up. They even had trouble orienting themselves. It wasn't the heat. Sun was already dipping over Syuhtun. It was late. Somehow they managed to stagger down the steep dune and back to the beach.

"It's too bad we have to go back," said Alow. "But I'm hungry, aren't you?"

He looked over at Ponoya. She did not look like the person he had always known. She was transformed. She seemed somehow exotic and strange, wonderful, like someone he might have met at a big festival in a distant village. Then he remembered: they had first been drawn together on such an occasion.

PART II

CHAPTER 4

MONTH WHEN THINGS BEGIN TO GROW

hesiq momoy ihsha cpuun

Lyamlawinat, the wot's sister's husband and assistant wot of the village of Mishopshno, stood at the crest of the village hill on the pathway between the red-fenced cemetery and the large ceremonial ellipse. His back was to the ocean with its island wall. The breeze on his shoulders was light; he wore no cloak, but carried his bows and quiver.

On the field, boys and girls brandishing red-and-black hockey sticks were charging a small wooden ball. Lyamlawinat looked past the naked children crouched on the grassy hillside who were cheering their elders at their practice. A young runner, not part of the hockey game, was running the length of the field, guiding a small ball with his feet. When he reached the far end he turned, kicked and glided back, all without stopping or losing his rhythm. Overhead, the hockey players' small toyon ball flew like a red-breasted robin. Lost for an instant in the background of dark oak forest, it alighted near the distant goal post.

The players of Mishopshno—nearly everyone old enough to have power and young enough to move freely—were strong competitors, at least against the coastal teams. As one of the coaches of the younger athletes, Lyamlawinat viewed the game with a sense of responsibility as well as satisfaction. Lyamlawinat thought the team might make a good showing on Hutash Day in the fall when they celebrated their seed harvest. But now it was only spring, time for people to come out of their burrows and stretch their legs.

He turned his hawk's eyes to the archery grounds carved out of the woods on the far side of the playing field. The wot's two young sons were there, standing together, almost leaning on their bows, talking. His own son, Halashu, was on one knee, his distinctive scarlet bow held horizontally to the ground. He was aiming at a target Lyamlawinat could not make out.

The coach climbed down the hill and headed toward the oak grove. Halashu had several questions. Lyamlawinat demonstrated what he could with his own strong sinew-backed bow. While he instructed his son, the wot's sons lolled around restlessly. Their father and uncle paid more attention to cousin than to them. Well, they had their mother's attention and their sister Nacha's. They didn't envy their cousin; they admired his skill. But they preferred hunting. A war would be more interesting than all this tedious practice. Moving targets were more stimulating.

Their uncle suggested a practice competition. The boys grumbled but stayed. Lyamlawinat tossed out a small target made of bound reeds. From a distance of forty feet the young men took turns shooting at the small bundle. Only Halashu succeeded in hitting it more than once.

His cousins looked at the ground, more bored than discouraged. Halashu was an outstanding marksman. How could they be expected to compete with one who had taken a prize at Syuhtun at last year's Hutash Festival? At that festival a few charges had been whispered against him by foreigners, from Shuku and other villages, charges that he had bewitched the bows of his opponents or had caused their arrows to deviate at long distance, even hints that he had used poison, ayip, against a certain individual. The complaints were practically a formality, half-believed only by the losing side. On the day of the Hutash Festival Halashu had earned his high reputation—and also his fine-looking scarlet bow.

Lyamlawinat wanted all the young men to develop their strength. He gave them a closer target, but demanded that they penetrate it as deeply as possible. His nephews shot in turn, crouching and drawing, more out of respect for their older cousin than to please him. Their competition had sharpened Halashu to his present keenness. They were expert, too. They would help one another. The cousins' toyon arrows hit the mark, penetrating slightly beyond their flint tips. With disappointment, they examined their bows—fine recurved specimens—as if searching for the cause of their weakness in them.

Halashu shouted encouragement: "Pretend it is a deer! You are good hunters!"

"Animals move. They breathe and tremble," complained the older cousin. "It's too difficult to pierce something so still."

"Nevertheless, even a target has life," said Halashu. "Watch me!" He lifted his prize bow of the beautiful scarlet color. It was made from elderberry wood and was said to have come from beyond the northern mountains where the best bow makers live. He was still getting used to it. He had not yet tried it out on a hunt. He withdrew a long flint-toothed arrow from the quiver at his waist. He set it on the left side of the bow and assumed the shooting position on one knee. He drew back the beautiful backward curving bow with all his strength.

The bow cracked. The noise was like thunder.

Halashu was stunned. He was immobilized like a bird hit with a blunt arrow. His cousins stood silently, gaping.

Lyamlawinat moved immediately to his son's side. "Woi, no good! No good!" he cried.

The words brought Halashu to his senses. With deep concentration he examined the fine fissure that had spread through his cherished possession. He was quiet and thoughtful.

Suddenly, Halashu was on his feet. He kicked the bow away from him into the rough brush that surrounded the well-kept shooting place. "Poison!" he exclaimed with disgusted finality. He ran off into the darkness of the oak forest. The way was tangled with bracken, berry bushes, and poison oak; he was not following the usual path. He nearly stepped in some human excrement. But despite his unbalanced condition his heart led him directly to the sacred spring in the depths of the wild grove. The spring's name was Deer Urine because of its slightly yellow color. Its waters were healing.

His hands shook as he opened his fur carrying pouch. Somehow he managed to extract a clump of eagle down, a little powdered tobacco, a few black hutash seeds. He offered them to the spring. When he spoke his voice was cracking with emotion. "Grandmother," he cried to the power of the spring, "bow has deserted me! Bow is poison! It has turned and become my enemy. Who is it that is trying to kill me?"

The grandmother of Deer Urine Spring told him to wash his hands and face in her water. She instructed him in purifying himself and asked him to fetch the wounded bow and bring it to her.

At the archery ground Halashu found his kinsmen standing in a knot whispering with the long-eared alchuklash and the wot. Tilinawit approached his nephew cautiously, checking to see whether he was kilamu, out of his mind, as the assistant wot had described him. The young man appeared calmer. "Listen, nephew," he said, choosing words to demonstrate his affection and support, "the alchuklash has examined the bow. He finds no trace of ayip or other poison on it."

"If there were poison you would already be on your way West. Or gravely ill," the alchuklash asserted.

"But I must take the bow to Deer Urine Spring!"

"Yes, you must. You must immerse it. I cannot discount any contamination, the possibility of bewitchment. Tonight you must come to my house so I can heal you."

"I feel strong," said Halashu, with surprise, as if just discovering it.

"Yes, you look fine," said the soul doctor. "Most likely, the person who bought your bow was deceived by a dishonest guildsman, a stranger. I advise you to have a new one made right away, a good toyon bow from Mishopshno."

Halashu retrieved the defective bow from the bushes and wrapped it carefully, so he wouldn't have to touch it. He offered it to the grandmother of Deer Urine Spring. Her cleansing water neutralized its contamination. Halashu sat by the spring breathing deeply, watching the red bow floating in the pure water. For the first time since the incident he felt the possibility of safety. Between the grandmother of Deer Urine Spring and the alchuklash he would be healed.

The old men doctors restored the souls of the terribly ill, even of the dead themselves, year after year. Halashu would have liked complete assurance, but he thought his alchuklash wise not to offer it. He was wiser still not to have ignited the suspicion ever smoldering between neighbor villages. He had been ready for war. But it was possible that Shuku had nothing to do with the incident. The alchuklash was a man to trust.

And the bow? Had it really come from beyond the northern mountains? Who had made it? Could it really have been a man from the bow makers' guild? And who purchased it? An ignoramus? A cheapskate? Maybe the ksen, when he returned, could help him trace it. At that moment, gazing into the dark pond, the future wot vowed that this knowledge must be his. He must know more than his enemy. He trembled that his power might be diminished.

He felt heavy in body and limb as he walked back through the woods to the playing field and up to the hilltop summit of his village. He would have to wait until nightfall to be cured. He thought of the ksen and of the ksen's report from Shuku. The report—and now this—oppressed him like a cloud hanging over the barren and illusory island of Anyapah. He went down to the sweathouse and spent the rest of the afternoon lying silently by the fire.

Halashu stood staring into the cemetery. A few fresh-looking red poles marking gravesites had risen about the time of the winter solstice. They were capped with baskets, bowls, fishing gear: the distinctive accessories of the former people's occupations.

The young man, waiting, peered between the fence posts at the weathered grave markers. He saw the no longer identifiable remains of the once wealthy and notable. The graves of commoners—unmarked from the beginning—he knew to be plentiful. Ghosts had a great power. It was fitting that they should be given the best residences in the village, high on the hill beside the sacred ellipse. As neighbors they had the most holy of all living people, the caretakers of the dead, who were available to converse with them if necessary. He had no doubt that if he were to die now Konoyo would be there to talk to his troubled spirit. With her grandmother's ghost to protect her she would be immune to any harm. That pleased and consoled him. Anyone but a caretaker would be destroyed by having close contact with a ghost.

The outer door of the caretakers' large house opened at that moment and Konoyo ducked out. She was freshly groomed, brightly painted in red with a few black stripes, and self-possessed. She was as tall as the budding wot. Her shoulders were strong, her figure attractively rounded.

When he saw her and her small red-painted breasts Halashu prayed that he might live a little longer to enjoy more contact with her.

"She says I may go out with you for the afternoon," the youthful apprentice announced.

"She is a wise woman. She knows I will be wot some day… if I live."

"She always says the antap should keep together."

They walked slowly to the top of the hill where it overlooked the game field below. They were experiencing the pleasure they always felt on first being together. Their steps were leading them in no particular direction.

"What's wrong?" said Konoyo, suddenly. "You don't seem quite yourself."

Halashu looked down on the playing field. He saw his two cousins, Tilinawit's sons, contesting with red flashing sticks. Red, the beloved color of joy—of the playing stick, the tomol, of Konoyo's shoulders, and of her soft fringed skirt. It was the color of shrine poles and grave markers and of his broken bow. The color of Shimilaqsha. "Ichantik, you are fortunate to be so intimate with death, to know the secrets that no one else can know," he said.

Konoyo was puzzled. "All who are initiated know the way to the Sky World. We all have this consolation."

"Yes. There is no question of the eternal life at Shimilaqsha. But before then, the way it comes… by drowning… or a fall… or poison. Who can tell when their power might suddenly leave them? Can you, ichantik? Can you see that future?"

"Not often, no." Konoyo was modest. "Remember, I am still young. But why are you asking me these things, my dear friend? What inauspicious thing has happened?"

They were heading for the creek now, just passing by the deserted archery field. Birds were calling loudly to one another. The sky was blue.

Halashu explained about his bow, about its breaking.

"Woi, no good! No good!" she said just like his father, Lyamlawinat.

"Do you know what made it break?" he asked.

"Oh, I know nothing at all of bows. We women depend on others to hunt for us."

From the time she could remember she had been raised as a girl. But she could recognize the signs of things being out of balance. She could always tell when men were worried, even if they said nothing. "Let's pay a visit to the shrine tree," she suggested.

"Just where I was heading," he agreed. "But first I want to see the creek."

Away from the trail the dark oaks grew close together, nearly blotting out the sky. The two picked their way through the oily-leafed new poison oak and the prickly berry vines. The pleasant smell of decomposing sycamore leaves drew them toward the creek.

Beside the running water willows and alders flourished along with the tall mottled sycamores. New leaves were appearing on bleached skeletal limbs. Fuzzy seed balls hung from skinny twigs. The creek was flowing well.

"Any day now snakes will be out," said Konoyo taking a seat on a pale sandstone boulder. "You'll have to be more careful."

"I'm always careful," said Halashu, sounding annoyed. The broken bow wasn't his fault. That was the problem. He twisted the crystal hairpin in his flowing topknot. It was a gesture he didn't seem to be aware of, but which Konoyo recognized as a mark of inner tension. "It's the others who need to learn more care. Especially, those without atishwins on their side."

"They have the snake doctor."

"Yes, they do."

Halashu wore little that he had to remove before jumping into the creek. "Iyi, that's better! I was too warm," he sighed as he joined the frogs and small fish and the insects that danced on the surface of the water.

Konoyo watched him bathe in the golden sunlight of the mossy pond. Her look was warm and attentive, something like that which a momoy giver bestows on his patient, or a mother on her infant. Sticking out of his black hair, the crystal ornament twinkled in a shaft of sunlight that fell through the new leaves. Rainbows sparkled on the gushing water.

Halashu pulled himself out onto a warm sloping rock. "Now I feel clean," he said, smiling at his companion, his iwu. He lay back, allowing Sun and the breeze to make him dry.

After a time a gray sparrow with a striped breast hopped onto a willow branch just a few inches from Halashu's chest. She sang and sang to him in a sociable way. Finally, the bather sat up on his elbows and said to the bird, using human words, "Ichantik, you have almost convinced me that in all the Earth World there is no poison! Are you inviting me to see the house you are building?"

And the gray sparrow proudly showed it to him.

At the tall shrine tree the two friends prayed and tied strips of rabbit fur to the tips of the branches. They spoke to the winds. They were beginning to feel close to the center again.

They followed the trail up. Sparrows sang and woodpeckers called. Hawks swooped. They stooped to gather feathers, edible greens, attractive stones. A lizard ran across their path, and they came across a sunbathing skink. But there were no rattlesnakes.

Halashu said, "I always like the time just before the snakes."

"And before the bears, too."

"I have fewer concerns for the people once the rains come. It's the only time I am almost at ease… usually."

"Come," said Konoyo. "Sun is taking his rest now. Let's follow his example." She led Halashu off the trail to a little clearing where there was a clump of cactus and a cluster of large tan boulders. She climbed right up one, rearranged her skirt and said, "What do you mean 'usually'? What makes this spring any different?"

"I'll tell you. Of course, you know everything, anyway," whispered Halashu.

Sitting on the hillside, the gentle slope before the high mountain wall, they talked and ate the cresses and sprouts they had gathered. They gazed down on the valley. The valley was dotted with dark oaks but cleared all around. Out of the charred black Shup came a fuzz of new green grass. The first flowers were blooming: gold, purple, and blue. Sun was shining his torch full in their face as he ran toward the west. Beyond the parkland that the people had groomed by burning lay the hill of the village, the blue smoke, the green shimmering sea, and the islands topped with clouds.

Konoyo rested her hand on her friend's thigh. "Now?" she asked.

Halashu moved away. "The alchuklash told me to… observe restrictions," he said.

Konoyo drew away, compacting herself like a turtle. "So it was serious—with the bow—then?"

"Serious enough."

"How long are the prohibitions?"

"Not long."

A silence. A black buzzard soared over the valley.

She said, "The ksen went out."

"Yes. And he returned, too."

"I didn't know that."

"Because he left again, that very day."

"Oh, where did he go?"

"Ichantik, I admire your discretion. Your will is stronger than flint. You know even the secrets of the dead. Tell no one what I say."

She pouted. "Do I ever?"

"Well, no. I guess not. But things seem to get around. I don't know how…"

Sun was shining his torch full on their faces as he ran toward the west. They could see the blue haze of Syuhtun town in that melancholy direction.

Halashu said, "Ksen went to Shuku. Now my father wants me to go, too."

"For what purpose?"

"I'll tell you everything," he said. He told her how they came to know that the intruder, the Wokoch at the Winter Solstice Festival, was the bear doctor of Shuku village. He told her—without divulging how he learned it—that the bear doctor had killed the late paint maker, injured the son, and threatened the rest of the family. He endangered the whole village. "We have no choice: we must destroy the evildoer. The only question is how? By whom? When? The problem is how to do it without initiating war or more serious destruction."

"So you go to Shuku to gain their co-operation?"

"That's what we hope. Their wot will see the threat to himself from his own kilamu achana."

"It is dangerous. It will require trust. Is the wot trusting…and trustworthy? His family has not been our friend. The balance is easily upset."

"Yes, I am aware. I don't know who poisoned my bow. My father says the wot is greedy and conceited, but he has not proved to be deceitful. Yet."

"How will you behave there?"

"I'll begin the discussion that the ksen arranged. I'll represent my uncle."

"It's tricky, tricky. Do you have Coyote…"

"Oh, ichantik, I know it is bad, bad. The ksen has learned that the bear doctor—the Wokoch—has been trying to incite the people of Shuku to fall on us by surprise. He lies, saying the late paint maker was poaching, stealing their wot's feathers. He says some of us are sneaking in and robbing from their people's granaries. What can I do?"

"Do the people of Shuku believe in their bear doctor?"

"The ksen thinks they may not or they would have fallen on us already. The achana is not popular with them because he lives apart, in the woods. He uses his power in eccentric ways."

"And Aleqwel—the former paint maker's son—would he like to kill the evildoer?"

"He is burning to do it. My father can hardly restrain him. But if he were to do it now there would be certain reprisal. Their wot seems neither to believe nor to disbelieve his own achana. But Shuku relies on him for the Bear Ceremony. They need his protection."

"Ichantik, you must be strong. Make their wot see that the Wokoch is lying. Persuade the leader to put a spy on him. Tell him you will hold him responsible if any further harm comes to our own people. He must know that, though we are small, we have powerful achanas, too."

"I should arrange it so that he sees the Wokoch's bad character for himself."

"Exactly! He will think himself clever to discover it."

The shadows were growing longer, the ocean painted with a golden path to the west. The water was pale. The two noticed the lateness of the day for the first time. Halashu noticed bats beginning to dart about in the evening sky. The circlet of shells on Konoyo's head stood out like a phosphorescent wave on the night tide.

They headed back toward the village. The trail was shady and quiet. They walked quickly, Konoyo leading the way. "When will you go?" she whispered.

"Soon. Right after the Rattlesnake Ceremony, if the ksen is back.

A silence. Rocks in the trail. Snapping branches. New growth.

"Where is he now, then?"

"Looking for Piyokol… and around."

"I heard he was going to a village over the north mountains."

"Where did you hear that? I thought you said…"

"Ichantik, I have been spoken to. There are those in your family who believe I do you little good."

"What? My aunt? Nacha? My cousin! I'll…"

"Hush!"

"Listen, iwu, believe me, this trip of the ksen's means nothing to me. It's not your fault. It's my father's idea. He thinks we need allies. I told him I was too young to marry."

Konoyo laughed. They were approaching the shrine of the sky-reaching sycamore tree. She tried to keep herself still in the sacred place.

But before they were fully beyond the range of the holy precinct the wot's son burst out. "Keti! How I wish the restrictions were over! I would show you!"

All the way home Konoyo reassured him, "Yes, yes, I believe you" and "It's best that you be cured."

As they came to the playing field and the hill of the village where they would have to part she added: "Have courage, iwu! You will succeed! Alishtahan!"

At the crest of the hill between the cemetery and the ceremonial ground, neither speaking nor touching her, Halashu gave her a last look that seemed to defy the intention of the prohibitions. Then he turned his dusty feet and ran toward his home.

It was peaceful in the sweathouse now that the bard had retired for fear of rattlesnakes. The sound of the late spring rain was muffled by the sod roof. The men lay by the fire snoring or talking quietly. Some played the bone game. Some threw stick dice.

Aleqwel had spent the night in the warm subterranean men's place. But it hadn't protected him from his dream. These past nights she had begun to pursue him again. She reached out to him with long sharp fingers that were smeared with dirt and blood. Her vulva flapped like wings. This time Aleqwel awoke, struggling for breath, his heart racing, in the company of men. It comforted him, in a way. Each night he had to run farther, and faster, to escape the woman and her vulgar challenge. This night had been the worst. The refuge he had always found in the dream—in the man-woman Konoyo, or in a solid rock of safety—had disappeared. Instead, he had been driven into the encircling arms of still another woman. In the end, he recognized his sister's embrace. This had not reassured Aleqwel, as he might have expected, but was the cause of even greater alarm. He had pulled away from her and headed back toward his devourer. With dread he awoke.

Now, in the day, with last night's rain still falling, Aleqwel tried to catch up on his sleep. He was dozing near the fire when Alow stumbled into the chamber and threw himself on the sand beside his friend.

Aleqwel had difficulty responding to his question: "How are things going?" He felt drained of vitality, almost devoid of will after the night's visitation. But he didn't want to speak of it. Only the alchuklash knew. And he had explained to him that the woman—who had come also on Solstice Night—was very likely an assistant of the evil bear doctor, trying to poison him. Aleqwel did everything his great-uncle recommended to strengthen himself: he fasted, stayed away from women, walked alone in the hills at night. It was only these things that kept his power from being depleted. What could he say to his friend?

"Oh, just like that," he said conventionally, if a little wearily.

"Yes," said Alow. "I see. Tell me, has the wot given you the word?" Since the night of the yucca feast Alow had paid close attention to his neighbor's welfare.

"No, nothing," said Aleqwel tersely. It was this waiting—as much as the night-time visits—that kept him taut and tense and tired. "Not from him, or his son, or the poisoner. No news from the other village." He peered around to see who was nearby, sleeping or eavesdropping. It would be terrible if gossip spread and the whole village went into a panic. Incidents would proliferate. The wot might lose power. They might all die. The two lay by the fire in smoky comfort. At first they touched without speaking; then they dozed off. Under the circumstances nothing could have been better.

It was later, when the fire was low, that they both began to stir at the same time. The fire tenders were nodding. Aleqwel got up to throw on some more wood. He didn't want a big blaze like they had had in the morning. But he hoped to keep warm. He saw Alow rolling on his side and yawning.

"Oh, I forgot to mention," said Aleqwel cheerfully. "There is good news. I'm going on a journey as soon as spring camping is over. My father—my late father—used to make this trip every year to purchase pigments. Say, would you like to come along? I've never been so far away on my own."

"Sure, sure," Alow answered without thinking. "Where are you going? How many days?"

"I'm following the path of the pine-nut gatherers toward the Center of the Earth World."

"Mount Iwihinmu?"

"Not that far. It's a trade center I'm going to, Matilha, where they buy paint from the distant mountains. They have the best paints there: vermillion and scarlet from the other side of the world, brought by the desert people."

"Matilha? That's the place where tok, the red milkweed, grows."

"Yes. We have a trading uncle there."

"Well," said Alow, "that's fine, fine for me. I wanted to buy some tok to carry to the islands. The islanders have none, of course. Matilha. I have heard that the girls at Matilha.... Are you certain you are going only to trade?"

"There are doctors there, painting doctors," Aleqwel said mysteriously. "They work on rocks and in caves just like the paqwot at the winter's turning."

"Woi! You can't go in there!" said Alow with horror. "Those places are extremely dangerous. They're forbidden!"

"Alishtahan! Have courage. I won't sneak inside. But I like to be near them. To see the artists who can bring their atishwins—and even the gods—into existence with only their paint and brushes."

"I'd better go along with you and keep you out of trouble. Though your power now is evident, almost like an achana's." Alow considered: "You'd probably do all right traveling alone."

"But companionship is better, brother."

They curled up together like badgers in a burrow while an uncertain time passed by.

Aleqwel awoke when Alow tapped him on the shoulder.

"I think I had better go now, ichantik. I have promised someone I will play stick dice. I think they will have good food," he added crassly.

"Play with me sometime."

"Is it allowed? You are so difficult to find these days. I hear you are in the hills, alone."

"And I discover, when I look for you, that you are seldom alone. You come to our house, but you disappear with my sister with scarcely a word to me."

"I hope you are not offended by it, ichantik."

"No, I am not offended, not for myself. But my sister, she is not only an enhweq, she is a serious person."

"Am I causing her unhappiness? Don't you believe I am also a serious person?"

Aleqwel thought about the rude remark about food and the enthusiasm for the girls of Matilha. "May it prove to be true, ichantik."

Alow gathered up his net. "Kiwanan, iwu," he whispered.

"Come visit me soon, ichantik," replied Aleqwel.

There were cloudy days and wet days. Then Sun returned. After that it stayed dry.

The hungriest families began moving to their spring camps in the foothills. Some others of the common people soon followed. The people were like drops of rain water that splattered, diverging into various inviting paths. But, like scattered drops of water, they would all end up in the same sea at summer's end. Their sea was the village of Mishopshno.

One of the first families to go out was that of Aquyahut of the Rabbit Family, a lame man, originally from Shuku and father of several children. One summer he had come face to face with a bear in a berry patch. Though it had only been a common bear, not a grizzly, Aquyahut had turned in fear and run away. The surprised bear also ran—in the opposite direction. But before he realized what was happening the simple man had caught his foot on a berry vine and fallen headlong into a dry gully. He paid the bonesetter all the beads he had to set his broken bones right. But they had never mended properly. He could only hobble where once he could run. The poor man grew even poorer, and he relied on his wife's family to hunt and harvest for him.

Now, in spring, while he sat in the village twining tok rope, his wife and children set out to camp, to dig fresh lily and sihon bulbs. At the camp, on a distant creek that ran into the salt marsh, the Blackbird Family joined the other desperate ones, those who, in the last weeks of winter, had been reduced to consuming shellfish and grazing on blades of grass as if they were deer. These people now thankfully dug bulbs and plucked cactus fruit. They burned yucca spines and felled their succulent stalks. There, at the base of the mountains, the children burrowed with child-sized digging sticks. They ate all day long. They played in the creek and climbed the trees. They were as happy as the departed in Shimilaqsha.

But in Mishopshno, for those who owned their own boats, there was another and new kind of work. The first migrant tuna had arrived in the channel. Every morning, before sunrise, Mushu, Alow, Chaki, Chaki's father, and all the other fishermen set out toward the open channel beyond the smooth brown kelp. They returned at noon, baskets full of large striped fish. The well-to-do people of the village gorged, and they shared with their neighbors. A new energy moved through their limbs. They relaxed in Sun's rays. They set plans and put them into action.

The women moved outdoors to grind their meal and to coil baskets in the warmth of the sunshine. They chattered and sang like birds as they kept an eye on the fishing boats on the ocean. They laughed as the men tried to land their heavy boats through white-foamed surf.

The rattlesnake doctor, his dancers and musicians, began preparations for the coming ceremony. The old achana went into the hills to greet the first snakes.

Artisans came outdoors to practice their trades. The bow maker made bows. The woodworker turned out plates and bowls, and the paint maker ground pigments for their decoration. The tomol builder, working near the shore under the bank of hardened black tar, drilled and sewed wooden planks to create the first round of the new canoe's sides.

Alow fished with his father or from his own tule raft. In the morning he fished and distributed his catch and collected his money. At noon, he visited briefly with the altomolich concerning progress on his grandfather's tomol. He tried his hand at sewing the tough tok rope that bound the boards together. When he tired of that he went to one or another of his cousins' houses or to that of the Coyote Family to eat and spend the afternoon in congenial companionship.

One night he went duck hunting with Aleqwel. He wanted to catch some of the last fowl before the flock followed the coastline north in that dark fluttering tooth-point that took them far away to their summer camps. They roasted the birds for the women.

But, though Alow spoke regularly with his paint-making friend, it was usually only briefly. More often he sought the company of Ponoya, who was industriously making coiled baskets. Whenever possible he persuaded her to go out walking with him.

Aleqwel did not know precisely where they went. Perhaps they followed the creek trail, then wandered off into the impassable sagebrush and sumac. There would be nothing to do there but find a clearing and lie down. Or maybe they walked along the shore, south toward the damp low-lying sea caves, or north to the mouth of the salt marsh and the cradling dunes. He didn't know what to think or how to feel. It was beyond his knowledge. His friend had said he was serious. But what did it mean? He never spoke of marriage. He was young. Would it even be wise for Ponoya to marry him? Wherever she went, whatever she did, his sister was usually home before dark, in time to help with the evening food. She was exemplary in tending to the welfare of her brothers. And, of course, her companion was his closest friend.

It was hot. As on the day of the shellfish party the dry wind rushed down the canyons from the mountain passes. This heat was not pleasant like the warmth of summer—it was a nunashish. The wind creature turned people kilamu and made them do what they would not ordinarily do. Dust swirled in spirals in the lanes of the village. It blew through the houses. People shouted. They cast insults. But the wise withdrew to the ocean's coolness, throwing themselves upon the frothy waves.

Alow was a swimmer. All around him men, children, even women, played in the refreshing salty foam. He felt exhilarated out in the surf—as if he were an island-bound tomol surrounded by dolphins. On the beach he could make out a man—or woman with her skirt torn off—dancing with the sandy gusts. He—or she—spun like a whirlwind nunashish. Alow was full of undiscriminating desire. The feeling did not arise from his own wish, but from the Sky People. Experience made him recognize this imbalance; he knew the wind. As much as he half-loved the delirium and could happily have surrendered, he had learned something from other years, other winds. He dove under a pounding breaker and let the water shut out the rest of the world.

Alow's father, Mushu, was not among the wise who counteracted the madness by throwing themselves in the surf. Instead, he was walking southeastward down the beach, approaching the tide-lapped rocky point where he would disappear from his son's view. Mushu knew he acted in disequilibrium. But he felt encouraged when he looked up at the bright shrine pole with its feathers churning in the monstrous wind and saw that they still pointed east and west, to the origin and the end. The cold ocean water licked at his wandering feet. He recalled the days of his youth when he had come here to gather abalone and mussels and crabs from the dark rocks. It was in the days when his father was still an active seaman. Later, he had come here to fish and to hunt sea animals.

He meandered beneath cliffs seeping with liquid tar. It trickled like tears. Sand flew in his eyes. The wind was hot, hot. Suddenly, he remembered the nights of his early manhood when he had come here to walk alone, to strengthen himself. The walks hadn't gone on long. He had soon been found by an atishwin. And he felt easily satisfied with his power. He had begun to embark on big expeditions: to Syuhtun, Mikiw, Muwu, and then to the islands.

He married and remained on Wima Island. There was a son. He got homesick and came home. Then he became a widower, and the new baby was lost too. Now, in his present condition he found the sweathouse lonely and uncongenial. For one who cannot—or dares not—sleep it is not a great comfort. But even in earlier years he rarely spent his nights with the men.

He stalked his own tracks once more, walking here, alone. He returned once more to the familiar places, places he had been drawn to revisit in recent nights. He was not finding strength in solitude. He was being drawn toward human companionship. But it was day now, Sun was oppressive. And he was going to their place, going without purpose or volition, without consideration for his own safety. The wind was sucking him away.

It happened just as he knew it would. The woman, who had told him she was called Wenla, was standing on the cliffs of Shuku searching across the invisible boundary toward his land, toward him. White seagulls, sliding through the air, were shrieking dizzily below her. Her soft buckskin skirt flapped invitingly in front of her like a feather banner at a festival. Her hair waved like seagrass, disguising her features with its windswept tendrils. She wore no cape, carried no net. Above her, a bald eagle tried to keep his center over some interesting object on the shore, gave up and glided away on broad noble wings. His eye remained fixed on the small things below.

When she saw Mushu, the woman gestured and called out.

As on the day of the shellfish party, he pretended not to notice.

As on that day she ran down the cliff trail and pushed her body up against his. "Not in the daytime," he cried, as if he had been brought to the place against his wish. The situation felt like a recurring dream. "What do you want?" he asked, not harshly, but furtively.

"To be with you," Wenla shouted. She had discovered his difficulty in hearing. Her seafaring husband suffered from the same problem. But he was old.

Mushu would have given in to her. With the wind he would risk anything. But some power he had forgotten he possessed was protecting him. "Come into the ocean," he said. "If we turn our noses to each other and bark a little we will be indistinguishable from the seals."

They went out where the water was deep.

"I have always been afraid of the ocean," Wenla said. "But, look, here I am with you."

"I can't believe you are afraid of anything," said Mushu.

"Only of the sea, of drowning," she shouted over the undulating swells. "Nothing else frightens me, not even violent death."

Mushu looked past the woman, out toward the channel and the gold-green islands. He knew now that this woman—Wenla—had been born at Michumash, the largest island. Her words were like waterfalls: outpouring at times, dried up at others. She had been pushed to marry a wealthy Shuku merchant whose family origins were on the island. Like so many islanders she longed to see the expansive world of the mainland, the rivers and tall mountains, the boundless valleys filled with deer and bears and wildcats. Though she knew they should remain in her village and she had expected that he would finally settle there, she had agreed to move to Shuku with the merchant and leave her family behind. She had seen a portion of the vast world now and lived in wealth and comfort. But she could never be happy with that man. He was old and interested only in the work she could perform to increase his wealth. His evenings—when he was not at sea—were spent with the men in the sweathouse. She was homesick beyond endurance. Yet he would not let her go. She ran away. But who can swim to the islands? She was captured. Mushu, in the short and limited way he had known her, had watched her twist like a fish on a line. She turned and flailed, shifting from resignation to rebellion to desperation.

One night, when she had asked him what he was called and he had answered "Mushu," she had laughed and said, "Fisherman, yes, of course. But that's an island word. You're not an islander."

"I spent a little time over there," he had answered laconically. "At Silimihi?" Her home. Her island home. "I passed through there once."

"Stop looking past me like that, as if I were a ghost!" she ordered now. "You're not afraid to be near me at night."

Recklessly, he reached for her in the cool darkness of the water. He knew her mystery now, her despair. He knew her body in its superficial contours, its pleasing contours, its assertive movements. But she still held a secret, some dangerous attraction that enticed him like a baited hook.

She moved close to him, stood on his feet, even began to climb him as if he were a pole ladder.

It was pleasing, pleasing in the water, especially on such a hot crazy day.

Later, when she spoke again, she said, "I know you are worried. I will go. But I want to tell you the truth—because I like you. You are good, good."

He let her words descend on him.

"You are a fisherman. You own a red tomol. Sometimes you go to the islands. Hide me away! Take me!"

"But you have the right to leave Shuku if you wish. Get your husband to arrange it." He was surprised by the hurt he felt. He ought to have known. How could it have been otherwise. He couldn't deny that he was disappointed. Yet it was for the best. If she tried to come live with him the volatile Shuku people would claim he had abducted her. There would be a war, or worse. Everything between them was impossible. She was using him because she was kilamu with homesickness.

"I can't trust him."

Mushu's voice sounded empty, drained by the voracious wind, when he said, "Listen, believe me, I do feel sorry for you." He adopted the long-ago language of the island people. "Listen, I know you are lost here. But I no longer cross the channel."

Wenla was knocked forward by a wave as she struggled for the shore.

Mushu let the next one propel him toward her. It was so dangerous for her to be walking around near the border. He caught her by the ankle. She struggled wildly. He let go.

"I'm not a swordfish," he said. "Please listen to me. It's true, I never cross over anymore, but others do. If you'd like I will see what I can do."

She was squatting on the shore in the wet sand. Her expression brightened like dry grass when it first catches fire.

He warned her: "You must promise me never to come here during the day again. Not to see me or even just to walk."

"But I like you," she cried and put her arms out to embrace him again.

Mushu's mind was effaced by the nunashish, by ghosts. But his mouth said, "Se, se. No, only at night." He pushed her toward her clothes.

At the shrine pole the fisherman climbed the steep trail to the top of the bluff. From the pouch in his hair he removed down and scattered it in the four directions. It dashed away to the extremities of the world. But the path it followed was winding and indirect.

He entered the village through the neighborhood of the commoners, paying little attention to the things going on around him. He was thinking about his son, Alow, and his nephew, Chaki, and his own vanity. Was it injured? There was little left to injure. No, he hadn't wanted to marry her, Wenla, the unquiet one, even though she was of the Seal Family and hence the Earth Team. He felt gratitude to her; he cared.

Head to the ground, thoughts swirling like the wind, he crashed into his curing doctor, Anihwoy. "What?" he said as a greeting.

She laughed. "Even on warm days people get sick, even injured."

"It makes them a little kilamu. Crazy, like they all drank momoy. I know; I feel that way myself."

Anihwoy peered at him. He looked better than he had before she treated him. She pushed against her buckskin skirt to keep it from blowing around, a nearly hopeless procedure. She was aware of her short ragged hair. "Well, I must be going," she said with a hint of shyness.

"Curing doctor," he said, "I am grateful to you."

She smiled. My treatment is working well, she told herself. The thought pleased her so much that she sang a lively little song into the wind.

In a few days, the cooling fog, which had been lying over the ocean, rolled in and enveloped the debilitated villagers. They welcomed it like a healer. But the crazy wind had brought few serious injuries, at least none that showed. And Anihwoy's patients continued to improve.

But, while the sensible had been bathing their charged bodies in the ocean or creek and the afflicted had acted wildly in the village, one man roamed the hills, alone. As he roamed he explored the chaparral, the streamside rock clusters, the barren ledges of the hillside. He searched and searched. He peered into small holes in Shup and observed the stars at night. Finally, he found what he was looking for.

When the old man, head of the Rattlesnake Family, returned to the village he found the damp gray fog subduing the people. He went directly to the wot's house. The people who saw guessed the meaning of it. Even before the crier came to announce the ceremony, the villagers were spreading the word: the rattlesnakes had come out of hibernation. The snakes were out! No more telling of tales and histories. It was time to assess the coolness of one's blood, to reflect on the diligence with which one had bathed all winter. It was time to attend the Rattlesnake Ceremony.

The old achana had the rattlesnakes' ears. He could read their intentions. He knew who might be vulnerable to their attack, and he knew how to cure—in advance. In the hills the snakes were emerging from the ground, hungry, with yellow poison in their fangs. They had saved up the poison all winter. The rattlesnake doctor could protect the people and keep them safe.

Sun went home to rest for the night, and Moon, in her full cleansing power, rose up over the deep gray mountains. She shone on the people of Mishopshno who were gathered in the sanctuary. She shone on antap, fishermen, guildsmen and women, on commoners and children, on every one of the people. Only the poorest of the poor, who had been pushed by extreme hunger to an early encampment in the hills, were denied the benefits of the ceremony.

Grandmother Moon smiled with her clear-faced benevolence. Together with Grandfather Sun's afterlight and the flames of many fires in the western part of the ceremony ground she kept dangerous beasts away from the village. All but one.

The rattlesnake achana, dressed in his feathered skirt and feathered headdress, his body painted red and black, stood in the center of the enclosure. He danced with split stick rattles. He stood in front of a large, tightly lidded basket. He stood at the exact center of the ellipse, in the spot that replicated the Axis of the Three Worlds. He prayed to the four directions, the forces of change and changelessness, and to Shup, the nourishing earth at their feet. He offered the prayers in the ancient tongue of the ceremonies. Three times he uttered them.

The antap played on their flutes and whistles. They sang long songs with archaic words. The songs were slow, rhythmic, monotonous. They were unlike the lively tunes of everyday life. These songs stretched far back, almost to the beginning. They transported the villagers to the time when animals were still people and people barely more than animals.

Abruptly, the music ended. The old achana began to address the crowd using the common speech. He talked about the rattlesnake and his power: "Rattlesnake is a nunashish. He is feared, even loathed. But he must be respected for he has a will. My great-uncle, who was intimate with the snake and who conversed freely with him, learned that if rattlesnake decides to kill someone he will sink his fangs deep into momoy root before biting, and the poison will be beyond cure. He also learned that the snake may bite simply, just as a warning, to scare someone away. This bite can be cured. There is no momoy in it. My great-uncle was given the ability to discern these intentions and to heal."

The doctor could read the snake's will, could distinguish a real snake from an evil achana in snake disguise. He said that from earliest days his people had been chosen to be the snakes' protectors. Because of this his family could associate freely and safely with the creature.

The repetitious music had lulled the people. And the words of the rattlesnake doctor were familiar. Nevertheless, the people stirred with anticipation. Children stood up and leaned forward to see. But the basket in front of the old man sat as placidly as it had all evening.

Night fell. The oration was ending.

At last, the achana indicated the basket. Yes, inside was a large coiled rattlesnake, one he had captured that very day.

Children crept closer. Adults peered and stretched their necks.

The old man cautiously opened the basket's lid and reached inside. Slowly, slowly, he reached. Gently, gently. Slowly and gently he lifted the big snake out of the basket. He moved fluidly, silently, like a snake. The rattlesnake was limp, fat, and blotchy gray with a pattern like the old man's paint. It was asleep.

The achana began to dance with the snake. It was a dance without music. His feathered skirt scarcely fluttered in the flickering bonfire light.

The people trembled.

The snake seemed to waken now. He seemed to be looking around. He pivoted his head, which was the shape of an arrow's tooth. He flicked his tongue toward the people and toward the fires. Then he began to travel. Sluggishly, he covered the length of the old man's painted arm. He moved sinuously like water, completely unlike the straight path of an arrow. His split tongue was still darting in and out as he mounted the achana's fleshy shoulder. The rattlesnake stopped moving just beneath the old man's left earlobe; four nostrils smelled the warmth there.

The people stared at their doctor, in awe of his power, praying for it not to fail. A young woman fell forward.

The dancer presented his other arm for the fat gray serpent to climb. He guided it up. It glided down. Now, he draped the long snake across both arms; he held it out in front, full length, toward the people. It was almost as tall as a man.

The rattlesnake hung there suspended, placid, dull, potentially deadly. Its flat arrowlike head turned toward the participants; its eyes gleamed. Its tongue flicked at them.

The dance was over. It had lasted only a few moments. With great gentleness the nunashish was returned to his basket. The lid was on again. The dance had been so brief that Grandmother Moon had not moved in the sky. Yet the people felt worn out, weak. They had trembled and sweated not only for their doctor, but for themselves. Their own susceptibility had been tested.

The woman who had fallen forward was still dead. After the snake basket was taken away, the achana came to her. She was a potential victim. While the people watched, the doctor cured her. First, he found the rattlesnake's fang marks on her hand. He tied a rope above her elbow and cut the afflicted place with his flint knife. He sucked out the yellow venom and spit it into a wooden cup of pure spring water. Everyone saw the poison.

The woman's soul returned. She sat up.

The doctor wet some chalkstones, snakestones, in his mouth and placed them in the wound.

Soon the woman was restored to her former vitality. She was cured. For that season she was safe.

The people breathed with relief. Their kinswoman was alive. They were alive. The ceremony was almost over. Having attended, they would be protected for the coming year.

Before they left, the old doctor admonished them: "Rattlesnake is powerful. Don't be conceited. Treat him with awe and respect. Never, never provoke or insult him."

Three times he repeated the words that concluded the ceremony. The people were free to go out.

Not long after the Rattlesnake Ceremony many more families began traveling to the hills. The days and nights were warm and green now, and it looked as if the rains were over.

There were several campgrounds, one on each of the three principal creeks. The poorest of the poor were already settled in. Common people, whose seed stores were low, went next.

Guildsmen, commoners who were especially important to the life of the village, lingered behind. Woodworkers, tar workers, bone workers, bow makers stayed at their trades. The tomol builder was occupied every day with sewing together, caulking, and tarring more rounds of driftwood planks on the new tomol. The paint maker remained behind preparing red pigment for the tomol while dreaming about a journey over the eastern pass. Sometimes, at night, against his wishes, he was visited by a red-haired woman.

The wot remained, too, and his first wife and daughter Nacha and her younger brothers. His younger wife had gone up to their family camp with the smaller children. The wot stayed in town waiting for the return of his ksen. In the meantime, he sent his first wife's brother, Lyamlawinat, to the hills to keep an eye on things.

Young Halashu stayed with his uncle and carried out the duties of an assistant, going here and there. But he was restless because his best bow was broken and he knew he would have to go to Shuku. To pass the time, he went fishing with the other tomol owners.

The lame man, Aquyahut, sat in the village with the infirm and the elderly. His wife's brother's family set out to join Aquyahut's wife and children at the westernmost camp. They were commoners who had no trade or specialized tools and no atishwins to protect them. They went to the hills to gather their sustenance. On the way, they passed the tall shrine sycamore, which was beginning to reclothe itself in pale green leaves. These members of the Blackbird Family had no fur or down and only a few acorns with which to make an offering and a prayer. But their hearts were peaceful; they had survived the winter and saw promise all around. They pointed to the tough-leafed oaks that had sprouted shiny new leaves and oak flowers sprayed out like dancers' feathered wands.

They broke away from the creek trail and followed the edge of the salt marsh. Fewer birds flew away from the water than at the turn of the year. But the reeds and cattails grew tall. Sprouts of ilepesh and hutash broke through last autumn's burned grassland.

The family pursued the rushing west creek trail up into the hills. They rested in a rocky clearing and shared their piece of cooked fish. They chewed slowly and gazed down on the grassy land that had been groomed by fire and the dark oaks, on the great lagoon, now silver with high tidal water, and on the hill of their village. Their homes on the oceanward side were not visible, but they saw rising threads of blue and a blue smoke blanket covering the settled area. It gave them comfort. Blue was the color of human habitation, of civilization. They saw more blue in the west, not far away on the lagoon's other side, hovering over Qoloq village and farther away over Syuhtun town. And down to the east they saw it again, out over the ocean where Shuku's creek and its high hill marked the boundary of the villages to the east.

The ocean glinted gray, etched with white foam at the reef across from the estuary mouth. The near-shore kelp beds made a dull red mat. Most of the boats were already in. Across the channel they could see the four islands stretching out in a line on the edge of the world. Waterless Anyapah Island was humped like a whale. Many-peaked Michumash was long and furrowed, a big land. Wima, the place where the best redwood washed ashore, sat on the main island's tail. Farthest west lay Tuqan, a flat land, famed for its abundance of sea animals. The brother of Aquyahut pointed out the islands and their attributes to his children. His children would never in their lives be able to cross over and harvest for themselves any of the island bounty. But they needed to know.

It took only a day to reach the camp. When they arrived they were greeted with enthusiasm by their kinsmen. No sooner had the adults exchanged information and filled the water basket at the creek, no sooner had the new arrivals spread out their blankets and gathered some downed wood for the fire than Aquyahut's oldest boy, Shunu, grabbed his favorite cousin by the hand and ran to show him the place where he'd put up the rope swing. Shunu's small sister and several younger cousins toddled along as rapidly as they could. The children were excited to be out of the village, away from the confinement of their smoky houses.

Shunu, naked and barefoot as always, ran like a mountain lion up the crusty limb of an old oak tree. At the top of the branch he sat down and hauled up the fat tok rope. He had made several large knots in it. Then, as the others cried "Iyi, iyi! Go on!" he jumped out and away from the tree. His feet wrapped tightly around the lowest knot and his hands grasped one of the upper ones. He swang out almost to the sky, and back, then out again, and back.

"I want to try now!" cried his favorite cousin. "My turn! My turn!" And he ran up the tree. Shunu dropped off the rope under the rough old gray limb and allowed his young cousin to take a turn. With a little practice the younger boy learned to swing out into the clear just as Shunu had done. Soon the little ones began clamoring for a turn. And the big boys humored them by hoisting each one up on the knot and pushing him or her around a bit. Everyone was having a good time on the swing.

While the children played, their elders prepared food for the evening. Sun began to drop lower and lower over Syuhtun. All at once, the children in the clearing began to feel hungry. Shunu, the leader, flying out over the new green grass on the fat tok swing called out the word, "Let's go back to camp and get some food."

Shunu abandoned the swing in his favorite way. At the very height of his highest swing he just let go. He dropped straight to the ground. It wasn't terribly far.

He landed right next to a hunting rattlesnake.

Like lightning, the flathead's fangs pierced the boy's ankle. Shunu felt a hot stab like sharp needles. He shrieked with surprise, as well as pain. He had been out playing in that field every day and he had never once seen a snake of any kind. Now, he lay on the ground hunched up.

The snake crawled away into the grass.

In a few minutes, with the help of his cousin who had come running at his cry, Shunu was able to stand on one leg. He tried to follow the path toward camp. Surely someone there would have herbs or snakestone to soak up the poison. Unless…and now Shunu's ankle, which had begun to swell, grew fierce with pain. It was a pain stronger than flint arrows, hotter than fire. Shunu, though a child, knew that the snake had been coming for him all along. It had been tracking him, watching, waiting, planning, maybe ever since it had come out of the ground. But why? It was his last thought before darkness rose up to greet him and he fell.

Soon all the adults who had been in camp arrived. They had heard the boy's screams, screams sounding so much like those of a struck rabbit. They came running, crying frantically, "Woi, woi! No good! No good!"

Shunu's mother now saw for herself that it was indeed not good. The boy lay on his side, already dead. His lower leg was black and swollen to twice its usual size.

There was a woman in camp who had brought snakestones. She tied the boy's leg above his knee, sucked on the chalk pieces and put them in the wound where the flesh had partially dissolved. She did it without conviction. "Only if the snake was merely defending himself will your son live," she said.

The mother showed that she understood. Then she touched her oldest son. She felt him all over with her hands: his face, his chest, his hands. Suddenly, she began to wail. She grabbed handfuls of dirt and threw them into the evening sky. The mother could see that her son was truly dead.

Then the children began to wail, too. And the men. The small children came and stared at the body. Some wandered whimpering into the brush. Grandparents forgot to run after them.

Men and boys, with Shunu's cousin thrashing wildly in the lead, searched the broad field for the rattlesnake. If it was an evil achana in disguise it must be killed before it struck again. But it was already growing dark. An adolescent boy, a good runner, traced the shadowy trail back to the village. Perhaps the rattlesnake doctor or the alchuklash could restore life to the poisoned boy.

The rattlesnake doctor grumbled, "What can I do if a rattlesnake made up his mind? It's no good, no good." But he consented to come. He even ran, the folds of his old skin flapping as he tried to keep up with the youthful messenger and complaining, "The boy was not at the ceremony, you say? Why don't parents protect their children!" The venerable achana was not entirely aware of the problems of the poorer people.

But he was right. There was nothing he could do, though he tried anyway, knowing he would probably never be paid by the boy's family. He wondered, irritably, why the people had not caught and killed the snake. It might be a disguised sorcerer who would strike again.

But after talking to the boy's uncle he felt differently. It was difficult to learn anything useful, for the poor man seemed afraid of him. He stuttered with a mixture of awe and grief. But he did discover that the boy, called Shunu, was known as a late riser. He could often be seen making his ablutions in full daylight. Why? His mother said he worked so hard she couldn't bear to wake him. These commoners, thought the doctor, how distorted were their priorities! To let their blood run warm all winter as if there would be no consequence to it. Well, they were born with that sort of carelessness in them. They would have to suffer the results of it. Still, he hated to see a child die.

The late boy's uncle—after he admitted the boy's lazy habits—had the foolishness to ask, with long empty spaces between each word, "Could it have been a bad... a bad doctor? I... we... have heard of an achana... not here... and a bear, an imposter. My sister's husband is from Shuku. Why us?"

The common people were always full of gossip and unfounded rumors. The wot of the Rattlesnake Family had not heard about a bear imposter. He told the troubled man that the snake had undoubtedly been a real snake, that the family's sorrow was of its own doing. He sent for the caretakers of the dead.

Konoyo, young and strong, came up from the village to carry the body. She had not fully accepted her part in the final care of children, even if they were small and light and easy to handle. She still wanted to cry like the kinsmen and throw rocks and dirt. But she had to present a dignified image. She had to impart confidence, even if she had little. What hope could she have about a child too young to have drunk momoy and too poor to have ever had the prospect of doing so? Any atishwin this one had ever possessed had abandoned him. He would never make it to Shimilaqsha.

While the late boy's mother and aunt stumbled along behind, wailing and throwing dirt, Konoyo trudged down the trail, conserving her strength. The little lifeless legs—one swollen—flopped against her back. The arms around her shoulders were growing cold. But the corpse never made himself a nuisance. Shunu, she knew, had been a good boy. He was kind, hard working; he followed the right path. Likely, he already accepted being a ghost.

Konoyo thought: cruelty, selfishness, misuse of power, these are dangerous things; everyone knows. But carelessness, uncleanliness, disorder, these are dangerous, too. Sometimes we forget. The commoners forget. On the trail just ahead, Konoyo thought she saw the face of her beloved friend. The vision brought steadiness and calmness and distracted her. Before Nacha spoke to me, she thought, I was almost forgetting too. Of course he must marry, and from outside the village.

The apprentice delivered the small corpse to the old caretaker, her teacher. Together, they found a spot among the graves of the commoners and reverently removed the old, old bones that were lying there in the crowded ancient place. Konoyo wrapped the little body in tule mats and carried it to the grave. She consoled herself with a piece of truth. Young and old, wealthy and common, the antap and the ignorant, all are alike in one thing: when they die they all become ghosts.

The funeral was held in the ceremonial ground. The wot, the alchuklash, and the rattlesnake doctor all spoke and prayed. They blew tobacco to the four winds and scattered offerings. They sang the death songs to the accompaniment of doleful deerhoof rattles. The people cried and cried and cried until their leader admonished them to have courage and to carry on.

The body of one who had been a boy, but who had now become a ghost, was buried with the common ghosts on the sloping side of the cemetery. The Blackbird Family showered his remains with a little money and some hutash seeds, sacrificing all they had for his safe journey.

After several days, the ghost went on its westward way. The lame man and his wife came to stand by the new grave, their hair shorn in bereavement and their faces blackened. The tomb was covered with boards and stones, but it had no expensive redwood pole to mark it. There were no possessions to indicate the former person's identity. What could they have hung up? A little digging stick? Dried sihon bulbs? A tok swinging rope? A boy has no real belongings. They concentrated on the peoples' saying, that children have an easy road to the Sky World. But they could not help but worry how he could find his way. They wept and wept until they remembered the wise words of their leader. "Alishtahan! Alishtahan! Have courage! We shall endure!" he had said.

Then they tried to forget.

It was the time of Grandmother Moon's darkness. But at midmorning the sky was filled with spring's light. Halashu stood, full of life, in the yard of the chief caretaker's house where Konoyo lived. He had spent the morning trying out his new sinew-backed bow, and he had come to show it off to his woman friend.

"Look here! Look here!" he cried. "See how beautifully the bow maker has crafted her. See how well he has glued the backing. We have good woqo here. Don't you think this is better work than anything the people from over the mountains can do? And it's made of good strong toyon: I chose it myself."

Konoyo sat with her deerskin skirt tucked gracefully between her legs. Her stone work bowl was in front of her. She looked up and smiled but went on grinding the meal in the bowl with her long tapered pestle. The old woman, her teacher, worked beside her cracking acorns. For a few moments, Konoyo broke the rhythm of her work to admire the new bow and to say a few words. "Yes, it is beautiful," she said sincerely. "It has a graceful curve and the color is vibrant."

"Oh, the color," scoffed Halashu. "The color is fine, of course, the work of our friend the young paint maker. But the true art here comes from the bow maker and his guild. That man is an uncommon commoner, don't you agree?"

"Yes," Konoyo agreed, but uncertainly. "I guess so. I trust your judgment. He's like Piyokol, the storyteller, yes."

Halashu looked not quite pleased. He was remembering why he had come. "Piyokol is no longer a commoner," he said curtly. Then he demanded, "Konoyo, come walk with me for a while."

Konoyo looked at the old woman. "I don't know. Today I have double work. Have you failed to notice? I am one of the few women of my age who is not hiding in the pit now."

The wot's son looked as uncomfortable as a young man of his poise could. The old woman saw it. "Go for a while," she said. "Go ahead! You are strong, child of spring. You have accomplished much already today. Go with him until Sun reaches his peak."

The apprentice finished grinding the meal in her bowl and transferred it into the leaching basket. She cleaned her pestle and mortar and put them away.

While she tidied up Halashu dashed home. It was only a short distance across a small clearing. He wrapped his new bow in tule matting and stored it away in a safe dry place.

Then the two young people walked where they most liked to go: under the oaks and sycamores, the alders and willows that grew near the village creek. Though the creek trail was often busy, being the main route to the foothills, they preferred it to the bright openness of the seaside cliffs or the sand on the shore. They loved shade and fresh water.

They walked right down to the big creek and perched on two warm sandstone boulders that were close enough together so that they could talk quietly. It was a warm morning and the water striders were dancing on the surface of the singing creek. On a nearby rock a lizard pushed up and down on its warmth. They did not see any snakes. They breathed deeply of the air, which smelled heavily of decaying sycamore leaves. The odor was as distinctive of home for them as that of rotting kelp. Pungent and beautiful, they agreed. But how else could it be?

Halashu said what he'd come to say. "My dearest friend, the ksen has returned."

After a pause, Konoyo ventured, "Do you know his news?"

The ksen's reports were secret, but Halashu trusted the young caretaker's gift of silence. "Piyokol was not at Syuhtun. The ksen was told that he had been so popular there that the wot from Mikiw—the biggest town of the lands to the west—who is our paqwot's brother, took him back to the western lands for a while. What can he be telling them at this time of year but trivial stories and jokes?"

"You know, ichantik, he is at his best with those ones. He has all the tales of the common people." Then, troubled, she added, "Do you believe, iwu, that we will ever see that man again? I miss him. He is Mishopshno's greatest artist."

"I miss him, too. He has unusual experience."

They sat for a time silently watching the sunlight shooting through the trees on the yellow-looking stream water. Halashu bent down and cupped his hands to drink. Above them, a red-headed woodpecker drummed loudly on an old oak tree.

Konoyo glanced over at her friend. He looked entirely different from how he had on an earlier day they had spent together. Today he was very alive and unpoisoned. His topknot was more neatly wrapped. She said, "The ksen visited some village over the mountains in the land to the north, too, didn't he?"

The wot's son might have smiled. "Yes, he did. He went to a place called Mistumukun."

"And? What happened?"

"The wot's niece is a dog!" he burst out with a laugh.

Konoyo looked horrified. Then she blushed. "You don't mean… Woi! No, it can't be." She was thinking of Dog Woman in the ancient stories.

Halashu saw her expression and laughed harder. He knew exactly what she was thinking. "No, she doesn't eat excrement—at least ksen didn't see her do it. But her manners are bad, bad: uncivilized. The ksen even heard it said that she only bathes before a big festival."

"Oh, that could be nothing but slander. Who said it?"

"Well, he, himself, saw her eating porridge with her left hand!" He made a grimace of disgust. "And with all four fingers, at that. The ksen nearly became ill right there, in the wot's home."

"Keti, how revolting! Is it possible all the people in the villages in the north are so barbaric? I cannot believe it."

"It doesn't matter to me a bit," said Halashu. "I'm only concerned about one of the wots in the north—the only one with an eligible daughter, at least as far as my parents know. And now my parents no longer consider her eligible."

Halashu's whole body spoke of relief, and Konoyo smiled for him. He was behaving as if he believed his difficulty was over. She knew better. She reached across the flowing water with its sparks of Sun and touched his shoulder. The two sat listening to the sound of the creek gurgling in its cobbles and to invisible frogs croaking all around. "Let's go into the brush," she said.

Halashu's face clouded. He seemed to be remembering something. "First I must tell you: I must be very careful. Soon, after the ceremony of Moon's rebirth, I must go to Shuku to speak with their wot. Our lives depend on what I do there. I must demonstrate the truth. Or, if I fail in that, I must attempt skillful hints, even threats. Yet, if I antagonize the wot, we are dead. On the other hand, if I am not strong enough the poison will go on and on and destroy us, anyway." For the gracious orator, it was an awkward twisted speech.

"Why does your father, the wot, leave this tortuous diplomacy to you?"

"He says that it is time."

"But will he, himself, intervene?"

"He will do whatever is necessary."

"Iwu, what a great responsibility you have! But I know that you, also, will do what you must. What other course is there? You have long studied diplomacy and persuasive speech. Your knowledge has grown, not only from study with the antap, but in practice with your own estimable father."

He touched her warmly and ran his fingers through some leaves. "You speak better than I do. I've never gone alone to a foreign village. I'm not even sure my southern tongue will be understood."

"What outcome do you most hope for?"

"That Shuku will see that the perverse achana in their midst harms them as much as he does us. That they will permit him to be stopped."

Konoyo spoke solemnly: "My kinsman, have courage that it will be so."

Halashu looked up from the dry leaf he had been tearing apart. He looked for Sun in the sky beyond the trees. It had nearly reached its peak. The young man stood up. In his eyes were not tears, but only shining admiration. He seemed to be calm and said, "Let's go into the brush now."

CHAPTER 5

MONTH WHEN THE FLOWERS BLOOM
hesiq momoy an capipquees

The foreign woman ran through the brush. Her black hair, snaking over bare shoulders, was as tangled as the chaparral undergrowth through which she fled. She dodged between twisted gray tree limbs. Her red body paint was smudged and streaked. Her buckskin skirt shifted to one side, exposing muscular buttocks. She stumbled on, through the vines and high grasses, panting and glistening with sweat in the pathless wilderness.

The man had no idea where she was going or why he felt compelled to follow her, his night-time familiar. She no longer seemed to offer the fulfillment of every desire. She appeared much more likely to lead him to his destruction. He told himself, "She is not real; she is a creation." He drew close to her, so near that he could make out the orange circle on top of her head, her identifying mark. The patch grew right underneath the place where she would wear her epsu hat. She carried no burden basket. He found himself nearly touching her sleek back.

Abruptly, she stopped running and swung to face him. Her small red lips parted and bubbles of saliva formed at the corners of her mouth. The look of her small bright eyes was wild and penetrating—and remote, as if she were peering down at him from a great height. Her body began to expand outward. It spread wide. Her looming breasts nearly engulfed him. Her breath was strong, almost foul. It sickened him.

He turned and tried to run. But his feet were bewitched and could not move.

In spite of her bulk, the woman's hands remained small. He saw that they were nicely shaped. A long hand reached out. It landed on Aleqwel's left shoulder.

Instantly, he felt a burning, like the burning when he was shot by the bird arrow. He knew, without looking, that her hand had imprinted his flesh. She had never before come so close to him, not since Solstice Night.

The enormous woman moved even closer. For a moment, Aleqwel stood staring at her, confused by her searing touch, which somehow bound him to her, and by her overwhelming odor, which repelled him.

Then he remembered his atishwin. Grasping the lizard's foot around his neck he called out, three times. He began to sing.

"Impressing your hand on the rock…
My hand.
Lizard…"

At once, the paint maker was transported to his own house, where it was night. He found himself crouching by the embers of the fire. He examined his fingers in the dim firelight. There was blood.

His sister had awakened and come over to the fire. She saw him wounded. Saying nothing, she cleaned the cut on his shoulder and dressed it with herbs. She led him to his bed place. He slept deeply then as if he had taken tobacco.

In the early morning, when Aleqwel arose, he felt tremendously weary. He staggered to the sweathouse and to the creek. When he inspected his shoulder he found only harmless scratches. But he felt built-up tension like thunderclouds massing over the high mountains. The encounter had been dangerous; over time he would lose the struggle.

After washing thoroughly, Aleqwel spent the remainder of the early hours walking the creek trails. He praised his atishwin. He prayed loudly, so that gods and nunashish could hear. He shouted: "Stay clear, you dangerous beasts!"

Aleqwel then remembered the sweet melody of his own dream song and he sang it over and over to calm himself. He sang until Sun's torch appeared over the highest peak of sacred Tsismuhu. He experienced dawn's full radiance.

When he went to the house of his great-uncle, the alchuklash, later that morning, the young paint maker was still filled with his song's airy lightness. Lizard had protected him.

The old man had already sweated, bathed, and groomed himself. He wore his many necklaces, those of abalone and olivella shell, of serpentine and huya beads. His earlobes hung down from the weight of his ornate earplugs.

They left his great-aunt at home to cook the acorn soup while they went for a walk together.

Aleqwel told the old man his dream.

The alchuklash had heard the others. He knew of the pursuit, the fear-desire. "It is not good," he said. "It is dangerous, dangerous. You must not let her touch you."

Aleqwel looked worried. She had touched him.

"In a way, it is also good," continued the achana. "It means the time of confrontation will be soon. And also that you have not been forgotten by your atishwin. Tell me, what beast was the woman?" He assumed she was a created being, an invention of their enemy.

"I can't say. At first she seemed... she felt like a large bird, a bird of prey, a buzzard or an eagle. I sensed her above me, looking down. Yet, later, when she grew, she turned massive and sinewy, more like a mountain lion or a bear."

"I see. And she was never anything like a snake or a black widow spider?"

"I don't think so."

"Then it is clear," said the old man. "It will soon be time to test your powers. The wot has been working for you, but the time is not ready. You have followed a prudent path. I foresee that you will have a dream, a different kind of dream. Your atishwin will speak to you. He will prepare you for the confrontation. It will be like the day you were initiated with Grandmother Momoy. Your atishwin will come to your aid. Perhaps Grandfather Coyote will be there, too.

"Listen, listen well to your dream. Your protector will tell you everything. You must follow his instructions exactly. Then you will be invincible to your enemy."

He added, like a tail on a mouse, "The woman, yes, she is dangerous, a poison. Do not let her touch you again. But she is not the enemy. She is only a lure to bring you to him."

Aleqwel wished the talk had allowed him to breathe more freely. His great-uncle had spoken to him with knowledge—but not complete reassurance.

While the two men walked and talked they had circled the outskirts of the village. Now they found themselves back at the alchuklash's house. The old man laid his strong hand on his grand-nephew's shoulder, right over the place where he had been scratched. "Alishtahan," smiled the doctor. "Have courage! Be happy, your power grows stronger every day."

The younger man felt a surge of strength, but he wondered: Was his power strong enough? Was it as fierce as that of the bear imposter—who was not afraid to kill human beings in the chaparral? He felt sure his power was insufficient to see over great distances and into the future. It could not yet create alluring women out of the air. Could it inflict poison?

T he trail to Shuku ran along the ocean bluffs. Halashu was not alone on the short journey. Some archers had come as a bodyguard, along with the ksen and his father Lyamlawinat, the assistant wot. Nevertheless, his father wanted Halashu to do most of the talking, since he was of the Eagle Family and would one day be wot.

In the early morning, the men followed the cliffside route. They were immaculately groomed and draped in their best bearskin, fox, and otter capes. Their hair was neatly dressed in topknots with feathered pins, rattles, knives, and money. They wore their most expensive jewelry, their nose and ear plugs and dark huya necklaces. Their limbs were carefully painted.

The spring wind blew little clouds across the blue sky, and scavenger birds sailed all around them. Young gray-winged seagulls screamed, while high above hawks and white-headed eagles circled.

The level field on their left side grew lushly with fresh green grasses and wildflowers of many colors. The blue ilepesh brought joy to their sight; the seeds, beaten from the bushes in fall, would cook into their favorite porridge. But the poppies, gleaming bright like Sun, outshone all other flowers.

Here and there, wherever there was a depression in the broad green valley, water had collected in vernal pools. Ducks and black mud hens swam in them.

Southward, on their right, spread the vast ever-changing sea, its deep gray-blue broken by tufts of white foam, brushed up by the wind. It was as if Golden Eagle, wot of the Sky World, had scattered his down on the water while soaring on his heavenly travels. A few abalone-decorated tomols bobbed in Shuku's red-brown kelp beds.

The path passed near the rise with Mishopshno's vermillion shrine pole. The black condor feathers continued to point to the east and the west, the origin and the end. The men stopped and made offerings of seeds and money to Shup, their nurturer. At the cry "qeqeqe" Halashu looked up to see a large duck hawk with pointed wings beating rapidly. It swooped down—with nearly invisible speed—on one large pool. The wot's nephew looked at his father. Duck Hawk was second only to Golden Eagle; he was assistant wot of the Sky World. The two men watched as the swift falcon remounted the sky, carrying his prey. Lyamlawinat said it was a good sign.

The rest of the journey was uneventful. It was nothing more than a morning's walk, as far as distance went. At the approach to town, the arriving men were greeted, first by a pack of barking dogs, then by Shuku's assistant wot. They were treated according to custom and offered the hospitality of the wot's home.

All around them, curious villagers peered, eager for a closer look at foreigners—foreigners who were neighbors, and enemies as well. There was a woman among the crowd who, by now, knew much of Mishopshno's men. She even recognized the three leaders, from the many times she had observed their doings. She stared so hard that Halashu turned to look, but all he saw was a well-to-do older woman, who might have been one of his mother's friends.

There was one inhabitant, one of a very few, who was not among the crowd of the curious. Shuku's bear doctor lived alone out toward the hills and did not seem to feel the need to associate much with the townspeople. They stayed clear of him, anyway.

The next morning, when Halashu awoke, his companions were already crouched by the fire. He looked around. The place seemed so much like his uncle's home, but larger. It was spacious, well-furnished, full of people. The floor was covered with clean white sand. He saw many blankets of bear and fox and fewer of plain rabbit skin. The huya cooking pots looked larger than those at home, and there were more of them. Halashu slipped down from his sleeping place onto the soft cool sand.

He considered his circumstances as he ate a handsome bowl of porridge. He thought, "This is the home of my neighbor, Shuluwish. It's true, then, he is a wealthy, wealthy man. These children—and young adults, too—who sit beside me and stare as I eat with my best manners are the wot's sons and daughters." They were undoubtedly hostile to his people, he thought, yet they appeared harmless enough at morning meal. Last night, one of them had spoken to him in his own language. Yet, Halashu knew he had to be careful to remain proper and straightforward at all times. If he needed to be as clever as Grandfather Coyote in his dealings with the leaders of Shuku, he must try, here, to appear as unlike shifty Coyote as possible.

Halashu stood in the front of the doorway of his host's great house and looked down on the village and the beach and the sea to the south. Shuku looked so much like Mishopshno. It lay on the east side of a good flowing creek and sprawled down a gentle hillside to the shore. The wot's house stood at the top, beside the ceremonial ground and the cemetery. The sweathouse was a grassy mound next to the creek, and red tomols floated near the brownish kelp. Across the channel lay the islands.

But some things were different. There were more canoes. And, though the tule domes of the houses were in the same neat rows as they were at home, there were more of them. Halashu had counted over sixty. The people at Shuku seemed to own more things. Everywhere he saw them dressed in expensive furs. The women who had been born men—and there were several of them—were attractive in a way. They were elegantly attired, yet somehow they didn't really please. There were many storage houses behind the dwellings. Halashu was certain they were full. And—how often!—he heard the strange tongue of the islanders. Even now, on the beach, tomolmen were unloading what looked like seal furs and worked stoneware from the islands. Shuku proclaimed itself a prosperous center of cross-channel trade.

The hospitality began. On that day and for several more all the visitors had to do was feast. Halashu was given no chance to speak privately with the wot. All day long the guests were stuffed with porridge, meat, fish, and delicacies. When they weren't eating they played games. They tested their skill and their power. Halashu demonstrated his archery. He played hoop game with the wot's sons and the wot's nephews. As the umpire rolled the hoop along the flat ground of the playing field—which had been cleared on a high plateau behind the village—the boys lined up along the route and tried to spear it with long poles. Then, Halashu showed them how they did it at Mishopshno, how they shot through the rolling hoop with their arrows.

Throughout the games Halashu's power was strong, but his partner's wasn't. In the evenings he played stick dice and hand game against the wot's brother-in-law and sometimes even the wot's wives.

On the third night of feasting, when teams formed to play hand game, the people were in high spirits. Halashu impressed them by doing well. He not only saw the hidden bones in his opponents' hands but he saw into his partner, the wot, himself. He penetrated his character. In a sudden flash he understood why his host was called vain and arrogant: he was a poor loser. Undoubtedly, he was cheating—and still losing. That was not so unusual. But what he did that was characteristic, transparent to Halashu who was seeing well, was to try to make it appear that his losses were due to his own disinterest. He wanted to seem sleepy or bored, even careless, anything but lacking in power. With Shuluwish it was the impression he made that mattered.

Long after sunset, when the evening play finally concluded, Halashu prepared for bed. He was glad he hadn't won money from the Shukuans,

even though he could see well. He needed to stay modest, if not weak.
Tomorrow, come what may, he wanted to bring up the purpose of his visit
with his host. But if Shuluwish was insistent on feasting there was little he
could do. Halashu knew, as well as he knew the boundaries of his own land,
that to decline hospitality was to invite retaliation.

He wondered whether his gifts—the fine woqo and the baskets made
by his mother and cousin Nacha—had been adequate. "If Shuluwish…" he
began to think. "Does he know that I know his true name?" And, as he fell
asleep, a question troubled him: "Does he know mine?"

The next morning they talked, Halashu and Shuluwish alone. The wot
initiated the conversation, and as it progressed Halashu found himself
surprised at how well they understood each other. Their sentences, at least.
The people to the south did speak another language, yet it was not so different.
In fact, many of the words were the same. Halashu had learned enough of the
southern tongue from his father to give him confidence in the talks.

Shuku's wot gave every impression of being straightforward. And yet,
the younger man realized, he never admitted or promised anything. He was
undoubtedly suspicious, wondering if the visitor was a spy who had come
to rob him of power. Instead of relenting, he would offer some more baked
yucca or cherry-nut delicacies. And Halashu never dared to refuse.

At last, the highest achana of Shuku acknowledged something. The man
whom Halashu called the Wokoch was not a favorite of his. He was not
a native. In fact, most believed he had come originally from Mishopshno.
Maybe he was even a spy for that village?

At this charge, Halashu responded indignantly: "That is ridiculous,
ridiculous! That one is our enemy!"

The wot replied slowly, deliberately. "Well, my kinsman—for we are both
of the Eagle Family, are we not?—I do know one thing. The bear achana has
protected us well. He has placated the bear nunashish, and that is no small
accomplishment. He deserves my protection. So do the people." Then,
craftily, an eye on the young man to discover just how young he was, he
added darkly, "And besides, he claims that your people have been poaching
feathers. And now, he says, they are stealing seeds from our granaries. Might
he be telling the truth?"

Halashu was tempted to speak of his own people's poverty, and their
good sense. But he would not be put off-balance. He was surprised to find
how little fear he had—now that he knew this man's inner weakness. He
proposed calmly, "I can guarantee our people will not trespass on Shuku

lands, if you can promise that the Wokoch will not be allowed to do us more harm."

The wot, perhaps a little startled by so blunt a proposal, agreed to it. He began the preliminary remarks for the conclusion to the talk. However, Halashu stopped him with a gesture. "No," he said. "We need more than your word. You, high wot, must put a spy on the powerful achana. See if he puts on the bear disguise. Follow where he roams in the western hills. See for yourself if he is guilty. For there is one in my village who has evidence and a vengeance."

The older wot looked annoyed as he reset his hairpin. Halashu again saw the flash of vanity and arrogance. At length, the wot of Shuku said, "You ask for a great deal, young wot. Perhaps we might better settle this little trouble through war. An organized contest is so much more civilized. Simpler even."

It was true. War was clean. It was just. The men would line up and shoot at one another. Few would be hurt. But Mishopshno would lose. The wot's son took a deep breath. He said, "Our village is smaller than some. We do not need war. But we, too, have ways of stopping evil. Our achanas…" He stopped, sensing he was going too far.

The wot glared at him, eyes shining eagle-like under bushy brows.

Halashu changed his tone. "A bad achana is no good for Shuku, either. His power goes wild. Watch for yourself."

Shuluwish was not appeased, though he recalled that he, too, often negotiated by threats. He said, "In Mishopshno do they teach you to be impudent to your elders? Do you speak this way to your uncle and father, whom I had believed might be a reasonable men?"

"I am speaking as a representative of the wot, who is your contemporary. I beg your forgiveness for any impropriety on my part."

The wot calmed slightly. He responded, "I have no reason to fear your family, my kinsman. But some of your grandfathers have not been so prudent. Do you remember the great earth shaking? No, you weren't born then. Houses were destroyed in Shuku, in Mishopshno, even Qoloq. So many lives were lost. And why? It was the doing of Mishopshno's sorcerers. Is it not probable that your present problem is caused by one of your own too-powerful achanas?"

"Wot," replied Halashu, "it is well known that the great earthquake was caused by the family of your own bear doctor."

Again, Shuluwish was offended, or pretended to be. He sat in silence, perhaps as a rebuke. But he was thinking that certainly he could attack Mishopshno without tremendous sacrifice. The leaders did seem to have power, but their numbers were small. Perhaps he should insist on a war. But something prevented him from saying these things. If the young visitor really had true knowledge, then the bear doctor was operating independently from himself, who should be in charge. "Is there anything more you want?" he said finally, expecting a grateful withdrawal on the part of his guest.

"Yes," said Halashu. "When you find that the intruder has indeed used his power to threaten and injure, even kill our people, we have a man who is ready to destroy him."

This was more than enough. The wot indicated that he heard and understood. But he could not speak. After a passing of eagle-like silence it became obvious that the substantive conversation had ended.

The two exchanged the customary polite remarks. Halashu thanked the wot abundantly for his hospitality. They stepped outside together. But they went separate ways. It was clear that the visitors would be leaving for home that day. Halashu felt the presence of those at home who were thinking of him. On the day of his departure from the hostile village, he had no idea what fruits, if any, would grow from his meeting with the wot of Shuku.

Grandmother Moon waxed in strength. She looked down on the people and gave them health. Not a woman remained in the smoky pit house. It was a good time for beginning a trip to the hills.

The old alchuklash, wot of the Coyote Family, prepared to lead the family to their traditional camping ground. He and his aging wife were still fit enough to make the journey. His sister, the mother of Anihwoy and Kanit, had the same strong bones and would also be going. Grandmother Moon smiled on them; not one of them had bad pain. During the fog, a twinge of rheumatism might slow them down. And, like everyone, they suffered from toothache. But for such old people they were remarkably mobile. It's a real blessing, the old man thought, as he went around the house gathering up everything that was indispensable for the trip, everything from bows and arrows for hunting to huya pipes, tobacco, power stones, and quartz crystals from his healing kit. The blessing came, in part, from his calling. As an achana he spent much less time in the ocean than many other men. And the ocean ate into a person's bones.

While the venerable old man packed at his house, his old and esteemed sister did the same at hers, just a short way down the hill. The older women made the difficult decisions: deciding which stone utensils were necessary and which were too heavy, how much seed and meal would be needed. Now a grandmother, she had given birth only to daughters, three of them. The old man had treated them as nephews. He had taught them even more than he had his own sons. Two had stayed near him: his favorite, Anihwoy, who had become an herbalist, a curing doctor, who had married the paint maker from Heliyik, and little Kanit, still without a husband. The other had found her way to Shimilaqsha. He had spoken with her there; she was happy.

As they prepared for the annual trip to the hills Ponoya and Kanit chattered more excitedly than ever. How cold would it be? How many blankets and capes would be necessary? How many cakes of red paint, they asked Aleqwel, would they need? And they must not forget the paint grinding cups. They packed all their jewelry—and their treasure baskets. The outsiders might raid the village in their absence. In whispers about the people from Shuku they used that word, "wokoch," intruder.

The flat-bottomed carrying baskets grew fuller and heavier. "Now will be the test of your endurance," little Anakawin challenged the older girls. Kanit reminded him, "Everyone knows that women are as strong as men. After all, don't we run the household and perform the most arduous work? We are certainly stronger than little boys." And she twisted his arm behind his back and held it for a moment, until he agreed to help them with their packing.

Then, Kanit and Ponoya grew still more excited as they tried to find room for all their basketry supplies. They could not imagine an empty moment, morning or evening, without weaving or wrapping baskets to fill it with purpose.

Aleqwel, looking up from his own preparations, noticed the young women in a way he rarely did. Maybe it was the spring with all its new shoots and seed-bearing blossoms. The young women appeared beautiful to him that morning. They were radiant and tender like spring poppies. Ponoya, especially, seemed to glow. He looked away again. There was pain in losing her as he felt he soon would. Instead, he busied himself searching for the things he needed. His needs were few. He took down his sinew-backed bow and his ordinary bow and the wood arrows and the cane arrows and even the fur quiver. He took them down from the high place where they were kept, wrapped in tule mats to be safe from smoke and damp. He packed an extra blanket of woven rabbit skins and some paint pigments. Most of all, he was careful to bring along—and secretly—that thing that Lizard and Coyote had given to him in his recent dream, the big dream the alchuklash had talked about. The object just fit in the pouch at his belt.

When he had finished packing, Aleqwel went to his mother and spoke to her in a quiet voice. He informed her of some news he had heard, that the wot's nephew had returned from Shuku. He asked his mother what she thought of his going to speak with Halashu that afternoon. Anihwoy seemed to appreciate the deeper intent behind her son's casual question, and to approve.

But, when he was opening the inner door to go out, Ponoya caught a glimpse of her brother's face. His eyes shone and his body seemed to tremble with bound-up excitement. It made her think of the moment before the breaking of a rare summer storm. She found him attractive, just then. Yet she grasped that it wasn't desire that had polished him, that made him shine with this new beauty. She half-guessed what it was he was after.

Halashu and Aleqwel could not find a place to be alone in the wot's big house, so they went out. Halashu was glad to finally get away from his family, all those whom he had missed so much when he was away and to whom he had to report extensively on his return. One always had to seek the balance, and he needed to be with someone other than family.

The two young men walked the village lanes to the bluffs above the soft tar springs. The beach was busy with fishermen hauling in their laden tomols. "The pohoh have returned," commented the wot's nephew, naming one of the most important of the tunas.

Aleqwel regarded the boatloads of large silver fish that were his own favorite food, as they were for almost everyone. "We knew it would be a good year for the people," he replied with conviction.

Then they sat side by side on a weathered old log, observing village life in silence. Before Halashu could begin a graceful speech, the young paint maker rushed right to the heart of the matter, saying, "May I kill the Wokoch now?"

Halashu saw the young man's eyes glowing with fire. "Not yet," he was forced, regretfully, to say. "But I believe that Shuku's wot will put a spy on him. Then he will learn the truth and we will be on our way."

"How long will it take?"

"It may not be soon."

"Will he try to stall us?"

"Or it may not be long," said the young diplomat. Then he looked pained. "Unless, of course, I pushed him too far."

Aleqwel said, "My family leaves for our spring camp tomorrow."

"Go with them, ichantik."

"And after that, I must go east on a trading trip to Matilha. I can't avoid it."

"Go on your expedition, too. Your route will pass briefly through Shuku lands. I know you will be careful. But do not be tempted to leave the trail, not for anything. I will inform you—wherever you are—when the time is right to carry out your obligation. Remember the saying of the grandfathers: 'It's only by leaving your native home that you may find the fulfillment of your inmost desires.' Have courage, ichantik! Alishtahan!"

Aleqwel, who, before, had begun to look as discouraged as a fading ember, seemed to be renewed by these last words. Like a beaten poppy bouncing up after a spring rain he jumped to his feet. "I know that saying well, ichantik. And I know, too, that we shall endure."

Walking home from the bluffs, Aleqwel glanced down at the homes of his friends, Alow and Chaki, who were working alongside their fathers. They were carrying large open-weave baskets and nets full of silver-striped fish. He heard their voices—now near, now far—twisted by the wind.

At the door of the home that Chaki shared with his wife and his widower father a baby cradle was propped so that little Kelele could see around her. Chaki's wife, Pichiquich, holding a half-full carrying basket beautifully decorated with lightning pattern, called something to her husband. Aleqwel's disappointed heart gladdened, knowing that Silkiset's big family would soon be camping with his own. Soon his friends would be traveling with him two days beyond the double pass toward Matilha. Alow would be bringing lots of pohoh fish with him. It seemed to Aleqwel that he had fasted altogether too much that winter and it was time for a change.

The village of Mishopshno lay nearly deserted. None remained but the old, the infirm, some infants and mothers and several fishermen who kept their tomols filled with the first of the big pohoh fish.

Aquyahut sat in front of his house, weaving nets. He was poorer than ever now that he had no son to get him food.

Wealthy old Silkiset, head of the Pelican Family, sat by the smoky fire of the sweathouse, slapping himself with nettles. In that way he found temporary relief from the pain in his joints. Kinsmen had stayed behind to care for him, but he missed his favorites, Chaki and Alow. They knew how to carry him without jolting his old bones. Even his curing doctor, that admirable woman who had brought him comfort with her hot huya rocks, had gone to the hills. How nicely she had massaged him with seal oil, too. Now he would have to wait until summer—if he could—for the return of his caretakers.

Tilinawit was a lonely wot of a lonely village at this time of year. His kin, wives and children, even his assistant, were at the gathering camp of the Eagle Family, right in the heart of Mishopshno territory. Even the ksen, though he ran back often to keep him informed of news in the hills, had left him. The wot kept company with the feeble. But it was important to stay on and look after the village, especially now when a hostile blow from Shuku could fall at any time.

The wot stood at the top of the hill, not far from his house, under the blue spring sky and observed the profusion of pale green flowers on the oaks. From there he could appreciate the blue and golden loveliness of the ilepesh and poppies growing among the grasses of the valley. The little hutash flowers gave the valley a reddish cast. For a moment, standing on the hilltop, looking out in the direction of the gathering camps, he wondered which one was more beautiful, the blue and red food flowers or the shining golden ornament?

He thought of the people's remote ancestor, Sky Coyote, the Stranger, the paqwot spoken of in the histories. In ancient days he taught the people all the useful arts. As a descendent of the Stranger, Tilinawit knew that what is useful outshines all else. Yet, in that same history, did not Lizard and Coyote, both wise doctors, show their keen appreciation for the seemingly useless beauty of fluttering poppies? It must be, he thought, that everything in the Earth World has some function, even those things that appear only to decorate. Indeed, decoration—the poppy—does have a most practical use in winning a young woman's affections. He smiled.

The ocean channel was full of tomols pursuing the large schools of summer fish. Across the water, the pale outline of the islands was already screened from view by a thick blanket of fog. Soon the fog would be rolling in, shrouding the mainland and further isolating the village. The wot liked that time. It was quiet. There were no hot winds or cold rains. Yes, it was turning into a good year for the people. At least the flowers and fish were abundant.

Every day, the wot, who was responsible for the well-being of Mishopshno village, visited the people. He made certain that the old and ill were cared for. He brought food from his great storehouses for those too poor to provide for themselves. He did his job. But he was lonely for conversation. There was one man with whom he enjoyed talking: the tomol builder, Saqtele. Each afternoon, Tilinawit sought him out at the place, high on the sand, where he worked on Silkiset's new tomol.

The altomolich had installed the crossbeam in the middle of the canoe and was sewing together the last rounds of planks. These rounds were unique, for they did not meet at the hull or stern but left a deep notch for fishing and anchor lines to rest in. Mariners knew well that a line thrown over the side of a tomol could easily capsize the canoe. Saqtele sewed the tarred tok string while his apprentices followed, tarring all the holes and ties, inside and out. It was a tricky business working with the hot glue, a mixture of woqo and dried pine sap. After each round, while the tar dried, the master carpenter spent a few days waiting. He found things to do, but even now, at his age, he was secretly impatient.

"We must bring the head of the Pelican Family down to see his tomol soon," said the wot.

"I would like, at least, to get the planks finished, maybe even the ears on, before disturbing Silkiset," responded the guild master as he sewed away.

The wot, wrapped in his long bearskin cloak and topped by his elegant waterfall of hair, stood watching silently. Grandfather Silkiset was indeed old; he had drunk his first momoy with Tilinawit's wife's father, the late wot.

When the time came for Sun to rest in the sand dollar, the apprentices strolled down the beach to lie in the sand and talk and gamble.

The wot spoke with unusual abruptness. "You know my true name, don't you, elder brother?"

"Yes, wot, I do. You told me when you were young."

"Yes, I remember the occasion, and I don't regret it. You were like one of my own family. Do you know what the name means in everyday language?"

"Yes, it means 'Principal.'"

"Who else do you think knows it?"

"Only your family… and whomever you've told. And, of course, the alchuklash; he gave it to you."

"Might the wot of Shuku have learned it?"

"Not by any normal means, I'm sure."

"They have a bear doctor who once lived here."

"I remember him. He was called 'Choi'; he was small, still small when he left."

"And yet I know the real name of the wot of Shuku."

For the first time, the tomol builder looked surprised.

The wot continued, "Even the bard and the ksen do not know it. But my late uncle told it to me. And I have told my nephew."

The altomolich grasped the implied question. "I am not a person of great power. But I advise you like an older brother: do not be afraid to use the name if you must to save the village. But use it only if you must.... Are things truly so dangerous with Shuku again?"

"You have heard, I suppose, that there has been poison against us. I will tell you—in complete confidence—we are having secret talks with Shuluwish."

"My wot, little brother, may I say—will you find me disrespectful if I say this?—everyone is talking about the poison and the secret talks. People are tense. They don't know what to fear or whether to fear."

"Brother, your old nickname, Saqtele, is still apt. Like a hawk you see clearly and, like one, you descend on your prey swiftly and surely."

Saqtele quickly broke in, "But the golden eagle exceeds all others in these skills." Though he was known as crabby, he did know how to show respect, even to a childhood friend.

Tilinawit continued, "The people do have reason to be afraid. We have had wars with Shuku in the past, of course. But the wars were agreed on, structured; they came and went and few were injured and all was forgotten. I have considered war, but here is one problem: we always lose. Our grievance would go unsettled. The poisoning would not stop. What the people fear most are the raids. They have memories of past raids. Do you recall the great earth shaking of our childhood?"

The altomolich was sitting beside the wot on the lump of dry woqo. "No one alive forgets that. Even those who were not born then speak of it with tears in their voices." He recited the facts as if relating a bardic tale: "First, the rattlesnakes who hold up the Earth World were induced by our enemies to take a rest. Everything tumbled and fell. It was just like when a person drinks momoy. Rocks rolled down from the hills and houses collapsed. In the sweathouse some were crushed, and then..." the old man began to cry.

"And then," he began again after wiping away his tears, "then, before we could put things back together—we hardly had time to drive out the evil achana who had influenced the snakes—almost at once the Shukuans came upon us in the night. From the beach, the cliffs and the hills they swarmed like summer locusts. They stole our food and burned everything they couldn't carry. Everyone who was unable to flee across the creek to hide in the cattails and tules was killed."

Saqtele, the hawk, had remembered with pain. "So many of our old people, our treasure, were lost to us." And he began to shake with crying.

The wot consoled him. Then he said, "And now Shuku harbors a fiercely powered achana from that same exiled family. Yet I dare not consider organizing a raid against them."

"No, no!" exclaimed the tomol builder, collecting himself. "We would get the worst of it. They are many, many."

"Yet—to you only, Saqtele—I confess that I do not know what to do if Shuku fails to see the truth."

There was a pause as Sun emerged from his rest, glowing in the western sky. "Tilinawit," said the guild master, "if I may presume to say so, it is your calling, above everything else, to keep all forces in balance. You, yourself, are a powerful achana. You have maintained us in the center of the four directions and on the axis between the Three Worlds. Your clarity shines like sunlight. Your compassion heals like moonlight. Have you not consulted with your great ancestor, Eagle, who is wot of the Sky?"

"Older brother," said the wot warmly, "that is just what I had decided to do." And then he said, "Have courage! Don't forget me!" and departed.

A few days later, the wot was warming himself and eating his morning food by the fire of the big house. Except for himself and one of his mothers-in-law the house was empty. Both the outer door and the inner door stood open and he could see the ocean in the south from where he sat on his mat.

Suddenly and without sound a shadow filled the doorway. It was Saqtele's nephew, the ksen. He had run in from the hills, and his skin glistened in the morning light.

The woman poured the messenger a sycamore cup full of water from the basket. She handed him a matching bowl, stained red and filled with fish soup. The ksen accepted in silence. The woman retired to her work outdoors.

Only then did Tilinawit inquire, curiously yet calmly, about the activities in the hills. "Any news?"

The ksen was economical as always. "No and yes, my wot."

"No?" questioned the wot.

"No. All is well. The snakes are out, but are stying hidden. A few bear tracks by the creeks. But no one has seen any yet. The people are eating and they are happy. There are deer. The crops are good."

"No quarrels?"

"Only the usual ones, the kind that spring makes between men and women."

"You mean the men who won't wait for poppies to turn a woman's head—or open her legs?" He laughed an old man's laugh.

"That's one instance," replied the stony messenger, the man whose feet could fly like wings.

"And what is this 'yes' then?" prompted a less playful wot.

"This may interest the wot," he said. "There is a man camping on the west creek—I spoke with him myself—who says he has seen one of our fishermen seducing a woman whom he believes is from Shuku."

The wot's face clouded. "Where did this 'seduction'—if that's what it was—take place?"

"The man—Pashe, he's a commoner—saw them before spring separation. They were down on the beach near the southeast border."

"Were they on our side?" the wot asked sharply.

"So he says. Of course, he was there too, so I can't be completely sure."

"It isn't good," cried the wot. "Especially not now. The balance. But these things do happen. Are we not children of Sky Coyote?"

The ksen hesitated imperceptibly: "The man also said he heard them discussing plans for her abduction."

"Woi!" exclaimed the wot. "What!" He nearly lost his self-control. If such a thing were to happen, the whole balance he worked so hard to maintain could be overthrown in an instant. "Who is this kilamu fisherman?"

"He is the one called simply 'fisherman,' Mushu."

The wot startled. How little he knew his own people. Mushu had once been an outstanding fisherman and trader. But there had been that terrible accident when his wife and baby had fallen off the cliff. His power had declined. Even so he made a fair contribution—though he seemed to have no social interests at all, not even lustful ones. "Mushu is not among the fishermen remaining in the village," mused the wot aloud.

"I believe he is far up on the east creek now."

"Yes, that would be right," confirmed the wot, who was supposed to know the family camps of all his people. "Will you ask him to come down and see me?"

And without even stopping to use the bushes, the ksen began to run toward the hills.

It was delicious to be at the campground. For the first time in nearly a year the people were surrounded by fresh food, by more food than they could eat. They felt content, optimistic, sociable.

The Coyote Family and the Owl Family, the Pelican Family and the Cormorant Family hiked toward the eastern foothills. All together they made a big party. The trip up exhilarated them. Everywhere along the trail evidence of the fulfillment of the paqwot's winter solstice foresight blossomed. The ancient oaks with their heavy twisted limbs were dark-leaved as always. But now they were also adorned with subtle plumes of pale green. Hikers called to one another, pointing with satisfaction, echoing those who had gone before. "Look, we have flowers!" And their companions replied, "Look, we shall have seeds!"

The gatherers walked through abundance. And, though much of the glory, the oak and ilepesh flowers, the small white flowers of fruits and berries, pointed toward the future, still the promise brought them joy in the present. Meanwhile, the spring harvest of bulbs and fruit awaited them in the hills.

In single file, carrying baskets suspended in nets that pressed against woven epsu caps, the people followed the easy trail along the village creek. As they approached the hills they came to a fork in the creek. Their party would follow the right hand, the eastern branch.

It was not a long journey to the campground—less than a day. But the women had begun to slow down with the weight of their carrying baskets, which were heavy with huya pots and stone pestles and wooden bowls. At the place where the creek branched the group sat to rest and drink.

They prolonged their rest, which they shared with Grandfather Sun, but they finally rose and parted from friends who would be taking up their habitual spring residence on the hill high above the west branch of the stream. The women, readjusting their burdens for the last stretch, joked that next time they would leave home that heavy huya pot that had once belonged to great-grandmother.

The final climb passed quickly. The families hiked the gentle canyon, a wide rocky wash whose sides were low but rising hills. They left behind the broad field of their valley with its green grasses and blue ilepesh clumped between spreading oaks. The shimmering poppies, the red hutash flowers, the purple lupine were behind them. On the banks of the stream that they followed white alders and cottonwoods flourished. The cottonwoods shivered in the breeze. Sycamores, with their ever-present odor of decay, towered beside the water. And a wild thick brush grew on the hillsides. The brightness of yellow sunflowers, the scent of sagebrush and pungent bay leaves, cheered their way. At the last the path grew dense and dark and the people could no longer see the valley or village behind them. They found the place where the creek turns to the left and climbs a steep canyon behind the hills. On the east side of this bend, on a flat cleared place, the people stopped and set up camp. There were mortars ground into the sandstone boulders near the camp.

Behind the place rose scrubby hills, still dotted with a few green yucca buds and many pale torch-like flowers. The lower hills were splattered with the green and red of cactus ripe with fruit, while the blue sihon flowers were mirrored by foamy blue ceanothus bushes. Warm brown boulders hung over them all.

In front of the camp lay a high valley, cut off on the south by hills. It was a valley like their home valley, but smaller, more of a meadow. It fronted no sea. It was full of deer.

As soon as the big group arrived at its destination the women began to unpack baskets and to organize their food and belongings. At the same time, the men built shelters and covered them with reed thatching borrowed from the walls of their coastal homes.

As he went down to fill the water basket at the creek, the boy, Anakawin, spied the first grizzly tracks. It had been less than a year since his father had been torn apart by a bear. The terrible thing had happened not far from this campground. And it was Anakawin who had discovered his father's remains, the yards of bowels strung out—like so many lengths of money beads—atop lemonade-berry and bay bushes. That first night at camp, after seeing the bear tracks, the boy behaved badly. He upset the pot of scarce ilepesh meal and burned himself. But nobody scolded him. They expected him to have memories. Anyway, he was a child.

Camping was a joyful time. But like all good times, it was never far from sorrow and fear.

Dinner that first night had a special flavor. There was acorn and ilepesh meal from home as well as fresh pohoh fish roasted on the fire coals. The women added freshly dug sihon bulbs, crisp miner's lettuce, tender roasted cactus fruit, all harvested that very day. But it wasn't just food that the people savored. Men let go of their concern for their work. They fussed with their bows and arrows. Women forgot how heavy the cookware in their baskets had been. By their fires people yawned as they watched Sun's willow torch disappear beyond the mouth of the canyon. Swallows and bats darted and swooped in the warm shadowy air.

They slept that night wrapped in furs beneath a cloudless spring sky. Swollen Grandmother Moon watched over them, while the wakeful alchuklash kept his eye on the familiar doings of the celestial people in their crystal houses. Eagle, the foresighted wot of the Sky World, and Holhol, the red-haired one, moved brilliantly in the west. To the north, Sky Coyote sat immobile and deathless. The wise creator was flanked by his Guardian Stars. The alchuklash kept track of them all, all those who made night their day. He watched them while they danced and gambled in the moonlit heavens.

In the days following their arrival the people worked and ate. The children dug sihon bulbs with little weighted digging sticks, and, what they didn't eat, the women roasted or dried for winter. The men hunted deer.

There was some surprise when the ksen came jogging up the trail saying the wot wanted to see the fisherman Mushu right away. It must have been something to do with the tuna fishing, the people thought. When Mushu returned from his summons his basket would be full of more mouth-watering pohoh. His companions thought little more about it. His son scarcely noticed that he was gone.

Alow and his girl were engrossed in their own pleasure. They now had the opportunity to meet easily and more often. In the mornings Alow would take Anakawin into the meadow and teach him the art of trapping quail. The plump birds waddled everywhere, calling out "takak takak" while their black feathered topknots bobbed and nodded like dancers' headdresses. In the afternoons he explored the canyon and the hills with Ponoya. There, they made light of the hazards of cactus picking. They deftly wielded the forked fruit pickers and plopped their treasure into tok cactus nets. There was time—always time—to lie together on Sun-warmed Shup or in the green grasses. Under skies fragrant with ceanothus they joined their bodies. More and more their hearts were united, too. They began to share a passionate tenderness. With each meeting they grew both more playful and more profound. At night, they felt that they slept near each other in the same house—for they shared the same starry and Moon-bright dome for their roof.

One day, the two decided to climb the hill on the south side of their meadow. They found the hilltop flat like a wooden plate. From it they could look across the canyon to the campground on a similar hill on the far side. They could almost make out the identities of their fellow villagers from their characteristic movements. So they played a game of guessing who each one was.

Alow and Ponoya sat on the hillside in the bright sunlight, accompanied by singing birds, by gentle sparrows, loud-mouthed mockingbirds, and flashing sun-bright orioles. They talked more than usual. Ponoya looked sideways at the strong young man as he chewed languorously on a slender stalk of needle grass. She found him satisfactory, and not just in his appearance. Perhaps it was true what Kanit said, that he was not old enough to be perfectly suitable. But his prospects were excellent. He was an adventurous tomolman. And a good friend to Aleqwel. He was as kind as an uncle to little brother. That was important. What is more, she loved to make love with him. She lacked wide experience, but she considered this especially important.

That day on the plateau, they talked about how well things were going—for the people, for themselves—and how good things could be in the future. Talking, Alow realized that he had never before felt so comfortable conversing with an enhweq, an attractive female. He had to admit he had never been inclined to do it before. He had known and appreciated many young women. But this was the first time he had felt this other pull, the pull to actually settle down with one of them. He thought: and she cooks well, too, stays home and works hard. Her baskets are lovely. Funny, he hadn't noticed before. Then he noticed something else unusual—he was laughing.

Below them spread the grassy fields and the dark oaks of their valley. Beyond lay the blue ocean and the island peaks.

"Look, iwu, see, the place of the islanders glows with a radiance as if Sun himself lay on the ground." Ponoya spoke softly.

"It's just as it was in the days when animals were people," he answered. "How I wish I could be like Lizard and swim all the way over just to bring you a single poppy in my flute."

"But it isn't necessary to be so heroic anymore," she laughed. "As you can see, poppies are now growing all about us, right here," she gestured.

"Are you trying to turn my head?" Alow teased, looking about him as if noticing the brilliant flowers for the first time. "Are you suggesting we gather some?"

Sometime in the midst of picking flowers, Alow came upon the enhweq, bent over, plucking the sunny fragile flowers. Her legs were strong and smooth and had a sunny shine of their own. He stroked her underneath her fringed skirt. And slipped into her as easily as he might board a canoe.

The night of the next day saw Moon in her fullness. Alow went down to the village that day to see how his father was. When the two returned together they brought many fish with them. On the trail, Mushu had seemed thoughtful, as if trying to decide something. He never mentioned his business with the wot, and Alow did not question him. Alow had reached such a peak of ardor that he thought of one thing only. His father's silence had been a relief. It did not even matter to him that he was having to forego deer hunting on account of his sexual activity.

When father and son got back to camp, it was already dark. But Alow took a chance. He stretched out beside Ponoya where she lay alongside Kanit in her open-air bed. He touched her as she slept and whispered urgent words. She did not hesitate to go with him down into the meadow. Kanit kept her eyes closed.

In the moonlight, the pair seemed luminous to each other, as they tiptoed, naked, beneath their wraps of soft fur. For a moment, Alow saw his beloved as a giant rabbit in her pale woven cloak. But her streaming black hair put a check to his vision, his moment of hilarity. "I am kilamu," he thought, "unbalanced."

Then they were disturbed by whispering in the trees. It probably was whispering. Had they imagined themselves the only amorous couple in the camp? Ponoya herself whispered, "Ichantik, my aunt has told me something worrisome. I must share it. Do you mind?"

Alow was scarcely listening. He had spent a lonely day in the village. He was stroking the fur of her robe.

"She says that when she goes upstream to bathe, she is watched by a strange man."

"Well, what sort of man is he?" asked Alow absently. "Is he strong and good looking?"

"She finds him so."

"Then it is fine, fine. Your aunt is still of a ripe age."

"But she is frightened of him… please don't touch me now, not yet.… She doesn't trust that man, that stranger. Why is he here?"

"Are you afraid, too, iwu? Of what?"

"I am afraid that man is a bear."

Alow suddenly become alert, as if he had just awakened. He knew very well that what Ponoya feared could be true. A stranger appearing by the side of the stream was a serious matter. But he could think of nothing to say. He held her close and was slow to move.

They lay in the field and Ponoya felt Grandmother Moon's powerful influence. The young woman and the man were united more completely, if possible, than ever before. For hours they huddled together, alternately hot and cold, sleeping and waking. They joined and parted while the widow Moon sped on her way. At last they rose and staggered back to their springtime camp.

Rising Sun found Ponoya still asleep, not usually a good practice. Her aunt, Kanit, was already up and bathed. Ponoya, when she finally opened her eyes, awoke happy. Yet she felt tired. She felt disinclined to move, almost as if a power had got into her.

I n the following weeks, the campers on the hill imperceptibly settled down to a life of more hard work and less frivolity. The people, at last, began to be sated with food and movement and sex. Once again they thought of their future. The people worked and ate. The children dug sihon bulbs with little weighted digging sticks, and, what they didn't eat, the women roasted or dried for winter. The men hunted deer.

Alow found less time now to be with his enhweq. But when they were together things went well. It was as if some agreement had been reached. And perhaps it had. For the first time, Alow talked with a young woman about marriage. More particularly, they talked about Anakawin, how they could care for him, provide him with proper guidance. Once, Alow had suddenly remarked that it might benefit his father to be cared for by a woman. And Ponoya agreed.

Each day, in addition to preparing meat and bulbs for storage, the women and children went out. They roamed farther and farther into the hills, searching for bulbs and root vegetables to dig, picking cactus fruits, gathering lettuce and hunting for eggs. Now and then they came across a flathead rattlesnake. But they faithfully carried their special root that was capable of stupefying snakes and diminishing their power. At each encounter the snake would warn them with his bony rattle. The sound, hardly louder than the rustling of wind in grass, would instantly attract their attention, for they were always alert. All accorded the snake respect. They backed away at his warning command.

Even more terrifying than snakes were the occasional sightings of bear tracks. They were footprints, like a man's yet as huge as a giant's, a haphap's. Most often, someone would spot the tracks near the creek. Old women said, "The bears have not been out long; they aren't even eating yet. But they have a big thirst, so they go to the creek. Just watch out when they begin to get hungry!" and "If a grizzly sees you, there is no way at all you can escape being eaten—unless you have a powerful atishwin."

At night, safely gathered around their fires, families whispered together about these things. All day long fires blazed in camp. The glow seemed to keep the bears away.

One evening, Nene spoke to Ponoya and Kanit as they cleaned the plates and bowls from the meal. The girls had been chatting about the good— mostly good—and bad features of marriage. Nene had heard of Kanit's mysterious admirer. All at once, she ordered emphatically, "Daughter, never speak to that man in the woods, not even if he appears handsome or kind or rich. He sounds like a bear. If he is, he will tear you apart and eat you." Kanit kept silent.

At last, Ponoya spoke up, "Nene, I'm sure you are right. If you call that man a bear, it is because you know. But surely there must be some men passing through the chaparral who are not bears, but really men. How can Kanit meet a man? Don't you want her to marry?"

And Nene replied, "Of course I hope she will marry. But she must be alive to do it, not a ghost wife on her way to the Land of the Dead. There are plenty of young men—and even better, older men—to be found at the festivals in the many villages." She repeated: "Always stay away from bears, whatever form they take. Especially if you are pregnant," she added enigmatically, glaring at them both.

The girls stayed silent. They were criticized. They were also aware that the old woman had lost more than just her son-in-law to the dreadful bear nunashish. Kanit's oldest sister had disappeared by a bathing pool one day long ago. They knew the old woman was right: bears did love to devour women, particularly pregnant woman.

The next day, while upstream searching for sihon, Pichiquich, Chaki's wife, suddenly began to shout excitedly, and Anihwoy came quickly. Pichiquich pointed to the soil. It was torn apart, dirt flung everywhere, as if attacked by a band of kilamu people with heavy digging sticks.

Anihwoy said softly, "Yes, it's the bear. He loves to eat the same things we do. He has torn the squirrels' burrow apart with his hands."

And they went forward, cautiously, in a group.

After that day the women never went out alone to do their gathering. They took along men armed with strung sinew-backed bows to guard them. For the first time, many of the campers began to wish for the safety of their coastal village home.

Each night Grandmother Moon shrank away, as if devoured by a bird of prey. Some mornings Aleqwel thought she looked like a ghost. Fortunately, the young paint maker had seldom seen dead souls in the Earth World, though he had visited the Land of the Dead in the Sky World. But he knew that ghosts were round and bluish-white and luminous. They were somehow weak-looking, like Moon when she was dying, he imagined.

Aleqwel had spent his time in camp doing many of the same things the others did. He hunted for his family, and he gambled too. He was pleased with the continued evidence of his power. He even won a considerable quantity of money. But, whenever possible, he had spent time with his grandmother's brother, the old long-eared alchuklash. They went for walks far upstream, where the canyon grows steep and the meadows turn to thick chaparral. They hiked to where the creek bends back toward the northwest and hides behind high hills. Sometimes they passed the night there, building their own fire with fire sticks and observing the world in the sky. The old man repeated things about the travels of the sky gods, the meanings of their movements, that Aleqwel had heard before as an antap student. Sometimes, though, Aleqwel thought he caught his uncle telling him new things about the star dwellers. But then, again, he might have been dreaming it.

Not once, day or night, in all their wanderings, did the kinsmen cross the path of a rattlesnake or a bear.

One day, after chasing deer unsuccessfully in the big meadow, the friends Alow, Chaki, and Aleqwel climbed the high southern hill. It was the same one that had come to mean much to Alow and his enhweq. Where they stood, the sky reached away, indefinitely blue and warm. The gods were up there sleeping. But below them, where they might have looked down on golden islands in a blue-gray sea, they saw only an expanse of grayish white fog. It obliterated all. The leading edges rolled up to the mouths of the foothill canyons like water at high tide.

The fog had come, and it shouted—though without a sound—like a wot's crier: Summer is at hand! The fog had come with its refreshing coolness that brought ease to workers and travelers. The fog had come with its dull gray pall, its silence and obscurity. And, above all, the fog had come for a long stay. "We had better make arrangements for our trip to Matilha," said Alow. "I can't afford to be gone long while the fish are here." He meant the migrating pohoh.

Aleqwel explained his plan, their route over the pass, what they would need. He told Chaki how glad he was that he would be coming, too. "Strong men are always good company," he said.

Alow and Chaki found the plan agreeable. And, although the three could have set off on the trail from their campground, they arranged first to return to Mishopshno to collect their trading goods. In a few days the coastal fog and its mild melancholy would be behind them. In each man, alongside the passion to trade and grow richer, dwelt a restless yearning for new experience. Beyond the double pass was the route of the pine nut gatherers, the trail that climbed eventually to the Center of the Earth World. They were going where common people rarely ventured.

Beyond the passes there was never fog, or so they believed. They ran down the hill, eager to be on their way. The promise of travel had brought out their coyote natures.

On the morning the young men had chosen for going back to Mishopshno to pack for their trip Aleqwel rose early, as always, to wash in the gray light that announced the arrival of Sun's torch over the eastern mountains. He climbed down into the little sweathouse they had built at their camp ground and, after a short time, ascended again to make his way to the creek. He traced the familiar path between berry vines and poison oak.

With care, he descended the low pathless creek bank, through vines and bracken. On the other side of the narrow creek, a dark shape loomed among oaken shadows. For an instant, Aleqwel and the grizzly stood still, watching each other.

The man made the first move. His actions seemed to flow out of inspired dance. He moved his feet. He sang. He did not try to run.   Even before the dishfaced grizzly could drop to all fours and begin to charge, the young paint maker had summoned his atishwin. Three times he cried.

Lizard came with his flute of elderberrry wood. And while the great bear, standing as tall as a man, began his own dance, awkwardly woofing and dipping his head, Aleqwel used his protector's flute.

He used the flute as a weapon. He stretched his arms out wide and stalked back and forth. He shouted the exact insults Lizard had taught him in his momoy dream: "Dishface," "Crackfoot," and worse. He waved the charmed flute like a harpoon at the furred beast.

The great brown nunashish stood still. He no longer moved in any direction, but continued to bark and nod and froth at the mouth. For a ferocious grizzly, he seemed strangely uncertain.

From where he paced, on the other side of the narrow creek, Aleqwel caught the animal's putrid odor. He nearly reeled into darkness from the foulness of it. Then Lizard tapped him on the shoulder, and—just in time—he revived. He was barely able to get out the three long high-pitched yells that were essential. They were terrifying shrieks, animal screams, Lizard's gift.

This time the beast took notice. He shut up and stared.

Then, Lizard borrowed back his flute. He went to sit on a rock in the middle of the stream and began to blow on the four-holed flute. He played the Song of the World. It went on forever.

The heavy old bear sank to all fours. He stood there, immobile, like an insect being wrapped up in a black widow's web. He was listening to the eternal song.

The song ceased.

The bear remained.

Aleqwel reached in his waist pouch and took out a small bird-bone whistle, another gift from his atishwin. He blew on it for the first time in his life.

At the first shrill note, the great bear seemed to come awake. His sunken face looked pained. He turned his shoulders to the creek and began to stumble, four-legged, toward the eastern hills. Branches cracked loudly under his feet.

At last, Lizard, handsome and heavy lidded, took his wooden flute and slipped quietly into the trees.

When the three young men walked into Mishopshno village later that afternoon there were people standing on the hilltop, waiting. They had already learned of the marvelous occurrence of Aleqwel scaring the bear away. They had heard about it from the mud hen's cry.

The wot greeted the three—Aleqwel particularly—with consideration. Children stared with open-eyed awe. It was rare, almost unheard of, for an unarmed man to frighten away a giant grizzly. With a plain bear, yes, it sometimes happened; that kind was timid. But grizzlies—they were monsters.

Aleqwel could see that people were looking at him differently. He was not prepared for it. It was hard for him to believe that he had done anything unusual. He was used to respect from commoners because he was antap. But now he imagined that he heard them whispering. And the oak leaves rustled: "There is a man with a strong atishwin" and "That one must be alatishwinich." Or maybe the people really did say it. He thought he heard a note of fear as well as wonder in the voices.

As he sought out his own home he went shyly past the people, speaking few words. But once inside, with his tools, his stones, he worried. Where once he had been able to go about cheerfully, inconspicuously, now he would always be marked as the one who had scared away the nunashish. There was no going back. Though he had only done what he had to, he could not stop the people from seeing it as a marvel. And he was not done yet. The enemy still lived.

CHAPTER 6

MONTH WHEN CARRIZO IS ABUNDANT
hesiq momoy an maishahuc

In the foggy damp morning the men packed their travel gear and their wares in big flat-bottomed baskets. Aleqwel carried chunks of dry woqo and lots of shell money—more money than he had expected since he had won so much at camp. Alow and Chaki carried this spring's dried fish, and Chaki brought some dark huya pendants that he'd traded for on his last trip to the islands. The stones were precious for they had come from faraway Huya Island, which was more distant even than their own channel islands. By the time all the trade articles and money were packed there was hardly enough room in the baskets for food, blankets, jewelry, and gifts.

Before leaving, Alow insisted on taking one last look at the new tomol. Saqtele had completed all the plank rounds and the boat had taken its final form. The wood looked good and the boards fit together perfectly. The sewing and tarring were tidily done. Saqtele told the young tomalmen the major work would probably be completed by the time they returned from their trip. He said to Aleqwel, "Be sure to bring back enough red paint. You won't get a big commission like this every day." And to Alow he said, "I have some pretty pieces I've been saving for the ears."

They set out at midmorning with carrying nets wrapped around their waists and knives in their hair. The burden baskets, set in carrying nets, were strapped across their foreheads. They carried their bows and arrows in fur quivers sewn of sea otter and mountain lion hide. They were a pleasing sight when the whole village came out to see them off. Though the fog was thick and gray people were still laughing and talking happily after the previous night's feasting and dancing. It was as if they had been chewing

185

tobacco and shell powder, but Aleqwel thought they were expressing their relief from great tension.

Once on the east creek trail the three friends were inclined to be silent. The colorless fog wrapped and muted all Shup like a tule shroud. The sycamore shrine tree was an extension of the quiet dripping world. They tied their squirrel skins on bony branches and scattered hutash and ilepesh seeds to soft prayers. They agreed that the cool of the fog made the best traveling weather. And just when they said it they moved up and above so that Sun's heat fell on them once more.

At the fork in the creek they took the eastern trail up the canyon. As they neared the campground, Alow suddenly said to Aleqwel, "Did you consult with Grandfather about the trip?"

Aleqwel knew he meant the alchuklash. "No, I never thought of it. There was so much else."

Alow looked nervous. "Then we don't know what to expect."

But Chaki said calmly, "It's only a short trip, not like the island trip. We don't have time to stop, not if we want to reach Koyo village by nightfall."

During their brief stop in camp the women filled their carrying nets with dried venison and fish, sihon bulbs and ilepesh cakes. Everyone wanted to touch them. As they were leaving Aleqwel said to Chaki, "You are a strong man, enduring. Your nickname is apt. What do you think of the mood of the villagers?"

"The villagers believe you have saved them from a terrible danger."

Aleqwel grew serious. He knew there had been a shift of power in the struggle between himself and the Wokoch. Still, the intruder was not yet defeated.

The men followed a narrow path through the tall grass of the high meadow. Woodpeckers with bright red heads drilled on gray oaks. The birds talked to their wives and babies, flying on flashing black and white wings between the trees crying to each other their own name, "Pulakak, pulakak."

Before long the meadow began to slope down to a good creek. It was the creek of Shuku village. The men called it Tsismuhu, meaning "it streams out." It came from their tallest mountain. They had to cross Tsismuhu's creek into Shuku territory. On the other bank a trail branched off following the creek up a dark canyon to the hills. Alow shouted, "Let's make an offering at the shrine pole of our holy mountain. We will be sure to have a good journey." And he set off up the trail.

But before he could get far Aleqwel called to him, "Brother, this is Shuku land. Let's not leave the main trail."

"But the path up the mountain is sacred and belongs to everyone."

"That's what we say. Maybe some other time. You know perfectly well that the trail also passes Shuku's storage caves. Unlike our reserves that we keep here and there in any little cave we can find, they have one great cavern—or so I've heard—filled with huge baskets of acorns and seeds."

"I don't want to steal their hoard," Alow asserted. "Wouldn't it be fun to have a look at it, though?"

"Se, se! No!" chorused Aleqwel and Chaki.

Chaki talked to his younger cousin as if to a child, "Their sacred caves are also nearby. It's too dangerous for us now. Wait for a holiday. Besides, the mountain would take too long to climb. We would never make Koyo by nightfall."

Perhaps it was this last argument that convinced Alow to turn back. "Well, brothers," he said, "I certainly don't want to be stuck out here at night. Grandmother Moon is terribly weak, not a favorable time for travel."

"It couldn't be helped," Aleqwel said.

So the three kept to the main trail, hauling their heavy baskets up a steep hillside. They felt as if they would never stop climbing. After some time, Aleqwel, the least hardy of the three, sighed and asked to rest. Alow who had been bounding up the trail like a jack rabbit said, "Tired already, brother? Bear up! Alishtahan!" He removed a cane nose plug and emptied out some tobacco and shell powder for Aleqwel to chew.

"Good, good," said Aleqwel as he passed the little tube to his companions.

The way went easier then, though always uphill. Chaki improvised a little traveling song, and they all felt light. They had left behind the grassy hills and had come to the chaparral, fragrant with blue-white ceanothus. They passed just south of another sacred peak, but they could not see the shrine pole high on top. They paused and looked down Tsismuhu Canyon toward Shuku village at the sea. But they saw only fog. Just below them they could make out the broad canyon that led up to the pass over the mountains.

"The route is easier over the pass," said Alow.

"Too bad we aren't going that way," said his cousin.

"You know," said Alow, "people blame the nunashish for everything bad. But the haphap did one good thing. When he was chasing Momoy's grandsons he sucked the dirt out of the hills and it made the mountain passes."

"It seems to me that every nunashish has his own virtue," said Aleqwel.

Chaki, the eldest, had the last word. His wisdom was unimaginative but sound: "The nunashish, who really belong in the Lower World, enter our world, too. And it's surely true that the whole world is sacred."

They decided to stop and eat. Alow made a little fire with his firesticks for the luxury of having a warm meal. After eating, they rested a while but did not sleep. When they rose, they began to attack the steep side of the mountain ridge. By steady perseverance they reached the top.

The new valley below them to the east was very large, grassy and dotted with oaks. It was like the valley of Mishopshno except that it was landlocked, surrounded on all sides by mountains. On the far side of the long valley, several days' walk away, was a wall of purple mountains whose ridge made a straight line. The young men recognized the range as part of the Toktok Mountains. There, the red milkweed, which they sought, grew in profusion. At this time of day the sandstone rocks on the sheer slopes glowed in the reflected warmth of setting Sun. Beyond those mountains lay the Center of the Earth World. At the foot of the ridge they had just climbed they saw the thin blue smokes of a small settlement. "Koyo," said Aleqwel simply.

Before descending they squatted a moment to rest and drink out of their water baskets.

"Iyi!" Aleqwel laughed suddenly. "Sometimes I wish I could travel like Coyote. How I'd love to leap from valley to valley over the mountain peaks."

"Use your atishwin," suggested Alow.

"Sadly," Aleqwel sighed exaggeratedly, "power is not what it once was."

"That is the way things go," said Chaki. "Power is fading. Someday our children's children may live in a world where there is almost no power left at all. I'm glad to be alive now, even if things are not so remarkable as they were in the old days."

All agreed. Still, thought Aleqwel, the days when people and animals were one must have been wondrous. In those days, people traveled easily between the Three Worlds without needing momoy drink or achanas to assist them. Each person, each creature, spoke his own personal language, yet all understood one another. How wonderful it must have been to live in that world all the time instead of only occasionally.

Chaki invaded Aleqwel's thoughts. He was saying, "If we traveled only in big leaps, think of all the little villages and streams we would miss."

As usual Chaki was right. The path down was rocky and the growth dense. Ceanothus and sumac and sagebrush slapped them as they went. Sometimes they were attacked by sharp yucca spears.

"Ow, are you sure this is the right way?"

"Yes, I came here last year."

"All right, then."

"Cousin, you ought to know the way yourself, you have been here, too."

"The pine nut harvest, you mean. I was just little then."

They went down, almost quarreling, sometimes joking, talking the rough talk of men who feel like Coyote. Before long Alow was complaining, "Keti, my bowels are twisting!"

"I guess it's safe," said Aleqwel, looking questioningly at Chaki. "We must be out of Shuku land by now."

"It's safe," said Chaki. "If my cousin can manage to avoid squatting on a yucca spear. In any case, we can't have him offending Koyo's wot by farting at him. He might throw us out."

"Except that the wot at Koyo is a woman," corrected Aleqwel.

"Even worse."

But Alow had already run into the bushes.

Sun had slid behind the mountains when the travelers approached the village, and Moon was absent, as she was secluded in the menstrual pit.

Though the village of Koyo, the first village of the valley, was small, the men were happy to find it. It nested in the fork of two good streams. They were greeted, first by the barking of the dogs and then by the wot, an old, old woman. Her skin was wrinkled and looked brittle.

"Haku, haku," she said and invited them to her house. She fed them well, if simply, on seeds and venison. Then they talked and shared the news. They spoke of crops and disasters and they gossiped. Aleqwel had to tell her about his late father, whom she had known because of his frequent travels. But he did not mention his own recent activities other than to say he was journeying to Matilha to look for more pigments. The wot looked sad, but she put them all to bed in her small house. Her house was almost as plain and cramped as a commoner's at home.

The next morning the travelers were eager to be on their way. The old wot could see their restlessness so she refrained from inviting them to stay. They presented her with some dried pohoh fish and a chunk of woqo and thanked her as they knew was proper.

"Don't forget us," she said. "Come back when you're in the neighborhood."

"I, i. Yes, yes. We will. We will."

And they intended to.

Aleqwel, Chaki, and Alow left behind the poor village of five or six domed houses that was no bigger than one of their gathering camps. They left behind the good flowing creek and the lonely wot. They headed northeast toward the light.

"Well, those people may be poor, but they are not mean," remarked Chaki.

"A good life.… began Aleqwel philosophically.

"Woi! Bah!" shouted Alow.

"Bah?"

"The fleas would eat you alive."

"But fleas are everywhere. We have them at home."

"Not like these ones. They must have been as big as sand crabs."

The other men had to admit they had been bitten, too. "Anywhere you go away from the ocean they're like that," observed Chaki.

"Well, I'm glad, then, that I didn't go off with that girl from Mupu," remarked Alow. "You must remember her—the playful one who pursued me at the Mourning Ceremony when all the villages were there? Her father is chief wot at Mupu and she said I might live at her house. But I thought, 'What good would a fisherman be so far from the sea?' So I didn't follow her. Now I know I made the right choice."

Aleqwel could never be sure when his friend was speaking in earnest. "Is it only because of the fleas that you don't regret it?"

But Chaki had another thought. "You must have had a dream, cousin. What would a wot's daughter want with you?"

Alow looked deflated. "She was his youngest daughter," he admitted.

"Very young, I'm sure. Probably about eleven years old," returned his cousin.

Aleqwel broke in, "I agree, the fleas here are terrible."

The way was not steep and hard as the day before. The path went straight through high grass and flowers, between oaks, across meadows, and over rolling hills. Up here there was no damp gray fog, but only Grandfather Sun. Some of the flowers had already begun to dry. The grass was still green, but pale. The three walked quickly through the long gentle valley. They talked loudly and sang. They did it partly to keep up their spirits and partly to frighten away the bears. For they could see grizzly paths paralleling and crossing their own, and they had even come upon some fresh tracks. But they saw no large beasts, and for company they had the raucous birds in the dark oaks: flashing pulakaks, blue jays, and noisy mockingbirds. Beside them, in the grass, silent butterflies—white, yellow, and russet—fluttered.

The men began to walk beneath a high range that had a great mountain. It reached closer to the sky than even their own Mount Tsismuhu. They passed this holy peak quietly, in wonder and joy at being nearer the center of things. The voyagers scattered seeds about them on the path.

The upper face of the holy mountain was covered entirely in sandstone, and it was this feature that brought the mountain's name to their tongues. The foothills in front of the mountain ridge, though thick with chaparral, were also encrusted, here and there, with large scales of beige sandstone. In one of these outcroppings Aleqwel recognized the form of one of the First People, one of the many who had perished in the Great Flood. When he had traveled with his father, the paint maker would always stop and point out the stony remains of that ancient being. Now Aleqwel halted to show his companions. Their enthusiasm at encountering the relic of one of their predecessors made him smile a little as it dulled the pain that had leaped up at the memory of those earlier journeys.

After a time they stopped to rest beneath a big shady oak. They eased their necks of the weight of the carrying nets and drank water and chewed tobacco. Squatting there in the cool they spied a small herd of deer feeding in the meadow nearby. Alow sprang to his feet and began to string his sinew-backed bow. But his companions reached out to stop him. They whispered that there was not time to stop, make camp, dry the meat, and cure the hide. Alow thought they could make the time. But he was not the leader of this expedition.

They walked on. And on. There were no villages to entertain them. Cottontail rabbits hopped in the high grass. Lizards basked on the trail. Red-tailed hawks and black buzzards and golden eagles circled slowly and patiently, bright-eyed in the heat of day.

At last the three came to a broad river, but the rocky wash was only partly filled up by the water. They agreed: it had to be the great river of Shisholop, the big town of the land to the south. Instead of following the river downstream to the ocean and great Shisholop, they turned north toward the hills. Sun had begun to rest in the sand dollar. After a good meal of dried foods, they cut tules from the river and made themselves comfortable beds to nap on.

Grandfather Sun had resumed his journey and was well on his way toward Mishopshno when Aleqwel opened his eyes. The wide-spread wings of a great black buzzard very high up nearly concealed Sun's torch. Aleqwel knew at once, from its huge size and white underfeathers that it

must be a condor. He had seen many of these powerful birds, birds gifted
with foresight and magical arts, in his life. But this one, master of buzzards
and rival of eagles, showed itself particularly forcefully, ominously even.
It peered down at him with its penetrating eyes. Was this what his little
brother had taken for a holhol bird on Solstice Night in Syuhtun? Up close
the huge bird might seem a nunashish. Although this creature flew far above,
Aleqwel had seen condors up close once or twice. Their skins, feathers and
all, were indeed worn by the holhol dancers. Up close you could see their
red-gold heads of a color like paint, yet different.

Aleqwel jumped up, terrified and liberated. More than ever he wanted to
hurry to Matilha, the village of the strong doctors. Though wildly impatient
he aroused his companions gently. He had no wish to frighten away their
spirits, which might have been wandering while they slept.

The other two rose quickly and set the carrying straps against their
foreheads. Going up the west bank of the river they again faced a hill.
The undulating valley gave way to low hills and then to shadowed paths
beneath the high mountain ridge. Aleqwel pointed out more holy peaks,
and the men vowed to visit them during their stay.

As they climbed, the river grew narrower, pushed together by the high
close walls of the canyon. The water rushed through a dark gorge. The river
sprouted clumps of willows, cottonwoods, and alder. The sheer walls on
the east side of the river wore lichen and moss as if they were blankets.
Following a narrow path on the side of the ridge the three basket-laden men
now came to a branch in the river. They followed the west branch to a place
shaded with sycamores and damp with ferns. The day was fading, but here
the river bank was low and easy to cross.

On the other side their noses were assailed by a strong odor. Aleqwel led
them to the source: it was a sulfurous hot spring. All springs were sacred,
being entrances to Shup, the mother, and they cast offerings of hutash,
ilepesh, and acorns on the water. They stood and prayed for a moment
experiencing the cool and damp of the mountainside and the vaporous
warmth of the springs, the dark shade and the day's lingering dry heat.
They had come to a new place.

Along the north side of the small river, they walked in near darkness
behind the high ridge called Kaspat. At dusk they came to a narrow ledge
above the river and the thatched domes of Matilha village.

The elderly wot who came out to meet them was frail looking and beardless. He was cloaked in a long bearskin robe and his thin grey topknot was laced with a fat hairpin. Also welcoming them was the man from the paint makers' guild who was a trading partner of Aleqwel's family. Aleqwel called the man "Uncle," and seemed to trust him as he would a blood relative, though he was not.

At the trading uncle's house the three guests rested on clean sitting mats by a fire of glowing oak coals. They sat under the shadow of the mountains. Their host's old mother served them acorn soup and venison, fresh bulbs and greens. They ate politely with two fingers of the right hand.

The paint maker uncle wanted to know everything they had seen on their way: the condition of the trail, the doings at Koyo, the movement of game animals, and the status of seeds in the meadows. The trading uncle, though he spoke a dialect of the eastern language, had learned to understand his trading partners both from the coast and from the high mountains of the interior. He nodded eagerly at their words. At last the host asked about the year's happenings at Mishopshno. Where was Aleqwel's father, his old friend, and why had he not come with them to trade at Matilha?

When the trading uncle learned of the elder paint maker's death the previous fall, he began to cry. The whole family, from his old mother to his young children, though they little understood the words of the Mishopshno people, began to cry and wail. They threw handfuls of river sand from the house floor. It struck the low roof and fell back on their heads, and a few grains flew out the smoke hole into the starry sky. They all cried together until they were finished and then sat quietly.

After a while the paint maker host said, "And you, nephew, have you come to trade then? It is good. You will be successful like your late father. There is much to buy here. Not long ago we had visitors from Kashtiq who were traveling west. They brought with them good loaves of red paint. Was it red paint you wanted? Tok, too? Naturally. The tok is ready just now, last year's, that is. But tonight, rest, sleep well. Tomorrow I will set up the trading. There is also a Mohave here, a remarkable man. He ran for half a month to get here, and already he's prepared to go farther. You will see… tomorrow."

Sun breathed gently, scented with sage. The dawn air, when they washed in the stream beneath the ridge, was cold but not damp. There had been fleas. The sky was clear and cloudless.

In an open area near his house the paint maker uncle had assembled all the people who wanted to trade: the tok gatherers, the basket makers, the people who had bought fine quality tobacco from the Kashtiq man, and the host who had obtained paint from the same man. There was also local paint. And the Mohave was there with his long hair flowing freely over his shoulders.

Aleqwel longed to talk with the man. A few times he had seen, but never spoken with, people from the Great River. He understood that they were pitiable, having to work for their food by growing crops. He also knew that they had feet like doves' wings and that they lived on their dreams.

The wot and assistant wot appeared. The villagers stood watching. The traders lined up with their baskets of goods on their ground mats. The singing began. Like the gambling songs, the trading song went on and on. First one side addressed the other, singing out their wishes and conditions. Then, the other side sang in reply. Eventually, the two groups achieved a harmony of intention.

After the trading song ended, the parties unpacked their baskets and spread out their goods. When he saw what was for sale Aleqwel felt glad he had brought so much money with him.

The trading uncle spoke for the villagers, and Aleqwel spoke for the visitors. It was his first time, and he talked slowly out of carefulness. Fortunately, his uncle was an honest man and helped him out when he made errors.

It took all morning to determine who wanted what and what they would give or pay for it. The information had to be relayed back and forth in two languages. Then it was time to measure out the money and goods.

Aleqwel measured off the lengths of bead money, two turns around the wrist and up the distance of his middle finger for each length. Big loaves of fine red paint as well as black paint made from pine soot and deer marrow filled his basket.

But the Mohave offered something better. He laid out a cake of a brilliant scarlet shade Aleqwel had rarely seen. The young paint maker was happy knowing the money he had brought with him was especially valuable, being nearly new and of good color. The Mohave seemed enthusiastic about getting his hands on the shell beads.

Trading went well for Aleqwel's companions, too. No, they really couldn't buy baskets this time, but they would like some of that Kashtiq tobacco.

Would payment in dried tunafish be acceptable? Could they use some carrizo cane, which was so plentiful in the interior this month? Yes, that's good, the islanders need it for their arrows. Look, here is woqo, excellent tar from Mishopshno, it sticks to or caulks anything. Will you buy some? Pine pitch? Yes, yes, with that our woqo will make tough sealant for our plank canoes. But, look, here is what we want most: tok, your local milkweed. Tok for string, for nets and lines, for tying boxes and boats together, for almost everything. And for the islanders who have none.

It seemed as if half the village had brought bundles of tok dried and ready to twine. The three traders gave them woqo and dried fish and huya jewelry and loaded their baskets with tok.

And then they spied the cotton blankets of the Mohave. Rare and finely woven, they would bring a fine price from the wealthy rulers of Michumash Island. The Mohave collected more and more lengths of beads, beads from Alow's hair and beads from Chaki's neck. It was a good bargain.

By midday the buying and selling was over. Everyone appeared satisfied. The trading uncle had earned his percentage. When he saw how well things had gone, the gracious wot addressed the visitors. He invited them to stay on.

"Will you join us in hockey?" he asked. "We have much food here now. Tonight, eat, eat. Then unpack your hiding bones and let us test our power."

Naturally, they agreed.

The wot concluded, "It is the weak time and there is little hunting. Of women only the old and very young and those who were once men are out. You must see our fine enhweq. Stay with us until they are out of their pits."

They would not have dared to refuse the invitation. Nor did they wish to.

A nd so they stayed on at Matilha. During Grandmother Moon's dark time they occupied themselves in playing field hockey on the broad square of dirt that had been squeezed in between the mountains and the creek. Recently rebuilt, it spread out smooth and level and was enclosed by a low rock wall.

The whole village came out to play or watch. The visitors joined their host's teams. The games were long, noisy, messy, and rough. They consisted mostly of running up and down the long dirt field. With red and black sticks in hand the visitors charged the field, running with the herd. Occasionally, one player would display his unique talents, hurling the wooden ball a vast distance with a single swipe of his playing stick.

The visitors felt exhilarated. Each afternoon after the game ended a fire would be built in the sweathouse and the men would climb down into the dark mouth to relax with their brothers and to scrape off their fresh sweat with their sweatsticks. Afterward they ate.

At night they played hand game. They sat outdoors beneath the stars. Around a big fire the two teams—Earth and Sun—sang and sang, taunting their opponents.

Everyone was impressed with the young paint maker's ability to see the concealed bones. Even his teammates were surprised as night after night his vision penetrated all secrets. The wot was mildly alarmed. The alchuklash, ancient uncle of the paint maker, noticed the power, too.

But Aleqwel's friends did not see the hidden bones so well. They failed in nearly every kill. Their fingers, thrust out like arrow points, inevitably indicated empty fists. Maybe it was for the best: had they been as strong as their companion they might have won the wealth and wives of the wot himself. And they might never have lived to return home with their prize.

As it was, most people were satisfied with the betting those dark nights— save for two bewildered and worried fishermen from Mishopshno.

The days passed and Alow continued to play field hockey whenever there were enough people to make teams. He competed in every sport in which he could find an opponent. Much of his day was spent aiming poles through rolling hoops. He had not entirely lost his aim.

Chaki, too, loved to play, but he found another interest. Though he had seen much tok in his life, both as string and in dry bundles, he had never seen the famed Toktok Mountains where it bloomed in abundance. It was flower season, and he wanted to see them.

The strong hunter found a young man to show him the way. They hiked upstream, following first the canyon and then the mountainside. Here Chaki discovered the white-sapped herb, thriving and in profusion just as he had always heard. He felt pleased, but not satisfied, as he chewed the wad of thickened milky tok juice that his guide gave him. He liked the gum and bought some to take home. He did not feel like playing at sports, though, and he was still restless and worried. He liked exploring. He convinced his guide to take him to Kaspat, the sacred peak atop Matilha's ridge.

The next day Chaki climbed to the shrine pole on a clearing at the summit. The stake stretched into the sky as if holding it up. It was vermillion colored like the poles at home and feathered with black condor above and buzzard below. Chaki made his offering and prayed to the six directions. He centered himself along the axis of the Three Worlds. And yet his confidence was still weak. For several nights now he had failed to kill a single hidden bone in the power contest.

Chaki looked above him into the clear pale sky without end. He saw buzzards and a condor soaring high and far away with their wing-tips spread like fingers. Below rolled the river valley that he and his companions had climbed coming to Matilha. To the west lay the trail home. The air felt hot and dry and dusty in Chaki's nostrils. Absently, he touched the mountain lion's paw that hung on a hair braid around his neck. The seaman felt a call to go farther into the hills alone. He needed to climb them all, to travel far into empty places, to make new discoveries. He decided to go hunting.

While his friends played sports and explored, Aleqwel sought out the Mohave, only to discover that the man had left the village the very next morning after the trading. The young man had hoped to talk with him, if only through an interpreter, for he longed to expand his knowledge. Passing the soul doctor's house on his return from the wot's he encountered the thin old man sitting in Sun's warmth in his yard.

"Mohave travel fast and rest little," said the wrinkled alchuklash, as if reading his thoughts. "He has a long way to go. His sister is married to one of us, one of the people of antap. She lives many days west. Perhaps he will return one day."

Aleqwel was surprised to find it easy to talk with the old man. In previous years he had been intimidated by the small man's assortment of feathers and his claw, tooth, and crystal necklace. Each object in some way called up a power. Now, these atishwin inspired confidence more than fear. The achanas of Matilha might have more knowledge than those at Mishopshno. Aleqwel had heard it whispered that they were truer doctors. They worked frequently in mountains and caves far from the settled village. Aleqwel felt a sudden trust in the shriveled old man, who was called Chnaway.

They walked together to get water. At the streamside, grandmothers and children were filling water baskets and gathering fallen oak branches. Chnaway took Aleqwel's hand and led him upstream. Before he knew it, Aleqwel had confided in the doctor the facts surrounding his father's murder and the subsequent developments. From the healer's comments, Aleqwel had the sensation that the old man had seen all the events that he had described to him. He knew details ignored by Aleqwel himself. He seemed to know the intruder like a kinsman.

Before long, Aleqwel was telling the old man about the solstice woman. He said the woman had seemed to offer everything, yet instead she was taking more and more. He uttered his fear of her touch. He even confessed his attempts to conjure her in the daytime. Then he shared the excitement he felt on the journey to Matilha when he spied the orange-capped condor and recognized the woman for what she was. Chnaway saw it all clearly. "Of course she is in substance a condor," he said. "You ought to have guessed it on the first night. But sometimes it's hard to see these things for yourself. I, too, have consulted doctors. You do realize, don't you, that she is not merely a condor but Holhol, the condor nunashish, as well? She is one who eats people. Holhol is a very powerful sorcerer."

"Why didn't I see it!" cried Aleqwel in dismay. "Is it too late?"

"Without doubt you were bewitched. This is what I see: this Holhol, this woman, is really the assistant of another sorcerer. She is, indeed, his creation."

"Someone has made her? My great-uncle alchuklash says that also."

"Yes. Who might that creator be?"

"It can only be the intruder, the Wokoch. Is the bear doctor powerful enough to do such a thing?"

"If he has been practicing in silence for years, he can be very strong. But, before you give way to his power, remember: you have forced him to back down."

"But only once," fretted the recently proud Aleqwel. "Tell me then, is this woman, the one who draws my strength away, is she no more alive than a ghost?"

"She is as insubstantial as a ghost. Yet, like a ghost, she can be very dangerous. Don't forget, if ever she steals your semen while you sleep you will die."

"I have been afraid of that," Aleqwel admitted. "But I know no way to prevent it. Yet even my own alchuklash advised me not to worry about her. He said the woman was not my real enemy."

"Your uncle sees clearly. Though she is dangerous, as long as you are vigilant you will be safe from the Holhol. Now that you recognize her she will find it difficult to deceive you and your resistance will be strong. But be careful: she may try coming to you in another form."

For the first time since the Winter Solstice at Syuhtun Aleqwel felt satisfied on the subject of the identity of the redheaded woman, though the menacing Wokoch still oppressed him. He thanked the old man for his advice.

The young man wondered as he stood in the shadow of Kaspat Peak and imagined bright Mishopshno why it was that the doctors at home, though powerful and wise, did not have the easy vision, the inspiration of this simple Matilha achana? Was it his very simplicity that made him strong? His own great-uncle, without question, could heal; yet sometimes Aleqwel, in watching the cures the old man performed, sensed that there was as much form as substance in them. Sometimes he had not even been able to see the atishwins come, though undoubtedly they had come. And then there was the money: the achanas on all the coast were rich. And they demanded many lengths of beads before they would agree to breathe on anyone. Their homes were comfortable, luxurious even. Aleqwel thought of the plain dwelling of his present companion.

"Chnaway alchuklash," he said, "what do I owe you for your service?"

Instead of replying, the wizened old man, shrunken by the dry years, told Aleqwel that he was moved by his power. "You have exhibited great clarity at the bone game. Do you always play so well? No? I thought not. Had you been so thoroughly dangerous I would have spotted it years before when you visited with your late father. And yet, it is apparent that you have a potential greater than just for trading and grinding paints."

"I am antap, Grandfather."

"That explains some of it, but not all."

"My mother's kinsmen have many spirit helpers," he replied. "They are alatishwinich. Her side is strong in me. Still, my late father's half is also strong. I want most of all to carry on his work, my work."

"Yet circumstances arise that draw us away from what we most desire."

"I can see that is sometimes true, Grandfather."

"Have you aspired to paint on the rocks as the doctors do on the solstices?"

"Yes, alchuklash," said Aleqwel, flushing. "I have painted the shrine pole for the winter solstice. I believe I could do more."

"Have you drunk much momoy?"

Aleqwel felt challenged as he had when trained by the antap. "This winter was my second drinking."

"Did it make you ill?"

"Not very."

Then the wrinkled man said, "In a short time the longest day, the summer solstice, will be with us. Do you celebrate at home as we do here?"

Aleqwel assented. It was nothing like the Winter Solstice Ceremony, but it was duly observed. Inside he trembled at the invitation that was to come. Outwardly, he remained serene.

The question came with the inevitability of a wave breaking. Chnaway was going to the caves. He would journey to the sky. The chief wot would join him, flying on Sky Eagle's wings. It was time once more to visit Sun's house. Would Aleqwel the paint maker assist in the preparation of pigments that would record the voyage?

Without hesitating, Aleqwel replied, "Yes. Yes, of course."

"Good, good. I will show you the caves. We will go early tomorrow."

"Aren't the caves terribly dangerous?" asked the young man. His voice trembled slightly though his expression remained impassive.

"Only for the uninitiated," said the old man. "You will be safe with us. I would not endanger you or anyone by sending them unprepared to the caves. For the unauthorized it could mean death. But for you it is only duty."

A chill spread through Aleqwel even though the day had begun to burn so hot that the air rippled. He knew he had discovered the true reason for his coming to Matilha.

While the men were away Nene, Anihwoy, Ponoya, Kanit, and the other women in the gathering camp kept busy. Though there was less deer meat to dry on the frames without the men, there were still sihon bulbs to roast and tender lily bulbs ready to be dug as well.

Ponoya gathered downed wood by the creek and kept the water basket full. She ground acorns in a basket mortar stuck with tar onto the great rock slab near camp. She cleaned the mortar with her fiber brush and poured water over the fine meal to leach the bitterness out. She gathered food and cooked and cleaned the baskets and bowls. In the random moments between her much-needed household chores, she worked on a cooking basket she was coiling. Anakawin often demanded her attention as he wavered between being a proud hunter and a spirited mischief maker.

Although Ponoya had plenty to occupy her hands and time, her mind often drifted far away to a place beyond the double pass somewhere in the parched interior. In the dark time of Grandmother Moon, when normally she would be entering the makeshift heated pit, she found she was not ready. She went on with her work, without Kanit's companionship now, and earned Nene's praise for her industry. Her appetite was good. In fact, she stuffed herself as she never had before with sihon and lily bulbs, cactus fruit, ilepesh, and acorn porridge. But, even though she was able to work hard and never become ill, Ponoya felt low in energy. Her grandmother looked at her a certain way and warned her again about bears.

During the dark time, Ponoya felt somewhat out of place walking around with the children and old women. Though it happened to some enhweq to be late for the pit it had never before happened to her.

After much of her work was accomplished, one morning she decided to climb the southern hill that overlooked the valley and the sea. The day unfolded warm and blue. The fog had settled in the channel, stopping just short of the coastal shore. Around her, birds sang and flowers bloomed. Ponoya sat for a moment on the hilltop looking down into the empty valley. Impulsively, she wove herself a garland from the flowers around her, mingling red hutash with purple-blue lupines and golden poppies. Her straight hair, held in place by a shell circlet, fell tidily around her shoulders. Before the grieving period it had been long. That morning she had singed her bangs, and the line they made across her brow was only slightly less neat for lack of Kanit's advice. Before putting on the flower wreath, Ponoya brushed her hair once again with the soap plant brush that she kept in the soft pouch at her waist. She liked to keep herself clean and well groomed. She glanced approvingly at the paint on her arms and breasts. When she placed the garland atop her head she looked ready for a celebration. She felt as if she had put on an antap's feathered headdress. She was all set to dance.

So Ponoya danced. And sang. She sang a wildflower song, a song of colors. Then she sang a calling and answering song with the birds about her. She touched the dried bird around her neck and danced her Hummingbird dance. After a while she felt better than she had in a long time. She sat down and straightened out her skirt. Sitting quietly, she began intoning her dream song. Quietly, she teased her atishwin to see if she would come.

She did come and quickly, too. Soon there were several hummingbirds whirring around her and sipping nectar from the flowers in her hair. The little darting birds, never still, shimmered iridescently. Violet, green, red, they adorned her like animate flowers. Ponoya spoke to her atishwin: "Are you happy? Did you like my dance? I didn't call you frivolously, you know. I was afraid you had deserted me. My power feels so weak. What is happening to me?"

Hummingbird, who had come as an ordinary bird, answered while hovering on invisible wings. She looked like a very large dragonfly. She said, "Look, daughter, I am over here. You have kept me happy and I will not desert you. There is no flaw in your power. In fact you are strong. I and my power are with you. Just see if you cannot still fly."

But the girl felt strongly reassured and did not feel the need to test her flying ability. "But why, then, do I feel so weak?"

"Maybe you have enemies who are also strong. Or perhaps what feels like weakness is part of your strength." And Hummingbird darted away as quickly as she had come.

Ponoya returned to camp along the creek, walking through the tall grasses, puzzling over her atishwin's words.

That evening, after taking soup to her aunt and mother in their little sweat pit, Ponoya went to see Pichiquich, whose family shelter was erected no more than several tomol lengths away from her own.

Pichiquich was helping her husband's mother cook over the outdoor fire. The baby, Kelele, watched, laced on her willow cradle, which was propped on its one leg against a massive oak. Pichiquich had not been to the pit for a long time because she was nursing the baby. And her mother-in-law was beginning to grow too old to go.

Ponoya approached Kelele and talked to her thickly in baby talk. The baby smiled with shining pink gums, amused by the silly Coyote words. "Iiii," she answered. Ponoya gave her the circlet of flowers from her hair. The baby laughed and began to eat them.

Ponoya said to Pichiquich, "Ichantik, do you need help with the baby? May I wash her for you?"

"I just cleaned her up," responded her friend. "There will be another time, do not doubt."

"I would like to help you more to care for her."

"I can always use help," laughed Pichiquich wearily. "Though Mother is very good."

"May I keep her for you sometime?"

"Truthfully, with my husband away I feel better keeping her beside me. What has gotten into you, ichantik? I know that you like children. But aren't your hands full now with that little brother of yours? Soon enough you will have your own." Pichiquich stopped stirring the porridge and looked up suddenly at Ponoya. For a moment, the two women stood looking at each other, wordlessly, as if they were curious strangers who spoke different tongues.

"I don't know," responded Ponoya vaguely, at last.

Later, eating together outdoors by the fire, sharing porridge, Ponoya asked the women how they felt when their men were away. Chaki's mother said that when a woman is young such things matter to her, separation is very difficult, but that after a while it gets to be not so bad. For an older woman there are even certain advantages, she implied mysteriously.

Ponoya, who was feeling undecided whether to cry or yawn, replied that for her part, since the men had been gone, she had had a pain in her stomach all the time.

"Are you sure the pain is in your stomach?" the older woman joked coarsely as she rose to get the unfinished basket she was working on. The basket was a giant storage basket shaped like a sea urchin. The woman said she regretted bringing such a cumbersome project with her to the camp.

When Chaki's mother was out of hearing Pichiquich said in a serious tone to Ponoya, "Sister, I know the pain you are speaking of. When you first love someone the pain of their going is very strong. But the ache grows smaller with time until it is hardly larger than a new-formed ilepesh seed: the pain remains but sleeps without disturbing you. Even so, it can spring up like a bush if the water of misfortune should fall upon it. If you marry anyone but a commoner," she warned, "you must accustom yourself to absence and worry. There are journeys that will be longer and farther than this trip to Matilha."

Ponoya knew: the islands. She complained fretfully, "I feel I have no one to keep my heart going."

Pichiquich scoffed. "There are plenty of old people who need care. And babies, too." She added, "What still frightens me about the men traveling is that their power diminishes in distant lands."

Her mother-in-law heard this last sentence as she returned with her half-completed basket. Her husband was safely roasting in the sweathouse, but Chaki, her youngest child, and Alow, her nephew, were absent, doing unknown things in another land. "We must trust in the strength of their atishwins," she said firmly.

Grandmother Moon was like a newborn baby. In the dusk people gathered in Matilha in the sacred enclosure. The people shouted and the dogs howled while the ancient alchuklash conducted the ceremony. She appeared, at last, swaddled in milky light. Health and strength would be renewed.

Early next morning Chnaway came for Aleqwel at the guildsman's house. It was still dark and Alow slept on. Chaki had gone out already with his sinew-backed bow and his mountain lion quiver tied to his waist string. The alchuklash took Aleqwel to the wot's house. In the cold predawn light the three, leaning on toyon walking sticks, picked out the upstream trail. As they walked, the wot, who proved to be spry despite his fragile appearance, explained that the cave was an entrance into Shup. But while Shup was a nurturing and healing mother, down inside of her there lurked all the nunashish of the Lower World. There death ruled. Only people with the strongest atishwins could survive the caves. Even they had to drink momoy.

Abruptly, in midsentence, the wot veered off onto a narrow path. It was more like a rabbit or coyote track than a human trail. It was overgrown with sage and laurel sumac. The track led steeply up a rocky hillside. It never went far from the creek yet was high above it.

The alchuklash spoke to Aleqwel now in the language of the antap initiates. He told him that the place where they were going was only one of many powerful places known to the doctors. They were places where they could more easily reach the Lower World and the Sky World. All the caves were forbidden to the uninitiated for their own protection. Yet Aleqwel should be safe as the apprentice of the achanas. Of course, he ought never to come there by himself. The caves were not for individuals to use. They were only for the spiritual descendents of Grandfather Coyote, the first benefactor of the people. They called Grandmother Moon "Momoy." Aleqwel had heard these things before. But he had never before set out to enter an opening into Shup.

They had come to a dead end high on the hill. They stood, leaning on their staffs, looking about them. Aleqwel stared at the dark mountains that curved around the stream's canyon like a curved shard of a huge mortar, broken perhaps at a rich woman's funeral. The mountains were a wall, a termination, and the people could not see west beyond them. Far away a coyote howled at the end of night.

In the east, before them, the sky thinned out pale and glossy as a wet abalone shell. Then it warmed and flushed purple and pink like the wild roses in the canyon.   In front of the three was the hidden opening. It was a small gap, a sandstone ledge high above them. A tall toyon shrub grew beside it on the hill. The two old men showed the young man the way. The old men climbed the vertical rock, using the natural and blade-carved toeholds like bobcats, and Aleqwel followed as best he could.

They spent the day up there. Sun warmed them in the morning on the cave ledge. Aleqwel saw for the first time the reproduction in paint of the journeys that Momoy provided. Wot and achana were transformed into their atishwins. All the animals of Sun's house lived in that hidden enclosure and the Sky People, too. Everything beneficial to the people was represented there. All was made real in red, black, and white pigment. Sun blazed and Moon shone, fish swam and bear loped… and it rained. The sky was filled with the wot, Sky Eagle, and Holhol, the monster condor.

Aleqwel felt dizzy, almost ill. He was in the presence of incredible power. He longed to leave—even if it meant jumping from the top of the ledge. The alchuklash gave him some tobacco to calm him. Then he and the wot began to explain how the paintings were executed. They showed him the paint cups ground out of the sandstone floor. They extracted small pestles, paint cakes, binder, and fiber brushes from their carrying nets.

And so Aleqwel was absorbed for the rest of the day. Because of his occupation he forgot his first terror. The priests mixed paint and taught him brush techniques, which he practiced on small hand-held rocks. At Mishopshno he had secretly made attempts of this sort in less sacred places. Now he was, at last, enlightened by tradition, and as he worked his confidence grew. They showed him how they got water and cooked and where they slept. At night they told him how they transformed their momoy dreams into waking reality.

In a few days Sun would be at his strongest. The help of powerful people would be needed to maintain the balance. They would have to keep the world from going to flame. Was Aleqwel prepared to stay with them, to assist at the caves, to grind and mix the red ochre and charcoal?

He felt he had no choice. He had always wanted this. Yet somehow he had imagined painting caves as simpler, less terrible, more like painting a bowl or a tomol or like the secret drawings he had made on cobblestones in the sand dunes. He wondered how he could have thought such a thing.

"And you will have to drink momoy, here, far away from your home," said the old, old momoy giver. His transparent skin gleamed in the firelight.

"I am prepared for it," the young man replied.

Alow had spent all his days at Matilha playing sports and gambling. On this trip, though, he had won hardly at all. Power came and went like the ocean tides. However, he had to be careful not to stake and possibly lose all his money and newly acquired merchandise.

One by one the girls had begun to emerge from their isolation and uncleanliness. Some of them were no less attractive than others he had encountered. With both Aleqwel and Chaki out in the hills much of the time, he had little competition as most desirable exotic stranger. He enjoyed talking with the girls, half in his language, half in theirs. They all joked together and laughed and then the well-bred girls went back home to work.

But some of the others stayed behind with Alow. They stared hard at the pelican's foot that he wore around his neck and asked silly questions about fishing. They invited him to play seed marbles and bat ball, and he consented. But he did not follow any of them into the brush, though several looked hard at him before going out. He never particularly wanted to. He began to wonder if maybe something was wrong with his power.

The girls grew more friendly with him, even aggressive. Then, when little happened, they became more distant. They began to joke together about him.

Chaki hunted deer every day now. He went up in the high range that was curved like a mortar shard, where the creek originated. He saw bear tracks by the water and deer in the hills, but he had no success. In the evening he would stride into the village, strong and large, with nothing more than rabbits and squirrels to show for his day.

Nevertheless, Chaki felt best in the hills. He went up to the top of the range, though it took him half the day just to get there. Above was a flat area of pines and meadows. The plateau was teeming with jack rabbits and pocked with ground squirrel holes. There were deer up there, too; Chaki saw their hoof prints and sometimes the flash of their white tails as they ran away into the trees.

Running after one of these white tails, Chaki came out into a low soggy meadow. In the middle of the meadow stood a great mound, a sandstone rock, larger than the wot's house at Syuhtun. Beside the rock was a deep pool, a spring. It was quiet in the meadow, a contrast to the pine forest with its screaming blue jays and woodpeckers. Chaki felt hot and thirsty.

In the soft sand below the spring Chaki saw the footprints of a bobcat. After praying and offering seeds, he drank. The water was cool and good and satisfying. He filled his water basket. He sat down on a low rock near the spring. He took out some of the food given him by the guildsman's wife: dried venison, cold ilepesh, cooked rabbit. While eating, he decided that perhaps he ought to abandon hope of catching deer that day and instead try to track down that bobcat whose tracks circled the spring.

After eating, Chaki felt renewed, optimistic. He followed the tracks. They soon disappeared, somewhere in the marshy area below the spring. He looked up ahead at the immense brown rock. He spotted a narrow fissure, just wide enough for a man, splitting the big stone into two. If the hole was wide enough for a man, then certainly it would be wide enough for a bobcat to slip into and sleep the day away. Chaki knew cats.

The strong man stepped up into the dark stone cleft. When, at last, he could see, he realized, instantly, that he was doomed. There was no cat. But Chaki saw, within the crevice, countless nunashish, cave on cave of supernatural beings. Some were Sky People perhaps, others, clearly monsters. Feathered, furred, horned, winged, toothed, and tongued, they menaced him. Though without the thought to do so, he had invaded a forbidden place, he had violated an entrance that led to the Lower World. He was as good as dead already.

Chaki leaped back out of the crevice. Instinctively, he pulled the mountain lion's atishwin from his neck and began to rub his body all over with it. He rubbed it on the mouth of the cave. He fled to the sweet spring where he broke his bow in half and his arrows, one by one, and threw them in the water. Then, he, himself, jumped into the purifying spring, quiver, carrying net, and all. He held his head under the water. Everything swirled around in confusion.

Some time later, Chaki pulled himself out onto the grass. He lay still, heart pounding, numb, waiting to die.

Sun drooped in the west. When he recovered his senses, Chaki believed he might still be alive, though weak. He began to hear singing coming from the fissure of the cavernous rock. It was a chorus of human voices, a beautiful human song. The once strong man, cat's paw still grasped in his hand, rose to his feet slowly. He began to walk toward the inviting harmony. After a few steps his feet stopped of themselves and would not go on. Then he turned and ran.

That evening as Aleqwel and the two achanas were returning from their own cave they were met by a wild man running down the mountain trail. His hair was flying, his bow missing. His eyes were set. Bewildered at first, Aleqwel sickened when he recognized his mighty friend. The man was trembling, kilamu, like a person who runs from a bear. Aleqwel peered up the trail and prepared to climb a tree.

But the alchuklash caught Chaki by the arm and led him down the trail to the village. He said firmly, as if to a child, "You have violated the sacred and you are suffering. But there is a chance that you may still live." He took the empty man to his own home and made him a bed by the fire. "I will take care of you," he said softly. "You must eat nothing at all until after the summer solstice. Here's some tobacco for strength. Chew it. There are restrictions you must observe until the winter solstice. Then, when you are pure again I will give you momoy drink. Do not be afraid. You are a strong man. The monsters may forgive you."

And Chaki seemed to understand, though he said nothing but stared past them all into a dark world. It was a world they acknowledged but did not share.

It was their last night at Matilha. Grandmother Moon had grown round, as if pregnant. Chaki gained strength. The drinking of momoy root had reconciled him with the nunashish. It turned him around from the road to Shimilaqsha.

The three travelers spent their last evening at the home of the old wot. The trading had gone to everyone's satisfaction. Burden baskets were heavy with loaves of paint and cotton blankets and heaped with bundles of dry tok. The wot's ancient wives and grown sons, Aleqwel's trading partner and all his family, joined them in a small feast. They sat around the red glowing fire in the center of the house enjoying venison and acorn porridge, rabbit meat and squirrel, sihon and lily bulbs, cherry-nut balls and pine nuts. The guests communicated their gratitude formally to their hosts, according to the rules of courtesy, but the words were also heartfelt.

Chaki had paid Chnaway for helping to save his life, and he had no more shell money left to wrap in his hair or around his neck. Financially, the trip had been a failure for him, as it had been a psychic disaster. But it never occurred to him to wish he had not come. Inevitably, he had come. He had made a terrible mistake at the rock—but he still lived. Now he had only to follow the stern restrictions and prohibitions the alchuklash had given him while his spirit regained force. With dignity, Chaki thanked those who had cared for him.

The wot and alchuklash were seated on twin whale vertebrae stools. Alow wondered who had lugged the heavy bone discs to this high inland village. They looked ancient and valuable like the two men who sat on them. The expedition had been financially profitable for Alow. His power had weakened, yet no ill had befallen him. His cousin had survived almost certain destruction. Alow gave his thanks.

Then Aleqwel thanked his host, the paint maker, for his hospitality and for arranging the trading. He affirmed his willingness to reciprocate at any time. He thanked the women for the delicious food. He turned to the two achanas and told them how honored he had been to assist in their sacred work. Aleqwel was now convinced that these men were inspired with the ancient gift.

In reply, the doctors urged Aleqwel to return at any time. They flattered him by saying how hard it was to find a talented apprentice. Until he came again, they advised him to use what he had learned to bring strength to the people of the coast. Aleqwel promised to do so.

Then the thin-haired wot gave the young men advice for the road. They listened. They considered it carefully, though it was the same advice they had been given on leaving Mishopshno: stay on the trail, mind your own business, be polite to strangers and grateful for hospitality.

By the time Sun first showed himself over the eastern mountains next morning, the three young traders were up and ready to set out on their homeward journey.

Before leaving, Aleqwel paid a last visit to Chnaway's house. He explained how, in the night, he had seen his sister very clearly at the bathing pool. It was the one at the creek by the gathering camp. It was early morning, dark. She was naked and up to her waist in water, washing her hair with soap root. Lather clung around her eyes and she seemed to be having trouble seeing. Just then, a stranger approached the stream with two young children, identical twin boys. The woman spoke to Ponoya in a peculiar dialect, saying that she was lost. Her eyes were unnaturally round, shining bright and black as the well-ripened berries that bears like to eat. Ponoya seemed not to have heard and moved closer to the mother of the twins. Watching from the sky Aleqwel had felt that something dreadful was about to befall his sister. But before he could intervene his spirit flew back to Matilha and another morning.

The alchuklash looked grim. "It is bad," he said. "Bad. But I do not know your sister. Is she a weak one or is her power strong?"

Aleqwel explained about her first and second experiences with Grandmother Momoy.

"It sounds like she has a strong atishwin," said the old man. "Perhaps it will save her. But you must get home quickly. There, you may be able to help her, to warn her. Tell me, is your sister pregnant?"

"Not that I know of."

"Possibly?"

"I suppose so. She is female." If Ponoya was indeed pregnant it would account for Alow's inability to see the bones at hand game. Fathers-to-be often lost their strength, their luck. And Pichiquich, could she be pregnant, also? Aleqwel stopped speculating. "My sister is young and unmarried, but I suppose it could be true," he admitted. "Do you think the lost woman is a bear?"

"The twins make it very likely; bear children often come that way. You know that grizzlies can't resist killing pregnant women."

"I was afraid it might be like that." With tears in his eyes Aleqwel hurried to the others, feet itching to get started.

Before the departing guests had reached the place by the great river where the trail turns to the west, even before coming to the split where Matilha's creek rushes into the great river, the enhweq of Matilha had begun to gossip about the men from the coast. As they went for water at the creek and leached their acorn meal, as they sat in front of their houses in the early light cracking and grinding seeds, winnowing and parching, preparing food for the day, they talked together, forming conclusions.

Mostly they laughed. Those men from the coast were certainly strange. Did they know how rude they had been? No doubt they were attractive and strong, refined, wealthy even. Yet they were naive as babies. First one enhweq made the joke, then it flew from girl to girl like a flame leaping from blade to blade in a dry meadow. Soon all the village was alight with it: the men from Mishopshno were the incarnations of Momoy's famous ward, the Big Child. Appearing to the world to be strong and brave and manly, the Child was nevertheless entirely ignorant of sex. Like him, those young men from Mishopshno probably believed that sex was a baked stalk of yucca. The girls, commoner and well-bred alike, laughed heartily, guffawing louder than was becoming.

The three friends spent the night at Koyo under bright round Moon. The fleas bit as fiercely as before, but at Matilha the men had grown accustomed to them.

The female wot drank up all the news from that village as if it were spring water and hung on every word of the message they brought from Matilha's chief. She did not show the disappointment that she felt over their hurry to get home. She abstained from giving invitations.

The next morning began clear and cloudless. It promised to bake the men as they had been baked every day of their stay in the interior. Secretly, they longed for familiar fog.

Yet Alow wanted to bring a special present to his enhweq. The sumac of Koyo was renowned as an ingredient of certain fine baskets. He insisted on picking some, though there was hardly space atop his own basket to lash it. His companions grumbled, even cursed. But they helped him cut the pungent branches. Aleqwel gave no hint of his dream or his urgency for his sister's life, though he was more restless and insistent that usual.

At last they were ready to depart, laden with sumac branches atop milkweed bundles. By the time they surmounted the overgrown trail that rose to the top of the ridge, Sun blazed overhead. They stopped to drink and eat and to look, for the last time, behind them, on the fading green valley shimmering in the heat of early summer. That long eastern land appeared familiar to them now. In some ways it even appeared hospitable, in spite of its terrors. But their hearts were already turned toward home.

They followed the hilltops singing, joking, and talking tough to lighten their load and speed their feet. By midafternoon they could see below them a sea of gray sand-colored fog. It drowned the ocean, shore, and their own land. They regained the refreshing scent of ocean air just as they were approaching the sacred Tsismuhu on their right-hand side. Observing that Sun was about to go into the sand dollar, the men felt it wise to rest at least a little bit.

Instead of bothering to eat they emptied some tobacco and shell powder from their earplugs and chewed it. It restored their energy as they cooled their faces in the breeze. They were not far from home now, though still in Shuku territory.

All at once Alow jumped up. The other two reached out to stop him, fearing he had once again set his mind on climbing Mt. Tsismuhu.

"Don't leave the trail," warned Chaki.

"But I must," cried Alow. "I must go out for a moment."

"Truly, you must wait," commanded Aleqwel. He was torn with empathy for his friend's condition. "You can wait a few miles until we cross the creek to our own land."

"No," replied Alow. "No, I cannot. My bowels are twisting now." And with that he abandoned his carrying basket to his friends and trotted a short distance down the path. Then he scuttled like a ground squirrel into the chaparral below the trail.

There was nothing to do but wait, however impatiently, for their kinsman to lighten his load.

Aleqwel took out his four-holed flute and blew into the end. It made a sound like the world breathing.

Chaki listened attentively. After awhile Aleqwel stopped playing. Chaki said, "The voice of your flute is like the sighing of my own mind. I wish I could play like you, then I would always know my hidden thoughts. Who taught you to do that?"

Aleqwel told him.

Then they both observed that their friend had been away a long time.

"His bowels can't be blocked or he wouldn't have been in such a hurry to leave us," said Aleqwel.

"True, true," agreed Chaki and he sprang up. "Wait here. I will find my cousin. It won't be the first time."

An animal path wove through the chaparral. Chaki ducked under the snapping boughs of sage and sumac and ceanothus. He had not crept far downhill when he came to a small clearing. It was a medium-sized rock pile beside which grew a scrub oak tree. The rock pile was surrounded by a thicket of fallen oak branches, poison oak, and vines. An area of empty dirt encircled the clearing. Chaki thought it was a likely spot.

The leavings were near the side of the rock pile where the thicket was least dense. Flies were already on them. Chaki spotted traces of his cousin's footprints in the brown dust. They went up, then headed downhill, widely spaced. The elder cousin followed the footprints down to the lower edge of the clearing. There he could see another set of prints, the tracks of his atishwin, the mountain lion.

At once Chaki could see what had happened. His cousin had chosen a nice clear spot to empty his bowels and had disturbed a sleeping mountain lion. The drowsy cat had run out of its rock shelter. Alow in his typically carefree enthusiasm undoubtedly pursued the cat with the intent of bringing home a spectacular trophy.

Chaki swiftly climbed the scrub oak. The tree was low and bushy and it was only with difficulty that he could see over the brush to the hillside below. First he observed portions of the animal trail that the mountain lion must have followed with Alow bounding along some ways behind. Then he could make out the form of a man bending over at the edge of another clearing near the low trail of the valley floor. In the clearing stood a fair-sized oak tree. Chaki guessed that his cousin was stringing his bow. Then he noticed two figures walking down the low trail—Shuku hunters. They carried recurved bows that were strung.

Chaki went down the tree as fast as he had run up. He sped down the hillside through open parts of the chaparral. Before he reached the tall oak he could see Alow facing the spreading tree. He was kneeling, bow held horizontally, flint-toothed arrow in place. From his higher position Chaki could also see what Alow could not: two figures on the trail not far from

Alow's left side, standing quietly, evidently listening to some sound as they drew cane arrows from the quivers at their waists.

Chaki touched his atishwin and silently called the unseen mountain lion.

The mountain lion sprang out of the highest branch of the thick oak in one long hard leap. Had there been an animal underneath it the men would have heard the snap of a broken spine. Then the lithe, strong-limbed cat loped, with head down, ears back, shyly to Chaki's side.

Alow turned around in amazement, for he saw no one. He pursued the tawny cat, which he prized for its teeth and claws and coat. He came to an abrupt halt before his older cousin.

Chaki was scratching the backs of the mountain lion's ears. It was coiled at his feet, wrapped in its long brown tail. It licked its paws. The broad pink tongue scraped and lapped at toes and between terrific claws with a noise that rasped like sharkskin sanding a new tomol. The lion looked at Alow with round blinking eyes. It purred loudly.

Alow was furious. "You ruined my hunting," he began to shout. Chaki, wordless, turned and ran up the hill. The narrow but powerful hunter, the color of sandstone, slinked along by his side.

Alow followed. At the clearing where Alow had first spotted the cat Chaki released it. The mountain lion bounded off into higher hills. Alow followed Chaki to the main trail.

At last Alow had the opportunity to unfurl his anger. "Cousin, why have you done this thing to me? This was my first mountain lion, and I know I would not have missed my mark."

"Did it ever occur to you, kinsman, that you were trespassing? Cousin, you may be brave and strong, but if you are not much more careful your impulses will get you killed. At times you behave like a troublesome little brother."

Alow stood silent, stung.

"What are you likely to come across on Shuku lands... besides valuable game? Yes, that's right, Shukuans. Their bows were drawn, aimed in your direction. If you had shot the mountain lion, they would have been justified to loose their arrows at you; you were poaching. It's what they always accuse us of. It's their excuse. They might have shot you anyway. Of course, you didn't see the men, you were only envisioning your own future prestige." Chaki relented. He could see his cousin's remorseful posture.

"Were there really Shuku hunters there—by the tree?"

"Look down there," Chaki pointed to the low trail beneath them before it faded into the fog.

Alow saw two men, their long hair tied with money and knives. They wore quivers at their sides and were heading southward toward Tsismuhu's creek. The hunters looked as if they were progressing cautiously. "And they were really aiming at me?"

Chaki turned and headed back up the path to the spot where Aleqwel waited. Chaki was afraid of finding Aleqwel pacing as restlessly as a tethered bear cub. To his surprise Aleqwel looked as if he had been dreaming.

By now Sun was very low in the western sky. He hovered in the mist over an invisible Mishopshno beyond the hills. "Let's get going. We can't stay here tonight," said Chaki briskly. And even though two of them were worn out with exertion and emotion, they all lifted the laden carrying nets and hurried in the direction of home.

Aleqwel hardly seemed to hear the cousins' exciting story. Chaki could not resist chastising his younger cousin: "Don't you know that if you get killed you won't be able to revive as easily as Grandfather Coyote? You have responsibilities!"

Suddenly Aleqwel lost control, as if writhing out of a nightmare. He cried at Alow, "What sort of man are you? Do you think you can marry the way you are? Or don't you even think about marriage at all?" He trembled.

Alow walked silently the rest of the way home.

Moon rose large at their backs. At Shuku Creek the path grew shadowy. Now they were traveling only by moonlight. They had finally reached their own lands. But, silently, all three wished they had already made camp.

The people were sleeping when the travelers arrived at last. They unloaded the pack baskets from their carrying nets and hung up the nets on oak tree limbs. They undressed, climbed under their blankets, and went to sleep.

In the early morning Aleqwel woke to discover that his sister was gone.

PART III

CHAPTER 7

MONTH WHEN THINGS ARE DIVIDED IN HALF
hesiq momoy an spatata

Grandfather Sun was already on his way when Aleqwel awoke. His little brother was straddling him and tugging on his short beard.

"Time to wake up! Time to wake up! Don't let your blood get too warm or Rattlesnake will find you."

"Get off of me, will you!" Aleqwel growled as he wrestled free from an exhausting dream of bears.

"What happened on your trip? Did you meet a girl? Did you bring me any gum?" Anakawin began to search his brother's waist pouch that lay by the sleeping place.

"Stay out of that, would you! I think Uncle Chaki brought you some. It's good to see you again, little brother. At least, I think it is." Aleqwel looked around him. The women were by the fire circle, not far away, ladling hot rocks into the mush pot. All the women, except Ponoya. They chattered cheerfully together, "pepepepe," not yet noticing that the returned traveler had awakened.

Aleqwel sat up and rubbed his eyes. He felt dusty all over and his neck ached. He was tired from his dreams. "Where is our sister, Anakawin, little coyote?"

Anakawin, appearing not to hear, skipped around, peered up and down, spun on one foot and never once looked at his brother. He picked his nose. "Something happened to her," he replied.

Aleqwel felt dizzy. He strangled a shout as he grabbed his brother's wrist. "What do you mean something happened! Is she ill? Lost?… Dead?"

"I don't know," answered Anakawin sullenly. "Ask Nene. They won't talk to me about it."

Aleqwel felt crazy, kilamu. It had not been so many days since he had drunk momoy and faces and trees still changed their shape on him at times. Had he come home in time? He tried to force himself into balance with a prayer. The world shuddered into focus. With relief, he noticed that the women by the fire still had their hair unshorn. And their faces were painted red, as usual, not blackened with mourning soot. Ponoya must be alive, then. Aleqwel rose and went to them.

They greeted him warmly, tearfully.

"What has happened to my sister, Nene?" He addressed the old woman first.

His grandmother seemed calm. "She is all right. She is in the roasting pit."

"Is that all? Nothing bad has happened to her? But why is she in the pit at Moon's fullness? She is never in at that time."

Anihwoy broke in. "Yes, son, there is more." Kanit began to cry. Anihwoy continued, "Yesterday afternoon—before you got home—your sister had a dreadful scare. She was in the creek washing her hair."

"Did the scare make her bleed so that she had to go into the pit?" he puzzled. "I don't understand women's things."

"Your sister probably is—or was—pregnant. The scare brought out blood."

"And now?"

"We are waiting, working to stop the weakness."

"It was a bear that frightened her, wasn't it, Mother? A mother bear with two cubs?"

"So you have heard, already?"

"I have seen…. The mother bear did not kill her. Why not?"

Nene spoke again, "She is blessed, like her older brother, with a powerful atishwin."

Anihwoy elaborated, "Her atishwin made her fly from the place of danger. Keti, she is a brave girl! She has never doubted her power. She only trembles when she thinks of losing the baby."

Just then Alow arrived, rubbing the sleep from his eyes. He greeted Aleqwel's family amiably, "My father seems to have left," he said. "My uncle says he has gone back to fish. The yellowtail and bluefin have arrived, he says. I can hardly wait to get back." He stopped abruptly. He looked around the packed dirt camp, as if scanning the beach for a mislaid fishhook. "Where?" he asked.

Aleqwel stood up and took his friend's arm. "Brother, let's go bathe before Sun is high. There are things that you should know."

Aleqwel and Alow left camp for the main village the next day. It was difficult for both of them to leave without seeing Ponoya. Yet Anihwoy, who spent most of her time in the small pit with her daughter giving her herbal drinks and massaging her, told them that she might have to be isolated for a long time—even if the bleeding stopped. Aleqwel felt obliged to return to Mishopshno. Silkiset's tomol required painting, and he carried the newly bought paint.

Alow, when he learned that Ponoya was possibly pregnant—or aborting—set out to climb into the pit to see her. But Aleqwel put an arm on him. He reminded him of the damage that could be done to the health of them all—Ponoya and Alow and their child—by such an act.

"But I have visited enhweq in the pit before," Alow pleaded, "and no. harm was done."

"Are you sure there was no harm? In any case, this situation is entirely different. It's serious, not some bit of play." Aleqwel felt that more and more he was taking the elder's role with his friend. He had never done so before. He wondered if Alow had recently become more childish. Or had something changed in himself?

When it was made clear to Alow that he could not see his enhweq just then, he agreed to go back to the village. He conceded that he might as well be fishing. And the sooner the tomol got painted the sooner he could take it out for a trial.

Once again, the travelers packed up their carrying baskets and put the bands against their foreheads. On a pleasantly warm morning they said "Kiwanan, kiwanan" to their families. They had barely had time to briefly recount their adventures in the interior. Reluctantly, they parted from Chaki. He wished to remain with his wife and daughter while he waited out the prohibitions and prescriptions that his fateful encounter with the nunashish demanded.

"No deer hunting for our friend," thought Aleqwel as he began the hike down to the coast. "How difficult for him, a great hunter. And not even any fishing. No eating of meat. The requirements are hard," he told himself, partly in empathy and partly as a warning. For Chaki, the most difficult proscription might be keeping sexually away from his wife, with whom he had just been joyfully reunited.

As if thinking his friend's thoughts, as they followed the creek, Alow spoke up, "My poor cousin, no intercourse for a long time."

"Nor for you either," said his companion dryly.

"I know," Alow sighed. Then, after a short pause, he added, "But at least I can fish."

They climbed the low hill of Mishopshno in the late afternoon. A few barefoot men were kicking around a hockey ball on the packed-dirt playing field. The grasses near the field and on the hill had paled in their absence and were rustling lightly in the breeze. The day's fog had recently blown out into the channel where it hung like an ash-covered mat, screening the mainland from the lonely islands.

"The women ought to begin beating seeds soon," Alow observed, eyeing the drying flowers around the half-deserted village. He then walked directly to his own home in search of his father, while the paint maker continued on down to the beach.

How good it was, thought Aleqwel, to inhale the ocean smells again—the salt air, the rotting sea kelp, and the damp pine boards of the canoes hidden among the tules near the shore. He spotted the tomol builder squatting beside the nearly completed and inverted tomol.

"Haku, haku!" cried the young man.

Saqtele turned his head without rising. His eyes squinted with what Aleqwel took to be pleasure.

Aleqwel sank down beside the older man, easing off the weight of the carrying basket. "How has it been?" he asked.

"Oh, like that," replied the altomolich.

"Good, good," said Aleqwel. "I've brought the paint."

Saqtele inspected the loaves of red ochre. "They will do," he said. "Listen, I have finished the paddles. I worked hard while you young men were having a vacation." Aleqwel smiled. "Wait. I'll run up and get them."

Aleqwel waited, doing nothing, glad to be home. It was one of those long summer afternoons that seem never to end. The seals basking on the glowing offshore rocks weren't doing anything either. Sand fleas hopped about the paint maker's ankles and legs in random delirium. He scratched his scrotum.

The altomolich returned and triumphantly held up three double-bladed paddles. They were expertly carved, the blades sharp and angular like chipped flint.

Aleqwel examined them and expressed artisan's compliments.

Then, the old man said, "Come, eat with us tonight. And tomorrow we will begin to paint. I hope I've enough pine pitch left. Say, did you notice, the Bang-Wearers have come."

"As I was arriving, I thought I saw smokes above the bluffs. How have they been? Well behaved?"

"You know how they are. They're so happy to get here they practically pay us just to use the water. The first thing they do is run into the ocean with all their gear on. Probably ruin most of it."

"You have to forgive them that," Aleqwel said, leaning back against the unpainted tomol. "The Great Valley must be miserably hot now—and full of fleas and lice—if it's anything like the valley of the Matilha."

"I know, I know. But these Yawelmani are so dull-witted," the tomol builder replied. "Their talk is more like the jabber of scrub jays than human speech. How is it our enhweq seem to find such exotic music in it and abandon their husbands and lovers for these creatures? All day long these people frolic and fish in the surf, entirely satisfied without ever pulling in a big fish. They become hysterical at the idea of going out in a tomol."

"I understand they have a terrible fear of the surf, of drowning."

"Such nonsense," said the altomolich, warming his hands on a beach stone. "They could get a lot of fish if they'd just go out in the kelp. They're so ignorant they can't even distinguish useless tar from good woqo!"

The paint maker smiled. "You have to admit, the Yawelmani manage to get enough money," he said.

"They make up in energy what they lack in brains," conceded Saqtele. "And they do bring aphid sugar. What would life be without something sweet now and then? I guess we do need each other. Are you hungry, nephew? Shall we eat?"

Aleqwel was hungry. He put on the carrying strap once more and followed Saqtele to his house.

That evening Alow sat with his father by the central fire. Mushu was roasting tuna over the coals while Alow did his best to reheat some acorn soup that one of the women from Silkiset's house had brought that morning. When Alow finally got all the hot rocks he had dropped picked up and deposited into the mush basket he sat back on his mat and observed his father. He looked more energetic than his son ever remembered him. He seemed revitalized, like a coal from a dormant fire that someone had begun to blow on. Yet he still wore that vest of sadness over him, as if part of his spirit was longing to be elsewhere.

Mushu seemed genuinely pleased by his son's trading success. He examined the tok and the woven blanket that Alow had brought back. He cried when he heard the news about his nephew Chaki. Why was the flow of power so fickle? he wondered aloud. What error had Chaki made? Or was there someone poisoning him?

Alow could name no enemies.

For a brief moment Mushu looked as if he were beset by a ghost.

Alow decided not to mention Ponoya's trouble. His father would hear of it soon enough.

As they ate their bowls of acorn soup and their platters of roast tuna Mushu told his son about Wenla's plight and for once asked for help. What he emphasized most was Wenla's unhappiness with her husband and her determination to return to the islands.

"Father, I'd like to help. What can I do? Shall I take her with us when we leave for Michumash? I won't be able to keep her a secret from my companions, though. Everyone will soon know. And Shuku will be very angry."

Mushu made a deep-throated sound like a dog beginning a growl. He explained that the wot had already learned of his intention to aid the island woman, and how he had vehemently forbidden it, forbidden him even to see her again. He cursed the ever-present spies who had reported him.

Alow said, "I'm sure you know the Shukuans are trying to poison some of us. Some very close to us. The wot is right. Listen to him! This is a dangerous time."

"What time is not dangerous? The woman will die if we do not help her soon. She is wild and careless. She will do something foolish."

"She already has, I believe," Alow suggested weakly.

Mushu ignored the comment.

"If she goes back to the islands, how will you be able to see her?" Alow asked.

"It doesn't matter," said Mushu dismissively. "She wouldn't stay with me anyway."

"Well, then, if you still want this done for her, what can we do?" concluded Alow matter-of-factly. He had given up on trying to understand his father's motives. He cleared away the dishes and cleaned up. He threw the fish bones into the garbage basket and the scraps to the dog.

His father unfolded his new plan. Alow listened to it. The sky was dark now. The doors of the house were closed and Alow sat on his mat watching the thin twisting smoke from the fire. It ascended the way a ghost must rise, first to the roof of the house, then out the smoke hole and into the boundless night.

Mushu got up and withdrew to his sleeping place. Alow thought his father had begun sleeping better lately and it was not only because of Anihwoy's special herb treatment. Alow, too, stood. He dug some tobacco powder out of his deerskin pouch. He chewed it and chewed it, thinking and thinking as he watched the disappearing thin blue smoke.

Finally, he had to go outside to vomit. In spite of everything, he felt robust in spirit.

The next morning Aleqwel began to paint. He mixed his red pigment with woqo and pine tar so the plank canoe would be tightly sealed as well as beautiful. He and the altomolich worked all day in the quiet of the fog. On their break they shared a lump of aphid sugar.

They painted every day for several days. And then they were done. The tomol was now a pleasing deep red color like the other tomols on the beach. People passing by stopped to admire it. Saqtele had only to decorate the ears with shells and the plank canoe would be completed.

Aleqwel was paid and he felt full of power. This was the most money he had ever earned on his own. He could afford to buy food, tule rafts, bows... even poison. He approached suitable men of the Earth Team and invited them to gamble. Alow was now unavailable since he was a father-to-be, though not yet a husband.

Saqtele pieced the abalone inlay work on the tomol's high curved ears. He carefully laid the pieces in the distinctive shape that belonged only to Mishopshno. At last, after many months, the tomol was shapely and finely finished.

Old Silkiset, the head of the Pelican Family, was brought down to see it. The summer fog had been hard on his bones and he leaned heavily on his grandson Alow. His dim eyes lit up when he saw the tomol. It was, he declared, one of the finest he had ever seen: "Its form does not deviate from that of the tomols of our grandfathers, and in that it may be perfect. It follows exactly the model of its inventor. Congratulations, makers! The tomol is beautiful." It was equal to the last one he had commissioned, the one now used by his grandson Chaki. He added, "Still, we can't know its true worth until we have been in the water with it. They say a tomol is like a house, a house of the sea, but in this way it may be more like a woman." He cast a sly look at his aged wife. "I wish I could take her out myself," he said.

"You have spent more years on the ocean than any of us," Saqtele responded. "You have given much to the people. We cherish your opinion of this tomol as in other things. Thank you. For myself, I am glad I gave up the sea life when I did. I have constant pain in my bones, even while doing carpentry."

"When we enter the waves we offer seeds and money to Swordfish, wot of the Undersea World," old Silkeset replied. "But the biggest offering we make is with our lives, or if we are stronger, in the pain of old age. From this sacrifice the people can be well fed and content and wealthy with goods from across the water."

Without sounding ironic the tomol builder amended, "And from that sacrifice tomol owners are wealthy and respected, leaders on a level with the highest wot."

Silkiset was philosophical. "The balance will always be maintained, and I do not complain."

The speeches over, the old fisherman made arrangements to pay the altomolich in beads now and in fish to be caught in the future. Then he instructed his grandson in the subtleties of testing out the new tomol. Finally, he spoke of the coming trade trip to the islands. He told the young captains to depart soon, immediately following the Bear Ceremony if possible.

Alow felt a rush of energy. There was so much to do. But he made an appearance of sedately escorting his grandfather up the path to his comfortable hillside home.

During Moon's dark time things were quiet in Mishopshno. The early summer fog hung heavily in the mornings. Fishermen from the hill camps had come home to their boats. They took advantage of the smooth waters to paddle to the kelp beds, tie up, and throw out their fishing lines. Or they ventured beyond, into the channel itself, in pursuit of the tunas. By fall they would all be gone, on their way to their winter camps in the Undersea World. For fish and birds had seasonal camps just like people did. By midday the fishermen returned with their planked canoes or tule rafts lying deep in the water, heavy with their catch.

Chaki's father, fisherman and hunter of the Seal Family, and originally from Shalawa, came down from the hills. The man, without his son to help him, had his guild brothers help carry his red tomol into the gentle gray surf. A kinsman paddled with him. Mushu went out, too. He fished with a young nephew, while his son felt the first excitement of lifting a light, never-wetted tomol into the surf.

The tomol Saqtele built needed surprisingly few corrections. It floated, was well balanced in weight, and nicely centered. There were a few leaky places that needed sealing, but what planked canoe was without leaks? The craft was thin and light, yet it felt strong beneath the young fisherman's knees. Alow soon made himself comfortable and believed he could travel more swiftly in it than he ever had in his father's old patched tomol. He had always felt Mushu's timeworn canoe lacked speed, though its noble endurance could not be denied.

For the first time, Alow rode the new tomol in through the light surf and was met by his fellow fishermen. Together, they pulled it ashore. The young man went to report to the tomol builder, who promised to make the adjustments as soon as the boat was dry.

Alow wandered through the village that was empty of young women. He thought of Ponoya in the hills. Had she stopped bleeding? Was she out of the pit? Was he still going to be a father? He wanted to marry the enhweq, he knew it. The matter had decided itself. Yet he was worried. This poison that was being directed at her family—at everyone in it, it seemed—should he expose himself to it? Would he become a target for that unscrupulous bear doctor? And his father's request? He did not want enemies in Shuku or anywhere.

In the streets of the village the old women were drying fish for winter. They split and cleaned them with their cane knives and dried them on racks. The young fisherman felt hopeful, as was his nature, especially when surrounded by the abundance of his trade.

The next day he fished with his father while the repaired canoe was drying.

Finally, the tomol was ready. Alow took it out with his usual Duck Hawk fishing partner. This time the tomol handled perfectly. After that he went out fishing every day in the new tomol. His power was strong and they caught many big fish. One morning Alow even lured his friend, the paint maker, into going fishing with him. Aleqwel was not a proficient angler, but that day the two were able to forget their worries. At noon when they came in they brought the altomolich a good installment of fish toward payment for the craft. Every morning Silkiset leaned by the door of his woven house and watched his grandson navigate.

Alow now believed that the new tomol had been well tested at fishing. It was time to make a short voyage. Mushu had a brother who had married a woman from Qoloq, the village opposite Mishopshno on the other side of the big salt lagoon. Silkiset, who had no nephews, planned the expedition to the islands, so that his three grandsons, Chaki, Alow, and Kulaa, the son of this woman, could make the voyage together. The cousins understood and agreed to take their three tomols in the same expedition.

Alow decided to paddle to Qoloq to visit his cousin and make arrangements for the trading enterprise. Alow's fishing partner and mate for the island voyage was also a Duck Hawk Family cousin of Kulaa and accompanied him on this trial journey to the west end of the lagoon. They had no difficulty in finding an eager young cousin to bail for them.

The ride to Qoloq went smoothly. The sky hovered with the usual gray fog. The ocean swell was weak and the water was warm. Little cousin kept up a steady action with the bailing basket, while Alow, in the stern, and his partner, in the bow, propelled them with their long double-bladed paddles. At the lagoon they passed between the mouth of that estuary and the offshore reef, which was revealed by a line of white foam and a collection of brown sea otters. The men followed the coastline westward, first along the salt marsh, which was part of Qoloq land, then past its little ten-house outpost. At the small village there were tomols, but Alow did not see his cousin. He expected to find him in the main village.

They glided beside white sandy beaches to rocky shores and sandstone cliffs and the mouth of Qoloq's creek. It was not yet noon. The three leaped out of their tomol, and, with the assistance of some fishermen who were unloading their baskets onto the shore, pulled the new tomol high up on the sand. They took the short dusty path up the pale bluff to the village. It sprawled on both sides of a lazy shallow stream. Qoloq, though slightly smaller than Mishopshno, was familiar in layout. Extending back from the ocean crest, its lanes ran nearly straight and were shaded with sycamore and oak trees. Its sinuous creek, which divided the town in half, had a reputation for being bitter.

As they could have guessed, Kulaa was not at his parents' house. "How can you have missed him?" asked his mother. "He's out fishing beyond the kelp with his father and his uncle. They ought to be in soon."

Alow and his paddlemate accepted his aunt's hospitality, though there was only a little cattail seed soup and some mush and fish in carved oak bowls. After eating they sat outside while Alow's aunt spread apart the coils of a cooking basket she was wrapping. It had black triangles around the rim and a strong black pattern. Even they, as men, were able to appreciate and comment on the basket's harmonious composition. A group of children played near the thatched domed house. Several of them were Alow's younger cousins. As soon as he had a bite to eat, the little bailer boy ran off to play with the children.

The young men from Mishopshno and the basket maker exchanged gossip and news—with some significant omissions—until Kulaa and the older men arrived carrying big open-weave baskets brimming with large yellowtail. Kulaa smiled when he saw Alow. "Haku, haku, cousin!" he called out.

Kulaa was more like Alow in temperament than he was like his other cousin, Chaki, or his younger Duck Hawk cousins. For one thing, they were both Earth Team people and used to cooperating on the same side in games. He, too, was unmarried and eager for adventure. Because of this, the two were very fond of each other. And, because they did not see each other every day, they were able to remain good friends. Had it been otherwise they undoubtedly would have soon led each other into disaster or perhaps mutual antagonism.

The young fisherman from Qoloq greeted his cousin, Alow's mate, with casual warmth. The two visitors then lent a hand to their hosts, helping to clean the heavy fish. They used the flint knives from their hair.

As evening came on and Sun slid over the bend of coastline that was Syuhtun, Alow and his cousins discussed their trading trip: when to leave, where to stay, what to take with them, how long they should stay. Kulaa had been collecting trade goods on forays up and down the coast. He felt prepared. Alow, too, said he was ready. He mentioned Chaki's restrictions.

Major issues agreed on, the cousins lapsed into exchanging sea stories. The stories covered their own uncertainties; this was to be Kulaa's, as well as Alow's, first channel voyage as a captain. Alow's mate listened attentively. He was learning what he could. Then he said his bowels were beginning to twist and excused himself to go for a walk down by the wooded creek. This was fortunate for Alow, and he hurried to get everything said before his tomolmate returned. What he had to say was secret. In a low voice he presented Kulaa with his father's request. He phrased it in a general way.

"Cousin, listen closely: I must ask you something, a big favor, something which must be done even before we leave for the islands. It must be done quietly, too. There is an island woman who lives on the mainland. She is terribly homesick and wants to go back to her island village. She will pay to be taken. Do you understand me, cousin?"

"I suppose I do," answered Kulaa. "If she will pay enough, then, surely, we can take her as a passenger. Is that so difficult?"

"No, it can't be done that way. It must be carried out by someone not connected to us, by someone from the west. Her husband in Shuku will be very angry, and it could be big trouble for everyone."

"You mean you want to kidnap the wife of a Shukuan?"

"Yes." Alow held his breath. "But not by you. Not by someone connected to me. By someone farther up the coast."

Kulaa hesitated. "It's risky, risky."

"It is. But, cousin, it is important to our family. Not only for the money. I can't explain more."

"Well, I always try to help out a woman in need. How old is she?"

"About as old as your mother. Do you know anyone who would do it?"

"Well, on my mother's side I have other cousins besides those in your own village, of course. Some are in Shalawa, some in Syuhtun. They are members of the tomol guild, too. I'm sure you know who I mean. Perhaps one of them is going to the islands this summer. Where does the woman come from?"

"From Michumash. I believe one of the smaller villages. I'm sure it doesn't matter where she lands, as long as she is on the other side of the channel from Shuku."

"Hmmm. Well, cousin, I'll tell you what I'll do: I will be going up the coast again soon; I will inquire of my maternal cousins. How much will the woman pay?"

Alow named his father's exorbitant offer.

"Hmmm," sang Kulaa yet again. "They just might do it. And you and I will have no connection with it."

At that instant, Kulaa's mother came out of the house bearing round basket platters of fish and bulbs and greens. Children and dogs immediately appeared from the brush and lanes and garbage heaps. Soon Alow's tomolmate cousin materialized out of the shadows, and they all spoke, once more, of other things.

During the time Alow was testing the seaworthiness of the new vessel and conspiring with his cousin Kulaa in Qoloq, two people who were very important to him returned to Mishopshno.

The first was his cousin and protector, Chaki, who had returned with his wife Pichiquich so that she could harvest ilepesh and hutash seeds in the parklands of the valley of Mishopshno. Chaki seemed to have gained much in strength while in the hills with his family. He must have been scrupulously following all the restrictions that Chnaway, the old Matilha alchuklash, had imposed. Back home again he resisted hunting and fishing and eating delicacies. He minded his little girl and swept in front of their house. He organized the island trading voyage.

While Aleqwel awaited his own family's return he spent time in front of the woodworker's house playing walnut shell dice with the man's attractive daughter. He considered the practice of denial, while Chaki and his family settled back into village life. He was impressed with Chaki's good health. Aleqwel, who sometimes sought power through injunctions and difficult practices, never felt quite able to carry them through just as they should be. He was always prone to self-endangering lapses. Aleqwel concluded that Chaki was a man of great power. No doubt that he had a strong atishwin. He thought of his friend Alow and how he rarely tried to augment his power through disciplines. He was known for occasionally breaking the rules. And when it was necessary for him to follow a prohibition, he did it more for the sake of form than out of any rigorous commitment.

Aleqwel witnessed his family's arrival over the crest of the hill as he sat in front of their home winning at stick dice from the woodworker's son. His heart jumped up inside him when he saw his sister. Ponoya, who had always been thin, looked so light that her dusty feet seemed as if they might take off from the Earth World. She might be released to fly to the Sky World like a duck or a heron. Aleqwel felt tears of pity springing up within him. But he soon saw how well and strong she was, despite her airy demeanor, and he was glad. He cried aloud as he greeted her. But his mother Anihwoy said plainly, "We have come for the seed harvest. Your sister is well, do you see? She is strong. She has been frightened only, not touched. And what's more, she is clean. The life is still growing within her."

Ponoya blushed.

Aleqwel appreciated that his mother knew the truth of these things. He admired his sister's tranquil carriage, in spite of her ordeal. All at once, he remembered the sumac boughs that Alow and he had collected at Koyo for Ponoya to make into seed beaters. And now she was asking him, as if divining his thoughts, "Brother, where is our friend?"

The wot sent his messenger to invite Chaki to his house. The next day he sent the messenger for Aleqwel. The wot wanted information on their backcountry trading trip. Still, the older man surprised Aleqwel slightly when, after greeting him kindly like an uncle and inviting him to sit down, he began by inquiring about his sister.

The wot had already spoken with the alchuklash and knew the outline of what had befallen her: Ponoya had been accosted by bears while bathing but had saved herself by calling on her atishwin. She was perhaps pregnant. The wot wanted to know if Aleqwel could add anything to this report. Were the bears, indeed, only bears or were they guided by some human?

Aleqwel confirmed that as far as he knew his sister had been and still was pregnant. He then confided his Matilha dream, as he would only to a powerful doctor like the wot. Those bears had first appeared as a human woman and her children, he told the wot, and because of that his sister had approached them. They were definitely involved with sorcery. Who they were he could not say for sure. He could not be certain that they were from the bear doctor of Shuku. Yet, who else could have sent them?

Aleqwel believed that his sister's attack gave him the evidence he needed to put a stop to the killer, the Wokoch. But he had no definite sign to show to the world. When they next met, what would the wot say to Shuku's wot? Would the thing be settled? He wondered, but he dared not ask.

The earthly descendant of Eagle, wot of the Sky, now shifted to inquiring about the details of the trading party. He had heard the story from Chaki, but he wanted all versions. What exactly had happened to Chaki in the hills of Matilha? How had he behaved while his soul was gone? Was he kilamu? How had he been treated? What was life like at Koyo and at Matilha? Did there seem to be any evil powers opposing them? How did the crops look? The game? How were his own relatives?

Aleqwel satisfied him. He had nothing to conceal. He also told him about his own work in the caves at the summer solstice.

The wot looked pleased. He flattered Aleqwel by implying that someday he might help his own villagers in a similar way.

Then Aleqwel forced himself to divulge the most difficult piece of his travel news: the account of Alow's attempted poaching on Shuku land. It was evident to him, as he told it, that Chaki had not mentioned the episode—no doubt, so as not to appear to brag about his own role. As he related the incident, Aleqwel emphasized that nothing had actually been taken. However, he could see the dark angry look in the wot's eyes. Maybe he even saw fear. Aleqwel looked away.

For a long moment the wot bent forward, silently, as if planning a speech. Who was it for? For the mighty wot of Shuku? For the troublesome fisherman of Mishopshno? Aleqwel sat uncomfortably on his whalebone stool, waiting. Would the wot lecture him as the organizer of the expedition? Aleqwel wished he could have avoided reporting the event. But the wot needed all information in order to do his work, especially at this ill-poised time. Aleqwel could not help feeling somewhat disloyal to his friend, even if he had only done his duty.

The wot, grand in his full-length sea otter robe, roused himself from his thoughts. He offered Aleqwel some porridge made from the first hutash seeds of the season. Then the wot related what had gone on at Mishopshno while Aleqwel had been away. For an instant, Aleqwel felt as if he was still a small child, observing the wot addressing his father—his late father—while he peered up from the opening between his father's legs. With a shock he realized that, since his confrontation with the bear, even the wot was treating him with heightened respect. Aleqwel felt like laughing. But he did not.

At the summer solstice the wot had visited the house of the Sun and the wot of the Sky World and had been given foresight that increased his confidence. But before Aleqwel could uncover even a vague detail of it, the wot had switched to talk of the Yawelmani nationals who had come over the mountains during Aleqwel's absence. The wot recited the trading that had gone on and still went on—how much aphid sugar Mishopshno traders had bought, how much arrow cane, how many badger and fox furs, how much tobacco, and how many strings of pine nuts. He enumerated what was paid in return and in what amounts: money, fish, woqo, and ornaments. It was a long and detailed account, and Aleqwel tried to follow it.

Finally, the old man commenced his annual complaint, one that must have been his great-uncle's great-uncle's before him. The Yawelmani brought more than their trade goods and their land-use fees. They brought their foreign ways, their strange speech, their crude habits, and their ignorance of the life of the sea. He told Aleqwel a story of a borrowed tule raft torn apart on rocks and of seals butchered without ceremony. He bemoaned the overstepping of limits both at Mishopshno and at Shuku: the foreigners seduced—some said bewitched—people whose allegiances belonged elsewhere. At the Summer Solstice Festival there had nearly been blows. Foul tempers were so hard to avoid—yet they had to be kept in control. "Every year my diplomatic ability is tested to the limit," he said.

The paint maker had heard this story every summer for as long as he could remember. The Bang-Wearers were good for the economy, but their price in disruption was high. Their foreign ways were attractive to some but often led to conflict, even violence. It was always a relief when they left in the fall.

However, no ill had as yet befallen anyone on account of the summer visitors. The wot concluded by saying, "They are not all bad, you know. It is only a few of them who make trouble. They are not people of antap as we are, and their words sound strange. But they understand the things that are important." The wot spoke these last sentences in the secret antap language, emphasizing the bond between the initiate and himself.

Aleqwel responded in such a way as to show that he understood both the wot's words and the wisdom behind them. He realized that his interview was over. Before leaving he asked for news about the wot's wives' kin, especially his friends Halashu and Nacha, who were still in the hill camp.

Instead of going directly home, Aleqwel walked to the crest of the hill, not far from the wot's house, beside the sacred enclosure. Walking, a new idea occurred to him. At Matilha he had heard it said that the people of the Great Valley, the Yawelmani, were the first to have been given the secrets of cave painting. Perhaps Aleqwel could get to know some of these people, find someone to teach him their peculiar language. He could acquire rare knowledge. For the first time in his life, the paint maker considered the Bang-Wearers as potential friends.

From the low summit between the sacred ground and the red-staved cemetery he could see boys playing hockey on the dirt field and men shooting at target practice. Aleqwel had an impulse to join them, but it was overcome by the greater desire to go home to his new pigments, to transform the beautiful loaves into saleable body paint. And perhaps some image-making paint, too. He wanted to ponder the best way of using the money he had earned staining the canoe for the tomol builder.

Before turning away from the view of the valley, Aleqwel scanned the wide sunlit expanse that lay between the village and the high blue mountains. The flowers among the parkland grass had withered in the dryness of summer. Sun was doing his work. Golden poppies had vanished along with the sweet red hutash and the blue of the ilepesh flowers. The beauty of the flowers had been transformed into a greater good. The women in the parkland, their black hair like strokes of charcoal paint on the paler brown skin of the grassland, were bent over their seed-gathering baskets. Some of the women were so distant that they were only black dots. Others were close enough to the village so that he could recognize them and identify the patterns on the small baskets that hung around their necks. He watched the women, young and old, hooking the seed heads and bending them over their baskets. He watched them knock the seeds loose with firm strokes of their curved openwork beaters. The women of his family however were in the family's precinct, which was distant.

For a lingering moment, Aleqwel wondered at the mystery of women. They were so vulnerable and yet so brave. They went out gathering, all alone, far from the safety of the village. Women were physically strong, yet they were subject to periods of fearsome uncleanness, weakness. He considered the possibility of uncovering the secrets of women. He sensed it would be a dangerous enterprise. And yet, it would be an important skill for an alchuklash, one who must heal the souls of both men and women. Perhaps he would talk to Konoyo about it when she returned from the hills. Who could better interpret women's ways than one who had known both sides? Then he caught himself. Women were liable to be destructive illusions. They were like ghosts. His future work would surely be the same as his late father's. He turned back toward the fog-shrouded ocean and his apprenticed trade.

I n a few days, Alow departed from the home of his father's brother. He had gone fishing with Kulaa and his tomalmates and had lain outside and napped. He had enjoyed having food served to him by his aunt. But now it was time to return to his village. Every day he had been thinking of the girl he would marry. And there were things he had to take care of.

After their rapid conversation on the subject of the homesick island woman, Alow and Kulaa had not had another opportunity to speak privately. It was as if the exchange had never taken place. Yet, on the day when Alow and his tomolmates left the village of Qoloq, Alow's farewell speech at the shore contained a hidden meaning.

"Kiwanan," he said. "Come and see us, cousin. In any case, I shall meet with you again soon—shall I not? Before Moon dies we'll meet, didn't we agree? Do you remember your promised mission?"

And Kulaa replied, "Cousin, before long I shall be traveling westward up the coast. My mission will be performed. Kiwanan, kiwanan."

Alow and his traveling companions had an easy trip back to Mishopshno. The beautiful new tomol was thin and well balanced; it handled well. The two men paddled a small distance offshore and dropped a dragnet off the stern. It sank at the end of a long line. Periodically, as they slowly paddled their way home, they pulled up the net and checked it. They arrived at their village with an openwork basket full of big fish.

The kinsmen made a fair division of their little catch and distributed it as was proper. They took some to the altomolich and the rest to their relatives. Alow saved a good fish for his friend, the paint maker, though he was not yet one of his family.

His friend was out in front grinding and blending his pigments and oils. The first thing he said to Alow was, "You have been away a long time."

Alow decided to hear this as a factual statement. He replied, "I did what I had to do."

Aleqwel looked at him closely. "My sister was disappointed to miss you when she arrived."

Alow jumped up like a delighted child. "She is here? Now? Is she well?" And he ran into the darkened domed house. There was no one inside, not even Nene, but the house was filled with women's belongings.

The paint maker said cautiously, "Yes, she appears to be well. She was not injured in her body."

"And her spirit?"

"Yes, it, too, seems strong."

"And," Alow paused, looking down, more uncomfortable than his friend had ever seen him, "and… the blood… did it stop?"

"I understand that it was no great amount."

"Then?"

Aleqwel made a gesture indicating that such things were out of his sphere of knowledge.

Alow demanded to know where Ponoya was.

She was in the parkland with the other women, collecting hutash, Aleqwel told him.

Alow was too impatient to wait for their return from their long daily trek. He ran to the top of the village and looked down on the valley of dry grasses and dark oaks. He spied village women here and there, but Ponoya's family were far away. Like the thunderous breaking of a summer storm, Alow's mind was suddenly drenched with the thought of the bears that came down, even into the low valley.

He ran out to the flat land of the valley, along the trampled trails and through the tall unbent grasses. When he came upon a woman alone he would stop and ask her where Ponoya was. But the women were usually too frightened to reply to this sudden apparition. Anyway, they did not know where she was other than the general direction of the family's field.

Ponoya was not alone. She worked on the other side of the village creek, not far from the salt marsh, and she was with Kanit. Ponoya still had bad times when she felt the world whirling around her, and once she had even fallen. Besides the dizziness she also tired more quickly than usual. She needed to rest and eat more often than Sun did. It was clear to the family that she was still open to attack. So, her aunt insisted on working beside her in the seed field.

The two women bent over the dry hutash flowers and beat showers of shiny black seeds into the small baskets hung around their necks. When the baskets filled up they dumped them into the large burden baskets that they would carry home on their backs. It was uncomfortable, hot work under bright Sun, and the women's red body paint smudged and ran.

But Ponoya had kept herself happy, thinking of her baby and her future husband. He was handsome and would be a tomol owner one day. She walloped her seed beater cheerfully as she recalled the sumac boughs he had brought back for her from his trip over the mountains to Koyo. If only she could have seen him when he returned.

Kanit was glad to be beside her niece. Not only was she concerned for Ponoya's health but she had never been comfortable going out into the fields alone. This season, though, she had developed a fierce dread of being alone in the valley. The aversion, which was so intense as to appear, to others, as something like a longing, was not exclusively of bears. It was as much one of being carried off by a strange man, a coarse Yawelmani perhaps. She had felt it ever since renouncing her admirer at the camp. Kanit was tremendously relieved to be obliged to help Ponoya by never leaving her side.

It was almost dark when the women started for home—not long after Alow had given up his search for them. The flat-bottomed burden baskets were heavy with seeds, and the women, wearing their little epsu caps, bent their heads forward against the carrying straps. They groaned with relief when they set the baskets down. Then they poured the fine black grains from the carrying baskets into the fat storage baskets. The small, dark seeds rushed like poured sand. Everyone was thankful to see the quantity of seeds. With new hutash and ilepesh and the coming of the fish all would be well for a while.

Little Coyote was sent to tell Alow that the women were returned. The boy found him, at last, by the mouth of the creek, watching Sun find his way home.

When Alow and Anakawin arrived they found Aleqwel already roasting his large fish. Ponoya looked worn out. She was streaked with red ochre sweat. Alow felt sorry for her. He determined to leave her alone to her sleep. But, when they had eaten, she insisted on going for a walk with him.

The reunion was good for them both. It was not of the sort that Alow would have hoped for—or even expected—when he went off on his trading expedition. But it was tender and they seemed to understand each other. They shared what they could of their lives when they were apart. Alow strained to grasp what had happened with the bear and for what reason. He tried to turn his thoughts from the problem of why someone might be trying to kill his enhweq. Instead, he made her laugh by telling her how terribly his gambling had gone at Matilha. But she was serious when she asked if he minded her being pregnant.

Why would I mind, thought Alow, as he returned home later that night. It would be good to have a family—a wife, a mother, a child. Wasn't his cousin Chaki happy? Wasn't it the proper thing to do? And he would soon be rich. Ponoya was the best woman in not only Mishopshno and nearby villages but the whole Earth World.

His father was sitting by the fire, not lying in his bed sleeping, when Alow ducked into the low door. The older man looked as if he had been waiting for a long time. Alow had not been home since he got back from Qoloq. His father did not criticize him for it. He just wanted to know what had happened with his brother's son, Kulaa.

Alow had to force himself to recall what had happened. It seemed so long ago. Mushu made him repeat it. In a few days Kulaa would speak to kinsmen in Shalawa or Syuhtun to see if they could abduct Wenla.

"And you will hear his answer before the end of the month?"

"Yes," he confirmed.

"Good," said Mushu, satisfied. "Good." And he climbed up on his bed, pulled up his blanket, and slept for the first time in several nights.

During the days that followed, the men fished and the women went out to gather seeds. Life was abundant. The fog had begun to roll out into the ocean channel even before noon. The days were warm and clear. Alow announced a new plan: he would take the tomol to Syuhtun, testing it on a longer trip and he would trade, too. He would do it soon, when Moon was full, when travel would be most auspicious. His kinsman could use the opportunity to get to know the new tomol better.

On the day before they embarked, as he was heading down the beach, Alow was stopped by the wot. The man wore the concerned look of his paternal office. But otherwise he appeared calm. He told Alow that it was urgent that they talk—in that very spot.

One of the wot's responsibilities was to encourage people to marry. Now, it was Alow who was being encouraged. More accurately, he was being politely ordered to marry the daughter of the late paint maker. The wot held forth in a long and convincing speech enumerating the girl's virtues and extolling Alow's qualifications as a husband. He implied that in spite of Alow's youth and his youthful indiscretions—what could he be referring to, Alow wondered—there still was a spring of potential strength waiting to flow from him. The leader concluded with a flourish, "You must marry the enhweq because she is pregnant. It is not good for a baby to be born without a father."

Alow was moved by the speech. He nearly wept with the emotion the wot had stirred in him. He felt swayed, overcome by the fine flowing words. And then he remembered that he had planned to marry the girl, anyway. "I will marry her after my voyage to Michumash," he told the wot. "Then I will have enough money for a family and, perhaps, even my own tomol."

"It is good that we agree," said the wot. "I am pleased that you see why it is best for us all if people marry when the time is right. You are young for a husband, but you already earn a good living. And you have experience with women."

"Keti! My notorious experience," sighed Alow. "My experience has shown me there is no woman as good as Ponoya. She works hard, stays home, and takes care of her family. And she makes fine baskets. In my recent trip to Matilha," he bragged, "many women were attracted to me, but not one was as desirable as the girl I plan to marry."

"Fine feelings, fine feelings," the wot said approvingly. "May such sentiments remain constant with you. Have you made arrangements yet?"

"Not yet. I prefer to wait until we return from the islands. I shall then ask my aunt to speak to her mother."

"It is well," said the wot, "though sooner might be even better."

It was the thick of summer, warm and blue every day. For many days at a time, the fog would struggle in the morning and then wither and drift to the four winds. But fog was well known for its constancy. It returned, periodically, with its white fingers, damp with grief, urging, ghostlike, "Do not forget me!"

On the day that Alow embarked for Syuhtun the skies had been clear and the air hot and dry for several days. Alow painted his face with charcoal to keep his skin from burning. When he and his kinsman, with the aid of little Anakawin—who had begged to serve as their bailer—launched the bright new tomol, the surf was of a moderate size but smooth as flint.

As planned, they paddled rapidly, in the manner that they would need to follow when they crossed the wide, wide channel to the islands. They flew past Qoloq, on the other side of the salt marsh, almost before they were fully awake. Then they passed the high mariner's hill, with its tall vermillion shrine pole, black feathers pointing the way. Before long they found themselves off the coast of Shalawa village, which sprawled along the shore. Alow wondered if his cousin's cousins had been questioned yet. But it would not be wise for him to stop there at this time.

At Shalawa they had come more than half way to Syuhtun, and before Grandfather Sun had reached his hottest hours the tomol had slipped past the high brown bluffs of Swetete village and the marshes of the big town. The men had made good time, even though the smooth ocean swell had gone against them. Getting to the islands, however, would require endurance of another order.

There were dozens of fishing boats near the kelp beds at Syuhtun. Alow tucked his two-headed paddle into his canoe and let the undulating waves roll them toward the shore. He marveled, as he always did, when he came to the big town. There must have been over a hundred houses. But, especially, he was awed by the number of tomols tied up to the offshore kelp and drawn up under shady sycamores near the beach. He felt proud knowing that many of the boats had been built at Mishopshno. He turned to Anakawin. The inexperienced boy had been bailing constantly throughout their trip. He was limp from the work, but his eyes shone with happiness.

They rode the surf in, hanging back, waiting for the calm spell. They were met by brothers from the tomol guild, who helped them carry the boat to a shady place. Then, on foot and with knees trembling a bit, they skirted the lagoon below the hill of the village. Alow knew exactly where to find the home of his trading partner in the guild.

At the trading uncle's they were offered food. Then they went to meet the wot. He was not so grand a wot as the paqwot, who also resided at Syuhtun, but still he was an important leader. The old man surprised the navigators by speaking in praise of their village and especially of its bard, Piyokol. Now that it was summertime Alow had almost forgotten the man so appreciated by all Mishopshno during winter. Where was Piyokol? Might Alow speak with him? But the old wot could not arrange it. Piyokol had been extended an honor. The wot of great Teqepsh, a town beyond the northern pass, had heard Piyokol speaking at Mikiw. He had invited the storyteller to meet with his own bards. He hoped the Mishopshnoan could impart some of his skills of memory, delivery, and related arts. Alow sighed. All this was fine for Piyokol, whom he loved, but the man was becoming almost like one of his own heroes—more often heard about in story than seen in the flesh.

Syuhtun already possessed nearly everything Mishopshno could offer. Alow and his cousin traded some large cakes of woqo with Alow's partner in return for white clay for his friend the paint maker, who had requested it. He also acquired some dark green beads with special qualities.

The visitors lingered a few days. They rested, ate, and played games. They took Anakawin to the top of the shrine hill, where they scattered new hutash and ilepesh seeds and money. They could see the expanse of the ocean as it stretched between the mainland and the three islands that stretched in a line and were misted over with thin fog.

Grandmother Moon ripened to fullness and beyond. Alow stood in front of his host's comfortable house watching the moonlight reflecting on black water. It spread westward like a trail, inviting him to the Land of the Dead, or perhaps only to Tuqan Island in the west. The fog had crept farther across the channel and hovered just beyond the kelp beds. A succession of warm days, even in midsummer, was often followed by fog. What he experienced as a light mist in Syuhtun would be a gray shroud back home. He thought of his friends and family, but particularly of his father, who waited in solitude for the abduction to be arranged.

In the house, Alow's kinsman was listening intently to the guildsman's sea story. Alow joined them beside the leaping fire. The tale was the old one of the deadly dilemma faced by some earlier navigator who had been caught by night while still at sea. He shuddered as he imagined the peril involved in trying to land a boat in the dark.

That night in Mishopshno the fog did indeed roll in. Mushu sat by his fire looking out the open door at the black wall. He longed to be with Wenla, to let her know the things that were being done for her. He wanted to touch her. He could almost see her, waiting—for him?—near the dark sea cave. But the wot had forbidden him to go there. So he continued to sit and wait. At last, he stretched and went out to smell the damp air from the channel. He could see nothing distinctly. The star crystals hid their night sport behind a screen of fog. Grandmother Moon was concealed, yet her diffused glow lighted the world in an indefinite way.

There were times when Mushu found rest in fog's gray cloak, a kind of concealment of his own nature. But, more often, it brought him ghosts. Ghosts who would not go west, as they ought.

There was a woman ghost—the perfect woman. So much better than himself. This superior woman must have come to him from a quirk of power. And gone the same way. And against all wish, he saw another ghost, a child. It was a young girl child, barely old enough to walk. The mother carried her in her arms. Mushu shut his eyes against the fog. He could not bear the waiting. If he kept still, the ghosts would take him. Precipitously, he set off for the path along the bluffs. He soon realized that his way would not be easy, for a band of Yawelmani were camped nearby. He saw their shadows among the shrubs and even in the stately shrine pole. And the ghosts pursued him.

Now he began to doubt that Wenla would be at the cave. Even she might be afraid of alerting the Yawelmani. Then, he saw the ghost woman, ahead of him, on the edge of the cliff. Suddenly, she slipped and twisted her ankle. She lost her balance. Weighted more heavily on one side by the child, she crumpled. Then she plunged into the void. The fog engulfed them both. Mushu heard a startling cry. The shapes of two blue herons flew high over his head, winging westward to their home.

Surprisingly, Wenla was still waiting, huddled, by the entrance to the cave. Mushu, who had run outdoors without his robe, embraced her in the soft fur of her otter cape. They clung to one another. The feelings had held strong.

Later, when he had regained his awareness, Mushu asked himself what would have happened to the woman if he had not come. What would the Yawelmani have done if they had found her? Had she been waiting there every night? His concern made him ask her these questions, but she gave no answer to them. She behaved as if she were dumb, as if she had lost the understanding even of her own language. She stared into the foggy nothingness.

Softly, Mushu told her what he had come to tell her. He told her how he, himself, was unable to help her but that his kinsmen were working on a plan for her safe removal from Shuku—and the mainland—forever. He told her it should be arranged before Moon's death. Until then, he promised to meet her every night.

Wenla looked at him and held him in the shelter of their little dark cave, so recently scrubbed by the tide. She cried.

Mushu wished he could have cried, too.

She told him now in strangely broken words how she had grown so desperate that she had again pleaded with her husband to take her to Syuhtun to visit the only friend she had. The woman was from her home village. He had always refused her this kindness before, but this time, for some reason, he had readily agreed. They would leave, immediately, the next morning. It was for that reason that she had come, to make a farewell. She might be gone a long time.

"But when you return?" he asked.

Her own look was questioning.

"Or perhaps you—or we—could arrange it from Syuhtun?"

"Perhaps," her voice brightened.

They made love once more. Afterward, they lay damply together, clasped in silence. After a time, unmarked by the observance of the Sky People, they stirred, knowing by their complacency that it was time to separate, to go home.

Mushu watched Wenla's small figure, wrapped so as to give her the appearance of some sea animal, as it disappeared into the wet night. He realized she could not be a good woman, for she seemed to have almost no dedication at all to her home or her duties. Instead, she roamed freely, anywhere she pleased. He knew that but could not keep from admiring the wildness and tenacity of her female being.

The day before he was to leave Syuhtun, Alow heard another tale of disaster at sea. This mishap, however, had occurred not in the distant past but very recently. The scene of the unfortunate event was the waters off Shalawa village. The way he understood the story—which came from a Syuhtun fisherman who claimed to have heard it from his cousin in Shalawa, who saw it—was that two men, wealthy leaders, and a female passenger were traveling west toward Swetete when something caused their canoe to capsize. The men were able to right the tomol and pull themselves aboard, but the woman could not swim and sank below the water leaving behind no trace. The men—one was quite old—were so overcome with grief that they immediately turned their craft around and hurried back in the direction from which they had come.

When Alow heard this tale from the fisherman on the beach, he felt uneasy, sick in the pit of his stomach. Tales of drowning always made him ill. And this one, in particular, unsettled him.

"Who were these voyagers?" Alow asked.

The fisherman replied, "My cousin did not know their names or faces. But the men were surely very wealthy, for they wore bearskin capes. The woman looked much younger. The emblem on the tomol's ears was one from a southern village. That's all I know."

When Alow was reunited with his father and giving an account of his stay at Syuhtun, he saved the tomolman's rumor for last. The news had a powerful effect. As if surprised by poison shot from an achana's invisible weapon, Mushu clutched his stomach and fell. Alow had to run for Anihwoy to revive him.

With her powerful herbs she worked to bring him around. For a curing doctor, her abilities were strong. She gave him seawater as a purge. And he lived. Yet he did not recover. Anihwoy built his fire up high and prepared him healthy meals of thin acorn gruel with rabbit meat, but he did not eat. His soul was roaming.

Alow realized that what he had dimly feared when he heard the report in Syuhtun could be true. His father had recognized the drowned woman as Wenla. But how could he have been so certain it was her? There were many wealthy wots from the coast.

Mushu lay by the hot fire, neither awake nor asleep. Sometimes he muttered fiercely. Anihwoy, who had been called away from the seed fields, stayed by him most of the day. Each morning she cleansed his insides with seawater. She prepared his herbs. She warmed his abdomen with hot huya slabs. In the evening she returned home, and weary Kanit and Ponoya would come to replace her. The sick man's son wandered in and out, not wanting to go out to fish, yet feeling helpless in the house. In the evenings he sat talking quietly with the young women.

This continued for several days. Grandmother Moon waned in her health-bringing strength. Anihwoy began to doubt her ability to cure the man. She went to consult the alchuklash.

Alow knew that he would have to pay his return visit to his cousin at Qoloq. It would have been more convenient to send a messenger, but Alow's message still remained secret. He was not yet convinced of the futility of his effort, and he carried on with the plan out of respect for his father. Alow felt certain that if Kulaa had traveled to Shalawa and Syuhtun he would have heard the news of a drowning. Perhaps he would have learned the name of the drowned woman's village, or even what she had been called.

On the night before his excursion to Qoloq, Alow sat up as usual with his father after the young women had gone home. Typically, his father would sleep or thrash with nightmares. It frightened his son to see him so. He appreciated the danger of the situation. But, this night, Mushu did something unexpected and entirely different. He sat up and talked to his son in a thoroughly coherent manner. Alow felt bitten with a chill, despite the hot blaze of the hearth.

The old man made a simple statement: "I have killed her."

To be absolutely certain of his father's meaning, Alow asked, "Who have you killed… the island woman?"

The old man persisted in condemning himself. "If I had acted sooner, she would be alive, free. I have lacked courage."

But his son argued, "You have done what your wot advised you. Besides, you could not have known this event would happen. These things occur as they must, on their own accord. Even now, you cannot be certain who the drowned woman was."

Mushu disagreed, "I know. I knew. She told me. She was going to Syuhtun—that very day—and her husband was taking her. And now he has murdered her. There is no doubt of it: he capsized the canoe and pushed her down. Everyone knows men do such things. Why else would he have left so quickly? And it is my fault. Wasn't it because of me that her husband was enraged? Otherwise, wouldn't he have just let her go?"

Alow listened carefully to the monologue, though he never felt it was addressed to him. He answered: "As you, Father, have told me, Wenla lived a wanton life. Any husband might have despised her. Even you could not have prevented her, if she was determined, from going to Syuhtun. She probably suspected what he would do—and didn't care. She was an unquiet, desperate woman."

Mushu neither agreed nor disagreed. When his last speech came out he sounded spent. "If I had acted sooner..." were his final words of self-reproach. His body shone with a thin skin of sweat. After a struggle, he threw off his blanket, the way a lizard shakes off his dead skin. He began pacing around the small house, circling the fire. Then he flung open the doors on the foggy night. Again, he saw the herons flying west.

It was late when the agitated man quieted down. Alow fell on his own bed and bathed himself in sleep.

In the early gray morning, Alow looked down on his father as he lay by the fire: Mushu was motionless as if asleep. But his eyes were open, staring. Alow whispered, but there was no reply. He was very frightened.

Anihwoy was already on her way. Calmly, she observed and felt her patient. She listened for his breath. She tried to reassure the son that there was life in the man. However, his condition was clearly grave. The alchuklash should begin working on him as soon as Grandfather Sun went to sleep. She, herself, could not say whether Mushu had been poisoned or attacked by nunashish or ghosts or whether he suffered from something else. That was for the specialist.

Alow told her it was imperative that he go to Qoloq that morning, but that he would make every effort to return by nightfall. He wished he could tell this woman, who was like a mother to him—he would never be able to shun her as a mother-in-law—what he had learned from his father the previous night. But he decided it would be wiser to keep silent. He believed his father would not wish to have his doings known.

This time, Alow ran to Qoloq. He crossed the creek and skirted the high edge of the salt marsh. Reeds and cattails loomed above him. The fat brown catkins had already begun to turn white and blow their down to the winds. Alow sang his dream song as he ran, keeping a steady pace for the full distance. He passed women on the trail, heading to the far-off parkland with their baskets and seed beaters. He crossed the creeks of his own territory and arrived, at last, at the bitter creek of Qoloq.

There was no one at his uncle's house. He ran down to the beach. The mouth of the creek cut a little gorge between bluffs, and Alow would have to follow the trail down the side of the cliff. From the top he could dimly see his cousin and several other fishermen unloading their day's catch from their boats. The breeze blowing on his face, as he stood atop the cliff, made Alow aware, for the first time, of the tears streaming down his face. He waited a moment, observing the activity on the narrow beach and the patterns swirling in the deep-blue ocean, while the tears dried in the wind. The breeze was tearing the fog apart, and blue patches were opening up in the sky. Alow scanned the sea for the movements of fish. Then, he went down the path to his cousin.

Kulaa had to finish unloading the tomol. Alow watched him divide the catch with his mate. He automatically noted, with interest and a little envy, that they'd brought in a big load of yellowtail. Kulaa and Alow carried the openwork basket, dripping, up the steep trail to his house. When, at last, they were alone, Kulaa spoke up with energetic enthusiasm, "I have done my mission, cousin. I did it as you asked. I have just come from my cousins at Shalawa."

Alow looked glum. "You can forget it; it is too late. Listen, my father, your father's brother, is very ill. His spirit is drifting."

Kulaa's expression changed. He looked as if he might cry. "We had better find my parents."

With resignation, Alow agreed. But before they had gone far, Kulaa brightened a little. "I want you to know… this favor you asked me, it can be arranged. The tomol will be leaving in a few days."

"No, I am afraid it is too late. The woman is dead," said Alow, deeply sadly.

"Woi! No, I think you are wrong, cousin," contradicted Kulaa. He stopped among the dry flowers and grass. "When I arrived at Shalawa I heard a story that I cannot believe is coincidence. Not long before I arrived at the village, one of the fishermen there found a woman lying on the kelp bed. She was wet as a seal, but crying with a human cry. He rescued her and brought her ashore. She said she was from the islands, yet she cannot have floated over—unless she is one of the First People. Do you think that possible, cousin? She, herself, insists she has no place on the mainland and that she only wants to return to her true home. Beyond that she is vague."

"When did she appear at Shalawa?"

Kulaa named the day.

It was the same day as the drowning. "Did you hear anything of a drowning that same day, cousin?"

"Yes, I did. Another man witnessed it. It was a tomol from a southern village, he says. But now the villagers believe that Seal Woman is the woman who appeared to drown. They want to help her. They suspect she may be a mermaid."

"What did you do?" Alow asked excitedly.

"I spoke to my cousin. He is leaving for the islands with the birth Moon—not long from now. I told him I would check to see if Seal Woman is the woman to be taken. I told him the fee. He is very agreeable."

Alow's face now shone like Sun after a month of fog. He wanted to run back to Mishopshno that instant, to fly if he could. He looked down at the atishwin on his chest. It was a bird, but one more noted for diving than flying. He felt certain now that this found woman had to be Wenla. He said, "Did you learn what the woman is called?"

"She gave no name. She seems content to accept what the villagers call her—Seal Woman."

Alow gave his instructions, trying to control his dancing feelings. "Tell your cousin to take the woman. We will see that he is fully paid. You, too, my kinsman, will get your share as soon as he returns. But, remember, it must all be done quietly, quietly."

It was already sunset by the time Alow dashed into Mishopshno. The first evening of Mushu's healing was about to begin. Alow was relieved to find his father's condition had not worsened, but neither had it improved. The fisherman had remained mute and staring all day and eaten nothing. Alow wished he could speak with him to give him his inspiring news. But the man was laid out by the fire. The alchuklash and his interpreter had already arrived. The old doctor, painted and robed, was shaking his clamshell rattles. His eyes were closed in concentration.

Alow felt a little ashamed to have not arrived sooner. He was Mushu's closest relative. But he was relieved to see that Mushu's sister and husband and their son and even his old uncle were there. Anihwoy and her children had come to watch, too. His father must have felt their presence.

The old alchuklash worked. As he shook his rattles he sang his dream song. He called on all his atishwins. He shouted. Then he sang the strange, low song of his special condition. His assistant interpreted in a loud clear voice so the patient and his family might hear. Alow observed the session carefully. He was fighting fatigue and the dreaminess of the rattles. Still, with a howling and beating of wings, he saw the atishwins appear. He saw the alchuklash bend over his father's mouth, his chest, his abdomen. He saw the patient covered with breath and tobacco smoke and egret down. Alow believed his father would live.

When the spectators finally left, Alow examined his father closely. His appearance was little different than when Alow had left for Qoloq in the morning. Perhaps his features were more relaxed, accepting. The young man was aware that it usually took two, sometimes many, evenings with the alchuklash before all the diagnoses could be made. And then, the damaging powers would have to be individually neutralized. It was rigorous work for the doctor. The young man knew that cures rarely took place in a day.

Nevertheless, when Alow spoke to his mute father the next morning, ignoring his continued stillness, he saw some movement. When he told him all that he learned and done in Qoloq, something happened. The spark of Mushu's soul seemed to ignite. Before noon, the tormented fisherman was beginning to eat and to speak a few words. His life seemed to have rekindled. Even the old alchuklash looked a little startled when he came to visit his patient late that morning. And he had to agree with his niece Anihwoy that the man was making a remarkable recovery.

CHAPTER 8

MONTH WHEN LEAVES SHED AND EVERYTHING BLOWS AWAY

hesiq momoy an smahatam

The ksen who appeared beside the central fire of the Shuku ceremonial enclosure this morning was Yawelmani. His hair was long and flowing and his bangs were singed. His body was daubed with red and black paint to resemble Coyote. He had the feathers of the ksen, yet he was only a caricature of a real messenger.

The crowd, gathered in the western curve of the ceremonial ground, recognized him at once: he was Bear's announcer, his clown. And though the ksen shouted in the peculiar Yawelmani tongue, the people knew, from their long experience, the meaning of his words: "Clear the way! Clear the way! Bear is coming!"

Three musicians with turtle-shell rattles began to shake out the rhythm. The mock ksen made a grand speech in his own language. The people understood that he was extolling the power of Bear, heralding his forthcoming dance and advising them to remain calm and quiet lest they be devoured.

There, in the warmth of Sun, the people shuddered. They had assembled, at the time of newborn Moon of the beginning of Bear's month of power, to arm themselves against attack. They gathered just as they had done in Shuku and Mishopshno and throughout the antap lands in the season of Rattlesnake's ascendance. They hoped to be healed against the fierce Bear, who would soon come down from the hills to ravenously consume seeds and berries and fruits, which he despised having to share with the people.

The last thing the enhweq Ponoya desired was to see a bear impersonator, but when the village of Shuku invited the Mishopshnoans to their bear ceremony, Ponoya's family, along with the rest of the village, could not turn it down. And perhaps it truly would protect them. The family sat trembling, fascinated. Nearby huddled the Yawelmani summer visitors and neighboring villagers from Mishim and Chwayik to Shuku's southeast. Encircling the visitors was a ring, like a waist string, of the greater number of host Shukuans and their trading guests from across the channel, who had nothing to fear from bears in their insular villages.

And now, the one who had been foreseen, the Big One, appeared at the seaward entrance. With a downy skirt and plumed headband that resembled a quail's topknot or a whale's foamy breath, he was garbed as a dancer, but the double bear paws hung around his neck proclaimed him a real bear doctor, a Yawelmani bear doctor.

The crowd remained silent, as they had been warned to do. No one wanted to attract Bear's attention. The powerful achana's dance exhibited all the wild gestures of the grizzly. He danced near Ponoya. She felt herself growing faint from the foul smell of his breath. Aunt Kanit reached out for her. Then, the animal stamped the ground. He moved away. He stood in front of another woman. He rocked from side to side. Sometimes he peered over his shoulder as if he, himself, were frightened. But he continued to dance. He groaned. He grunted. And while he danced, the musicians with the turtle-shell rattles followed him, singing. In their foreign words they described his movements and magnified his might.

To keep his mind calm, Aleqwel, who sat beside his mother, listened hard to the words of the Yawelmani song. He had made the acquaintance of some of the visitors and had found them willing to teach him their words and their ways.

Others in the throng sat or stood in respectful silence, though inwardly they might be quaking or wishing to hurl insults at the Bear dancer. They dared not show their loathing, because the power of the Bear was too great.

Now Bear paused and began to tear the dirt apart with his fat feet, and then he began to lunge wildly. He caused the ground to shake. Small children cried. Had the snakes that hold up the Earth World begun to weary of their chore? Fortunately, there were grandmothers present to whisper reassuringly. But Bear was as bad as an earthquake. In his hands he carried feathered wands. He extended them to the four directions, demonstrating the vast extent of his ferocious majesty. His dancing encompassed the entire arc of sacred ground between the people and the central fire. Finally, with a last fearsome flourish of the wands, he made his exit. He followed the path of the Milky Way over the blue morning mountains.

The people let out a collective sigh. They had come face to face with the terrible beast and were still alive. They began to murmur relieved comments to one another. The Yawelmani are certainly the finest bear dancers, the most exquisite, the most authentic, they said. They breathed their approval deeply. Their appreciation of superior dancing, voiced like this, had a soothing effect.

All morning there were ceremonial songs, bear songs. The Bear Family from Mishopshno presented their song to the accompaniment of split-cane rattles. Others sang songs from the southern villages. Even the islanders had a bear song, a solo, tremulous and moving. Although their far-distant home sheltered no bears, they remembered him from their oldest history, and their hearts knew him still. The morning ceremonies concluded with high emotion.

Caught among the crowd mumbling in diverse tongues like a heterogeneous flock of birds, Aleqwel waited his turn to squeeze through the southern exit of the ceremonial enclosure. It would be a long, difficult day. Shuku's bear doctor—whom he thought of only as the Wokoch or the intruder—had been absent from the morning ceremonies. He had neither danced nor appeared as an observer. No doubt he would appear at the evening ceremony when Grandmother Moon would be reborn.

Coming out into the everyday world and smelling the women's cooking, Aleqwel supposed he would have to partake of the festive meal. Any breach of polite manners could be disastrous. Still, his sister looked queasy and he had no stomach for food after the vivid memories aroused by the morning's dancing. Though the dance was supposed to provide protection he had not been reassured at all. Anakawin looked uncomfortable and restless. He did not envy his wot. Clearly, the event had a wider purpose than neighborly sociability—to demonstrate the wondrous power of Shuku's own bear doctor. There had been so many misunderstandings between the villages recently.

The Coyote Family from Mishopshno made an appearance of enjoying the Shuku women's culinary hospitality. But as soon as they could they withdrew to the beach, as far away from bears as possible. They lay on the sand, as lethargic as if they had spent the morning taking tobacco. Shuku beach was lined with red tomols that bore the glittering emblems of several countries. Eventually, they were discovered by their friend Alow. His presence seemed to have a beneficial effect on the women and even on wild-eyed little Anakawin. Then Alow and Ponoya and the boy went for a walk on the beach toward Mishopshno.

The southern clouds were in a hurry to fill the sky. Aleqwel roused himself and dove into the warm summer waves, swimming through schools of small tickling fish out toward Shuku's famous offshore rock that was said to be the home of a mysterious fish called Piyok. He was not a strong enough swimmer to reach it. He floated on his back for a time. With only the fish and gulls for company he imagined the liquid life of the sea otter. At last, not eagerly, he flopped over onto his stomach and swam for the shore. The village on a bluff above the place where the coastline turned hovered in a smoky blue haze. Aleqwel let the surf carry him in to the pale gray sand.

He emerged from the ocean, naked, with his beard dripping and his hair dressing ruined, but he felt fresh. Walking eastward where the sand ended in high rutted hills, he saw a man and a woman walking down the beach. Aleqwel recognized them at once. The man's crystal hairpin glittering from Sun and the woman's gracious stride gave them away—the wot's nephew and the caretaker's assistant. Both had returned from their gathering camps in the last few days, and Aleqwel had not had the opportunity to speak privately with either of them. Halashu, especially, has been almost constantly in the company of his family.

For no special reason, Aleqwel suddenly felt as he stood dripping wet in the summer sunlight in this hostile land that he was in the middle of a prayer. He felt balanced in the center of all opposites. And, where he had been tense with the situation he was in and anticipating worse to come, and raging with the desire to extinguish his father's poisoner, now he felt only cleansed and centered and empty inside. He was half content, half depleted. He went back to his mother and aunt and grandmother and slept on the sand until the renewal of the ceremonies with the dusk of reborn Moon.

Tilinawit, wot of Mishopshno, headed for the great house of Shuluwish, his host. He hoped some definite conclusion could be reached with Shuku over their differences. The power position of Mishopshno was perpetually weak in relation to her southeastern neighbor. They were like common people beside wealthy wots. Tilinawit accepted such inequality as the natural order of things. Still, even the weak and the strong experience fluctuations in their power and at the summer solstice he had been granted a vision of the future in keeping with his hopes.

As the lean, long-robed man climbed the hill of Shuku, he lifted his eyes to his adversary and host's great reed dwelling and to the fat houselike granaries that stood close by the screened walls of the sanctuary. He looked up at the slopes of the high hill behind the town that were the southeastern visual wall of Mishopshno. Above and beyond the hill were steep blue-green mountains. In the distance rose sacred Tsismuhu, the high peak revered in both villages. Clouds billowed up behind the high mountains like mounds of sea foam ready to fall. Tilinawit was not a weather achana and he could not be certain whether the thunderheads would pass innocently over the Great Valley beyond the mountains or darken and descend, drenching the evening celebrants in a summer storm. He was relieved that his people were with him at the ceremony grounds and not out roaming in the hills or exposed at sea. He noticed down toward the creek an enhweq of his common people. She was just slipping among the pale shady sycamores. She was being followed closely by a young man whose long black hair flowed loosely over his shoulders. Things never change, he thought.

But at once his conclusion was contradicted by the appearance of Mushu, the prosperous fisherman. This man was, to the wot, the embodiment of change itself. He was like the southern direction, from whence arises all that is unsteady and impermanent. Though they had grown up at the same time, Tilinawit had never understood Mushu, and it disconcerted him. He prided himself on knowing his people. Ever since the man's ill-fated sea voyage, when he washed ashore on the islands, his moods had been peculiar. He brought his wife back to Mishopshno, which perhaps he should not have done. But he seemed divinely happy. Then, after his wife and baby daughter's death, he began to flounder in diminished power, no doubt beset with ghosts. And then one day, this lonely man began engaging in dangerous, provocative activities. And when he, Tilinawit, had learned of them and warned him of the possible consequences of such behavior, the man, who had recently been so active, slipped into severe illness. The alchuklash had to be called. Inexplicably, though, Mushu's health was suddenly restored with little doctoring, and he became whole again. There were no happenings without causes, yet Tilinawit was not able to understand this man's. He prayed that Mushu was following his injunction; spies had brought him no information of his doings. It would be dreadful if Mishopshno were caught off balance in this sort of affair. There had been, as yet, no complaints from his host about abducted woman.

Walking casually down the lanes of Shuku village, the man the wot could not understand was caught up in his own emotion. He was exultant like a man on Solstice Night who has watered the ground for future abundance. He noticed his venerable wot making his way to the top of the hill, but he thought little of the leader's concerns. Wandering past the thatched domes of the common people and now, higher on the hill, by those of the rich, Mushu burned to learn which was the residence of the wealthy wot who had tried to drown Wenla off the coast of Shalawa.

There could not be so many older men wealthy enough to wear bearskin cloaks. And yet, as he looked around him, it seemed to Mushu that nearly everyone dressed in just such luxurious attire. He could only gaze and guess. Most of all, now that he was in alien territory and vulnerable, he wondered if the man he sought knew about him, recognized him, spied on his every move and gesture. So what if he were poisoned, he thought. His whole life seemed to be touched by poison. But only he and a few others knew that the woman, once called Wenla, the unquiet, and now known as Crying Seal, had already embarked on her journey home.

Shuluwish's cavernous dwelling was chaotic inside. The greater part of the feasting was over. And now, in midafternoon, his wives and daughters, sisters and nieces, grandmothers and guests were going in and out. They were washing, scrubbing, and putting away enormous huya cooking pots, huge sandstone grinding bowls, basket dishes and wooden bowls, platters, ladles, and spoons. Some women were still grinding seeds and cooking.

Shuluwish greeted Tilinawit politely. He was almost convivial. He thanked him for sending his nephew, Halashu, to visit in spring. His words slid out like liquid tar on the water. The leaders paid each other compliments and inquired about the health of their respective relatives. Indicating the crowded doorway the host led his guest out to talk in the nearly deserted ceremonial ground next door. As heads of the Eagle Family and achanas of the Sun, both men were the sanctuary's highest officials. They spoke in the antap language. Shuluwish asked Tilinawit how things were going with the Yawelmani. Tilinawit answered that they went as always—not easily, yet for the most part peacefully. Then, he confided to the wot some events of the summer solstice, which had nearly led to violence. He realized that by so doing he was exposing, to a potential enemy, a weakness of his own village. But he believed he needed to make an offering of trust if they were to negotiate. Shuluwish accepted the news complacently. He remarked that their situation was similar in regard to the foreigners. Tilinawit took the occasion to compliment his host on the smooth flow of the gathering. He commended the variety and beauty of the dances, the quantity and quality of the food. Shuluwish responded with a knowing glance toward his neighbor: "We have many wealthy wots here; there will always be plenty of food. You only have to know how to get them to pay their share. Isn't that right?"

Tilinawit agreed. "It helps to have a highly skilled poisoner." Was he being too explicit? he wondered. But he held fast. "Tell me, my colleague, we have not yet seen your bear doctor. Will he perform for us this year? Or has he grown intolerable to you?"

"Oh, he will come tonight. I want you to see for yourself his great power, why we need him, why you might value his service, too. Do you know, last year we had no bear fatalities? Not one. It is remarkable. He is indispensable to us." The leader enunciated the last words carefully.

Tilinawit spoke out bravely, "And, yet, if he goes against your exhortations, defies his own wot, roams about on his own… ."

"What are you suggesting?" Shuluwish retorted sharply, casting his eagle eye as best he could upon the elder and taller man. "We have done what was agreed. The doctor has been watched. He does not leave Shuku land. We have found no hint of poisoning, none. Such insinuations can be very dangerous."

"I mean to insinuate nothing," said Tilinawit plainly. Then he related, as clearly as possible, the details of the attack on the late paint maker's daughter.

Shuluwish, taken wholly by surprise by this account, managed to bluster out a denial. "We had a spy on the achana at that time. He reported nothing, nothing of the sort!"

Tilinawit continued in a calm voice, though his heart beat impatiently, "No doubt, the doctor is assisted by a spirit helper. Not only his many atishwins, but by some kind of woman, one of his own creation. Don't deny it; we have seen her. Perhaps you have seen her, too, flying at night, like some great condor in the sky."

"A holhol!"

"Yes, exactly, a holhol, redheaded and far-seeing."

"A nunashish," the wot of Shuku spluttered, this time at a total loss for words.

Tilinawit felt as if he were bailing water out of an ill-sealed tomol. "The woman may fly where the achana dares not go," he said.

Shuluwish took the offensive. "Be careful when you mention trespassing. We have proof. Not only have your women crossed over again," and he emphasized the word by repeating it, "again to harvest our hutash and ilepesh, but now I've learned that one of your men has entered our territory to hunt wildcats. We have witnesses. What reply have you for that?" Shuluwish was flushing darkly, making himself look angry and, therefore, foolish. His glittering topknot shook.

Tilinawit knew this was a crucial moment. Shuluwish needed no further pretext for war, if he wanted a war. Carefully, the wot of Mishopshno outlined Alow's case. He admitted the trespassing, but he denied any intention to poach or hunt. "Frankly, the man's bowels were twisting, as any man's might, and he stepped off the trail, as is only polite."

With this unpretentious explanation, Shuluwish shrank away like a dog retreating to gnaw at a bone. Tilinawit, too, thought it best to withdraw into silence. Again, talk seemed to have accomplished little. Yet, an unsteady peace apparently was preserved.

Tilinawit remained standing, tall, lean, impassive. Actually, he was frightened and dreading the coming evening. The sanctuary seemed to hold the Wokoch's unchecked ferocity in store. As a wot, he had perhaps failed by not acting in time: now bear season was coming into full fruition. Anyone could easily be killed. His only pale hope was that the bear doctor's duties would now take up so much of his energy that he would not have time to spend tearing through the hills, terrifying people on his own. Before taking leave from the wot of Shuku in the ceremonial ground, Tilinawit made a final plea. "Please, my kinsman, do not remove your spies. Watch the achana. Watch for an assistant, too."

And Shuluwish, suddenly conciliatory after his shameful loss of composure, replied, "Certainly, certainly, my kinsman, we will do that until we are entirely satisfied. Should what you say be true, some action would be called for." He spoke these last words as if that circumstance's coming to pass was as likely as a return to the world of the First People. Still, the wot of Mishopshno knew it had been a significant concession, an admission, at least, of his neighbor's desire for peace. Then, the son of Eagle saluted his host and brother in the sacred enclosure and stepped out into the diverse and disintegrating world of time.

Grandfather Sun, having followed his thread to the edge of the Earth World, now began his invisible eastward journey home. But his torch must have shed sparks behind him, for twilight's gray clouds glowed like the ochre-colored rims of heaped leaves at autumn burning.

The participants joining the evening Bear Ceremony jostled their way through the narrow southern entrance of the windbreak. As they found their places beneath the dim and burning sunset sky, they heard the sound of distant rumbling. Some believed the thunder arose from the sea while others imagined that it descended from the mountains, though there were more than a few who were convinced they were hearing the fierce footsteps of Bear himself as he approached the sacred circle.

The master of ceremonies, Shuluwish, gave a grim speech suitable to the occasion. And the music began once more. As the western sky deepened in color from ashen embers to dark charcoal, the celebrants relied more and more on the central fire to illumine their sacred arena. The flames glowed like a memory of red-orange Sun departing at the end of his journey as they flicked shadows across the faces of the feathered, painted musicians.

The far-off rumbling that had persevered throughout the early ceremony like a rhythmic accompaniment now increased in volume. Some found the sound ominous. Young Anakawin, huddled with his family in the humid night, heard in it the warning growls of a great protective dog, though he well knew that dogs had lived too long with people to have any supernatural power. Still, his ears roared with the low throaty grumble, and he clutched in his fist a pretty rock of quartzite he had found on the beach that afternoon. He held it like an atishwin.

Shuku's ksen appeared in the dancing firelight. Like the ksen of the Yawelmani he had come to announce the arrival of Bear himself. But, where the Yawelmani messenger had come as a clown, jesting and grandiose, this ksen flung an awesome cloak of awe over the arena. The Bear was coming: they had better watch out. Not one word. Not one sound. He is dangerous. He will bite. He will eat you alive. Be careful. Hide. Show your respect.

As if to emphasize these injunctions, thunder crashed like some nunashish arriving from the Lower World. A haphap, perhaps, was stumbling around the mountainsides. People started. Aleqwel moved closer to his sister's side. Little Anakawin trembled in dreaded anticipation. He felt the touch of the first drops of summer rain as the Bear Doctor arrived. His appearance terrified: the long-clawed paws, the dark paint, the feathered wands. How pointed his nose looked.

The singers began to sing, accompanying themselves with turtle-shell rattles. Thunder rumbled. The Bear danced. He moved gracefully, beautifully, like the dancer of the Yawelmani. Every move, every gesture was true. The audience showed its appreciation.

Then the Bear began to circle the leaping fire. And in the flames a transformation took place. The gentle rain abruptly ceased. The dancer's face began to sink inward, while his beady eyes grew rounder and his snout more pointed. The grizzly head began to wag from side to side. The creature that emerged from the firelight, hunched on all fours, was no longer a man. It was not a dancer but a splayed-foot beast that began to charge the crowd. There were gasps and stifled screams. The music never faltered while the Bear lunged through the mass of spectators.

Some held their ground. Others died for a moment. Small children yowled.

When the monster charged the guests from Mishopshno, Aleqwel instinctively placed himself in front of his sister. She must be spared the leer of those shining dim-sighted eyes. Despite metamorphosis, they were the same eyes that had stared at her not so long ago while summoning by name the ghost of her dead father. Aleqwel was thankful that his father—so far— remained with the dead at Shimilaqsha. He felt a tremendous impulse to leap upon the Bear with his knife and kill him right there. But a small brand of radiance from the daylight world reminded him of the sacredness of the present setting and the ceremony's importance to the people. Even now, the bear dancer was performing his duty, just as he ought. "Soon," Aleqwel promised his clenched body.

No one seemed to notice when the thunder subsided, for the ground still shook with Bear's heavy tramping. Aleqwel, who had been thinking foremost of his sister, had momentarily forgotten the rest of his family. When the terrible Bear had dared to approach them, Anakawin had gasped and gagged, tasting the creature's foul breath. Now, as the beast began his retreat, Anakawin began to recover himself. Half in rage, half in blind defense, the boy hurled his lovely pale stone at the monster. It struck the giant hard on the brow, stopping him where he stood. The boy exhaled relief and vindication. But only for an instant. Almost at once, Bear recovered and found him out. Before the child had time to feel the energy of fear, the ferocious killer was upon him. He was torn away from his family. He felt crushing teeth in his shoulder. There was the rip of flesh, the coming of blood.

The crowd watched in horror as Grizzly Bear reeled and exalted around the ring. This boy was evidently vulnerable to bears. But now they expected he would be healed, protected for the season, as one might be at the Rattlesnake Ceremony. This type of thing sometimes happened, and Bear would soon spit up the flesh.

As expected, a Shuku curing doctor appeared with a basket of seawater to purge the boy's tender flesh from the animal. Anihwoy ran to her boy's side. Her rage at this particular bear achana was without limit. As a curer she had participated in such a ceremony before. But this one had dared to touch her youngest child.

Bear swallowed the seawater in great gulps and danced wildly on. People now began to throw rocks at him. But he ignored them as would a flesh-sated animal. Others threw gifts of shell money at Anakawin, whose shoulder was still bleeding despite his mother's ministrations. Bear would not give up the flesh. He never vomited at all. This part of the ceremony was not going as it should have. Anyone observing the master of ceremonies would have noticed that he looked more nauseated than the monster.

Somehow the wot recovered his balance, and the people, theirs as well. After all, things did not always go as they should. Overall, the performance was tremendous. The boy bore up well. Every direction had its own influence. Sometimes it is time for the South, with its changes, its summer storms, its swells and winds, to predominate.

When the weary participants made their way out of the ceremonial ground, they found the soil beneath their feet barely touched with moisture. The clouds had vanished from the summer sky. On that mild warm night, they were greeted by the reassuring horns of newborn Moon as she was taking her leave. It was as if the storm had never happened.

T he visitors spent the night in the foreign settlement, though, to some at least, the dangers of the empty darkness seemed less than those lying in the heart of their host village. The women of the Coyote Family applied themselves with frantic determination to the care of their boy. Anihwoy did her best work. She cauterized the bite with burning mugwort and concocted an astringent poultice out of oak bark. Anakawin's wound was not large, but the women were sick with fear for him: Bear had not given up the boy's flesh. And the young boy, though open-eyed and apparently awake, moved stiffly as if in a dream. He was able to hear and answer questions, but no one could truly assess the condition of his spirit.

Even though he was too young to have drunk momoy brew, Anakawin now was experiencing himself as a person neither asleep nor awake but just waking up. He felt as if he were waking for the first time out of the world of momoy, of which he had often heard, into the life of the people. He felt himself shedding old memories like dry leaves that begin to blow away after the seed harvest. At the same time he was beginning to remember. He recovered all those things that had been lost to him for a long, long time. Throughout the process he could only vaguely recognize his family. In their voices he heard a song growing stronger.

Much as Aleqwel wished to keep vigil beside his immobilized brother, there was little he could do. He had a late-night appointment. He decided it would be best to keep it.

The camp of the Yawelmani, near the fresh water ponds on the bluffs midway between Shuku and Mishopshno, was only a half hour walk from where Aleqwel's family was encamped on the western bank of Shuku's creek. Darkness had grown thick after frail newborn Moon went to her sleeping place, but with the aid of his torch, the young paint maker found his way along the cliff trail to the small area occupied by the summer visitors. He trod carefully, if confidently, for on his back he carried a basketful of money.

The thunderstorm had rolled northward, leaving the expansive sky above him vacant and black as the pupil of an eye. The eye was flecked with the radiance of star crystals shining through. There was no trace of treacherous fog to lure or deceive him over the precipice of the bluffs. Aleqwel could identify the visitors' settlement ahead by the low glowing of fires. Most people would be asleep already, in spite of the excitement of the evening's ceremony. He walked toward the camp. He felt secure knowing he had an honest engagement there. After several visits in recent days, he was well acquainted with several of the bang-wearing men and could speak the rudiments of their peculiar tongue. No longer was he afraid of their spies and sentries.

Coming near, he saw the water of a pond, shrunken now by summer's drought, congealed, impervious, and black as a spring of malak. Around it the paint maker could see the outlines of cattails and basket reeds, tall thick cane and cottonwood trees. He imagined the ducks and mud hens and all the other animals sleeping in the protective warmth of Shup's natural thatching.

He slipped into the memory of his first visit to the Bang-Wearers. He had approached one of the men fishing on the beach. The man's appearance had repelled him slightly. His dress was crude, his beads oversized and roughly finished; his grooming seemed careless. That time Aleqwel had been afraid. But the man had proven helpful, if not skilled in graceful manners. The shore fisherman had even been able to express himself in bits and pieces of the language of Aleqwel's own people.

After Aleqwel had been taken to meet the Yawelmani paint maker, things became easier for him. The man understood, at once, his desire to purchase paint, and when he had indicated his interest in learning to speak their difficult tongue, he began to treat the local resident almost like a long-time trading uncle.

So Aleqwel had returned to their camp. The Yawelmani paint maker taught him their language by talking about his own people and how they made their life in the Great Valley. Because rattlesnakes were still above ground the man dared not share the timeless history of his people, but he told simple stories. Aleqwel came to have an appreciation for many of their ways. Their paint maker, who was not an achana, invited their alchuklash— who was called differently in Yawelmani—to meet with Aleqwel. Aleqwel began to feel comfortable. The doctor openly admitted to being ignorant of the ways of antap, though he seemed to grasp the fundamentals. He seemed, also, to like and admire Aleqwel. He asked provocative questions. He did speak openly and enthusiastically about painting on rocks and declared that his people had been the first to practice it.

Every time Aleqwel left the camp of the Yawelmani he felt filled, the way he did after a feast. He also felt as though he had been given a gift—though he knew he had paid quite adequately for the few cakes of red paint that he brought away. The emotion he experienced was more that of the satisfaction of a longing. It was one he had had ever since he saw the Mohave traveler at Matilha. The yearning was unrequited at that time. Aleqwel was in his thoughts. What had the Yawelmani achana told him? It was something important. It was about their atishwins. What did they call them? Anetwal? Something like that. It was about their spirit protectors. Some of their pigment makers specialized in painting, and by doing so...

What was that sound? Aleqwel heard a rustling and saw movement in the high cane as the trail passed close beside a smallish pond. He paused, senses alert. Had he startled sleeping birds? He saw a hunching in the dry bent leaves, then a rising form.

Aleqwel scarcely had time to experience panic. Almost immediately the growing shape showed itself in the uncertain light of his torch to be that of a man's contoured back. Its nakedness was draped in long flowing hair. Though he had been returned abruptly from his own thoughts, Aleqwel understood at once what he was seeing. He was not surprised to soon distinguish another form in the feeble light. This person was smaller and wrapped round with a rabbit fur blanket. Aleqwel suspected that beneath her fur, the enhweq was completely naked.

Aleqwel remained still, but they must have seen him. The two scrambled off into more distant brush. The pair never looked back and spoke no words, but the swishing of the cane as they stole away broke the quiet spell of the warm summer night. Ducks, mud hens, and herons flew up on noisy wings. Aleqwel was certain that he recognized the girl—though she was only one of the common people. He could not remember what she was called. He was not angry with her. But there was something he didn't like about her behavior. He wondered, surprising himself, if he was envious. It was only this summer, for the first time, that he had come to appreciate the attraction that might exist between a civilized villager and one of these simple foreigners. He appreciated it and even felt its power. But he knew the action of the two young people was, itself, dangerous. It went against the interests of the people. Wouldn't that near-naked enhweq already have a local suitor? He, himself—no matter what his inclinations—would, of course, never consider...

He resumed his forward steps. It was not far to the quiet campground. He did not care to think about the powerful attractive force of women—or even of strangers. But his earlier thoughts had fled from him as surely as the lovers had fled at the faint patter of his approach. It was only as he neared the sleeping place of his new trading partner—a man he called "kinsman," though not yet "friend"—that he recalled the purpose of his visit and the terrible events of the evening.

The man was awake as promised. He crouched beside a dull fire with a fur blanket flung over his shoulders. When he saw Aleqwel in the distance he was able to identify him by his elaborate waterfall of hair. He sprang to his feet and ran to meet him. He motioned his visitor to a rocky place away from the other sleepers. Together, they swiftly built a comforting fire. They began negotiations.

A few days before the Bear Ceremony, Aleqwel had come to a decision. His luck at gambling, which had been so miraculous, had begun to drop off. He still possessed, for someone as relatively impoverished as himself, a considerable amount of money. He decided to invest a portion of this money in more paint, paint that he could send with his friends to the islands to sell for him. Money to make more money. The visitors from the Great Valley had brought a quantity of red ochre to trade. It had not yet all been sold. Aleqwel had examined some loaves and found they were as good as he had been told they would be. He and his "uncle" arranged a private trade. He had come laden with a large basket that bounced with shell money. The transaction went as quickly as formal trading manners would allow.

The two men sat back in the rocky clearing in the night. The little fire they had built of driftwood played modestly. Their faces were half concealed; to each other they appeared content. But for Aleqwel something had changed since they had made their appointment to trade. Now, in the dancing smoke, he saw a vision of his younger brother. The boy's shoulder was torn. It was festering with the poisonous saliva of the Bear. He saw Anakawin's startled eyes, disbelieving. At the time of his parting, as strongly as at this very moment, he had been convinced that the women alone would not be able to cure the boy. He, the older brother, as much as an uncle or father, had the responsibility for the boy's care and very survival. Thoughts, memories of the Bear began to crash down on him. He felt as those drowning might feel.

Aleqwel, like everyone else, had heard that the Yawelmani traded in poison, ayip. It was not the sort of substance he had ever purchased before. Ayip was for powerful doctors, for sorcerers. He felt certain that his father had never procured any. And now the late paint maker's heir, suddenly knowing what he must do, could not conjure the words for asking for it. What words could he utter that would avoid offense?

The blue smoky wraith floating between him and his partner began to pull apart and dissolve in the late evening breeze. Aleqwel saw his brother—with a bewildered look—fading from his gaze. Fading perhaps forever. He found the words. Yawelmani words. His own native words. Ayip. Poison. His mouth was dry.

The Yawelmani paint seller did not appear at all offended—or even bewildered—by the request.

"Ayip. Of course. Yes, we have ayip. What kind do you want? What color? You don't know? But what do you want it for? There are many kinds of ayip."

Aleqwel flushed in the dark. How should he know what color ayip? Did the man think he bought the stuff every day? Were the Yawelmani so free with poison themselves? "I don't know," he said. "Just the usual kind. The strong kind."

"For killing, you mean?"

Aleqwel could not answer.

The man continued, "You know it depends on how the ayip is burnt, how it's prepared, whether it comes out black or brown or some other color. One type will bring back a faltering love and another will bring success in competitions. But black will kill. It's expensive, of course."

Aleqwel was swamped with confusion. He had never even seen ayip. Its use was the greatest mystery to him. He knew it was small, no larger than the ball of a person's finger. He knew it could be put on arrow points or rubbed on the skin or hidden in the house. It was made of ground rattlesnake and something else. Was it seashells? His great-uncle had some kind he used for healing. That was all he knew of it.

The Yawelmani rambled on, as if with pleasure, describing the proper application of poison both on the body and apart from it. It was clearly a subject about which he had much knowledge. Aleqwel listened without hearing. These people, without any doubt, possessed all kinds of ayip. Aleqwel, in his daze, wondered if he had really been planning to buy some. After all, how could he use it if the wot did not give permission? Still, he yearned to have it, to have it at hand when the time came. For the time must surely come—and soon. But the young man could not summon the strength to say, "I want some of the black kind, the kind that kills." Instead, he chose a color at random and then, having quickly paid for it, he stored the little ball of influence carefully in his pouch. He offered his profuse thanks. He lighted a new torch and began the trek back to his family. Relieved of his money, he was burdened only with a basketful of paint cakes, regret for his own weakness, and a small pouchful of dark substance that was created to return a man's wandering love.

I chantik, why is it that we have not been able to meet like this," complained the wot's nephew, as he leaned up against the warm yielding sand dune. He faced a sparkling blue-green sea and closed his eyes to better hear the rhythmic breaking of the light summer surf.

"Iwu, you know very well the reason. While you were out hunting on the middle creek and seeing to your father's duties, I was helping at our own family place."

"And you know very well, I don't mean then. I mean since we have returned." He opened his eyes to the quartz-like sparkle of Sun on the waves. Plank canoes and tule rafts rocked in Mishopshno's offshore kelp beds. The islands rose out of the south as outlines softened by the thin fog, which lay in midchannel.

"You would have found me, ichantik, if you had looked in the fields. Though I have my special work, I am not exempt from the hutash harvest."

"I looked for you but could not find you."

"Your uncle was taking up most of your time, I imagine. You have seen more of him than of me during these long months."

"That is true. That is true," said Halashu with a hint of irritation. He felt as if he were beginning to lose the trail. But Sun shone so warmly and soothingly that he had not the will to regain the disappearing path.

Konoyo witnessed his discomfort. She smiled. She ought not to torment him. "I have missed you, too, ichantik. Surely you know that." She straightened her long thick hair. She gave a little expression of annoyance. Her face paint was beginning to run a little. She broke her own spell by adding darkly, "But you do realize, don't you, we must become accustomed to separation? Can we expect to be always happy, like babies?"

Halashu now began to grow so gloomy that his friend regretted speaking her last words, though they did express the difficult truth in her heart. Why did men—even powerful ones—insist on deceiving themselves?

Halashu sat up. He stared hard at his toes. They sifted slowly through the gray sand.

For a moment, Konoyo, in fascination, watched the dribbling sand. Then she reminded her friend, "Don't you remember our day together at Shuku? Before the Bear Ceremony? It was not so long ago."

Halashu remembered. How could he forget? It had begun for him as a day of long-awaited consolation. But Shuku. His skin prickled.   "I never feel I have privacy at Shuku. Do you? I can't feel safe there. And now, after what happened."

"Yes, yes, that was horrible," she agreed. "It still is. I'm sorry I mentioned the place. But I thought our being there together made things better, more endurable."

Halashu looked at his beloved, "Of course it does. Can't you see? That is what I've been trying all afternoon to tell you."

The young woman, special by birth, and esteemed among women, did see. Naturally, she saw. She saw and had always seen, even when they were children growing up together, before she had left her family and gone to live with the caretaker of the dead. Konoyo was a person of great ability: she understood men and women; she could handle ghosts; and she knew the way to the Land of the Dead—and back. But one thing she could not easily see was the future, much less arrange it. She guided her friend back to the painful place, to Shuku. "What is going to happen now? Will the bear doctor be poisoned?" She uttered the dreadful word softly.

Halashu rolled onto his left side and leaned up on his elbow. He drew strength from the contemplation of his friend's strong beauty, streaked by Sun's warmth. "Shuku's wot does not consider the biting attack provocative behavior."

"Woi!" Konoyo exclaimed. "Can they get away with anything at all, then?"

"It is because the attack took place in the ceremonial enclosure; the bear achana was performing a sacred act. Their wot asserts such doings are commonplace."

"Yes, yes. We know they are," Konoyo cried impatiently. "Because of such acts, people who are vulnerable can be cured, protected. But Bear always gives up the flesh." She lowered her brows in indignation. She despised the abuse of anything sacred. It was a violation of trust with their grandparents' grandparents.

"What you say is very true," said Halashu, "but Shuluwish insists this act is sacred, because it was without human volition."

"Woi!" she cried again. "The boy's family live and wait in anguish. I have seen them. They are afraid to let the boy out of the house. They watch for signs of coming death. They listen for owls and coyotes at night. That family has suffered more than is endurable. If they are not allowed to defend themselves, I'm afraid they may all perish and the poison will spread to us all."

"I am aware of these things. So is my uncle. Since the bears have become active, I hear he no longer sleeps well. I, too, am more easily thrown off-balance. Can you have missed seeing it, iwu?"

The elegant woman laid a hand on his forearm.

Halashu felt himself returning to the center as if he had said a prayer. "All we have is the word of their wot that the Wokoch is being observed carefully, and that if he attempts any purposeful harm…"

"Are you certain the family will not act on its own? The way they all feel?"

"The paint maker is my friend. I trust him, more than almost anyone I know. He is quiet natured."

"Everyone has his weakness. Look at our great Chaki, even he…"

"Yes, yes."

Konoyo could see she was only distressing her lover. So she turned her conversation away. She told stories from her days in the eastern gathering camp. She omitted from her tales all mention of bear tracks seen or even of rattlesnakes found beside the creek. Instead, she amused him with accounts of the interactions between individuals, the humor founded on the deep knowledge they both had of each villager's character. Konoyo portrayed herself in these stories as a gullible old maid, somewhat like Coyote in always being surprised or fooled, the victim of her own fallibility.

Halashu laughed—or he tried to laugh. But the sound came out broken, hollow as the barking of a seal. He did his best to reciprocate with anecdotes of his own encampment. He did not wish his own unhappiness to spread to his treasured friend. He described how he had bumblingly performed his duties in the beautiful springtime campground of the middle hills, how colored flowers and green grasses blinded him to certain unfortunate goings-on. Then, recloaking himself in pride, he told of the game animals he had brought down with his new sinew-backed bow.

Konoyo listened, taking pleasure in the sound of his sweet voice. His melodious voice harmonized with the monotonous onward rush of the ocean waves and the occasional screeching of scavenging gulls. The voice was bred for diplomacy, for convincing, for pleasing. She had faith the people would always love him; he could charm their ears, even if his policies failed.

Halashu grew serious again. Once more, he told Konoyo how much he missed, in camp, having someone who understood him with whom he could talk. He admitted how much he had dreaded, every day, hearing the news of a raid on Mishopshno by their enemy. Or of a killing in the eastern camp. Or of the failure of his negotiations. The only thing that kept his heart beating was the knowledge that, in the height of summer, he would be reunited with his friend. Halashu reached out toward the young woman.

Konoyo held him and spoke, not teasingly, but kindly. She felt his muscles soften. She asked Halashu if he had not found comfort or guidance from his uncle or father.

"Yes," sighed Halashu, enjoying his physical contentment. "Yes, my uncle is a fine teacher and my father is as well and a good friend. But the wot is always correct; he knows everything. With him I experience all my imperfections, my ineptitude. It's not like when I'm with you. With you I discover my strength, find wisdom, if ever I do."

Konoyo began to cry sedately. The tears made her paint smudge even worse, but she seemed not to notice. In any case, the perspiration of their bodies had already ruined her decoration. Now she sat herself up, trying to avoid any impression of pulling away. "I wish I could be always so for you," she said.

Halashu sat up, too. He glanced out over the ocean. A string of brown pelicans was cruising by looking down into the depths for fish. Sun was high and bright. Because he did not even want to think it, it took courage for Halashu to finally say, "My uncle—and my mother, who I thought loved me—have decided that I must marry as soon as they can find someone suitable. I told them I was too young, but they say things go differently in the Eagle Family than with others."

Konoyo replied with a certain downcast relief. "Oh, ichantik, haven't you always known this is how your life must go? You must make an alliance. It will be best for you, if you can face it. It will be best for both of us."

"In what way can it be good—for either one of us?"

Konoyo explained firmly, as if she had considered the matter beforehand. "A marriage—a new bond—is always good for the people. Don't you yourself counsel that? It's especially good if it makes friends of strangers. What you must do for yourself is seek out a wife of your own before you are handed one by your family."

"Do you suggest I marry you?" The wot's nephew sounded incredulous.

The woman who had been born a man, sensing the pain behind his surprise, tried to not feel personally hurt.

He added more gently, "You know I do not have free choice."

"Of course not," she answered. She was unable to keep a little sadness from her voice. "What I mean is you have some choice in it. Why not pick a wife you find congenial, one who is able to respect your ways, your needs?

Do you understand? If you fail to do this—if you just give up and leave it to your mother—your happiness—ours—could be destroyed."

Halashu looked at Konoyo in amazement. She was so wise. Why had he never thought of such a simple resolution before? He would try it. Though, perhaps, the plan would not work. Nevertheless, in spite of his deep worries about the peace of the community, he felt lighter than he had in a long time.

He felt hot, too, he suddenly noticed. And sticky with Konoyo's red paint. He looked to the cool channel. Masses of dead sardines were heaped on the shore. Their odor was strong. Farther out, a tremendous pelican was plummeting from the sky. His mighty beak fell first, like an arrow, aimed at the body of an invisible prey that swam in ignorant serenity somewhere beneath the sea. Halashu bent toward his friend and encouraged her to rise. The beach, in their remote area, was nearly deserted of people. "I know you can swim," he said to her. "Your belongings will be safe here." He reached over to help her with her skirt.

Konoyo looked eagerly at the refreshing ocean water. Then she turned to her revitalized companion.

Kulaa arrived at Mishopshno to join his cousins for the island trip. There were goings on at the shore where fishermen mingled with commoners hauling in dip nets full of slippery sardines. The small fish were piled in large mounds on the sand. The fishermen, their uncles and fathers, brothers of the tomol guild, momentarily left their easy but rewarding work and came out to meet him and his crew. They helped lift his heavily laden canoe out of the water.

As always when he came to his grandfather's village, Kulaa admired the hills of hardened woqo fronting the beach. He peered into bubbling pools of the liquid tar. He appreciated the universal utility of woqo and woqo glue. As he stopped by the black tar spring, he made a prayer to all directions and scattered new hutash seeds on the sandy soil.

His cousins, who could make their fortunes trading in the black adhesive, greeting him warmly. Alow was especially friendly. They shared a secret bond beyond kinship. In addition to the profits from the trading trip Kulaa could soon expect a reward of beads for his part in arranging Seal Woman's departure. He wondered where the money would come from but did not ask.

Alow and Chaki began to poke around in his tomol, guessing the contents of his neatly secured baskets, boxes, and bundles. Great storage baskets were stowed in bow and stern, and his cousins rightly supposed that they were filled with many epsu of seeds. There were large bundles, well wrapped against the elements, that looked like they contained cured deer hides and fox and rabbit blankets.

"Is that badger fur I see in there?" Alow called out.

"Yes, it is. Don't you remember, cousin, we discussed everything?"

"Just making sure. Did you bring money?"

"Some. But I plan to bring more home—straight from the mint," he boasted.

"I've always wanted to see that place where our money is made," Chaki said. "The villagers there don't even fish. They do nothing but shape and drill and finish shells."

"We will see it!" cried Kulaa, then turned to Alow: "And you, cousin, are you bringing a lot of money?"

"Se, se. Only what you see me wearing. I can't gamble anyway, so what use would I make of it? Better to use the space for pine nut necklaces."

"Where are those cotton blankets you told me about?"

Chaki broke in politely, "Let's go eat first. Afterward, you can help us load. You'll see everything then."

Kulaa left his bailer boy beside the tomol and led his tomolmate to Chaki and Pichiquich's house that they shared with his father. Pichiquich provided a good meal with lots of variety. "Enjoy it!" she urged. "On the islands you will only get seal meat and swordfish, an unbalanced diet."

"Where did you learn island cooking?" asked Chaki, amused.

"I have heard about it. And it's true, isn't it, father?"

Chaki's father gave a noncommittal cough and turned his attention to his granddaughter. "See how well she walks, and she makes words, too."

Kulaa was delighted with the baby. "Come to your uncle," he said and opened wide his arms. "Do you remember me, my little limpet?"

Kelele smiled with her one tooth and lurched into his lap. She reached up for his nose ornament, pulled his head down and dismantled a cane earplug. The tobacco powder came spilling out. Everyone laughed.

After eating, the men walked back to the tomols. Kulaa brought some food for his bailer and encouraged him to go play. Alow and his Duck Hawk cousins and Chaki and his brother-in-law began carrying goods from their houses to the beached canoes. First they laid out protective matting, and then, working together, they heaved in the large baskets and boxes. They were carrying a great many seeds to the islands. Then they stuffed in bundles of hides and furs. Alow and Chaki displayed for their cousin the fine light blankets they had bought from the Mohave.

Every so often one or the other of the traders would look out at the ocean to check if the fair mild weather was holding and that the waves were still rolling in low. A strong swell would show up long before any sign of bad weather manifested in the sky. Rainstorms were not typical of summer, but the calmest spells could be abruptly broken by a brief southern storm. Though they were very astute they would depend on the word from the weather doctor before setting out.

The rest of the afternoon was spent in carrying, loading, and securing their cargo. The weather remained warm and pleasant, the surf placid. The tomols filled up with chunks of woqo and pine resin, the raw materials for sealant, and with boxes of tobacco and bird feathers as well as the loaves of red and white and black paint. Last, the men stowed baskets of fresh spring water for the voyage.

As Grandfather Sun slipped farther and farther toward the horizon, in the direction of Syuhtun's smoky bay, their industry became tinged with an unspoken reluctance. It was as if the excitement they felt surrounding their departure was turning into its opposite. Without knowing it they were clinging to home and certainty.

Alow rarely made effort to know his feelings, but he found himself wondering if home truly was more secure than abroad. He had always believed it, yet the sea was not always dangerous. While he paddled uneventfully across the channel, his whole village could be burned to the ground or destroyed by arrogant Shuku. Still, a great energy propelled him forward.

"Alow! Alow! Haku!"

"Don't shout, little brother; it is very rude. And you must not call out people's names, either!" Anakawin's older sister admonished him.

But Ponoya's brother paid no attention as he ran to Alow's side. He peeked into the neatly packed tomol and exclaimed, "Keti, how I wish I were going with you!"

"I wish you were, too," responded Alow. He thought it was wrong to keep Anakawin captive in the village, away from men's doings. He knew the boy's family was terrified of bears, but the boy's wound was healing well. And there were no bears at sea or on the islands. "Someday you will come with me and be my bailer," Alow consoled him. "But first you must get more experience. You must build your endurance like my young cousin here," he said, indicating his bailer, a boy little older than Anakawin.

"And Chaki, does he not need a bailer?" the boy implored.

Chaki answered gently, "We promised my nephew he could go with his father and me." Chaki maintained a special fondness for his eldest nephew.

By now, Ponoya had joined her little brother on the sand beside the tomols. Without preface, she presented captain Alow with a set of newly woven kneeling pads. She said this way the two of them would remain close throughout the journey.

"When I am at sea, anyway," smiled Alow, accepting the gift from his future wife. When Alow looked at Ponoya, she seemed very thin and vulnerable. She showed no evidence of the baby within. But he knew that she was strong to have survived at all. She endured the suffering of her whole family. He stepped closer to her side. He told her that whatever happened he would come to see her that night.

At that moment old Silkiset arrived, carried on the strong arms of his grandsons. And limping just behind him was his old, gray-haired wife, quietly complaining about the pain in her remaining molar.

The two old people, in their feeble way, made an elaborate inspection of the tomols. The old man told his grand-nephews and grandsons how pleased he was with the tomols and their cargo. He proclaimed his faith in the strength and courage of their youth. But he warned them of their deficiency in experience: only one of the captains, Chaki, had commanded an island-bound tomol before. He advised Alow and Kulaa to listen carefully to their older cousin and to do whatever he said. He advised Chaki, because of his relative inexperience, to pay attention to the advice of the others. And he warned them all to observe the world: the ocean swells, the hidden rocks, the winds and the clouds and the tides. He admonished them to pray earnestly at sea and on land, to scatter lots of feathers and seeds, and to heed all omens and weather doctors. If they did everything properly, the expedition would bring greater wealth to their family and to all the people.

From the eloquence of his speech, his grandsons concluded that their benefactor was making his farewell here and would probably not come down to the shore early next morning when they embarked. But that night Kulaa and his companions slept in Silkiset's large and well-furnished house. He took pleasure in accommodating his relatives.

Alow kept his word to Ponoya. Everyone in her house was weeping, presumably at his impending departure. But, through it all, the young woman kept a kind of serenity, based on her child-bearing condition and her certainty that with Alow's successful return she would begin a new life as his wife.

When they went outside together he told her, "Please look after my father while I am away. You know how he is, how he can be." Her future husband itched, as he often did after the evening meal. He wished he could ask her to delouse him; it was one of his greatest pleasures. But, because of her condition, he dared not let her touch him. This was tremendously frustrating but he resisted.

That night was Chaki's last with his family. His household was a cheerful one; everyone anticipated his trading success. They looked forward to having more money. Chaki and Pichiquich could build a larger house, and leave this one for his father. If some family members, including his mother-in-law, felt uncertain about Chaki's future on account of his terrible experience with the nunashish in the mountains, they did not show it. Chaki had followed his requirements exactly; he was still following them. His family trusted in his great endurance.

That night, when everyone had gone home and his father was asleep, Chaki climbed into his wife's bed to be near her. She was asleep and dreaming. Half waking, Pichiquich responded to him. It had been a long time but fit right in her dream. It would be another long separation. He pressed hard against her. She rolled over, automatically spreading apart for his entrance.

Before falling entirely asleep Pichiquich murmured to her husband, "Tell me again, when will you return?"

And he repeated softly, "If all goes well, I will be home in little more than a month, in time for the Hutash Festival."

"And by then your prohibitions will have expired, isn't that right?" She drifted off, peacefully, unaware of what she, and he, had done.

The nine seafarers rose early, in the dark, after half-grown Moon had already gone to bed. The three stars of Bear Constellation still dominated the sky. At low tide, the surf rolled tamely in to the shore and the ocean lay smooth and flat as a sitting mat. The shadowy tomols wore an eager look as they waited, fully loaded, ears tied up for strength. The voyagers' way was lighted only by their own torches and the glowing crystals of the high-roofed sky. They loaded their day's food and water, their cloaks, and their atishwins. At the rim of the sea the travelers and their achanas said their prayers. They threw duck hawk down on the water. Then, with the aid of their guild brothers, in an exultant rush, they launched the planked canoes through the murky waves.

At first, they could barely make out the outlines of one another's canoes. But they knew, as well as they knew the trails and borders of their own land, the safe route from shore to the deep water. On their left-hand side lay a shallow rocky reef. Their eyes, adjusting quickly to the dark, picked out the forms of seals and sea lions sleeping on the reef. They swept wide of the rocks as they swung out to sea. The seafarers found a beginning rhythm and glided southeastward through the fertile kelp beds of Shuku. They maneuvered to avoid the mysterious rock of the Piyok fish.

Chaki, their chief captain, felt relieved that their early departure meant they avoided the Shuku boatmen who fished off the coast in early morning. Rising had been more difficult than usual for him. His will to leave had begun to crumble like an ocean bluff in persistent rain. He depended on his wife more than anyone knew. But now, paddle in hand, he felt no regrets. The initial stiffness he always felt when beginning to paddle was beginning to work out of him. He felt his rhythm come as he pulled, first on his left side, then on his right. It began to quicken and smooth out. As they flew past Shuku village, he dared not call to the other boats and awaken possible enemies. But he looked behind and found the others closer than expected. He wished he could shout to warn his cousins not to throw away energy they might need later on. But he had to trust in their own experience.

The coming of dawn brightened their faces. It found them still slipping down the southeastern coast. They had sped past Mishim and Chwayik villages and had come nearly as far as Shisholop, the big town in the lands to the south. Their hope was strong as they paddled in the direction of Sun's appearance and new beginnings.

Shisholop was a wonder with its rows and rows of houses and high blue smoke cloud. Like Syuhtun, it looked crowded as it dominated the land along the river. Like Syuhtun, its many tomols and visitors' tomols and tule rafts filled the harbor. The voyagers made their way among the foreign boats. They responded to greetings without pausing. The early light started to warm them, although the iridescent silver morning was, itself, still cool.

South of Shisholop, where there was less activity at sea, the men stopped. They drank some water and had a bite to eat. Seagulls screeched round them, hoping for a wasted scrap. High above, the companions spotted the heavy wings of a white-headed eagle competing for the same prize. At this halfway point in their journey to the launching place, the men talked—or rather shouted—about what they would do next. Water separated the boats. The swell rose and fell gently and the ocean shimmered almost white. The sea reflected Grandfather Sun's early journey. It had begun deeply black-green, the color of huya stone. Then, with first light, it shifted to pale gray then lavender then pink and then to something deeper, the color of a flicker's feather. Then it had faded away, until now it glowed brilliantly but nearly beyond color. For the men this passage of colors, which had followed their southeastward progress, was something they witnessed most mornings. They commented on the clarity of the day, the sparkle of the sea. It was a good sign. As they resumed their journey down the coast, Chaki began to sing his dream song to himself.

It was hot by afternoon when the men made Wenemu village. It was situated on the point of the mainland that was closest to the islands. Seafarers spent the night there before departing for the islands and for that reason the town was called "the sleeping place." Wenemu specialized in assisting people in channel crossings. The tomol guild was strong there, and the finest weather prognosticators and manipulators worked there, too. Navigators not only departed the mainland from Wenemu but returned to it as well. Islanders landed there when they made their own trading expeditions. It was a busy port.

Chaki, Alow, Kulaa, their tomolmates and bailer boys enjoyed finding a place for themselves close by the surf. They listened to quiet lapping as they spent the rest of the day reclining in the shade, rubbing their knees, eating, napping, and even bathing. In the evening they sought their brothers from the tomol guild for a feast of food and information sharing.

The voyagers stayed in Wenemu for several days. Their first day was spent recuperating. It had been a long trip, nearly twice the distance as that from Mishopshno to Syuhtun. The rest gave the tomols a chance to dry out a bit and the boys some time to play and stretch their legs. Their elders were sore.

They waited for the right conditions for crossing the channel. Although the distance between Anyapah Island and Wenemu was less than between Wenemu and Mishopshno, the traveling circumstances were different. Tomols traveling inside the kelp beds along the coast were in relatively shallow water; the swell there, though it varied, was usually smaller than in the deeper channel. That is why, in Wenemu, the weather doctors checked the size and direction of the incoming swell every night and every morning. It had to be just right for a crossing to be safe. In the open channel, if the swell were to rise or a storm come up, there would be no neighborly port to steer into. The captain, his crew, and boat would have to rely on their own powers.

The expedition of Chaki, Alow, and Kulaa was well favored. They had chosen a mild time of year. Moon was waxing. The skies were clear by night and day.

On the night of their third day at the sleeping place their host came to tell them that the surf lay nearly flat. All the achanas agreed the coming morning would be auspicious for their departure.

Hearing the news Chaki felt something almost like disappointment. He had long wished to make this trip; he particularly wanted to increase his fortune. But now it seemed everything was happening too quickly. He had been prepared to bide his time at Wenemu for weeks awaiting the right weather conditions. He scarcely had the opportunity to feel thankful for living to make this journey—or to doubt his ability to carry it out. He had planned on using the slack time to set his mind for the responsibility of leading the expedition.

Next morning, the men were up early. They cleaned and groomed themselves excitedly. Chaki watched his younger cousins plucking their beards with clamshells. Even when he was younger he had never wanted to endure that tedium; it seemed like a waste of time. He had never sought to be physically admired. But he had learned to be more patient since his youth. He didn't hurry the others. All of them painted their faces red against the burning power of Sun.

Grandmother Moon had finished her night's work, and in the predawn the voyagers found their way to the tomols on the sand where they met their guild brothers and the weather achana. In the east, one of the Sky People served as messenger for the mighty wot of the Sky World. The low rolling surf was breaking as cleanly and sharply as a polished obsidian blade. The weather doctor prayed to the four winds and to the sea; he tossed a rock into the waves. As it bobbed and churned in the pale foam of the morning water, he read its motion. All was well, he said. They might, indeed, embark. Then he gave the travelers detailed advice on winds and currents. He forecast the conditions for the month ahead. All looked propitious.

It was the turn of the men to pray. They prayed to the south, the changing direction of the watery Undersea World dominated by the greedy Swordfish wot. They prayed to the east and the west, to the north, and to the zenith above and to Shup below their feet. Having encased themselves within the six directions they sought to align themselves along the axis of the Three Worlds. They scattered hutash and ilepesh and acorn seeds on the ocean as well as down and they prayed: "Make room for us! Make room! Make room! Give us courage! Help us persevere to our destination! Alishtahan! Alishtahan!"

"Ayaya! Ayaya! Ayaya!" they shouted at last in triumph. Then, together with their brothers from the guild, they heaved the heavy tomols into the ocean, paused briefly to await the calm spell, and, with its coming, gave a last cheer and leaped out of the cold water into their planked canoes, plunging out beyond the waves. They settled themselves among the blankets and kneeling mats and felt for their double-bladed paddles. They took out of their hair pouches their long thin cords of eagle's down and wrapped the magic string three times around their heads. The captains checked on their mates and bailers and turned back to call thanks and farewell to their shore-bound guild brothers, who were quickly receding on the other side of the curling surf.

Chaki led the way into darkness. He had no difficulty reading the star crystals, the Sun's sparks. His paddle cut cleanly into the calm waters, which were not only smooth and glossy as obsidian but opaque and black as well. He led the three tomols from the safety of shore toward the open channel. All was quiet but for the lapping of the paddle blades and the low singing of the captains as they kept up the rhythm for the strokes: "Rock and turn / Rock and turn / Side to side / Side to side."

The fullness of dawn came upon the nine voyagers beyond the safe confines of Wenemu's coast. They were deep in channel swells, which rolled stronger and longer than those near the seaweedy shore. The planked canoes dipped low into the salty ocean and rose high on peaked crests, so that at times they men seemed to be fighting an inexorable tide that made progress impossible. The water was unruffled by winds and the swells were untroubled by storms from the great sea beyond the islands. The men knew that in spite of appearances, they were getting ahead. Wasn't the shore receding? They had confidence in their strength. Chaki changed his paddle song.

"Alishtahan! Alishtahan!
Have courage! Our endurance is great!
We have the power to reach the place."

Grandfather Sun's torch burned clear and warm; it came close to them, drawing out their sweat. The men paused in midchannel to drink fresh water. Except for the gulls and pelicans and seals fishing nearby, the center was an empty, lonely place. The smokes of their own land were barely visible and the high mountains were but a line drawn across the sky. The islands, to their southwest, had the same look—a mountainous skyline and no human figures. The men were already tired. Even though they had been out for only a few hours, they had paddled hard and constantly against the natural motion of the sea.

Chaki shouted words of encouragement. He reminded his companions that, though the distance seemed far, it was really no farther than between their home and the big town Syuhtun. He exhorted them to consider how many times they had made that trip. They were making good progress and would soon reach their destination. The others were renewed by his speech. Their leader was wise and strong. He would look out for them. Nevertheless, each of them harbored a fear, not of the distance and difficulty of the trip but a dread at being so far from land—from Shup. Any mishap, any error, would be fatal. There could be no swimming to shore, no towing a damaged tomol into a convenient port. They must rely on themselves and their atishwins.

They were near, very near, the Land of the Swordfish. Bravely, they made more offerings of seeds upon the water. They remembered those who had drowned at sea. Then they looked ahead toward the high rocks of Anyapah Island. It loomed up like a mother whale followed by her young. The skies over Anyapah gleamed in the pale blue of summer. There were no clouds.

After the transition toward the other shore, the men began to feel more confident. Despite Sun's heat, which made red sweat drip down their sunburned arms, they believed they might arrive at their destination. Porpoises swam at their bows, their large dorsal fins dipping and rising like the red tomols themselves. Flying fish guided them on their way.

Before Grandfather Sun reached his daily zenith their small canoes, lying low in the sea, drew up beneath the red shrine poles atop the stark cliffs of uninhabited Anyapah Island, which had no fresh water. They were once more in the placid waters surrounding land. They made prayers of thanks and threw more gifts to the Undersea People.

It was not difficult, from the calm waters of Anyapah, to follow the coast westward. Crossing a medium-sized channel with mild swells, they found their goal—the large island of Michumash. They shouted with joy and relief. Men in red tomols from the easternmost village of the island came to meet them. Their planked canoes were filled with fish: the tomol guild brothers had been at work when they spied the foreigners coming. The islanders hailed them courteously. They addressed them warmly when they saw that they had come to trade.

The little curve of Swahil village was deceptively gentle and sandy. There were several rocks where pelicans perched and seagulls sat. There were more rocks submerged invisibly beneath the bay. The visitors had to restrain their eagerness. A disaster could happen even near the shore. In some ways, navigating in sight of this hospitable-looking settlement was the most difficult part of the crossing. But the fishermen of Swahil helped them, using universal gestures to show the way.

The men rested at the welcoming village. The inhabitants were generous with the limited food they had. The voyagers from the mainland went to sleep there that afternoon and awoke at dawn the next day. They agreed it would be best to head for the big town of Nimitlala as rapidly as possible. They regained their canoes and continued to trace the westward coastline. The day was again clear and warm. The coast wove gently, though it was rocky in spots. There were high bluffs and low sandy outlets. They passed small villages all along the way. Before long, they cut across a long curving beach, inhabited by seals and sea lions as well as people. Chaki showed the excited boys, who had never been to the islands before, the places where green water seeped from the cliffs.

Soon they spotted the tall red shrine poles towering above the northern and southern hills of the port of Kahas. Kahas village was on a sandy beach where the island's largest stream met the sea. Large though the stream might be, it was a creek no bigger than theirs at Mishopshno or the one at Qoloq. Now, in summer, it barely flowed at all. Yet, Kahas was well favored. There was good water there and greenery. Basket reeds grew thickly. The beach was sandy and the bay was without rocks. There were tall leafy sycamores for shading the boats.

The villagers they encountered were busy. Their chief occupation seemed to be making flint blades. They also shaped stone weights for digging sticks. Alow made up his mind to purchase some of these products before departing for home. All six men admired the villagers' diligence and craftsmanship as they recalled the islanders' reputation for making useful things. Everyone there seemed to be an artisan.

But the traders did not want to remain in Kahas, either. They stored their tomols in what they trusted was a secure place indicated by their brothers of the tomol guild. They found men and women they could hire to carry their cargo up the stream to the big town. And so, with porters, the six men and three boys from Mishopshno and Qoloq on the mainland set out, amid the dust of summer and under the shady curling leaves of tall sycamores, along the path for Nimitlala.

T he girl sitting astride the thick gray oak limb called down to her companion below, "I see them, cousin. They're coming. Six men and much cargo. Three little boys, too." She grew very excited and raised herself up so that she was standing on the branch, which grew high above the ground.

"Be careful! Remember you are a young woman now. You're not a boy. Not even a girl, anymore." Her earthbound cousin scolded like a jay.

The girl—young woman, rather—standing in the tree laughed and wiped the beads of sweat from her brow with the back of her hand. "Yes, I can see them plainly. They will be here soon. One of them is even handsome, I believe."

"Which one?" asked her cousin with serious interest.

"The fisherman," replied the girl, peering hawkeyed from the top of the tree. Despite her somewhat careless appearance, it was obvious that the girl, or young woman, came from a wealthy family. She dressed well and paid some attention to her grooming. Her necklaces and earrings were dark beads of huya and serpentine. She had painted herself tidily with red ochre, and both her singed bangs and her seagrass skirt were neatly tipped with black beach tar.

"But, cousin, aren't they all from the sea?" her equally well dressed and more fastidious cousin asked, puzzled.

"What?" shouted the high up one. "Yes, they're obviously from the mainland." Leqte began to do the steps of her atishwin's dance on the rough-barked tree limb. Mainlanders did come to her remote town, but not every day. This time she would be ready for them.

"How can you tell that the men are mainlanders?"

"By their hair, of course, my ignorant cousin. They wear it up—like a quail—with things in it, all sorts of things. Surely you know that."

"Yes, I guess I do," admitted Qupe, her soft otter's eyes glowing for the moment with their own excitement.

Leqte now scrambled down the oak tree as nimbly as a mouse (she had never seen a bobcat or a mountain lion). She stood in front of her companion; they were of equal height and were close to the same age. Looking her full in the face, she announced: "I am going to the mainland."

"I am sure we will. Our parents have promised."

"No, cousin. I mean soon, very soon. I am going to be married."

"Really! To whom?" Her confidante was startled.

"You'll see," said the sharp-eyed girl. And she turned and ran back to the village to tell her uncle of the arrival of the mainlanders.

A chorus of motley dogs rushed out to greet the new arrivals. The dogs were followed by the wot of Nimitlala. His hair hung long and straight like a Yawelmani's or a woman's and his bangs were singed. He was adorned with many shell and bead necklaces and he wore a nose ornament of bone. His cloak was of soft dark sea otter and it stretched to the ground. Beside him stood a man of about his own age who was similarly attired, except that his robe fell only to his knees—the assistant wot. On his other side stood the wot's wife who was wearing a beautiful fox fur cloak. Next to her was her daughter Leqte, the girl from the treetop. Beside her was her cousin Qupe and her parents and assorted uncles, aunts, siblings, and cousins. Their three families apparently made up a good proportion of the village's elite.

Leqte remained observant on the ground and did not cower and hide behind anyone. She surveyed the men of the trading party. The one exchanging polite words with the wot was, of course, the oldest and clearly the leader of the expedition. Leqte found him of solid build, full bearded, and not bad looking for a mainlander. He seemed like a trustworthy person. Still, she could see that he was old, perhaps even married already. She turned her attention to his words, trying to guess where the visitors had come from. The leader's command of the island speech was halting, slow. From this, she concluded that they were not from the land near Shisholop or Muwu for those people were quite good at island speech. Then she listened as her father made a welcoming address in a mainland language that she thought was that of the people around Syuhtun. With her burning interest in the mainland and its people, she had been studying languages with her cousin, the assistant wot's son, who should one day become wot. She practiced on every foreign visitor who came to the islands' biggest town. She imagined the big towns of the mainland—Shisholop, Syuhtun, Alkash, Sahpilil, and others—as exciting places. Her dreams began to take shape.

She caught herself. It was not the moment to dream. She had done that all winter long in the wet time when no visitors come. Now it was time to act. And she knew she hadn't long. She examined the other guests—five men and three boys. She ignored the boys, though they were not much younger than herself. The men were all strong and pleasant looking. But two stood out as having a prouder bearing and finer garb. Their beards were plucked smooth and they wore a great deal of money in their hair. Around their necks hung the dried remains of seabirds. The two young men looked so alike that Leqte identified them as brothers or close cousins. She had a difficult time choosing between them. But of the two one looked a little older, a little more experienced. Without knowing anything more about him, Leqte selected this man for her mate. With that settled, she turned her attention to the baskets the men had brought with them. There were many, some carried by porters. She coveted those exotic goods that came only from the other shore. She loved the rabbit and badger fur and the soft deerskin skirts. Her uncle, Qupe's father, was a fur trader. When she was smaller, one party of mainland traders had brought him a pair of brown rabbits as a gift. She loved watching them, especially their active ears and the astounding way that they hopped around. But they had trembled so and, not long after the guests had departed, one of the beautiful creatures died. Not long afterward, the other escaped from the wot's house and bounded off into the brush. He was never seen again.

Alone. Leqte had realized then that none of the wonderful creatures would ever take hold on the island. She had to content herself with the friendship of dogs and the tame foxes that lived just outside the village, the creatures that her mother's family was descended from. She would have to go on talking with the many birds that filled the trees and fields of her home—until it was time for her to leave. For she had made up her mind to leave the island for the wider world. Now, seeing the men, Leqte wished they would bring her something exotic and wonderful from across the ocean. A mountain lion, a deer, even a rattlesnake or a bear, would be all right; she wouldn't be frightened. Then she smiled to herself. She would get her wish. She was confident she would soon possess an exotic pet of a sort. A man from the mainland.

Alow's thoughts were not, for the moment, on great beasts or other animals as he stood and listened to the simple friendly speech of Matipuyuat, wot of Nimitlala, the big town of Michumash. He was welcoming them to the island, which he called Limuw, "of the sea." Alow found himself distracted by the birds. They sang loudly and everywhere, as if filling a void. He could not understand what they said—it must have been in island language. He smiled to think how gentle was this sea-born land where his mother had been born and where there were no bears or rattlesnakes or mountain lions. The people must be innocent and fearless. Perhaps they did not have poisoning, either.

He returned the looks of the villagers who stared at him. He recognized no one, not even the wot. For it had been the man's uncle who ruled when Alow had come to Nimitlala years before as a young bailer with his father. There were young people his own age; maybe he had played with them many years before. But no one looked familiar. He wondered about their skills in racing and archery. He looked over the women. They appeared crude to him in their grass skirts, not particularly attractive. One girl— perhaps she was even a budding woman, though her breasts were as flat as Konoyo's—was openly gaping at him. One of her front teeth was chipped. Alow met her stare, briefly. Then he looked beyond her to her small village of seagrass-thatched houses.

The visitor couldn't help but feel superior when he contemplated this miniature center of importance. At the same time he was charmed. It was as if the reality that he was in—the tiny village surrounded by mountain walls and edged by a meager stream—was but a ceremonial enclosure, a representation of the whole world, a replica that could become the world through magic. The grass houses with their blue smokes were the hut of the paqwot and the fires of the spectators, while the inhabitants of the village were the rays of Grandfather Sun himself.

Alow abandoned this vision when he raised his eyes to the white light of day and realized how hot and dry he felt. He was ravenously thirsty and hungry. These had been strenuous days. He felt that if he did not eat and rest soon he might lose consciousness. To keep himself alert he played the game of inventing insults. These he silently addressed to the audacious girl who had been staring at him. "Your cunt hangs as crooked as a crying baby's mouth," he thought. "Iyi, that's good!" he congratulated himself. Kulaa would laugh at that one.

Then, as if divining Alow's unexpressed needs, the wot concluded his address and invited them all to dinner at his house. He apologized for having only one wife and so little food. Chaki, as the leader, took this to be a good occasion for presenting the wot with many epsu of new hutash seeds. The wife looked grateful, though much of the gift would probably be used up in feeding the guests.

The entrance of the wot's house was an arch of whale's ribs. When the men had all passed through it, they found themselves in a crowded room. The wot's wife and daughter, that forward young girl, set down platters of fatty sea lion meat, seaweed, tuna, and swordfish. It was disturbing when their hosts crudely wiped the grease from their mouths with their fingers and smeared it into their flowing hair. For a while the meal was nearly ruined for them. Later on, there were small baskets of acorn soup and grass seeds, and no one came away from the meal hungry.

That afternoon Alow joined Chaki, Kulaa, Matipuyuat, his assistant, and their trading uncle to make plans for the trading. They settled the matter fairly rapidly. They determined to hold the trade in a few days' time, when the travelers would be rested from their voyage. After the trading, the wot said he hoped they would stay in his village as guests, for—he assured them—there was plenty of food. There were available girls for companionship and many people looking for sport and gambling. There were several interesting places to visit, he promised.

The men replied that they would be pleased to stay for as long as their host wished—though actually they intended to stay no longer than a month. Their visit seemed to be starting well.

That night there was more feasting, if that's what it could be called. The food selection was just as monotonous as before. Most of the guests played hand game with their hosts, though Chaki and Alow, for their own reasons, abstained from the power contest, and no person pressed them about it. There were many circumstances in which a man might be unable to gamble.

Later, there were dances at the ceremonial ground. Nearly everyone in the village participated. Matipuyaut was also master of ceremonies. His relatives were all antap officers and dancers. Others were musicians and singers.

The people of Nimitlala paid tribute to their guests by dancing the dances of the mainland: the Bear, the Badger, the Rabbit dances, sung in accompaniment with mainland songs. Then, the hosts, transformed by feathers and paint and firelight, presented their own dances. Leqte's uncle— Qupe's father—performed the comic Fox Dance. The dancer intimidated his audience by swinging his headdress, which hung like a tail and was weighted with a stone, in a wild and threatening manner. Leqte, her cousin and friend Qupe, and other adolescent girls presented the hypnotically flowing seaweed dance. Alow felt himself growing drowsy watching the sensuous movements. He swayed as he sat before his fire in the sacred place. Before he knew it he had fallen into the blackness of sleep.

T he beds at Nimitlala, like others on the island, were hard and damp. They were made directly on the ground, not raised on tall legs as they were at home. Nevertheless, Alow slept soundly, dreamlessly. Because houses were small, the guests had been sent to stay in different homes. Chaki was invited to stay with the trading uncle, Alow was given a sleeping place with the assistant wot, and Kulaa was a bit surprised to find himself at Matipuyaut's. The other men found accommodations with the brothers, sisters, and cousins of the wot and his wife.

The assistant wot's house was almost as crowded as the wot's what with all the children and adolescents and the grandmother. Alow enjoyed the company of the wot's oldest nephew, who was slightly younger than himself. He spoke the language of Syuhtun passably. The young man inquired solicitously after Alow's friend, Halashu, whom he had met at the Winter Solstice Festival in Syuhtun some years earlier. With his long stringy hair and bushy beard, this future wot bore no physical resemblance to the nephew of the wot of Mishopshno. Yet, when he took up his bow and spear with Alow in sport he soundly defeated him in all marksmanship contests, and Alow began to appreciate the innate similarity of all people of the highest rank. Perhaps it was the difference in their ranks that kept the friendship between Alow and his host's son from developing beyond the shooting range.

One morning after they had been in Nimitlala for a week or so Alow woke and got up quickly. He didn't like to be caught on his mat long, for he was bound to be discovered and descended upon by a basketful of Eagle Family children. He wrapped himself in an otter blanket and headed for the sweathouse down by the meandering creek. Inside, he met several of his own cousins. They began the new day together squatting silently by the blazing greenwood fire.

After bathing and making an effort to wash his hair and groom it elegantly, Alow felt ready for anything. The sky spread wide, clear, and cloudless, and the day promised to be a hot one. He couldn't decide what to do. Since the excitement of the big trading, with its singing and bargaining and his eventual success in selling all his wares, there had been no work for him. He had only to dream over the great amount of new money he had acquired, the otter skins, the fur seal capes and huya pots, the ironwood harpoons and heaps of digging weights and knives and blades.

He could spend this day as he had the others. He could play ball or race or shoot through hoops or into targets. But his constant losses to the wot's nephew had somewhat cooled his enthusiasm for sports. He could lie around and eat, gossip, and trade stories. Matipuyaut invited him in and suggested that his daughter and niece show them the sights of the island. There were great sea caves and a sacred mountain. The great man seemed to have a deep admiration for the foreigners, even though they were of lower rank than himself. Alow suspected that the high regard existed because he and his fellow traders had more money, if lower office, than their hosts. In spite of this suspicion, the wot's generosity touched him. He had not come to the islands to find a wife, but he would like to see the sights. It would be rude to say no, but still he hesitated.

Alow was standing indecisively just outside the whale rib door of the wot's house when Kulaa appeared. "There you are, cousin," he greeted Alow eagerly. "Are you doing anything? Come with me. I want to explore. There's a place I want to see. We follow the creek until it comes to the mountains: it's not far. And we don't have to carry our snake staffs or even worry about tripping in gopher holes."

"We are in a wonderful tame land," said Alow agreeably. His face took on a distracted look as if he were trying to recall a dream.

"I guess that's true," replied Kulaa brightly. "But I'd hate to live here all the time. It's too cramped, too dull really, impoverished of life."

"Of wealth, you mean," Alow teased. They walked to the stream with its wide flat bed of gravel. It wound under oaks and sycamores, creek willows and flowering elderberry. They crossed the lazy stream on stepping-stones, and Kulaa found the narrow dusty path between the willows beside the creek. They jogged on without troubling to watch their feet. Just in time, Kulaa spotted a vigorous momoy bush growing right in their way. The cousins apologized to it for nearly trampling it in their carelessness. The big white flowers looked up at them as Grandmother Moon looks down, but these orbs wore pinkish rings.

Alow returned to their earlier conversation. "I disagree. I believe I could live here forever," he said, surprising himself with his conviction. "The people are simple and seem poor to us, but they are strong and generous. Being here is like living in the Timeless Time."

"But your enhweq, your family at home, your money. Would you give that all up?" asked his cousin in alarm.

"No, of course not," said Alow, "I am only talking about a dream—if everything were different."

"Perhaps it is your late mother talking. Have you ever been to Wima, to her home?"

"I was small when I came as a bailer for my father. And he showed no interest in going to any other island than Michumash."

A hot dry breeze blew down the canyon where they hiked. From where they stood they could see no trace of ocean or mainland. They might have been at Matilha. After a time of silent walking, Kulaa asked his cousin how he thought the trading had gone. Alow was pleased with it and said so, though he wasn't entirely certain that he had made the best bargains. Kulaa expressed similar satisfaction. The two beginners congratulated each other—and their absent elder cousin. The mutual encouragement was like sinew, strengthening the bows of their novice's uncertainty. Alow thought back, contentedly, on the baskets full—and fine large baskets they were—of new money he had gained in the trading. He calculated how far it would go toward buying his own tomol. The huya bowls were valuable, too—they should last for generations. He would sell them for a profit, but he would keep one for his own household, for his future wife. He could see her now, crouched over it, stirring, large with his child.

While Alow was lost in his thoughts, Kulaa chattered on. He sounded almost like a girl. He rambled on about the exploits of their companions and the doings of the local people. The women had been out gathering odd-looking seeds in the fields. "Do you know that the administration of all the islands is taken care of at Nimitlala? That's why they don't need to go to the shore to fish and hunt. They are well paid. Did you know that the man Chaki is staying with is paqwot of all three islands? Even now, our hosts are preparing messages, invitations, for every village of each island for the Hutash Festival."

Alow had not been listening closely. Kulaa's sounds had blended with the chatter and cries of the birds around them. He had heard the bright shrieking jay, the soft droning doves, the loud and flashing pulakak, but little of his younger cousin. High over the mountains he had seen a red-tailed hawk circling. In the tops of trees he had spotted night-black ravens looming. And underfoot were more birds. It was the birds that returned him to awareness. He had to dance to avoid some bobbing top-knotted quail. They clucked as they scurried out of his way.

"The Hutash Festival?" queried Alow vaguely, unbalanced in time. "We ought to be home before then."

After a while they drew close to the wall of the small valley they were following. Tall hills blocked their view and their way. Little wisps of white clouds floated high overhead, riding easily over the mountaintops. "Where are we going?" asked Alow, curious, at last.

"We are going to a pool near the source of this creek," replied his cousin. "It's the principal stream of the island." He led the way to a path on their right, through a thicket of mimulus bushes with sticky orange flowers. The narrowed branch of the waterway wound up into the hills. "I know I can find the place," said Kulaa with a confident smile. "That Leqte may be a tease sometimes, but she gives competent directions," he added.

"Leqte?"

"Oh, you know, you opossum! The little tease, the daughter of the wot. I'm staying at their house, remember?" He mocked, but he sounded a little hurt.

"Oh, yes. Of course. The flat-chested one with the chipped tooth and the fox eyes," Alow appeased his cousin. And then, suddenly, for the first time since the day of their arrival at Nimitlala, he was reminded of the insult he had composed during the welcoming ceremony. How did it go?… like a bawling baby's mouth? Yes, that was it. Pretty good. He opened his own mouth to share the joke with his cousin. But seeing the peculiar expression on his face, Alow saved it for a later occasion.

They were mounting the hillside now, the part that fire had not touched. The chaparral was thick here, and the way was becoming difficult. Sun roasted them. Their recently washed torsos were now sticky with sweat and dust. Alow sensed they were nearing the place.

All at once, with eagerness and pain, Kulaa began to confess to his cousin. His phrases were rough and uneven but they shone; they were bright like abalone shards. He confessed his attraction to the daughter of his host. "At first I hated her," he admitted. "She followed me everywhere. Her movements were coarse; they repelled me. She spoke too loud, like a boy. And too much, like a girl. Either she was spying on me or she was asking incessant questions."

"Sounds dreadful. What made your opinion change?"

Kulaa stopped climbing and lowered his voice. "I don't know," he said. "I can't say. I think I just got used to her. And then I began to see that she wasn't so bad, really. Like any good woman, she works hard, gets up early, brings water, cooks. She fed me. And then I got a surprise when I saw her basketwork—it was exquisite, better than mother's even. I knew I had been unfair. Anyway, the girl turned out to be a good companion and guide, though she talked too much. We explored some interesting places…"

"Yes?" Alow prompted. He was giving his full attention now.

"Well, yesterday—I can hardly believe it—she enticed me out to meet her little fox friend. He is really quite tame…" His voice faded.

"And then?"

"Yes, well… I just all of a sudden definitely became aware of her for the first time… I mean as a woman, not as a child or girl, but as a complete woman."

"Keti!" exclaimed Alow.

"Oh, yes," continued his cousin heatedly. "That isn't all. Since that moment my desire has burned so that I hardly dare to enter her father's house, not even—especially—at night to sleep."

"Surely, cousin," Alow admonished, "you are aware that her father is the wot and her mother is of the Fox Family. That makes the enhweq one of the Earth Team, the same people as yours and mine. She is like your sister."

"I know it," said Kulaa bitterly. "I am constantly thinking of it. I know we cannot marry. And yet, the wot has hinted that we may go with any willing girl who pleases us."

"No, cousin," said Alow firmly, "he didn't mean anything like that. Even he cannot alter the way the world works. Screwing is nearly as bad as marriage with someone of your own half. It insults the balance of the worlds. Don't even consider such a thing!"

"I know you are right. And yet, I can think of nothing else. That enhweq has a power. Do you think it comes from the little fox that she plays with?"

"Cousin, listen! You must resist her. You have the ability to do it. But your impulse fights the strength of your own power. There are other girls. What about that cousin who hangs about with her? Oh, I wish our achana were here now! If you fail to resist, disaster will surely follow. Anyway, the daughter of even an assistant wot is too high for you. Has she thrown herself at you?"

"No," admitted Kulaa. "And that's the worst part of all." For all her friendly attentions, he could not tell if Leqte cared for him as a man.

"Ah, that's good," sighed Alow in relief. "Maybe she is not trying to put a spell on you." But in his secret thoughts Alow began to plead his cousin's cause.

The two kinsmen, in the course of this discussion, had come to a complete halt in their progress toward the source. Now they looked ahead. "Look," said Kulaa, pointing at a swarm of orange dragonflies hovering close above them, "I think we are nearing what we have come for."

The edge of the pond had been built up with rocks. The water beckoned, cool and deep. The pool was green.

On the side that was against the mountain and from which the spring originated, a tall sandstone boulder faced the two men. A small waterfall, indolent in summer, trickled gently down its face. Two adolescent girls were standing atop the rock. They were hand in hand, naked. They must have been preparing to jump into the green pool.

Qupe looked down while Leqte stared right at Alow. She smiled broadly.

Perhaps it was from the effort to understand his cousin's feelings that Alow felt himself suddenly set ablaze by the girl. He heard the singing birds. Were they laughing at him? He felt ridiculous. How could he admire this puny girl with the chipped grin? But the sunlight had begun to burn doubt away. She was a fact. Did it matter where her power came from? He smiled. Alow forgot entirely that he too was of the Earth Team. He made a quick prayer and threw himself into the translucent water.

At the same instant that Alow was being struck as if by lightning by Leqte's presence, his cousin Kulaa was overcome by a similar experience. It was the first time that he had seen either Leqte or her companion without their grass skirts and adornments. The peculiar experience he was having was not the intensifying of his passion for Leqte but the shifting of it toward her quieter cousin as suggested by his cousin. Why hadn't he noticed her soft beauty before? Kulaa was afraid he could not contain himself. He did not like it that the girls had noticed his excitement and were beginning to laugh and joke about it. He, too, dived into the cool green pond.

In a flash, the girls, still holding hands, leaped from the high boulder into the pool. They created a great splash and drenched the young men.

The four laughed and played together in the water for the rest of the morning. The girls pulled themselves out and jumped off the rock again and again. Their guests attempted it, too. Kulaa dove beneath the surface and nibbled toes as if he were a barracuda. Reticent Qupe shrieked with delight.

At last the four hauled themselves out onto warm rocks to dry off. Alow had managed to shake off the stunned condition he had felt on first seeing Leqte naked. He had not been able to resist touching her. He believed it was of his own volition. Kulaa, thanks to his cousin's dispassionate advice, seemed to have regained control of his own disturbing passion for the girl and moved toward one more suitable.

When they all had dried, the girls dressed themselves and then, as if by magic, they produced a whole carrying net full of food. They led their new friends up the hillside trail toward the high pass. Leqte led the way to the top. It was not a strenuous climb. Everything on the island was smaller and more gentle, even the mountain ranges. They walked through chaparral and ever-present orange flowers of the mimulus. Elderberries were blooming and simultaneously ripening in deep blue clusters. They reached out and ate as they walked along. Leqte chattered vivaciously all the way.

As they gained altitude they were met by a greater variety of flowers—red, yellow, blue, golden—still vibrant even in late summer. Grasshoppers and small yellow butterflies hovered around them. Though the sky opened overhead as clear and blue and pale as ceanothus flowers, the wind at the pass blew strong and cool. They felt refreshed and invigorated. The men took their first look as adults down on the long dry westward valley that sloped all the way to blue smokes at the farthest shore of the island. They saw distant pine forests. In the northwest they saw a high wooded peak. They—as well as the islanders—revered the sacred mountain. They contemplated it in silence.

At the crest of the pass the girls spread out food for their meal. From where they sat they could see not only the western end of the island but across a small channel to another large island.

"Wima," said Qupe.

"Wima," echoed Kulaa. "That's where the money is made, isn't it? Alow has family there."

Alow said nothing.

Qupe smiled, "The money is manufactured on the island, but it all seems to go to the mainland."

"My cousin Chaki, our leader, is determined to visit the place," said Kulaa. "And of course Alow wants to go. I'll go too," he added as he casually helped himself to more fish.

Qupe looked disappointed. "When will you go?" she asked.

"Oh, I don't know. It's barely past Moon's fullness now. We have plenty of time, don't we?" he said, looking to his elder cousin.

But, while Kulaa was stuffing himself with food and chattering with the girls in a comical admixture of languages Alow was carefully scanning the new view that had opened to the north. It was a view of the falling slopes of the island, of the ocean channel, and of the mainland beyond. Leqte moved close beside him. "Is it true that your father is an islander?"

Alow was caught between worlds. "No," he said brusquely. "But I have kin at Silimihi on Wima."

Leqte looked at him with an expression that her cousin recognized as her undaunted look. "No wonder, then, that our guest is so clever and has such a handsome profile," she said. Alow smiled at this obvious attempt to win his favor.

It was some time before he returned his gaze to the contemplation of the ocean and his homeland on the other side. It was the first glimpse of it since the day they had hiked out of the port of Kahas toward Nimitlala. It had not been so long ago, but when he stared across at the distant mainland it looked alien, blanketed as it was with thick fog. Only the high mountain peaks were visible, incised in shimmering purple, yet Alow had trouble identifying the sacred peaks. Tears sprang to his eyes. He turned away from his companions. He felt that somehow he had been deceived by this new place, and he made up his mind to remain aloof from every charm of Limuw Island.

CHAPTER 9

MONTH OF FESTIVAL

hesiq momoy an smahatam

As soon as Grandmother Moon was reborn and it was auspicious to travel again, the Coyote Family along with others undertook the short trek to their gathering camps. The days and nights were still warm, though sycamore leaves had begun to turn brown and curl and drift down from the trees. Aleqwel walked at his sister's side at the rear of the family procession and was happy to find her appearing stronger than she had been in many months. Her face was fuller, her expression less strained. Her waist, where she tied the string of her buckskin skirt, had begun to thicken. He wished to touch her for comfort. But he did not dare: her influence would be too strong now.

The Coyote Family's traditional campground near the creek was in the same condition as when they had abandoned it after Ponoya's escape from the bears. The camp was dusty and dry, exhaling a good smell characteristic of late summer. The ragged oak leaves were falling into a bed that crunched under their calloused feet. The green acorns were turning pale golden brown. Soon they would be ready to pick.

At camp Ponoya stooped to drop the heavy carrying basket. Her breath came out in a sigh. Then she bent to unload their gathering tools, utensils, bedding, the gear that she was so accustomed to bearing with her strong neck. She told her brother, "I feel like a turtle—always transporting my home on my back."

Aleqwel announced that he would forgo deer hunting to guard the women of his family as they beat the bright golden showers of ilepesh seeds into their flat-bottomed baskets. Ponoya said, "Are you afraid for us? Even

289

though I am vulnerable, I know that bears will not touch me. My atishwin, though small, has proven stronger than mighty beasts. I know she will protect me."

Aleqwel did not know how to answer. Why were women so much more courageous than men? "It was fortunate you were able to drink momoy a second time," he said obliquely. He did not want to refer too openly to her atishwin. Her words had come dangerously near to bragging, he thought.

"And you, older brother, I know you have grown strong lately. Your atishwin is great. All the people admire you. But didn't our uncle advise you to seek yet another spirit helper, because of what you must do?" She looked at her brother with so much tenderness that Aleqwel had to turn away. He thought, "Alow, ichantik, you had better be truly transformed in your ways."

He answered: "It's true. I shall speak with him about it soon. I drank momoy on the summer solstice at the caves of Matilha."

"Sometimes I forget what happened to you when you were absent. And, then, when you returned things have not been usual as they were when our late father.... Do you think our family can endure?" she asked suddenly.

"Have courage, sister. Alishtahan! We will surely endure. We can triumph. See how strong Nene and Mother are? Even the taniw is well; he has come out of his illness with strength."

"But I do worry about him so," Ponoya said with a tension-releasing laugh. "He has become so quiet and obedient; it is unnatural."

Aleqwel agreed. Anakawin was strictly forbidden to leave the campground. He offered to help Nene with "women's" work. It was peculiar for their mischievous younger brother to be so compliant. He said, "Maybe he is just beginning to grow up."

Ponoya took his words as sincere, although jesting.

The people had come to the hills in search of the last ilepesh seeds; the stalks were drying and the leaves were beginning to blow away. The golden seeds would sustain them over the long empty seasons. They also picked ripe manzanita and mountain cherry fruits. And with the birds they vied for berries that flourished along the creek. But birds and people were not the only ones who loved fruits and berries; the delicacies were also beloved by grizzly bears. No one could ignore the evidence of bear activity in the blackberries that grew by the creek. Aleqwel told the family he was going to the creek to get firewood and water. He wanted to search carefully for animal tracks.

In summer's last days when Sun made everything dry up, the women of the Coyote Family worked near one another in their family's plot.

They bent over the low-growing plants with their collecting baskets suspended from their necks and resting on the ground. They rapped the bushes expertly with their seed beaters, and the dry flower heads sprinkled out seeds like solar rain. When the collecting baskets filled, the women straightened up for a few minutes and stretched as they walked to dump the seeds into the larger carrying baskets. To relieve the monotony they shouted to one another across the brown fields and frequently burst into fragments of song. Aleqwel, carrying his sinew-backed bow, patrolled the boundary of his family gathering area, soothed by the familiar sounds. He had not seen bear tracks near the creek. He wondered, could he really kill—or even frighten—a grizzly bear with his bow and arrows? Arrows were said to bounce off the thick black fur. He would have to rely on his power.

Aleqwel fumed internally at the supernatural bear that had brought so much grief to his family. His beloved father had died in this very camp. The thought made him long to visit him once again in Shimilaqsha. Just to talk things over. Then he thought, no, it is not wise to disturb ghosts too much. Suddenly he heard once more in his memory, over the women's songs, the intruder at the Winter Solstice Festival invoking his father's name, his real name that no one should know. The Wokoch had no respect for ghosts. In his fury, Aleqwel determined that it was time for the Wokoch to become a ghost himself. He passed several hours in imagining the time and means of dispatching the evil bear doctor.

"Son," said Anihwoy, waking him from his scheming. She had just emptied her collecting basket, which bounced lightly around her neck. She carried her seed-bending hook in her left hand and the twined seed beater in her right. Her brow was moist with sweat. "What do you think of your sister?" she asked.

Aleqwel was startled by his mother's unaccustomed directness. He replied that his sister seemed well and brave.

"Yes," agreed Anihwoy. "I find her so, too. But still I am worried for her."

"She seems to put great faith in the power of her atishwin," he said.

"It is not her atishwin that worries me, Son."

"What is it then, Mother?"

"It's Alow, that roaming cloud, that one who made her pregnant. I like him, but I wonder how reliable he is. Will he return to my daughter, do you think?"

Aleqwel stood beside his mother while Sun beat down on them; they might have been insignificant seeds and Sun their harvester.

"Dear mother," Aleqwel tried to take a tone of balance and wisdom as his late father might have, "you have known Alow all his life."

"That is true," agreed Anihwoy, whose own opinion as a curing doctor was so highly respected. "I know he is sometimes as changeable as the southern ocean."

"And clear and positive as it is, too," added Aleqwel. But he, too, has doubts.

Anihwoy suddenly burst out crying. "Of course the young man is fine. It is I who have changed! Why do I think these things? I'm beginning to believe there are many poisoners. It is not good."

"Mother, do not upset yourself," Aleqwel reassured her manfully. "Soon we will have no poisoner at all. And Alow will come back from the islands with baskets of money. And he will marry Ponoya. Don't be concerned. Of course, you hesitate. It would be unnatural to be too favorable toward your future son-in-law."

Anihwoy returned to her work, relieved. Aleqwel resumed his rounds. He felt a little light-headed. He was surprised at his own efficacy in the delicate situation. But he was grateful that his mother, in her emotion, had not reached out to touch him. He wondered if perhaps he had been too quick in backing away from her when he said he had to go see how the other women were getting along.

After several days, the ilepesh seeds were finally all collected. The harvest had been a good one, for there had been adequate rain in winter and warmth in spring and summer. Big buckskin sacks of fine gold seeds filled the camp. The fire was kept high, and guards were ever present. Some had seen bear tracks. But, as yet, there had been no confrontations. Perhaps the Bear Ceremony had served them well.

To celebrate the conclusion of their seed gathering, the women toasted some ilepesh with hot coals and ground the parched seeds into meal. They winnowed the flour in basket trays, shaking the trays so that the coarser meal fell into mortars below, where it was reground. The women then boiled the fine meal in cooking baskets, pouring in water and heated stones.

Later, when the family sat eating together beside their own fire, Aleqwel noticed, with satisfaction, that his sister scooped the thickened porridge from her dinner basket almost as fast as he did. She even helped herself to more. It must be true that the baby inside her was going to stay. He wondered whether her child would be beautiful or plain, persevering or changeable, strong or weak. He supposed it would depend on the month in which it was born. It was too hard for him to calculate when that might be just now. He was sure his great-uncle could do it, or any woman. At the moment he just appreciated the good harvest and the women's labor.

"It won't be long now until the Hutash Festival," said Nene, her thought bending in the same direction as her grandson's. The look of eager expectation in her grandchildren's eyes made her happy, even though none of them would be able to fully participate in the games and dances. Their energies would be taken up with survival. Still, they would find the celebration a distraction. "It is important to show our appreciation to Shup in her manifestation as Hutash. It is she who gives us seeds and all the food we live on. Now, before she rests, is her greatest time," said Nene.

"I believe we will be able to fulfill our contribution toward expenses this year," said Anihwoy. She spoke to her mother, but addressed herself to them all.

Aleqwel felt proud of his achievements—and so prosperous that he readily helped himself to a third bowl of ilepesh. He began to dream about the Hutash Festival. Would the words of encouragement he had given his mother really come true—would Alow return by the Moon of harvest time? Would he come with wealth, and would he marry Ponoya? He turned to his sister. She looked radiantly well fed and unshakably confident.

Before returning to Mishopshno village, the gatherers picked all the fruits and berries in the hills. They devoured blackberries and fresh ilepesh cakes. They picked manzanita berries and crushed them into refreshing drinks. What they did not eat or drink they dried and stored for winter. Then they plucked the mountain cherries, dropping the dark fruit into bags hung around their necks.

While some men guarded others hunted. Deer also were coming down from the hills in search of food and water. Often, when they were out picking fruit, especially near the meadow, the people saw small herds of deer. The deer looked up at them with wide brown eyes. They moved their ears. They sniffed the air. But they did not run away unless someone made a sudden movement. The deer did not belong with the people the way that the dogs did. And yet they were not entirely wild; they were not separate from humans. The hoofed creatures kept quietly to themselves. But they offered themselves up for sacrifice on the right occasions.

Aleqwel finally felt satisfied that he could take off a few days to hunt. Although his usual deer-hunting companions were absent and he was not an outstanding hunter himself, it was one of his last opportunities to provide his family with meat and hides before winter set in.

Aleqwel did not need to use the deer head decoy that one of the other men had lent him because there were so many deer in the meadow. Even so, it was not easy finding a suitable animal, one willing to sacrifice its life. The search led him away from the meadow and up the hillside. He climbed the creek canyon he had followed the previous spring with the alchuklash.

At last, the young buck he had been pursuing, which had kept well ahead of him without disappearing into the dense chaparral, paused and put his nose to the ground. Aleqwel crept closer. The deer seemed to be scratching the ground like a dog uncovering a bone. Aleqwel pulled an arrow from his quiver. He knelt. He touched the lizard's foot at his neck and prayed that his aim might be accurate. He begged the deer's pardon for what he was about to do.

The small buck lay down on the ground as if preparing himself for sacrifice. Even Aleqwel was surprised by this peculiar act. Nevertheless, he set his bow crosswise and drew. The arrow struck the one-pronged buck in the chest. The animal fell back with a groan. But the arrow's point had struck the deer's sternum and did not penetrate well. Aleqwel did not enjoy having to make another shot. He begged the wounded one's forgiveness. The young buck stumbled to his feet. He staggered toward the hunter. When he got very near, Aleqwel was able to finish him off easily with an arrow to the throat. The buck carried fine mossy antlers.

After further examining the animal and determining that he had been an admirable creature, Aleqwel scattered seed and down on sacred Shup as a mourning offering for the child she had yielded.

Aleqwel thought he had better carry the dead buck to camp himself rather than leave it and risk its being eaten. A condor, buzzard, or coyote might tear it apart before he returned. He began to tie up the animal with tok rope so that he could better carry it on his shoulders. A breeze came blowing gently down the canyon. His nose caught a foul smell. Reluctantly, Aleqwel left his kill and followed his nose.

He came to the place where the buck had stopped and scraped the ground. In the clearing was a mound of earth, a heap of dirt and grass and stones. Aleqwel felt sick. He poked at the mound with his bow. The foulest odor on all Shup came steaming out.

Aleqwel kicked the soil in disgust. He had exposed the rotting remains of another deer. It was a bear's deer. And the bear could be nearby waiting for his dinner to putrefy. Aleqwel had to leave quickly.

He was angry. And the growing heat of Sun in the afternoon only made him angrier. He was tired of running from bears and bear doctors. As he returned to his own fresh kill and stooped to arrange it on his shoulders he felt somehow less pride in his accomplishment. He determined, right at that moment, to do no more hunting until he had killed the evil bear doctor, wot or no wot, permission or not.

As he struggled down the canyon, Aleqwel repeated the promise he made to himself. The weight of threats made by the murderous bear doctor was heavier than the heavy buck. Aleqwel knew there would never be an ending except through his own action. With this decision he felt free of his anger. He walked lighter, even as he struggled home with his kill.

As he entered camp with its dark oaks drooping and dusty soil packed down by generations of campers, a group of women simultaneously arrived from the low hills. Delicately, they balanced bags of cherries from poles slung over their shoulders. The grace and care of their movements suddenly brought Aleqwel face to face with his own imbalance. At the same time as he felt at peace, he knew the deed he intended was unwise for the community. It was too private. Yet he was in no spirit to give it up. He made a silent concession, though, to the graceful women. He would, at least, inform his mother's uncle of his resolve.

T he harvest was short and bountiful. Leather storage sacks filled up with seeds and dried berries and the pits of mountain cherry. These last would be cured and ground into paste for delectable cherry-nut balls.

The people looked forward to returning to the village. The annual autumn festival lay ahead. Everyone would have a part to play in the preparations for the celebration. Contributions of ilepesh and hutash seeds had to be made to the wot so that his wives could feed all the hungry participants. There would be guests as well as villagers. Firewood needed to be gathered in quantity. Men were expected to share the fish and deer they had recently killed. Aleqwel did not object to sharing his deer. He revered Shup, the earth, whom he addressed with honor as "Hutash" or "beautiful one" at her festival. Aleqwel was grateful to her as the source of all nourishment. The deer had been given by her. He, in turn, would offer some of it at her festival.

There was one last thing the people had to do before they returned to the coast. It involved fire, one of the sacred elements. The dry parkland of worn ilepesh and hutash, of seed grasses and flowers, had to be burned so that after the winter rains seed plants would rise again. They had to be burned so that tender shoots would not be pushed away by coarse chaparral shrubs. Every year the women undertook this vital responsibility, which had been handed down from their grandmothers' grandmothers: they set their own fields to the torch. From the flames and the blackened earth, from the killing, the women carried on the continuous creation of the green parklands of their valley. They shaped a land inviting to deer and other animals, lush with green grass and flowers in the spring, shady with acorn-bearing oaks that had the power to survive the fiery heat.

The weather was perfect. The days had continued hot and dry, so the withered stalks of vegetation ignited with just a spark. The air was still with only the slightest breeze so there was less danger of the flames spreading to the chaparral of the high mountains. When strong winds blew this could happen, and the lives of animals and people—particularly of the burners—were lost. But the women were expert at reading the wind and controlling the burn.

In these days of burning Aleqwel set himself up south of camp to grind pigments in his little mortar. The dancers at the Hutash Festival would need a great deal of body paint, and he was responsible for providing most of it. As he worked, great blue clouds of smoke drifted overhead. The air he breathed was heavy with ash particles and he coughed. It was very warm.

Aleqwel distrusted fire. Flame was cleansing like the gentle moonlight, but fierce and deadly like devouring Sun. It was unpredictable. Fire was another instance in which women proved more knowledgeable than he—and braver. His feet itched to carry him away from the smoke and the voracious hot tongues that grazed the valley below. He ached to run just as the other animals ran. But he trusted those who did the burning and stayed with his work.

In two days' time the women finished the burning of the upper valley. The women of his family—Ponoya, Kanit, Anihwoy—were at first unrecognizable with their faces blackened by soot. They looked more like performers from the Nunashish Dance come from the Lower World than like human beings or like the mourners they were. Though the Mourning Ceremony had come and gone nearly a year before, the elder paint maker had died just a short time before it was held, and his family's grieving had been cut short.

Now all that remained on the valley floor were scattered oaks and sooty stubble. Aleqwel joined the other men and boys on a spree, chasing rabbits, throwing sticks at them, and shooting them with their plain bows. Aleqwel tied many rabbits to his belt string. He found in the frenzy of this effort some sort of preparation for his deadly work to come.

Mishopshno village, after the burning and return of the gathers, bustled with activity. The ceremonial enclosure was refurbished by members of the antap in preparation for the Hutash Festival. Feathered costumes were unrolled from their places of safekeeping and carefully inspected and repaired. Women cooked and fishermen hauled in great baskets of pohoh, bluefin tuna, yellowtail, and perch, as this was the most abundant time for fish. Commoners waded in the surf, scooping out baskets full of sardines. The fishermen dried fish for winter as well as supplying the upcoming festival. The people would depend on the dried fish in the scarce months after the tuna migrated to their winter camps. Any spare moment was filled with sports and music, practice for the festival itself.

Aleqwel resolutely walked along the hill path to the intense cluster of activity beside the house of the chief wot. He found his great-uncle, the alchuklash, mending fences in the semicircle. Aleqwel greeted the old man with an insult, as was the inverted custom of the antap when working on the sacred grounds. Realizing the seriousness of what he was about to say and the sanctity of the place, he chose the best vulgarities he could to express his true sincerity. "Old Man," he said, "you with the withered balls. Haku. I have come to ask your advice—may it displease the Sky People—and to seek your encouragement—which is probably pointless. Still, there is some work I must undertake soon, some sacred work." It was difficult enough to tell the alchuklash his plan and to risk his disapproval, but having to phrase it in the other language and in ill manners besides was almost more than he could handle. "Old man," he hurried on, "what I plan to do is dangerous for me—and possibly for the whole people—and it is not authorized. How should I best go about it for the most successful results?"

The alchuklash had stopped working and listened carefully to what his grandnephew said. His answer gave no hint of either approval or disapproval: "I will speak with that miserable fool, our wot, about it."

"Woi, no!" cried Aleqwel, dropping the profane and difficult antap guise. "Se. Se, he will try to prevent me, and I cannot be prevented."

"Perhaps he will. Perhaps he won't. Our wot, lazy though he is, wants what is harmonious for the people. And you kilamu one, do not. You want only what is good for you. I have sympathy for your point of view: we are of the same family. Still, it is our wot who must decide. If people will not listen to the wot and follow his advice, but instead go their own individual ways, disaster will surely be the result."

Aleqwel heard these wise words—which, in his earnestness, the old man spoke with lessened crudity—with disappointment. It was not what he wanted to hear. He had planned to avoid the wot. Or, he wondered, was he a coward who secretly wished to be dissuaded from his goal. Or was there truly a spark of balance underneath his conflagration of rage? Aleqwel thanked the alchuklash in phrases of strident contempt and began to back away from the enclosure. "Don't come around, Old Man, Old Farteater…" He was caught in a whirlpool of confusion. He felt for Lizard's foot about his neck. But before he could escape, the alchuklash called him back: "Paint dauber, you homely creature, there is much work to be done here before Moon is in her fullness. Will you deign to lift a hand?"

It was with a certain relief that Aleqwel ran home for his paints. The song he made up on the way expressed not only his confusion and uncertainty but also his sense of security in being, in spite of everything, only one part of a greater social family.

The next day Tilinawit sent a messenger to fetch the young paint maker. In his house, he invited Aleqwel to sit on a whalebone stool. He offered ilepesh and hutash and condiments, aphid sugar and yellow juniper berry cakes. He treated the young bear charmer with respect, almost as if he were a tender tobacco plant he had transplanted and was trying to cultivate. Aleqwel was young enough to find it disconcerting.

The wot was well prepared and moving carefully. He could not afford to have this fine young man ruin everything. He said, "I understand your feelings and you are right. Justice is on your side. I give you permission to do what you have to do."

Aleqwel was taken by surprise. He had come prepared for an argument—something difficult to have with one's respected wot—but not for this.

The wot added: "I only ask you to promise one thing."

Aleqwel, off balance, promised readily. He would promise anything to be allowed to kill the Wokoch.

"Good, good." said Tilinawit. "You may do what you must. But you must promise to wait."

"Woi!" exclaimed Aleqwel, jumping to his feet. "What sort of permission… ?"

The wot stopped him with a clap of hands. "It's not so bad as it sounds. It's not forever. I have been given a message, a sign. But we must not disrupt the festival. Our mother, Shup, deserves our full honor. Later you may do it. Shuluwish has consented."

This was big news. So Shuku's wot was not altogether satisfied with his great vicious bear doctor. Why, then, had he invited all Mishopshno to that monstrous display of power at the Bear Ceremony? Aleqwel's head was racing.

"Yes, it must be done. If you prefer, our poisoner will do it. He is very skillful and subtle. No? I thought you might not accept that sensible offer.

Shuku will give a sign when the time is right. His spies are still investigating. If we hear nothing by the new year, then…"

"Then, I will poison the murderer." He spoke the words!

"And you will wait until then."

"You are wiser than I, wot," Aleqwel deferred. "I will wait until the last month if I must. But no longer." He was silent as if calculating his energies and his family's resilience and apportioning them over the coming season.

The wot indicated his dismissal with a graceful gesture. He was pleased with the outcome. "Your great-uncle has reminded me that you were to drink momoy again this year. It is not always sufficient to have only one atishwin."

Aleqwel took the advice and carried it with him out the door. Yes, he would need more power than he had at his disposal right now. His adversary, after all, was much older. He had not only Bear and Holhol in his service but unquestionably several other atishwins as well.

Aleqwel gratefully returned to mending and painting fences in the ceremonial ground. He sang the song that had come to him the day before when he was leaving the sacred ground. It gave him courage for what lay ahead. He had said the words aloud, and he knew now for certain that he would carry through with his resolve. Then he thought about drinking momoy again. He didn't want to. He did not believe it was fear. His last session, at summer's commencement, had left him with visual disturbance and confusion for some time afterward. It had impeded his senses and actions. He could not afford to have that happen again. Though, probably, he told himself, the doses brewed by that old alchuklash in the mountains were stronger than those his uncle dispensed.

A low's grandparents at Silimihi on Wima Island cried when they saw him. Generously, they shared their food and simple homes made of seagrass. But he had a difficult time communicating with them. Their poor village was isolated, and what mainland speech they knew had come from Mushu long ago. As for Alow, he had scarcely heard any Wiman language since the day of his late mother's fatal fall when he was very young.

At first the people of the small village had been suspicious when the foreign tomol came into their little bay. And when Alow announced his lineage he was not sure anyone believed—or even understood—him. Even so, his grandparents, who, though not aged, suffered severely in their joints and were missing many teeth, extended hospitality as they might have done for any stranger.

It was not until his late mother's brother, Tata, came to see him that he was positively identified. Tata was a strong and persuasive character. He pointed to Alow's physical attributes, demonstrating familial likenesses. Then, extending a weathered forefinger with a chipped nail he indicated the spout of hair that Alow wore high on his head and laughed. Alow heard him say something about whales and dolphins, and everyone laughed. Then his uncle cried. He seemed to have had a great love for his departed sister, whose over-riding desire to go to the mainland drove her to leave her proper home for her husband's in Mishopshno.

Alow brought presents—woqo and paint and seeds. He led his uncle down to the shore to see his tomol. He pointed out the fine center board, which had come originally from Wima Island. This pleased Tata since part of his livelihood came from transporting red pine driftwood logs from western Wima to Limuw Island. Tata and Alow went out fishing and enjoyed themselves. Yet, the older man never seemed wholly comfortable with Alow's tomolmate. Alow found it strange, for, as far as he could see, the young man was quiet and inoffensive in all ways.

Life in Alow's mother's birthplace was slow and uneventful, not marked by much ceremony. The people fished and collected driftwood and made things. They worked stone and wove baskets. Hills separated them from their neighbors, and the hills rolled on all sides to the sea. Their world was dominated by birds and sea and sky. Alow took his relatives on short trips in his tomol. They called him "Alapapa," their way of saying "free white cloud." They asked after his father and seemed happy to hear he was well. He wondered if his kinsmen, like Leqte, found him handsome for his island blood. On his own, he explored the hills and shores. He liked the tranquility. Slowly, he was coming to know his other family, and a sense of belonging was growing in him.

One day, two more red tomols appeared in the settlement's little harbor. They belonged to Chaki and Kulaa. Alow wanted them to know his family. The village wot hospitably invited the newcomers to stay. Although Alow feared the nine of them were straining the resources of this modest village, the next several days were cheerful and harmonious ones. They fished and scoured the beaches. The bailer boys ran around with the village children.

Chaki impressed all who were willing to listen with his descriptions of the famous mint, which he and the others had just visited. He amused them by demonstrating bodily and vigorously all the processes involved in the manufacture of shell money. Every person in that village was a shell worker, just as everyone at Kahas Harbor was a stone craftsman and his own people were fishermen and boat builders. He launched into a lecture on the importance of money: the virtues of using it, of possessing it, of trading with it. He claimed that money was the basis of peace among neighbors. He spoke so exceedingly solemnly that his younger cousins might have laughed had they not looked up to him as their admired leader.

When they were alone on the top of a fire-blackened hill that overlooked the hazy ocean channel Kulaa confided to Alow, "Actually, the mint was pretty dull. Yes, it was astounding to see so much money all in one place— very beautiful. But the enhweq had no life in them. I wanted to go right back to Limuw. Those were wonderful days—the hikes and swims, the abalone gathering. Qupe is really something. The girls over here are so free."

Alow replied with his own question, "So you got over that little seducer Leqte?"

"Keti, yes! With your guidance. But you seemed to grow fond of her yourself."

"Oh, in a way, I guess I have. She does have a power. Of course, I see right through her. She wants to find a man to marry so she can get to the mainland, to civilization. Like many island women, I suppose." Was his mother that kind, he wondered.

"Fortunately you and I are both of the wrong team to marry the little island fox." Kulaa then lowered his voice, "Don't you think it is time for us to be leaving Wima? Your uncle glowers at us as if we were thieves or poisoners. Why is that?"

"I don't know what you mean, cousin. He is strong, but I only experience love and kindness from him. And you don't have to whisper here. No one can understand our language."

"Well, I tell you, we had better be leaving pretty soon. I told them at home that we'd be back for the Hutash Festival. In truth, I wouldn't mind staying a little longer, not if we are at Limuw. But I don't want to frighten my family in Qoloq."

Despite all of Kulaa's secretive peering and peeping around, someone had managed to creep up on them as they talked. But it was only Chaki. He must have caught Kulaa's last words because he said, "You're right. They will be lighting bonfires for us every night at home. It is bad, bad to make them wait. They will worry that we have drowned in the channel. When we do get back they will not trust us. Since we are already overdue, all we can do is try to get back as soon as possible. We'll leave for Michumash Island tomorrow morning."

Chaki could always make decisions. And he had resisted adopting the islanders' name for their home.

That night, as they sat around the central fire in Alow's mother's parents' darkened house, the young visitor announced their intention to depart. Most of the family cried again, as they had on his arrival. He wondered if they had begun to look for a suitable enhweq for him. No matter, it was time for him to go home where he would soon have his own family. However, Alow's uncle looked relieved to learn they would be going. Alow could not understand it. Tata had been such a good friend to him. He would miss him more than anyone else. It perplexed and hurt him that his uncle sat with such indifference. They might never meet again in this world.

Later, as Alow was lying on his damp floor bed and beginning to drift off to sleep, he sensed that someone or something had come up beside him. He opened one eye, and the small fear that had begun to well in him quickly subsided. It was only his gentle grandfather. He must have noticed the glow from Alow's open eye, because, at once, he began to speak to him. He talked rapidly in a low monotonous voice. Alow caught a word here and there, distinguished a pattern of words. Grandfather spoke of his late daughter, Alow's mother.

Alow heard the term for "mainlander" and the name "Mushu" they had given his father. Then, in succession, he heard the names of his mainland cousins and tomolmates. The old man did not pause for breath in his narrative. Alow was startled to hear him utter the Wiman word for "ayip." Then the names came again. All at once, Alow grasped what the old man, his few remaining teeth shining yellow in the ember light, was telling him. He seemed to be saying that Tata, his mother's brother, believed Alow's mother had been kidnapped and then poisoned at Mishopshno. He thought maybe it was her own husband, or his family, who did it.

The young man sat up, "Se, se! No, no! That isn't true. To my father, she was everything." But he could see that his grandfather was not able to understand him. He felt terribly frustrated. He just repeated, "No, no! Se, se, se!"

His grandfather patted him with a soothing old hand. He said something that Alow interpreted as meaning that the old man did not feel that way himself, it was only his son who had this bad idea. He had suffered when his sister had left the islands with her husband.

Alow appreciated his grandfather's words as he sat up under his fur blanket. Still, he was upset. He had come to love his uncle, his kinsman. He wanted to talk with him about the misunderstanding. But he knew it would be futile to try until he mastered more of their island speech. He wanted to resist Chaki's call to leave. How could he go with the situation confused this way? Yet he now knew that his crewmates would be in danger if they stayed any longer.

Instead of sleeping more, Alow rose. He parted silently from his grandfather. Then he collected his gear and went to waken his companions. He tapped them gently so as not to frighten their wandering spirits. It would not be wise to make them call out in surprise, either.

By sunrise the cousins were paddling across the channel between Wima and Limuw to the east. They were gliding near the westernmost point of the large island when the first yellow rays of daybreak illuminated them. Chaki, in the lead tomol, rested his paddle for a moment. He had a vague sense of unease, of things not being as they should. Something was seriously wrong in fact. Something was missing. He looked around. He peered down over his full beard onto his hairy chest. He grasped the empty place. The lion's paw atishwin was gone. When the other tomols drew up alongside his resting one, Chaki said to the captains, almost choking on the words, "You go on ahead. I have to go back!"

A t Nimitlala visitors were already arriving from every corner of the three inhabited islands for the Hutash Festival. The wot was surprised to see his mainland guests returning without their leader. But he was busy overseeing the setting up of the sacred enclosure and taking in contributions of food and money. Alow and Kulaa, having seen their cousin's stricken expression and observed the empty hand clasped to his chest, understood that he had gone back in search of his lost atishwin. They imagined the fever with which Chaki must be searching. A person abandoned by his atishwin was as good as dead. But it would not help matters to speak of Chaki's lost atishwin, not even to the wot, so they gave a vague reply when he asked what happened. They dared not speak of the problem even among themselves. The power of an individual's dream helper was highly personal and delicate. They waited in agonized silence and watched for their cousin's approach on the trail up from Kahas Harbor.

With every night Grandmother Moon grew brighter. The crowd of people continued to fill the little valley of the big village. Alow and Kulaa wandered down the short lanes of Nimitlala, torn between wanting to stay on and needing to leave. Their young island friends were all antap and were busy preparing music and costumes for the festival dances. The visitors practiced with the village field hockey team.

The enhweq seemed to have truly missed them when they were away on Wima Island. Yet Alow felt more adrift when the girls found time to join them. For then Kulaa was likely to abandon him and slip out into the brush with his newfound love, Qupe. And he would be left devising projects so that he could avoid having to do the same with Leqte. Alow could tell from her look and manner that she would offer no objection if he asked her to go with him. He feared she might initiate something at any moment. He avoided her not out of distaste—not since the first day at the pool—or even entirely out of loyalty to his future wife, whose image in his memory had grown just a little dim, but because of the their being kin.

One afternoon, when Kulaa had gone for a stroll in the hills with the companionable Qupe and Alow was pretending to be repacking his gear, the wot approached him as temporary leader of his party and extended an invitation to remain for the Hutash Festival. Alow remembered with a pang his own promise to return to Mishopshno by then. Briefly, he glimpsed shadows and faces, the spirits of his friends and family. However, Chaki had not yet returned. He said yes, they would be honored to stay for the festival.

The festival took the same form as theirs at home—only in miniature. There was lots of good food. During the day there were field hockey matches and sports competitions of all kinds. There was intense gambling. Friends and relatives whose lives were usually separated by mountains and shores visited with one another. In the evening there was music and dancing in the sanctuary. And then there was more gambling, though Alow abstained.

Alow felt as if he were being reabsorbed into the timeless world he had experienced on his arrival. Everything here was complete, perfected. How easily he was transported, on entering the sanctuary, to ancient days. And when, in competition, he thrust his pole through a rolling hoop and defeated some new opponent, he thought that perhaps some of these contestants, these strangers, were, indeed, of the First People, those who later became animals. One of the men had the soft eyes of a buck and another the bright ones of a jack rabbit. One cackled like a crow and another shrieked like a jay. Alow felt the world shrinking about him. The images from home and of his blighted cousin Chaki dimmed. He was alive in the eternal moment and didn't want to ever leave.

One morning during the early days of the festival, Kulaa was surprised to come across Alow in deep conversation with a middle-aged island woman near the sweathouse mound. She was not from Nimitlala. The two were standing not far from the sweathouse, near the creek. The woman was leaning her brow against the strap of a bundle of brittle oak wood. Kulaa assumed the meeting was coincidental, yet the woman had tears in her eyes. And her speech was an emotional and rapid mixture of island and mainland phrases. Kulaa stopped unseen at the sweathouse door. He caught her vehement words, "My life is entirely changed. I am peaceful at last, among my family and in my native land. My gratitude to your father is boundless. Every day I praise him as my protector. He is like Sky Coyote." Alow stood still through it all. Kulaa thought the woman was kilamu, and he quietly backed into the sweathouse.

Kulaa, unlike his cousins, was able to gamble. One night he participated in a big team effort of hand game. He played beside Leqte and her family and against Qupe and hers. The Earth Team won most often. To young Leqte it seemed auspicious that Shup, whose power had begun to wane with the closing of seed season, should come out victorious in the contest. Others might think it was unbalanced, not giving Sun his due, but she, herself, felt empowered by association with the winning force. Taking pity on her defeated cousin and best friend, Qupe, she went to stay the night at her house.

Leqte climbed under the fur blanket of their shared sleeping place and snuggled up beside her cousin as she had done so many times before. Qupe had been silent all the way home. She had even ignored her young mainland admirer when he had addressed her in a friendly way. Now, when Qupe finally whispered to her cousin in the darkness of the warm domed room, there was a certain uncharacteristic edge to her voice that was almost spiteful. The hand game had been exhaustively fought, and the lead had passed back and forth many times before the defeat of the Sun Team. Now she whispered: "I can see you gloating, cousin, even in the dark. But I am as certain as I am that Eagle is wot of the Sky World that I saw you cheating tonight."

"Be still, cousin. I did no such thing. Perhaps it was you who did it. You know how it's done as well as I. Anyway, what if I did cheat? You could have exposed me."

"I didn't want to embarrass you. Not in front of everyone, especially not in front of that mainlander, Alapapa, whom you want so badly. Actually, everyone here already knows that you cheat."

"Well, little one, you certainly are a bad loser tonight. You know as well as I that the game can get pretty dull if no one takes any advantage. You're only throwing away your side's opportunity to win if you don't do what you can. It's the same as in the rest of life."

"I know, iwu, I'm sorry. And I do admire your daring. I likely will never expose you. But tell me, why is it that your man friend never gambles? We don't even know which team he is on. Why does he not go with you into the bushes? He looks at you in that way. Can he be married? Or is there some prohibition? What has he done?"

"Don't worry. Whatever the cause of his behavior, I will have the man from Mishopshno. I can tell that he is warming to me. Our cousin, in whose home Alapapa stays, says that he has spoken with him when they go to shoot and run. When he asked if any of the traders were married he replied that only the leader and his tomolmate were."

"And where is their leader, the married one? Won't he come here for the festival? Did he fall in love with one of those drudges at the mint?"

"I have heard—only by rumor—that he has lost something of vital importance."

"Keti! How terrible! He seemed such a good man."

"It's only a whisper; perhaps it's not true. But listen, cousin, there is something else I must confide to you." Leqte rolled over on her other side and listened for sounds of wakefulness from the rest of the house. She could hear nothing, not even a snore or a sigh. She put her trust in the privacy of the partitions surrounding their sleeping place. "Will you listen to me, but remain silent to the world?"

In the dark Qupe made an affirmative sign. She no longer felt so keenly the disappointment at losing at hand game. She was left with her curiosity—and a little anxiety. For her cousin sometimes confided disturbing things, unbalanced longings and actions.

"You know that our cousin, the future wot, is fond of me."

"Yes, yes. I know. I believe he would like to marry you."

"Never mind that—you know I could never stay here, I would die—but he is fond of me and will do whatever I wish."

"He and my father indulge you."

"Oh, shut up. You're making me lose the path. Just be quiet and listen. You know our cousin is powerful; his atishwins are strong. And his father's sister is a curing doctor of the Owl Family, an herbalist. He can get a hold of every strong herb and even charmstones. Well, he is working for me, on my behalf. He's helping me win the foreigner!"

"Cousin, it is too dangerous! Does he know what he is doing?"

"Of course not; he wants me himself. But he is doing no harm, no harm at all," she said sweetly. And, unburdened of her secret, Leqte yawned and dropped into deep sleep.

The festival in honor of Hutash and her bounty lasted nearly a week. On the last evening the most important of all the religious ceremonies was held: the speeches, long prayers, and the offerings of seeds from all participants. The most elaborate dances would follow. That afternoon some late arrivals straggled into Nimitlala village: Chaki, his brother-in-law, and the man's

son. Alow, Kulaa, and their tomolmates and bailers were overjoyed to
see them intact. But it was quickly plain that they had been defeated in
whatever they were attempting. They looked weary in spirit and they
hardly spoke. They drank a great deal of spring water and ransacked their
gear for tobacco to chew. Despite the terrific anxiety the others felt for their
leader, they were relieved to know they could finally go home. It was best
to face loss of power in one's native land.

That evening, when the sky began to darken and Moon at the harvest
festival shone over the eastern treetops, the whirring of the spirits and
the shrill whistles accompanying them called all participants to the dance
grounds. The wot, who led the ceremony, gave an eloquent speech in praise
of Shup. He called her "Hutash" in the ceremonial language and praised
her generosity, which made life possible. He admonished the assembled
islanders and their guests to treat her properly, respectfully. He told them
to scatter seed in prayer frequently and in all ways to honor her: "She is
half of the driving force of the worlds. And together with Sun she makes
the whole of life possible. Now, when the two halves of life are in perfect
balance, when Hutash is about to rest and renew herself in seclusion, now
is the time to acknowledge her. To remember and to remember always. To
remind the children. To teach them so that the seeds of truth might forever
fall on fertile soil and not be lost like ephemeral flowers blown away in
the wind."

The people were much moved by the speech and some of them cried.
The wot began to offer elaborate prayers to all directions, blowing smoke
after them. Then the material offerings began. While whistlers blew in the
small enclosure near the middle of the ring and the feathered banners from
every village fluttered in moonlight and firelight, women from all villages
and families came forward. Circling the most sacred enclosure, they offered
seeds from their recent harvest.

The Hutash Festival was indeed an occasion with special meaning
for women. It was they who tended the seed fields, beating the ripened
grain into their collecting baskets. When the grain was gathered it was
they who set fire to the brittle stubble. It was the women who toasted,
ground, and cooked the seed into the very foundation of life. Women
were the vessels of Hutash. Every year they came forward with their
baskets of seeds and returned them to generous Shup. That way her
festival was supported and preserved.

The traders from Mishopshno felt that peace that comes from
experiencing the repetition of a familiar ritual. Here they were, far from
home and family, perhaps even doomed, and yet the way of embracing

the sacred was everywhere the same. The sameness recalled to the heart the eternity of life. The visiting men were soothed and at the same time stimulated by the ceremony.

The songs and dances began. The guests saw some of the performances that had been presented for their entertainment on their first arrival. There were others, too, songs and dances learned long ago from the mainlanders. In feathered headdresses and skirts, with painted bodies and feathered wands, the dancers wove their spell. With faces daubed in red then traced in black and white, a pair of dancers, accompanied by singers, wound their way through the intricate subtleties of the Barracuda Dance. They blew bone whistles and waved feathers all the while. Then the nephew of the wot and other privileged young men presented the Arrow Dance. Leaping and twisting, they shot real arrows at one another but aimed to miss. The Fox Dance came again, the lone dancer, who was Qupe's father and Leqte's uncle, making his way to each fireplace. He shook his mussel-shell rattles and intimidated the audience with his long rock-bottomed braid. He sang many songs, most of them ribald and insinuating. The participants laughed and called out their own coarse verses.

Alow, totally absorbed in the night, recalled the insult he had composed in dishonor of Leqte. He was not surprised to hear himself, modifying it slightly, call it out as his own offering. The people laughed. He looked around for the girl, to see her response, but, of course, she was not there. As a dancer, she was not among the crowd but outside where the performers dressed. He was pleased with himself anyway.

Now the participants, who had been aroused by Fox, were awed by Swordfish and his dance. The sole performer wore a feathered headdress crossed on top by two egret feathers. His dance was as sedate as Fox's had been raucous. He floated slowly in circles. He sang a long, long song of praise and thanksgiving. Swordfish was wot of the Undersea World, and his watery kingdom was large.

Now, while wispy clouds sped across the face of Grandmother Moon, the people were joined together and with their ancestors in a cord of Timeless Time. They were back in that blissful age when animals and people were—and always are—one. They were returned to that age that came before the devastation of the Great Flood. Separation had not yet come into existence, and power was not only great, but all. In ritual they recaptured the Timeless Time not as a memory, but as a recurrence, a continuation. Here, now, animals and people spun together, singing, joking, dancing into one whole. The participants had come expecting to be entranced. And they were.

Alow, more than ever, was lost to the everyday world that existed beyond the sacred place. Gone was all sense of common time and home and boundaries. He saw everything as simple and beautiful as it had been on his first day. The intimations of poisoning made by his uncle at Silimihi were forgotten. Poison was without effect in this place, not only this sacred enclosure but this whole land. He was in another world. Instead of growing sleepy as he had the first night when he saw the island dances, Alow grew more and more alert.

The crystal houses of the Sky People followed their sky trails. The dancers wove on and on into the chilly night, and the singing and the rattles and whistles accompanied them. There was the Deer Dance from the mainland. And the Skunk Dance from Wima. There were dances of every being of power, not only animals but all living things. Alow witnessed, for the second time that month, the Seaweed Dance. The high-born girls of Nimitlala, sinuous and waving, weaving and beckoning, were transformed by dark feathered crowns, feathered skirts, and wands. They swayed. They sang. The songs were his favorites: the "Song of the Sound of the World," the "Song of Love of Home," the "Song of Endurance." Alow's passion for the little dancer with the sharp eyes and the soft low voice fluctuated with her liquid movements. Now he was lulled, now lured into depths.

The Seaweed Dance was the last dance. The star crystals had traveled far. But Alow, even more than the others, was unready to retire to his resting place. There was an excitement circulating among the celebrants. Couples crept stealthily into the bushes; others went openly. Older people gathered in knots to gamble. People wagered their most valued treasures. The singing did not stop. Alow recognized the melancholy flute playing of his own tomolmate coming from an oak grove east of the sacred grounds. The place was not far from the dancers' dressing area. He was drawn toward it.

After the Hutash Festival, Grandmother Moon began to rise later and later in the evening. The days continued warm but grew increasingly cloudy and humid. The last of the visiting islanders left Nimitlala. Yet the traders from Mishopshno and Qoloq of the mainland stayed on in damp and indecisive lethargy because of the indecision of their leader. Chaki was so morose he could hardly speak. He made no movement other than to roam endlessly around the hills that surrounded the village, retracing every step he had taken since their arrival. Yet his companions were certain that his atishwin was with him when he went to Wima Island. No one dared say anything to him about it. They felt for him strongly and only spoke words of encouragement. No one pressed him about leaving.

The other captains showed little interest in leaving, either. Kulaa was having such a good time at the village, eating, playing games, gambling, and going about with his island enhweq that he appeared in no hurry. And now, his older cousin, Alow, who had been so aloof in the early days and so dependable, had suddenly changed his path and was even worse than Kulaa in indulging lazy pastimes. Ever since the night of the festival, when his tomolmate had observed him stumbling out into the brush with the daughter of the wot, he had been oblivious not only to his tomolmates but to nearly everything else in the world except that girl. His friends argued among themselves about whether Alow was kilamu, trying to be polite, bewitched, or merely human. Some admitted that they would have liked to have such an opportunity with a wot's daughter. Alow was so taken with the girl that he even declined to come down with the men to Kahas Harbor to check on the boats. That was not good. Especially with Chaki refusing to come, too. The skinny little enhweq must have charmed the bait that captain Alow fed on. That's what they said.

Early one morning, down by the little trickling creek under the sycamores and the willows the skinny little enhweq encountered her slightly more shapely cousin. She was filling her water basket. "What shall we do today?" she asked her friend gaily, if a little sleepily.

"Oh, I don't know," Qupe replied. "I have a lot of work to do."

"What's the matter? You don't sound very enthusiastic. Has your boyfriend informed you that he's going back to his mother on the other side? Is he going to ask her to find him a civilized enhweq?"

"You don't need to be mean, cousin. It might come back to you. Actually, things are quite the opposite from what you imply. Only yesterday Kulaa told me that when he gets home he will tell his mother how much he likes me and that he wants to live here. He is sure she will arrange our marriage, if only we can persuade our fathers to take us over for their Winter Solstice Festival. What do you think? Can you believe it? I, who have no special power to assist me, may be going to the mainland in less than a season's time. I hardly believe it myself. And you? Will you be joining me? I couldn't bear to go without you. You seem to have finally caught the man you were set on."

Leqte's teasing twinkle faded from her eye as she confronted the truth. "I am happy for you," she said flatly. "For myself, I don't know yet. He has not spoken of marriage. I don't even know what family he is from. He's very mysterious. But I do know that he likes me. He is quite insatiable, actually." She continued in her chattering manner, "I wonder if the potion was too strong. To be honest, I don't know if I could keep up with it if we were married, though they say these things don't last. Oh, what am I saying, if we were married? I know he will speak of it soon, probably in just a few more days. He is certainly making no move to leave. I only hope he hasn't come to like it here so well that he will never want to go to the mainland. Then what would I do?"

Qupe listened sympathetically to her friend's disjointed speech. She held, for the first time, a more powerful position than her cousin and could afford an attitude of kind indulgence. As she loaded her filled water basket into her carrying net she said, "Have courage, iwu! Believe! You will be able to see it through. It is only a matter of time. You will reach your goal."

And Leqte had no doubt that she would. Though she was a woman, she was determined to know the wider world.

W hen the villagers on the mainland honored Shup after the harvest in the fall they often gathered in the big towns, in Shisholop, Syuhtun, Alkash, Sahpilil, and Mikiw. Some years, however, they joined together with their near neighbors, traveling little but inviting guests. Occasionally they would do both in the same year.

This year, the sacred ground atop Mishopshno village was swelled with celebrants from neighboring Qoloq and with representatives of the Yawelmani, who would be leaving soon for their homes in the Great Valley. Personal guests and kin of the wot who happened to be visiting him at the time of the event were also present. In addition there were passing transients, people who no longer had villages of their own. These unfortunates made little contribution to the wealth of the people, but they were harmless— unlike the hostile achanas who dealt in poison—and so the villagers fed them and welcomed them to their festival.

On the night Grandmother Moon was full the ceremonial ground was filled with Mishopshno's guests and inhabitants. As they danced at Nimitlala, so at Mishopshno the antap performed. Here, too, they danced the dances of the First People, the dances of those who survived the Great Flood to become animals. They danced Rabbit and Blackbird and Badger and Fox.

Tilinawit, master of ceremonies of the festivities, gave his own speech of thanksgiving. The year had brought an abundance of seeds—both those harvested and those still ripening on the oaks of the valley. He prayed to Shup as Hutash below their feet and to Sky above and to all the cardinal directions. His elder wife made a pleasing speech as well. Content with their lot, the people were responsive and exhibited a lively energy. They would need the energy to take them through the lean winter. The heaping baskets they saw all around helped give them confidence. If all continued well they might endure another year.

As elsewhere throughout the antap countries, the festival days saw intense field hockey matches, long foot races, and archery contests. Achanas vied to impress with their feats of power. They made trees sway and even move at long distances. The people marveled to see such wonders openly displayed. Day and night people gambled and traded. There were dances in the morning and in the evening, and there was feasting all day long. Acorn mush bubbled, "put-put-put," in deep huya cooking pots. Fresh fish roasted in coals. There were cakes made of hutash flour and of ilepesh flour. Cherry-nut balls and sweet and salty condiments gave savor to the meals. There was fresh venison and lots of rabbit. People ate till they felt they would burst.

But there were other appetites to feed as well. The bushes surrounding the village were often uncomfortably crowded. Yawelmani guests often went openly into the brush with young women or men from Mishopshno or Qoloq. In the early days of the festival little was said about this, though everyone noticed it.

Aleqwel scarcely paid attention to these activities other than to tell himself how glad he was that he was not born to be wot of the village. He would dislike having to deal with these delicate situations, while at the same time being so excessively admired by his own people. It was bad enough to have people turning away from him in awe just because his atishwin was strong. How would they act, he wondered, if he were to get still another spirit protector—as he soon hoped to do. What if he succeeded in poisoning a powerful doctor? Would he feel obliged to become an alchuklash? He thought that would be nearly as burdensome as being a wot.

But there was little time to ponder. The paint maker was engaged in his more modest trade in the service of antap. He ground and mixed a tremendous quantity of paint of all colors and assisted in decorating the dancers. He even applied black and white dots to the cheeks of his mother, who would be participating in the Seaweed Dance of the islanders.

And he was very worried. Alow had told him they would be back in time for the festival. Of course, things often came up, so it wasn't disastrous that they weren't back. But he would have to wait longer to know what happened, and he didn't want to. In addition, once he had made up his mind to kill the Wokoch, he found that the business of the festival days gave him little opportunity to plan how he would carry it out. There was not even time to fear the consequences of doing it, except in a remote part of his spirit, inaccessible to his thoughts.

On the last warm hazy morning of the Mishopshno Hutash Festival, Anihwoy, as partner of the wot's younger wife, danced the Seaweed Dance. She knew all the steps and words, which were in island language. Aleqwel, in the arena, admired his mother's performance, realizing, all at once, how proud he was of her. She was a famous doctor, she had even saved his own life. Even so, he couldn't help feeling, a little disloyally, that Ponoya might have interpreted the dance a little more charmingly. It was unfortunate, he thought, that Ponoya had not been enlisted in the antap. She might have been more suited to it than he was. He could be completely happy just traveling and grinding paint. But he was the eldest child so he was initiated.

When the dance ended, Aleqwel looked over at his sister, who was sitting near his side at the family fire. Her expression was concentrated on a distant point as if she were not wholly at the ceremony but wandering far away. The string of her red buckskin skirt had been let out a little more. It must have been obvious to all around that she was indeed pregnant.

Anakawin sat at her other side. He wore a serious look and asked, "What do the words of the song mean when she sings, 'In the land where I was born, never does the foreigner dare say that it is his'? Isn't wokoch another name for foreigner?"

When he heard this question, Aleqwel was struck as by crystal lightning. His younger brother, child though he was, was struggling with the same defensive hatred as he was. The boy's understanding was complete. Aleqwel bent forward to help his sister explain the line to him. In a serious and straightforward way he interpreted the phrase—not only the words, which were in Michumash speech—but their true meaning. Anakawin took it in solemnly. He looked strained, too strained for a ceremonial occasion. But Aleqwel had almost gotten used to the look. No doubt he himself wore the same face. Then, suddenly, the boy said, "When is Uncle Alow coming back? I miss him so!"

Older brother and sister exchanged a quick glance. Aleqwel said hastily, for the whistles had begun to play for the next dance, "He is still on the islands making money." And then the Dance of Coyote and the Nunashish began. The Nunashish had his face covered by a black feathered mask, and his cloak was also made of feathers. He danced and puffed on his whistle while Coyote pursued him with a toy bow and arrow. It was one of the dances in which the audience—the men, at least—could vigorously participate, shouting coarse verses and impressing their fellows with their wit. In the end—as anticipated—the Nunashish lifted his cloak from behind. While Coyote examined his backside, the Nunashish unloaded himself in his face. People moaned. They laughed so hard it seemed their sides would split. The children of the Coyote Family forgot all about their own troubles.

After the dances, when they returned to the everyday world where no one would dare consider defecating in public, let alone in anyone's face, Aleqwel and his family enjoyed the last of the feast. High clouds, some oddly shaped, drifted up from the southeast. The day was a hot one. While some people, perhaps inspired by the general abandon of the Nunashish Dance, were slipping off with their partners into the brush for the last, or possibly first, time, the rest ate and talked. They told their best—or worst— stories and initiated last-day trading arrangements. While eating, Aleqwel socialized with the bang-wearing Yawelmani, whose shy foreign ways kept them apart from many of the others.

Later, when they were alone for a moment, away from the festive circles, Ponoya and Aleqwel spoke together. Ponoya said anxiously, "Where is he, older brother? Where is the one who will be my husband? You heard him say he would return for the Hutash Festival."

"Don't worry, little one," soothed Aleqwel, who was equally anxious. "It has not been many days yet; things can happen. Perhaps a tomol was damaged and needs to be repaired, or the weather is not right. It could be anything."

"You speak just like his father. Mushu says, 'Don't worry; there are all sorts of things that can delay a seafarer.' I suppose he ought to know. But it's strange, isn't it, the old man reassuring me, while I'm supposed to be looking after him?" She laughed weakly.

"It's not so strange," said her brother. "Often the weak will grow strong."

"And the strong, weak," added his sister.

"Yes, that's true, too."

"Oh, elder brother, I am so frightened. What if he has drowned?"

"If something dreadful happened we would have heard of it, I'm sure. Have you talked with Pichiquich? Is she frightened, too?"

"Yes, I have. She appears very complacent. She suckles her child and imagines her new house and says she dare not think of her husband when he is away. But I don't believe her. She must feel something."

"My dear sister, it is probably all a matter of experience. You will have to learn not to be afraid when your sea-faring husband is a few days late."

"But that's the trouble. I don't even have a husband. What if he is killed? Who will raise my baby?"

"Taniw, don't upset yourself with these imaginings. I am strong. I will always take care of you."

"If you, yourself, survive," she burst out. She stared at him in a way that said she knew just what he was planning to do.

Aleqwel turned away. He felt tempted to brag about his atishwin, Lizard, who protected him. But, instead, he breathed deeply. He said, "I am concerned about the traders, too. Chaki is not the sort to give false promises. Still, they are not long overdue. Besides, what can we do?"

At that moment, their private conversation was interrupted by men's shouting and the shrill screaming of women. The outcry came from the direction of the beach. Along with many others, the two ran toward the sound. Not far from the sweathouse mound a circle of celebrants had formed. They shouted insults and encouragements at something in their midst. Some threw clods of dirt and others fistfuls of sand. Aleqwel instructed his pregnant sister to stand far back while he went forward to look. He peered over the shoulders of people in the crowd.

Inside the circle of people stood two men, one a commoner from Mishopshno, the other a handsome young man whom Aleqwel recognized, one of the Yawelmani. They were beating each other fiercely with sweatsticks. Sometimes they struck about the legs and chest, other times they beat their opponent on the head. It must have been early in the fight, for there was no blood and neither man appeared to be seriously injured. But both staggered dizzily and hurled slurred insults at each other between gasps and blows.

Near the two men, an adolescent girl stood—or, rather, hopped. Aleqwel recognized her as one of the common people of his own village. She was frenzied with emotion. She jumped up and down and screamed, her hair and tule skirt flapping about wildly. She was clearly an involved party, but Aleqwel could not determine which side she was on. Probably she does not know either, he concluded. It was only another brawl between individuals of different nations. It was unfortunate, but not a rare happening. The fighting man from Mishopshno was the brother of a young man—where was he?—with whom the wild girl was on friendly terms. And the other, a gentle-looking youth, was, of course, the foreign seducer. It seemed such an old story to young Aleqwel; but such stories, he knew, were not entirely predictable. Sometimes the fights flared into something more serious. He had heard of a village, not far away, that had, in earlier days, been burned entirely to the ground by Yawelmani after just such an incident. He looked around for Tilinawit, or his assistant, or Halashu.

The wot was the tallest man among them and he was striding down the hill toward the cluster of disputants near the shore. Aleqwel had faith that the situation would soon be under control. And when he heard the wot's first soothing words and saw how they calmed the combatants like salve on a wound, he walked away to find his sister.

"It's just the same as always—rivalry and seduction," Aleqwel told her with a slightly false air of understanding. "The jilted lover's brother has attacked the unprepared Yawelmani with his sweatstick."

"Imi!" cried Ponoya. "Is the foreigner even guilty?"

"Of course he is," said her brother. "Foreigners are always guilty. They have a great attractive power, you know. Besides, I saw them together one night."

Ponoya was impressed by her brother's knowledge. Still, she worried about the fighters' fate.

A fter leaving the scene of the brawl, Aleqwel and Ponoya walked down the path toward the beach. It attracted them because of the day's great heat, and, now, with these peculiar clouds, humidity as well. The ocean gleamed. Its surface was smooth, though there was a swell. No wind stirred to give support to the seagulls, who stood forlornly on the sand, first on one foot, then the other. They eyed the brother and sister expectantly. Aleqwel and Ponoya threw them a few pieces of seed loaf and directed the scavengers inland to the feast. But the patient birds just shifted feet and waited.

Brother and sister walked ankle deep through the cool ocean water. They could see schools of small fish in the crystal waves that broke beyond them. Aleqwel would have liked to have taken a swim, but his sister could not so they continued walking down the beach to the southeast. Like the village, the beach was alive with people, friends and strangers alike. The ocean was busy, too. Seals dove for fish, sea lions basked on the offshore reef, and otters played near the kelp.

But the young man and woman, different in many ways but alike in their devotion to each other, walked on through the crowds as if they were invisible. They rounded the rocky point where the tall shrine pole stood. Aleqwel proudly admired its bright red cloak. Though the tall stake had weathered since the winter solstice, it continued to stand through the seasons. He thought of navigators at sea who look for the colored poles to guide them when far from land. His sister must have had the same thought, for she whispered the name of their absent friend. And she paused to take a pinch of down from her pouch. She scattered it to the wind with a prayer. But there was no wind and the feathers fell straight to the sand at Ponoya's feet. Aleqwel pretended not to notice.

Now they walked the thin rope of beach between the ocean and the bluffs. They were not far from the cliffside encampment of the Yawelmani and the transients. They were quite alone now. And they walked in silence. They rounded one rocky point and then another. Ponoya had to lift her short skirts to keep them from getting wet in the ocean spray that lashed back from the landward rocks. Though he loved his sister more than anyone, Aleqwel was not accustomed to being much alone with her, and he hoped he would not have to talk much with her. Just then, she stopped right in front of him so that he nearly had to touch her. Before them both stood an old toothless woman wearing a dark feathered cape and an epsu hat.

The young people were both startled, though there was nothing to be afraid of. The woman greeted them civilly, if gummily.

"Haku, haku, Grandmother," they replied. They did not recognize her. Could she be one of the transients? Her feathered cape looked as if it might be valuable.

"Have you lost someone? Is there someone you wish to find?" the old woman asked.

"Who do you mean?" asked Aleqwel with a touch of suspicion.

"Oh, anyone. An iwu. A lover. Anyone at all," she answered with that empty smile. "I know where they are. I know where they all are. I can see them."

Ponoya made a move toward the old woman and began to speak, but Aleqwel clapped his hands. "Stop!" he commanded. "Who are you, old woman? Where do you come from? How did you get the power of divination? And what do you want from us?"

The old woman smiled blankly, as if she were slightly deaf and said, "I know where he is. If you want to know, too, I can show you." She stared straight into Ponoya's eyes. "If you want me, you don't need to go far to find me."

But Aleqwel said firmly, "Grandmother, go away and leave us alone. I know who you are now. You are no true diviner at all. You are only an apparition, the creation of a sorcerer."

"Oh, no. Se, se. You must mistake me for someone else," she protested, shrinking back. "I only want to help you. For a small price, of course."

But Aleqwel was convinced he had correctly identified the Holhol woman, the accomplice of Shuku's bear achana, although she no longer bore much resemblance to the voluptuous young woman who had abandoned his dreams when he finally named her. "You are not even a real person," he said. "You are a nunashish, and I can prove it, just allow me," and he stepped forward and reached up to remove her little basket hat.

But the woman turned from him sharply and ran. Quickly, she fled back down the beach in the direction of Shuku, her black feathered cape flapping. "See how she runs," said Aleqwel with disgust. "No old woman could run like that. Look, she is gone already."

Ponoya sat down on the nearest rock and stared into the swirling ocean water. At last she said, "Brother, I long to know the whereabouts of the fishermen. What if the old woman is a real diviner? How can you be so certain she is an imposter?"

"I recognized her," said Aleqwel.

Later that night, when the celebrants of the harvest festival had wearied of their pleasures and returned to their camps or homes to rest, Ponoya, in her sleeping place, found herself unable to keep her eyes closed. For the third time that night she threw off her light blanket and, wrapping her rabbit cloak around her, went out toward the clump of oak trees near her house to relieve herself.

Grandmother Moon had still not risen from her own sleeping place and was not there to help light the way. Ponoya had only her own torch to guide her. The oaks were dark and shroud-like, and the dry oak leaves crunched under her bare feet. The night was as still and warm as the day had been. She was glad there was no rustling in the oaks' branches. She prayed that there were no owls in the tree. Every night when she went out she dreaded hearing the sound of the great horned owl calling to her, crying that someone close to her was about to die.

As she turned to leave the wooded place her attention was caught by something dark fluttering near the trees. Ponoya's heart beat faster. She felt for her atishwin.

Just at that moment an old woman, harmless, wrinkled and toothless and bearing a small torch, stepped from the shadows. Ponoya put down her hand in relief. Then she realized that the old woman was the diviner, the one she had encountered that very day on the beach. She stepped back slightly.

"Don't be afraid, daughter," said the ancient creature. "Can't you see I am merely an old woman. I cannot hurt you. Really, you ought to show me more respect. Come here, taniw and call me 'Grandmother.'"

Ponoya stood her ground.

The woman in the black cloak approached. "Grandchild," she smiled toothlessly, "you came here to see me, didn't you?"

Ponoya hesitated. She couldn't be certain that what the old woman said wasn't true. While lying awake she had been thinking of the woman's promise. But her visit to the trees had been purely a call of nature. "No, I did not. And I am going home now. Kiwanan."

"All right, taniw, go! I must have been mistaken to think that you cared to know what Alow was doing."

At the sound of her lover's name, Ponoya froze in her retreat. She was like a small animal stunned by a throwing stick. She turned. "Can you really see him?" she asked.

"Of course, I can," said the old woman. "I told you, I have the gift of divination. I can see far-off places."

"But I have no money with me to pay you."

"Don't worry about money, granddaughter," said the old woman, generously. "You can pay me later."

Ponoya was like a bird in a snare. "Show me Alow," she said.

Without a moment's hesitation the old woman reached into a little leather pouch that hung at her waist. She withdrew a cord of twined eagle down and a loose arrow point. She stepped into a cleared space just beyond the trees. She looked around. No one was about. Then, in the flickering light of their combined torches, the old woman laid out the sacred cord in a circle on the ground. She placed the arrow tooth in the exact center of the circle and began to pray. All at once, in the midst of a muttered phrase, the arrow point leaped into the air of itself. It flew off into the dark. It flew south, in the direction of the channel islands.

Ponoya watched in amazement.

"Your man is on Michumash Island," said the old woman.

"But I already knew that," protested Ponoya, disappointment overcoming her awe.

"Were you absolutely certain?" asked the old woman. Then she opened her pouch again and took from it a large bird's egg. Ponoya thought it must have been a condor's. The old woman held the stone-like egg in front of her over the sacred circle. She appeared to be studying it. She frowned. Ponoya grew frantic with impatience, but she dared not interrupt.

After what seemed a long time the old woman spoke. "It is difficult to see over such a great distance—even with an egg. It's a good thing I have so much power," she laughed.

Ponoya could hardly bear it. "Do you see him? Is he well?" she cried out.

"Oh, yes," said the woman. "Oh, yes. Oh, very much so. I can see that. There is no problem with his vitality." And she proceeded to describe Alow's activities of that precise moment.

"I don't believe it," cried Ponoya on hearing the report. "My brother was right; you have only come to harm us. Haven't you done enough injury to our family already, you and your creator?"

"You do not believe my words, taniw? Perhaps you do not like what they say. Would you care to see for yourself?"

The old woman stretched out a bony arm and drew the disbelieving young woman to her side. "Look," she said. "Look into the egg. Anyone can see. It will not lie." And Ponoya had to look.

With a wave of nausea she witnessed for herself what the old diviner had described: her lover, Alow, asleep on the starry hillside of a foreign world. He lay entwined in spent embrace with some foreign girl. So, it was true. Words might lie, but this picture was severely honest. So it was this that prevented Alow from keeping his promise. This that kept him from returning to her. But what about Chaki, she wondered, where was he? Had he, too, lost sight of his native land, given himself up to such diversion? That she found impossible to believe, and she laughed.

The old woman mistook the laugh for a temporary madness. "I can help you," she offered, insidiously.

"What!" cried Ponoya. "Help me? How? Can you change a man's nature?"

The old woman seemed not to comprehend. "I can… take care of him. If you'd like."

Ponoya's bemused anger now flared into rage at the old woman. "What do you think, that I want to poison my own husband? If I wanted help, it would be to get him back—and soon." She turned her back and ran toward her house.

For days and days after her encounter with the diviner, Ponoya moved in a fog. She was well, but felt ill. She did her chores—and there was much cleaning up to do after the big celebration. She cooked for the family, and she found time to work on her basket, a little, but she did it all without interest. Yet no one around her seemed to notice.

The weather, which has turned from a cool serene fog to a motionless humid heat, gave everyone a wilted look. Thunderheads moving in imperceptibly from the southeast billowed up over the high mountains, while above the village thin clouds hovered in momoy-inspired patterns. The sultry ocean rolled to shore in smooth sharp swells. The high waves made it impossible to launch the boats. No one seemed to want to initiate anything—except swimming. People slept and waited.

Ponoya finally decided to confide in her older brother. She chose him even before a woman because he understood part of it already. One day, as he was sitting in front of their house desultorily grinding paint, she took up her basketry and went to sit beside him, making sure they were out of hearing of the others. She soon confessed what had happened with the old woman on the last night of the festival and that with the men still not returned she was even thinking of seeking out the old woman again. The confession came out on a wave of tears.

Aleqwel was angry. "Why couldn't you have listened to me? Aren't I your elder?" he said. "I told you that woman was no real diviner."

"You mean what she showed me was not true?" asked Ponoya with a twinge of hope in her voice. "What I saw looked so genuine."

Aleqwel crushed her hope. "I'm not saying it couldn't be true, what she saw. It certainly sounds possible, if you'll pardon my saying it. But it could be only a clever illusion of her own design. Her purpose in showing it to you was to give us harm and grief and not to help in any way." Aleqwel then sat silently for a long while almost like one accused. He bent over his small mortar as if intent on his work, but he never moved. Finally he straightened up and looked at his weary sister and said: "You are wise to come to me and so avoid further foolishness. Under these skies it is a nuisance even to move about. But what you tell me is important. I have decided what to do. I must find you a real diviner, a true one, and then together we will call the men home. How does that sound?"

"Thank you. Thank you," Ponoya exclaimed. "But where will you find another diviner? I know of none in Mishopshno. How expensive it must be," she added as an afterthought.

"Leave it to me," said her brother.

From contacts with his friends at the Yawelmani camp Aleqwel located a woman who promised to be an authentic diviner. He offered to pay her in shell beads, and she agreed to meet with him and his sister on the bluffs overlooking the sea. They were to bring a piece of clothing or ornament that Alow had worn next to his body.

Ponoya borrowed a necklace from Alow's house when she went to bring a meal to Mushu. She wondered if the man didn't suspect what she was doing, but he said nothing. Altogether, he seemed complacent about his son, though every night he, too, went with his guild brothers to the bluffs to build bonfires as guide lights for the absent mariners.

But it was under Sun's heat on the charred cliffs, not far from the Yawelmani camp, that the true diviner—who had learned the local language and ways from her Mishopshnoan husband, who had gone to live with her in the Great Valley—met with them and first began to sing for Alow's return.

Before commencing, she told Aleqwel that her singing was strong, but that things would go better if he could get some ayip, some poison of the kind that brought back negligent love. "What color is it?" he asked. And when she told him, he astounded all three by reaching into the pouch in his hair and extracting a thumb-sized ball of the very substance she had described.

"Then we will surely succeed," smiled the woman, who was not so very old and still possessed many of her teeth. "But first you must promise one thing," she said, turning to Ponoya. "When your man returns, you must refuse to speak to him until he swears never to do such a thing again. Do you understand? Next time, there may be no one who can help you."

Ponoya promised solemnly.

So the diviner sang for them. She sang over Alow's necklace and over the ayip, there on the desolate cliff in the enervating heat of early autumn. She sang the long song three times over.

The next day they met with her again, and she sang the persuasive song three times more. She did the same again on the third day. Then, after the last verse died away, the woman declared to Ponoya and Aleqwel: "He will be here in a few days time, however long it takes to get here from the islands." And she refused to be paid until Alow's return.

It was dawn. Alow woke out of a wandering dream. Its details were unclear, but he had the sense that it had gone on for a long time and that it had been strong. The new day was warm and breezeless, but the house was astir. Old women were cooking. A baby that was being washed cried loudly. Alow noticed that the assistant wot's wife was absent. He imagined she was steaming in the little sunken house with the other unclean women. The men had already left.

Alow jumped up. He grabbed his sweatstick and ran out. He feared being late. The island morning greeted him with perfect calm, stirred only by the cries of birds. High clouds loomed in the southeast. He didn't like their shapes. Standing there, in front of his host's door, contemplating the sky and the path to the sweathouse, Alow was suddenly overcome with the feeling that he had been on the island too long. The cloud shapes above him now took the forms of familiar places at home and of the faces of people he loved. He could almost hear the words of an insistent song, calling him, calling him back.

After sweating by the blaze of green willow wood, Alow scraped himself clean. At streamside, he washed himself thoroughly, even his hair. But he was not able to submerge his entire body because there were no pools in the shallow summer stream deep enough. For a moment, he stood there, knee deep in the lazy creek, remembering the green pool at the stream's source and the many happy days he had spent there. He saw Leqte and Qupe standing naked atop a boulder, holding hands. Leqte like a little fox, delightful and devious. Qupe modest and shy. The girls were now in the pit with the other unclean women. At least Leqte was not pregnant. He would have to leave without saying farewell to her.

When he was scrubbed and dry Alow sought out his kinsmen for a private talk. To keep up his courage he sang a song that came to him on the way. It hardened his determination, for he feared that the others would insist on remaining on the island.

To his surprise, Kulaa, who had been so taken up with the enhweq Qupe agreed to come home at once. "My family must be worrying," he said. "Frankly, I have wanted to leave ever since the festival, but you seemed immovable."

"So, the girl is not for you?"

"Quite the contrary. I want to marry her. But I must ask my mother—she will want to arrange it. It would be bad, bad manners just to bring the girl home with me, don't you think? I don't want to upset my people more than I already have. Our journey has stretched out so long."

"Good, good." said Alow. "Then you're ready to come home now?"

"Yes, of course, if Chaki is. I think I can arrange to see Qupe in the pit."

"Woi, don't do that! Send her a message."

They went to find Chaki. He looked up from the rock on which he was seated. He had such a sorrowful eye that Alow had to bend down to examine a feather on the ground to keep from showing his own tears. He knew as well as Chaki that without his atishwin working for him his remaining days would be few. Physical strength and endurance are of little use without the confidence that comes from knowing your dream helper is behind you. Even so, wouldn't it be better, thought Alow, for him to spend his last days at home with the people he loved?

Their leader said, "I would like to stay here a little longer. There are places yet to search. I'd like to make one more trip to Wima Island."

"Oh, my beloved cousin," cried Alow, "let's not stay here a moment longer. It's not good. Before many days the weather will turn bad. Look at the sky; see how many clouds there are already. Can't you think what everyone at home must be imagining?

Kulaa, watching one indomitable cousin trying to persuade the other, refrained from commenting. But it seemed to him that before that very morning Alow had given no thought at all to the worry and suffering of those at home. It must be a southern storm bringing change.

At last, after a long silence, Chaki modestly raised his eyes to Alow, as if to an elder brother or uncle, and consented. "You are right," he said sadly. "Why should we prolong their worry? If it pleases you, we will leave tomorrow."

"No, today," insisted Alow impatiently. "I beg your pardon, my captain, but we are already overdue. There can be no delay. Even now the day is heating up. If we pack now, we will be at Kahas Harbor by evening; then, we can be off at first dawn.

"All right, all right," said Chaki with resignation. He did not bother to try asserting authority. The details made little difference to him.

They had spent the afternoon loading their tomols with the wealth of their adventure. On one of their treks to the harbor Alow chastised his tomolmate, "Why did you tell the wot that we would return soon?"

"What else could I say? He was urging us to stay on with so much feeling that I couldn't deny him. He was so hospitable to us. I think he wanted us to stay always, to marry his nieces and rule at Nimitlala ourselves."

"None of us are of the Eagle Family. We had to go, and I thanked him cordially. But we're not coming back. Not soon anyway."

"And what about Leqte, his favorite daughter? You were so rude, going without even saying 'Kiwanan.' Do you want these people to be your enemies?"

"No, of course not," muttered Alow, as he arrived at the tomols and paddles under the sycamores where they had left them. "They are good partners," he added a little obscurely.

The night was dark and moonless. It was an inauspicious time for undertaking a voyage. Still, Alow deemed it more favorable than waiting for Moon's rebirth. By then the weather might turn bad. Worse, he—or the others—might lose the will to leave at all. The calm waters of Kahas Harbor were ruffled with a little swell. A soggy breeze came out of the east from the direction of Anyapah Island.

The men dressed and ate quickly in the dark before dawn. There was much limp kelp littering the beach. Perhaps it had been tossed up by rough waves and high tides. The air smelled damp, and the kelp mingled with sagebrush to produce a characteristic beach odor. The eldest of the faithful brothers from the tomol guild who had come to see them off said with misgiving, "I don't know what the great weather doctors of Wenemu would say, but at this time of year, with a southeast swell, there is always danger of a sudden storm." Nonetheless, he helped carry the tomols to the dark bay water. "Kiwanan. Alishtahan," he said.

As the traders left the peaceful harbor of Kahas, where people devoted their whole lives to working in stone, Grandfather Sun sent his first glinting rays, which struck the abalone inlaid ears of the three red tomols. This inspired Alow with courage and a feeling of exhilaration; he was longing now to be home, and he naturally took the lead. Before starting up the rhythmic chant that would guide their paddling for the next several hours, he quietly sang to himself the empowering words and melody of his own dream song. As he knelt on the grass mat in the tomol he instinctively touched the atishwin hanging at his neck. Then he rested the paddle across the tomol and unfastened the pouch that he wore in his hair. He extracted the long thin cord of eagle's down. He wrapped the magic string three times around his head. He was ready now to cross over.

The trip from Kahas to the eastern end of Michumash Island and across the channel to Anyapah Island was without incident. The swell was larger than they liked; they were doing too much work too soon. But the breeze was light and the clouds high. At Anyapah they saw something disturbing: beyond the island to the southeast lay a line of dark gray clouds. A storm was coming.

Alow thought they could make it to the mainland before the rain. Kulaa feared they might not be able to. The other men took one or the other side. The bailer boys looked scared for the first time on the trip. One cried for his grandmother. Chaki maintained an impartial and fatalistic indifference.

In the end Alow proved most persuasive when he pointed out that waiting on Anyapah Island would be little better than being out in the boats. If it rained, there would be scant shelter for them since there were no villages and few caves. If it turned out not to rain they would have a problem getting fresh water. With Alow's determined mood, no one dared suggest returning to Swahil on the east end of the big island to wait out the clouds. They were all tired of waiting.

The men in their low-lying planked canoes advanced into the open channel. The southeastern swell was indeed larger than usual. They had hard work hauling the tomols over the lapping crests and pushing in the direction of far-off Wenemu on the other shore. Opaque blue seawater like rolling hills hit them broadside, and it was difficult to keep oriented. The bailers worked steadily with great perseverance. Every one of the men had experience navigating in rough sea, and not one suggested turning back. But never had any of them had to face such waters so far out in the channel. They were caught in a southern squall, the most dangerous situation they could face at sea. But by the time they realized it they were nearly in the middle of the channel.

Even though Grandfather Sun had reached his zenith, the men did not pause to rest and look hopefully ahead. Instead of relief and accomplishment they felt only increased urgency. They scarcely had time for a drink of water and none at all for food. They scattered seeds and prayers. Blue-black waters, dense as huya, swallowed up all offerings. Somewhere in the depths, old gray-bearded Swordfish swam around and around hoping to indulge his greedy appetite. Kulaa took over the lead so Alow could rest a little. Chaki kept up but without initiative. All the time, the little bailing boys worked courageously to keep the white froth of the waves out of the boats. No one talked. The paddlers pulled hard on both sides, trying to keep from being pushed west of their goal. Broken clouds raced high overhead like an endless stream of fish bones. The gray line of rain hung over Anyapah Island.

The voyagers' bones began to ache as they paddled their hardest. Their knees were numb. Their faces dripped with humid sweat. Yet for all their labor, the waves rising and falling in slow deep undulation seemed, effortlessly, to push them back, away from the mainland shore.   S p r a y hurled into their faces. Kulaa struggled to keep his boat in the lead. Chaki brought up the rear with steady remorseless strokes. Then the wind began to pick up. The high dismembered clouds in a blue sky gave way to encroaching ominous gray. Hearts raced from exertion entangled with fear. Each captain did his best to keep his tomol aimed for the point of land that was Wenemu, their only hope. Still, no one spoke. Or if they did, it was carried away on the wind.

Time passed. But the men could not measure it by Sun's travels; all the sky had now become uniformly gray. But now the estuaries and bays and points of the mainland began to appear closer, larger and sharper. They were advancing. They could make out low smoke from many fires. Every man ached with exhaustion. But each paddled on—pulling on the left, pulling on the right—while the boys bailed. Their paddling songs were sucked away by the wind that had grown stronger. It seemed the captains might lose control of their boats. Alow called out to his atishwin.

Abruptly, the broad turgid swells of the open channel gave way to troughs of shallower sea. Mainland mountains distinguished themselves in purple and green. And, most wonderful of all, dull brown kelp beds began to shimmer before them like a mirage. A line of heavy brown pelicans rode the wind on their right-hand side. They could smell the land.

Then, in another swift stroke, low gray clouds crowded in on the men and boys in their red tomols. The way, though no longer far, grew obscure. A few raindrops fell. And then the wind grew stronger. It pushed them off course, twisted them askew. They heard a distant rumbling behind their backs in the southeast. The only things the captains could see at all clearly now were their own tomols and the line of spear-beaked pelicans to their right. They followed the seabirds. The navigators had no idea where they were. They were near the coast. But what coast? They were lost. They had no thoughts. No words. There was only power and hope.

Now the wind hurled rain at their backs. It was nearly impossible to keep the planked canoes bailed out; they were like eating vessels half full of acorn soup. Yet they remained afloat. The low rumbling in the east grew to a loud booming. And then to repeated ear-splitting crashes. Lightning crystals sparked between clouds, illuminating the desperate landscape.

The tomols, directed by the low flight of the pelicans, managed to enter the sphere of the kelp beds. The men had no idea how far off course they had been pushed; the heavy rain obscured their view, but they were not far from the coast. For a brief moment, they relaxed in the calmer waters inside the curtain of kelp. But their respite was short. The rain was increasing, and the growling din of thunder rolled closer. They could see fiery strokes of lightning as it flashed from cloud to sea, painting the ocean glowing white where it struck. The wind blew hard and chill. Already, the men were nearly drowned in ocean spray and rainwater, the boats brimming with both. They shivered. It was time to find the shore.

As he raised his paddle to stroke, Alow, who knelt in the rear of the middle tomol, was horrified to see the upper blade, which was high in the air, alight with dancing flames. He nearly fainted; he had heard stories of such things and he knew what the flames meant. Ahead of him he could see Kulaa's tomol barely visible in the storm, but with fires flickering like far-off signals on the tomol's ears, both fore and aft. Quickly, he turned back toward Chaki, whose boat still clung to the rear. That tomol, first in the line of the storm's attack, was aglow with tiny lights that skipped around the upper planks of its perimeter and all about the ears. Alow cried out at the sight of little sparks dancing in Chaki's hair.

The air crackled. There was a whirr and a buzz. At that instant, Alow's tomolmate, in the bow of the sodden tomol, called out in a shrill and terrible voice. He screamed for his atishwin. Alow turned toward him, and in that instant he died.

Seconds later, the blinding flash and deafening explosion existed only in a continuing low rumble. And in the vestiges of destruction they left behind.

Kulaa and his mates were the first to see again and to rise. Looking behind, they saw the singed tomol of captain Alow. No bodies were visible. Beyond that aimless craft, in the dark and squally afternoon, they could see nothing. There was no third boat. Kulaa cried with terror and exhaustion.

After an endless minute, Alow, his mate, and young bailer lifted their heads above the rim of their battered tomol. The dead had come to life. Kulaa cried with joy. The men had only been stunned and deafened. Trembling, he paddled toward his cousin's tomol.

Alow could neither hear nor see. The fierce crystalline light had blinded him. His hands were still dead. His shoulders ached as if a mountain had fallen on him. Without vision he was lost; he thought he must be somewhere on the road to Shimilaqsha. He began to shake violently. After a while, he thought he heard someone calling out to him from far away. He felt a hand on his sore shoulder. Who was calling him? "Kulaa, my cousin, are you dead, too?"

When they had stopped shaking and it seemed to Kulaa that Alow and his mates might be able to paddle, he indicated for them to follow him toward the shore. Though the head of the storm and passed by, they were still being swept northwest by intermittent slaps of wind and rain. There was no less rumbling than before, and the western sky blazed with the light of liquid crystals.

Alow made an effort to paddle, though he could not feel the wood in his hand. He spoke though he could barely hear. "Kulaa," he shouted, "are we really alive! Did you see it? Our atishwins.… But where is our captain?" He stopped paddling. "Where is the tomol?" He turned stiffly to look behind. Where last he had seen Chaki and his tomol shrouded in glowing light, he now saw nothing at all, only black writhing sea.

"I didn't see it," said Kulaa sorrowfully. "They must have been struck. It must have blown a hole in the tomol. There is nothing left."

"Woi, woi!" cried Alow, flinging water in the air with his lifeless hands. "No, No, No! Se, Se, Se!"

"I was never dead," cried Kulaa. "But when I first looked they were already gone. I thought you were dead, too."

In that moment, Alow vehemently wished that he was still dead.

"I think I saw their spirits, though," said Kulaa grimly. "There were three of them, small and white. One was smaller. It was while you were dead and I waited. The spirits floated right past your boat and came toward ours. We had to move out of their way; they passed right on by. Oh, cousin, we must find the shore while there is still time. Danger has not yet passed." And the younger led the elder toward the land, while the eldest went to the Undersea World.

What sand they fell on when they reached the shore they could not name, and they were unable even to lift the loaded boats far out of the water. Kulaa made sure each man was covered with furs. Then, in utter weariness, all six voyagers slept.

Next morning, some children, combing the damp beach for food and firewood, came upon the survivors. They were far north of the village of Wenemu, yet not near home.

The people of Ihsha, at the wide mouth of a river, took care of them until they were well again. With sorrow and tears, the villagers heard the story of their disaster and of their missing kinsmen. Every day they helped the men search the sand for bodies. The six survivors felt sick at the idea of the Swordfish wot claiming their cousins' remains. To be separated forever from the blissful land of Shimilaqsha—nothing could be worse for an antap.

They waited and waited, but no corpses floated in. The men, through the Ihshans' good care, began to be restored in body. Their tomols were singed, but remarkably intact. Their goods had mostly survived. It was time for them to face their people.

PART IV

CHAPTER 10

MONTH WHEN THOSE THAT ARE DRY COME DOWN

hesiq momoy an ciyam loqayi alahsiw

The two tomols rested for a brief spell beyond the surf before landing. The day shone warm and blue and cloudless. A little breeze ruffled the ocean water, but there was no swell to speak of. Alow raised his eyes to the eastern mountains. Tender young Moon was casting her pale infant light on them all. Nearly the whole village was out lining the shore: infants on cradle boards, children crawling in the sand, old people with aching joints bent over and supported by the young. He could even see his own father, his aunt, and his uncle. And he thought he could hear the people's sobbing, though their tears were too small to be seen. They always cried when the boats came back.

Once more Alow found himself wishing that he, too, had been struck by the deadly bolt. He would rather have died than bring grief to the people. He did not want to have to tell the news, though it was possible a ksen from Ihsha would have carried it first. He was afraid. Then he remembered: there was one person, at least, who would be glad to see him again. And the thought gave him courage. He made a signal to his cousin Kulaa.

The two canoes began to push in through the low surf to the sandy beach. They were met by the strong arms of the brothers of the tomol guild. Old Silkiset was among them. The guildsmen worked without speaking. Alow moved closer to the assembled people on the gray sand. They were sobbing uncontrollably. He still could not tell whether they wept from joy or sorrow. Chaki's father, his wife, and his sister stood dumbly looking out to sea. They

333

stared at a point beyond the line of waves as if they expected to see a third boat coming around the reef.

Alow, Kulaa, and their crew walked unsteadily on land. Not only were their knees stiff but Alow still ached in both his arms from the crystal bolt. His fingers tingled and his heart skipped and hurt. His memory of what had happened was dim. He, too, looked out to sea, searching for a third boat. He sought the leader.

Dignified and serious as usual and even imparting a hopeful air, the wot strode up to Alow, the elder captain. Sun glinted on the immense crystal hairpin in the headman's topknot; the stone was the symbol of Eagle, the Sky Wot, and his ability to transduce power. Alow shuddered at its flashing. The wot greeted him with great warmth. He congratulated him on his safe return and his valuable cargo.

On hearing these words one of the women in the crowd—Chaki's sister, who was married to his tomolmate, began to shout, "Yes, your cargo, your precious cargo. And what else did you bring? Where is my husband? Where is my son?"

Alow's mouth moved but he was unable to speak.

"No. No. Don't say anything! Only say are they alive? Show me their bodies! Where are the bodies?"

The wot should not be interrupted. But this was different. The crew stood in total silence. At last, Alow's bailer boy could stand the tension no longer. "They have drowned, cousin," he blurted out. "Your husband and son and your brother, too." Then he bolted from his captain's side and ran into the arms of his grandmother.

Alow confirmed what the boy had not been able to contain. "It's true. They have. There are no bodies." His words were hoarse and sad like the rasping of a flute.

His female cousin, the one who had demanded this dire information, began to wail horribly. Her children, mother, father, even her grandparents joined in. Pichiquich slumped to the sand like one dead herself. Both her husband and brother gone beneath the sea. Soon the whole village had heard the terrible news, which had been circulating as a rumor, and everyone began crying or wailing and throwing sand and dirt into the air. The dead mate's wife, Chaki's sister, began to beat her breast with a heavy beach cobble. It was impossible to restrain her.

Alow felt accused by the whole village. He turned as if to run back into the sea, but Tilinawit prevented him. He took the survivors aside to a separate place beside a pool of black bubbling malak. "What happened?" the wot asked sadly.

"We were hit with liquid crystal," said Kulaa. "It was near the shore—the mainland shore. The third boat disappeared."

Tilinawit did not sob, but he looked as sad as anyone could look.

Alow was unable to speak. His crewmate took the liberty of declaring, "The captain was abandoned by his atishwin." It did not need saying.

After a time, during which the five men stood silently apart while the rest of the village screamed and roared and the assistant wot and Halashu moved among them to try to bring some restraint, the downcast wot spoke again. It seemed to be painful for him even to breathe. "We saw the storm coming," he sighed. "The weather achana said it was a southern squall. Being warned by a diviner that your party might be returning, he made the ceremony to divert it. He was able to postpone the storm until late afternoon. It was the best he could do." Then, with resignation, he added, "But things happen, in the long run, as they must."

"The achana saved our lives," Kulaa hurried to proclaim.

Alow had his eye on the mourners, the grief-struck women. Chaki's sister was lying on the ground, her breast bleeding. She too looked dead. She might have crushed her chest with the rock. Pichiquich, the serene young mother, was seated in a heap on the sand. Tears poured from her like rain, while her little Kelele ran around in circles, throwing sand in the air, licking it off her fingers and crying because everyone else was. "There will not even be a burial," said Alow dejectedly.

The senior caretaker of the dead, an old woman of great esteem, had come quietly to stand beside the wot. She heard Alow's words and said, "It is always very hard for the family when the dead soul is unable to join the ancestors in blessed Shimilaqsha."

The fishermen knew it well. Their cousins would forever be in the Undersea World.

The days that followed were, if possible, even worse for Alow. Kulaa left him and their cousins and went back to his family at Qoloq. Though the village wailing had subsided, the young voyager was now confronted by the shorn heads and charcoal-blackened faces of his grieving relatives. He knew these gestures would admonish him for a long time, until the Mourning Ceremony. He felt an unspoken condemnation wherever he went. Worse, his beloved enhweq, his anticipated wife, not only showed him no sign of welcome or affection but she turned away from him and refused to speak. Although he returned with a valuable cargo, as he had hoped, Alow's vision of how it would turn out, the vision he had nurtured during the construction of the tomol, was shattered.

The days now were warm and blue and dry, crisp around the edges like the curling yellow sycamore leaves. There was no trace of humid southern heat. The valley was black with soot from the burning of the seed fields. The land seemed to Alow to reflect the black-faced grief of the villagers. Soon it would be time to collect acorns, the most important crop. But he had little interest in food. He felt listless and empty inside as if he were no longer leading a real life but only a temporary one, like a soul that had fallen off the bridge to the Sky World. He didn't know if the disaster had been his fault or not. Nevertheless, his tomol—his grandfather's tomol—had been damaged in the deadly storm and it needed to be repaired quickly, before the winter's rains began. And so he managed to engage himself in some purposeful activity, though it was Saqtele, the altomolich, who did most of the work.

Alow saw his father going out early to fish and he saw him coming home with heaping baskets of tuna to dry for winter.   But he did not want to go out in the water. As he lay by the sweathouse fire he thought of Chaki's sister, who was lying beside her home fire. Her rib bones were broken from striking herself so furiously with stones. He wondered if she would live. He wondered if she might try to poison him if she did survive.

His arms and ears gradually began to return to their normal functioning though his heart sometimes seemed to stop. Then his teeth began to ache. Every day the pain got worse. He felt that if it continued to increase it would soon become unbearable. He wondered if he dared consult his second mother Anihwoy, the curer. He wondered if he dared approach anyone. Why, why, why wouldn't Ponoya speak to him. She couldn't have known about the little fox girl.

Alow's days crept by. His nights were little better. The nights in this autumn-turning month were growing cold, clear and starry and cold. He could not sleep well and he took up the habit of his father before him of walking alone at night. He was not afraid of bears. He found no voluptuous friend. He found nothing. He would not be surprised if someone was trying to poison him.

More than a week had passed since the voyagers' return and Alow had spoken to almost no one—only a few words to his father, some to Saqtele, and a few more exchanged with his tomolmate. The Coyote Family didn't seek him out. He couldn't explain that it was Chaki who delayed them because of his lost atishwin. His behavior did not appear entirely unnatural, for no one in the village talked much these days. The lost men had had no wake or burial, and yet there was mourning. Mishopshno loved and depended on those who had died. They were good fishermen and brave merchants. The boy had been strong and promising. None was replaceable.

Alow made no attempt to sell his wares, and surprisingly little effort was made by anyone to contact him. The late paint maker's family stayed away. Villagers stuck close to the village and worked diligently at preparing for winter. They were drying fish and abalone and repairing the tule rafts and tomols and acorn baskets. Outside the village there were many bears and mountain lions and rattlesnakes about. It was so dry in the hills now that all animals were coming down in search of water.

One morning, while checking on the repairs to his tomol, Alow began to experience severe pain in his tooth. He could no longer endure it. He had to consult the curing doctor. With trepidation he took the familiar path to Anihwoy's house. Kanit and Ponoya were sitting out in front weaving loose mats of freshly picked reeds. Aleqwel was grinding paint. Alow greeted them as a group and all responded except Ponoya, who looked up but went on with her weaving. Alow's pain made him pass quickly into the house. He found Anihwoy kneeling by the fire stirring a pot of soup. Alow had not visited Anihwoy since his return. He did not know what to say to her. He finally blurted, "My tooth hurts!"

Ponoya's mother was still angry with the young man for his irresponsible behavior on the voyage. But seeing how unhappy and pained he looked, she took pity on him and agreed to help. She took a look at his tooth and saw, at once, that it was badly abscessed. She boiled up a tea of molar herb and red shanks. She gave him a cup of it to drink and a little pouchful of herbs to take home with him. She instructed him to eat only thin acorn broth and to lie with a heated slab on his jaw. And she gave him some cure-all root to improve his constitution. She told him to come see her again the following day.

Alow left the house feeling better, though the herbal cure had not yet taken effect. But in the night his tooth disturbed him again. He awoke from a dangerous dream. He was trembling all over. As soon as Grandfather Sun was up he went to Anihwoy's house. He did not stop to greet anyone.

Anihwoy said, "Your tooth is still not better. Did you do what I told you?"

Alow signaled his agreement.

"Then I'm afraid I'll have to pull it," she said.

He offered no objection.

"Afterward, you will have to stay with us for awhile." Anihwoy got down her dental kit and made the necessary preparations. She made up a tea and a poultice of poppy root to help numb the pain of extraction. Then she got some fine red tok string and wrapped in around the diseased molar. Alow did not flinch; he knew he would die if the sickness was not removed. Anihwoy had a delicacy that came of good hands and wide experience. This made the operation bearable.

After she got the tooth out, Anihwoy staunched the bleeding. Then she made up a sleeping place for the young man beside the fire. She told him not to eat anything for a few days and to abstain from meat for the next three months. She warned him also to abstain from sexual intercourse for the same period of time.

Alow could not speak. He was barely even conscious. He looked up at Anihwoy, whom he loved as if she were his own mother. He looked for malice in her expression as she gave the last injunction. He could find none. Nor any humor, either. He let the darkness take him over.

When his awareness returned the pain of illness had been replaced by the pain of the wound. He lay by the fire and slept again.

It was yet another day when he fully awoke. Aleqwel was sitting beside him offering a bowl of soup. Alow took it gracefully. His trembling and shivering had stopped, but his jaw was swollen. He was missing a part of himself, and he could not talk. They were alone in the house so Aleqwel talked to him. Aleqwel seemed to sense that his companion, his iwu since childhood, was now silenced by his own suffering and hardship, finally able to hear him. He confided his own experiences of the last month. Most prominently, he described the seed harvest, the deer hunt, and his irrevocable decision to kill the Shukuan bear achana. He admitted that he had never expected his life to go in such a way, that he never considered himself either a mystic or a warrior. But he said things were always going their own way without asking him and all he could do was to try to fit in and earnestly do the best he could.

From his bed by the fire Alow made signs of understanding and agreement. Though he could not say it, for the first time since his return he felt less alone.

Aleqwel said he believed that Alow might now see things as he did, that they had understanding. He said he hoped one day soon to hear the complete story of Alow's adventure. But he never mentioned the name of their late beloved companion, who was now a ghost and possibly dangerous to them.

Alow felt forgiven. He had no doubt that he had been accused in Aleqwel's eyes. Didn't everyone accuse him? Wasn't someone poisoning him? Why else would his tooth go bad? Even that sweet girl, Ponoya, who had told him so warmly and so often that she would stay with him always, even she…

Seeing his friend's eyes stray to some of Ponoya's creations, her baskets and mats, Aleqwel said, "Do you still value my sister and wish to marry her?"

Alow indicated that he did, though inside he was not sure now if he would make a good husband.

Aleqwel pressed hard on his friend's feelings, as if on a recalcitrant lump of pigment. "You are not good now, you know. Your power is weak. You are not reliable. But my sister still cares for you and the…" He stopped for a moment. "Why do you avoid her? Why don't you go to her and apologize? She is very unhappy. She knows what kept you on the island, and she is afraid you have forgotten her. You must ask for her forgiveness."

Alow sat up, distressed. He made sounds, "Se… se… se."

"No?" said Aleqwel. He felt clever in his handling of the situation; he forgot to give credit to his companion's inability to speak. "No? Good. In spite of your worthlessness, I have faith in you. I know you; you are my friend. It is because you have no mother, no sister to teach you, you are still like a taniw. But if you live, I believe you will learn to be good." He broke off again. Maybe his lecture took too much advantage of his friend's enfeebled condition. He said: "Ichantik, why don't you reconcile with my sister? You must swear to her you will never again do what you did. Then, I'm certain she will take you back."

Alow looked as if he would get up right then and run out in search of the enhweq. His friend pushed him down and offered him some willow-bark tea. "Do it when you are healed," he said.

Aleqwel went for the last time to the camp of the Yawelmani. They no longer showed any surprise at his comings and goings. He always talked with the people in their own words.

This afternoon the camp was filled with drying fish. Though the men from the Great Valley disdained to go far out to sea in boats, they were having success in kelp and surf fishing. They hauled in much food in their nets and on their lines and in their baskets. Soon they would return to their landlocked home and their summer's feasting would be only a memory preserved in the dried ocean fish they would carry back with them.

Aleqwel scattered seed at the tall shrine pole and prayed for a good acorn harvest. He begged the rains to have patience until it was over. Then he nearly stepped on a blotchy brown gopher snake that was lying across his path. He thanked his walking staff for warning him, for the creature could easily have been a rattlesnake. The pools of water around the encampment had dwindled, yet they still attracted every kind of animal: snake, deer, bobcat and mountain lion, even bear. He hurried on.

Just before coming to the camp he passed the place high on the bluffs where the woman diviner had sung for Alow's return. He scattered some money on that spot, too. She had done her work well. Too well, perhaps. Aleqwel knew he had not behaved in the best way in helping his sister bring Alow home; he should have consulted the achanas. The weather doctor might have advised him that the time was not propitious. And now three fishermen, one a good friend, were dead. The remembrance of his own rashness lingered like a devilish dream.

Aleqwel had a dual mission at the Yawelmani camp. His hair dripped with money beads and he wore many more lengths around his neck; he was going to spend the last of his gambling earnings. But the causes were good: he would pay the diviner for her expert services and he would make a necessary purchase for himself.

This time, when he exchanged greetings with his new trading partner and had accepted his condolences on behalf of the missing fishermen—even putting up with a stupid remark about the brutality of the sea—he looked up into the man's kind face, which was topped off by womanly bangs and which beamed down at him like Grandmother Moon herself, and said, "I want to buy some ayip. The black kind. For killing."

His partner neither questioned nor hesitated. He asked permission to withdraw for a moment to his shelter. When he returned he brought with him a small pouch. It concealed a carefully wrapped package. Cautiously, the man untied it; he displayed the thumb-sized black lump to Aleqwel.

The paint maker could not clearly distinguish the lump of ayip from a lump of prepared charcoal, though it did have a unique undefinable smell. If it was truly composed of pulverized rattlesnakes and ground mussel shells Aleqwel was none the wiser. He could easily be duped. Yet his life depended on its being the real thing. He scrutinized his partner. He did not offend him or display his own ignorance by saying, "Are you sure this is authentic?" He remembered the ayip for returning wandering love. It had worked. He began to bargain over the price.

When he departed from the Yawelmani this time, dispossessed of many lengths of beads, Aleqwel knew what sort of ayip he carried in the cane tube in the pouch in his hair. It was so powerful that he dared not touch it himself. It would be difficult finding a place to store it. Perhaps he would bury it in the hills. As he followed the path along the bluffs homeward Aleqwel thought: "After I kill the Wokoch our family will no longer have to fear for little brother. And I can walk freely in the hills, once more. I can return to my normal pursuits, after I kill the Wokoch. And Alow will not hesitate to marry my sister."

Suddenly, he realized how glad he was that the fisherman had taken his advice and apologized to his sister and that he and Ponoya were reconciled, though neither would tell him exactly how it happened. In spite of everything, the man did bring home with him from the islands a sizable amount of money. Perhaps his promise of faithfulness would even hold. Ponoya's belly was growing rounder every day.

A fter having his tooth out and setting things right with Ponoya, Alow began to feel a little more human, a little stronger. He still felt empty inside and bruised; it was as if he had fallen from a high place onto a pile of rocks and brush. And he was no Grandfather Coyote who could revive himself. It had almost been easier for him to push through the stormy swell and rain at sea than to raise himself from his present wreck. He could not imagine how he would ever be a worthwhile husband for Ponoya. But he was gratified that she was kind to him again. And he found some purpose in his life in going out to the kelp and fishing for the enhweq and her family.

At first he went out in his tule raft. Then, when it was repaired, he took his grandfather's tomol. Silkiset had taken Chaki's death hard. He had scarcely come out of his house since Alow and Kulaa's homecoming. Alow did not know where he stood with the old man, but since he did not even know where he stood with himself, perhaps it was not such an important matter. The storm-battered tomol stood up well, and Alow was still able to attract fish, though he had to expend more energy to bring in the same size catch. He had difficulty concentrating on the work, and it was only his desire to be useful to Ponoya and to repay her mother for her healing that kept him at it. Furthermore, he had a problem at sea that he never had on land: he was distracted by ghosts.

While pulling in a heavy line he would suddenly be confronted by his late cousin, hovering slightly west of his tomol. His presence made Alow angry. "Oh, my former cousin, why have you abandoned me?" he shouted. And then, incongruously, "Go away! Leave me alone! You are a ghost now. You do not belong here anymore!"

When he returned to land and had carried in the fish and split them for drying and had no more work to do, Alow continued to spend much of his time alone. He walked on the beach or sat by the fire at his father's house. Even on land he could not keep from feeling anger at his former cousin. Chaki had been like an older brother, even an uncle, to him, more influential than his own father. Who would be his guide now? Who would tell him what to do, how to behave? Who would teach him how to be a tomolman, a trader, a husband? Chaki had always been so upright and strong—perfect, almost. What mistake could the man have made to unleash such forces against him? What had led him to enter the forbidden cave at Matilha? For surely, thought Alow, that error must have been the cause of his downfall.

These questions were too difficult for the young man to resolve by himself. After all, his teacher had left him. When alone he continued to cry out, "Who will show me the way? Who will lift me from this fallen place?" One day, at a lonely spot on the beach he grew so desperate that he sang for his atishwin to come to him. Instead of anyone's coming, Alow began to feel very ill with a strangling sensation in his throat. He sat down abruptly on the sand where he had been walking. He felt as if he would die. It must be the ghost killing him. He wondered wildly if this was how Chaki had felt at the end. But it struck him that for Chaki it must have been worse, more frightening, more violent. His own memory of the fateful storm returned.

The young fishermen began to cry. He could no longer distinguish sorrow for himself from pity for his cousin. The living and the dead were joined. "My late cousin!" he sobbed. "You were so good. Always so good. You were kind to us all. What happened? I need you! Forgive me!"

The more he remembered his cousin—and his other cousins who had died—the more love he felt for them and the more he cried. He thought of Chaki's particular ways, his kindness, his endurance—and also his dullness, his priggishness that he used to make fun of. These last recollections strangely made him miss the man all the more. Situations and instances in which Chaki had been indispensable came rushing back to his mind. He recalled their journey in late spring and his own ill-considered pursuit of the mountain lion. Chaki's decisive intervention had saved his life. "How can we exist without him?" he cried, going beyond his own concerns to the life of the village. "He is part of us."

Somehow, in saying these words aloud, an invisible separation began to take place. Alow's cousin's ghost began to let him go. The survivor felt less choked, even as he cried. He began to experience a numbing relaxation and a fatigue. Then, a wave of loneliness swept over him like high surf. Yet the loneliness was more bearable than the emptiness and weakness he had been trying to endure before.

He sensed that someone had come and was sitting down just behind him. He turned around. It was Pelican, his atishwin. He looked strong and big-nosed and tough as always.

"I will guide you now," said Pelican with authority. "I always have." His message to Alow was stern but kind. "You must pay attention to me. You must not neglect me. You must be responsible. Sing my song every day and talk with my descendants whenever you are at sea. Feed me and dance my dance, and I will continue as an uncle to you. Did I not bring you through the storm? But you must always pay attention to what I tell you."

Alow cried again and promised that he would.

At Moon's fullness Aleqwel drank momoy tea for the third time that year. This was unusual for someone who wasn't a doctor. He had been abstaining from meat since newborn Moon and was in a pure state. He did not lie beneath the sacred sycamore, whose leaves were now parched and curling in autumn's dryness. Rather than seeking to hear the voices of the dead, he sought to strengthen himself, to find an additional atishwin so that he might better face the malicious poisoner.

Aleqwel's great-uncle, a spiritual descendant of Coyote himself, carefully mashed the root in its special mortar. The old man steeped the paste in cold spring water. Aleqwel knew how difficult it was to prepare the herb properly. He trusted the old man to bring him no harm; the alchuklash had long experience and few seekers had died under his care. Thinking of those who had died on their journeys brought Aleqwel little fear now—though it had at his first drinking. But now it seemed to him that there was really little difference between this world and eternal Shimilaqsha. This morning, this clear autumn morning, he felt strong and powerful, and though he had little fear of leaving the Earth World, he had no particular desire to move permanently to the Land of the Dead. He had contributed to restoring his sister's happiness and he had made a good profit on the paints he had sent with Alow to sell on the islands. He had purchased and hidden the weapon he would use to restore well-being to his family and village.

The alchuklash handed him the ceremonial drinking cup.

Aleqwel drained it in a single gulp. Then he composed himself on the sleeping mat to await his coming sickness.

He did not have to wait long before he began to feel the anticipated dizziness and trembling. He lost some of his composure and even began to be afraid. The crystal mansions in the sky were breaking apart and showering down on him. The sky was filled with their fiery rainbow fragments. Aleqwel did his best to hide, for he knew that when they struck him he would die. But he could not rise from his bed; his legs would not hold him. He felt as if he were being covered with a heavy blanket. It was pressing him down, suffocating him. He struggled. This was not how it was supposed to be. Aleqwel was drowning in fear. Finally, fatigue forced him to stop fighting. He had to give himself up. He gave up to whatever would befall him.

After an incalculable time Aleqwel became aware that the thick blanket that was enveloping him was made of down. It was piled high all over where he lay. He laughed aloud: the down was protecting him from everything bad, even from falling stars. He lay still in the muffled darkness, feeling safe. His eyes were of no use to him, yet he could see that his sleeping place was encircled with a long down cord, just as the Three Worlds are girdled by the Milky Way. He sank into the soft dark.

Sometime later, the young artisan found himself walking down a dusty path along high ocean cliffs. He did not know the place, but it looked familiar; it could have been anywhere. Soon he came to a small village set on the jagged nail of a finger of land that extended out and sank down into the ocean. No layer of blue smoke hung over the settlement, and Aleqwel concluded that the place was deserted. This displeased him, for he realized that he was thirsty, hungry, and tired; he had been traveling for a long time. Just as he was about to give up and move on he noticed a thin stream of smoke coiling up from a thatched house, one that stood near the high ground. He called at the open doors. Inside, two women sat by the fire cooking. They invited him in. "Eat! Eat!" they said and offered him a basketful of hutash porridge.

The younger woman was very clean and neat in her appearance and she worked busily, darting here and there. Aleqwel found her pleasing to look at, too. He admired her cape of iridescent green feathers. She told him she was Hummingbird Woman. Aleqwel recognized her. This attractive woman's sister, by contrast, was slovenly and lazy. She seemed only interested in eating and making lewd jokes. Her bare shoulders were draped with a black feathered cape. She eyed Aleqwel lecherously.

While he was greedily stuffing himself with their porridge, Aleqwel saw that this woman had a reddish patch in her hair, as if she had been splattered with paint pigment. He recognized her, too.

He said, "And you are Holhol, the Condor Impersonator."

The dark-feathered woman did not deny it. She smiled.

Aleqwel was frightened to be in the same room with this creature. But Hummingbird Woman pleased him very much, and it reassured him to have her there. He was tired, tired. He went to sleep in the house of the two sisters.

When he awoke the two women fed him again. They talked to him in a friendly way. They said they were lonely; their husbands had gone on a long trip to see the world. They invited him to stay on with them if he would help out by grinding pigments for their faces and hair. They said they wanted him to help keep Bear away. Bear was a dreadful hairy man with a ferocious temper. He lived in the mountains and had formerly been Holhol's lover. Now he came around threatening to reclaim her or to kill them both.

With some misgivings—mostly about grinding paint for hair— Aleqwel agreed to this proposal.

It seemed like the three lived together contentedly for some time. One day, when he was keeping an eye out for Bear while Hummingbird Woman bathed—Holhol never bathed—the painter was suddenly overcome with desire for her. He dared not act because he was afraid of her absent husband. But he had to tell her how he felt.

She said, "Yes, my husband is always vigilant, even when he appears to sleep. You could not easily fool him, not if he were here. Although, if he liked you he might forgive you. If you leave before he returns from his travels, however, he may never know we have been enjoying sex together."

Aleqwel was now so excited that he nearly fell on Hummingbird Woman right in the rocky brush by the streamside. But before he could accomplish it the young woman added, "If you do have me, though, you must have my sister, too. She is very jealous and will kill you otherwise. She is a powerful sorceress. But, if you love her and make her happy, she will be on your side, just as I am. My sister is deathly afraid of Bear and is grateful to you for keeping him away."

So the young man went back to the house with Hummingbird Woman. He found Holhol still lying down with her hair unbrushed and her feet dirty. He realized, then, that he wanted her, too, just as much as her sister. He climbed up on the sleeping place with her first and then did the same with Hummingbird Woman.

And so it seemed he continued to live happily in this way with both sisters for many days. Instead of feeling afraid or weakened by his contact with their power he felt stronger and stronger. It was as if he were absorbing their own qualities, Holhol's fierce magic and Hummingbird's goodness.

One day he said to Holhol, "Would your husband be terribly angry if he found out that I had been here with you?"

"Yes, of course. He would track you down," said the Condor Impersonator.

"But he's used to it," laughed Hummingbird Woman.

Just then, the three heard a calling—"wawawawaw"—in the distance. Holhol said, "I think I hear my husband now. You had better get lost."

So Aleqwel grabbed his carrying net and quickly thanked the women. At the low door Hummingbird Woman said to him, "Kiwanan! Remember, we like you. We will never forget you. But it is best that you do not upset our husbands."

Aleqwel ran out of the village, going in the other direction from the way he had come. He felt very well, very fine; the women had taken good care of him. Hummingbird Woman had even woven him a little treasure basket, and Holhol had promised to send him a present one day soon.

He traveled and traveled down the narrow path. But he met no one. The world was nearly empty. He marveled to realize that he was walking in the Timeless Time before the Great Flood, when animals were still people. Then he began to feel lonely. He kept himself happy by playing his elderberry wood flute and remembering the two women in the abandoned village.

One afternoon, he was resting, lying on the side of an ocean cliff. Sun napped in the sand dollar. Aleqwel thought he heard a distant sound like the sighing of a flute. He took out his flute and played an answer. The traveling musician came closer. Aleqwel looked up. Standing above his head were not one, but two men.

"Haku, haku," said the younger of the two.

Aleqwel jumped to his feet. "Haku, haku, uncle!" he cried. Right off, he recognized glorious Lizard, his ally, who had befriended him when, as a somewhat younger man, he first drank Momoy's tea. Lizard had not forgotten him, which filled his heart with joy. He begged Lizard to teach him the tune that he had been playing on his flute. Langorously, Lizard obliged, while his companion made up some scurrilous lyrics to go along with it. At the song's end Lizard said, "Nephew, you are wise not to accept too much hospitality from married women. But my friend was enjoying himself in my company and surely doesn't begrudge you some fun."

"Isn't that right?" he asked his shaggy-haired companion.

"Oh, of course, right," grunted the old man, who looked like a vagrant. He had his nose in Aleqwel's carrying net and was poking around like a dog scrounging for food.

Lizard continued talking in his worldly way. "Don't be afraid, nephew. I am your protector. Besides, life is a feast, and it is proper for you to partake of it. I hope you learned something from your visit. Don't get the idea, though, that it is wise to go around doing such things as you have done in the everyday world. You cannot have sex with an achana's wife or with your sister. But you are not stupid, you already know that. My oldest friend is here with me. He might even help you."

Aleqwel could not keep from noticing Lizard's companion's scruffy appearance and rude behavior. The old man could be no one but Grandfather Coyote himself. Clown, fool, scoundrel by reputation, he was also known for being a powerful doctor. Aleqwel laughed to see the mangy old man. But Coyote scowled: "Have you brought any food for me, nephew? I am starving."

Aleqwel gave him everything he had. He was not deceived by the man's silly ways. He knew how clever he was. He would be indeed fortunate if Coyote became his spirit helper. The old man— bedraggled as he was— possessed great powers. He could even revive the dead. No one could do more than that.

"Have you anything for me?" asked Aleqwel, surprising himself at his boldness.

"I should kill you," said Coyote. "But, since you already have seduced my wife you might as well have me, too."

"Keti!" wondered Aleqwel. "Does Coyote expect to have intercourse with me, too? This is quite incredible. I have not enough experience in these things."

But Coyote yawned, "Didn't you bring any cherry-nut balls? Listen, nephew: Holhol—that unfaithful wretch—gave me a good report of you. She asked me to give you this." He searched around haphazardly in a tattered gopherskin pouch, which hung low on his waist string. He paused to break wind. After a maddeningly long time he managed to extract a small arrow point, perfectly made.

Aleqwel understood what it was at once: it was a poisoning tooth, to use with ayip. His heart leapt with joy. Holhol had completely turned from Bear and was indeed on his side. And her husband appeared to be, also.

Coyote said, "Have you anything to use with it?"

"Yes, Grandfather," cried Aleqwel. And, trembling, he took down the poison pouch, which he had in his hair. He showed Coyote the cane tube and the lump of black ayip he had gotten from the Yawelmani.

Coyote sniffed the black thing and even dared to lick it with the tip of his tongue. He shook it and listened to it. He handed it back to Aleqwel. "It is good," he said.

By which he meant it had the power to bring death.

Many other things happened to Aleqwel. There were black empty places and troubles with several nunashish. There were a dozen other incidents that he could not remember. But the encounters with Hummingbird Woman, Holhol, Lizard, and Coyote were with him when he awoke to the alchuklash's singing. He related the tale to the old man when he could finally speak again.

The old man sang to him of his great good fortune in being chosen by such powerful atishwins. The old man might even have shown a little surprise, in spite of himself. He showed his young grand-nephew the gifts that Hummingbird Woman and Coyote had given him: the tiny treasure basket and the perfect obsidian point.

Later, as he convalesced, Aleqwel played Lizard's melody on his flute. He even managed to recall Coyote's ridiculous words to it. Such an outrageous dream song. He smiled.

Things were getting better in Alow's life since Ponoya and her family had forgiven him and since the day his atishwin had come to him on the beach. He felt stronger, as if he might, after all, some day raise himself up from his fall. He doubted he would ever regain the heights he had attained so easily before the disaster, but he had hope that he would someday move about with more confidence.

Along with the other fishermen, Alow paddled every day out to the kelp bed and beyond. He split and dried the fish from his heavy catch and put the tunas aside for winter. As he worked he watched families preparing to leave—and leaving—for the hills for the big acorn harvest. Soon it would rain—hadn't they been assured of it?—and more of life would take place indoors. People would begin telling the old stories again. They would work and sleep and depend on the acorns and the food he was preserving now. Alow fished carefully and steadily. His luck was not remarkable. But he encountered no more ghosts.

On land, he often kept to himself. Although he felt a renewed—even stronger—attachment to his enhweq, and was determined to marry her as soon as things were auspicious, he still frequently preferred to be alone with his grieving heart. When he was with Ponoya, it was usually in the company of her aunt or mother. He secretly admired her growing belly and tried to imagine himself the father of a child. It was very difficult for him to envision: their own child, a little taniw.

But since Ponoya was in such a dangerous condition, being pregnant—she could only touch her own person with a wooden finger—Alow could not find any comfort in being physically near her. When he went away from her he felt lonely. But he left with a sense of awe and wonder at her femaleness. He was glad for her strength and health. No poisoning had been attempted against her or her family since his return from sea. Her older brother, he knew, was planning some action to restore the family's security. Afterward, if it came out well, he and Ponoya would marry. And if it didn't? For now, he wanted to be alone, to build up his own strength.

One of the people Alow tried to avoid was Pichiquich, his late cousin's wife. It was not that he truly believed she was poisoning him. His deeper doubts concerned Pichiquich's other brother, who lived with his wife in Shuku: Chaki's sister's bones had still not healed. Pichiquich, though intact, was forlorn. Her ragged shorn hair and her blackened face always turned away when he approached. This turning away inevitably made him feel more miserable and lonely than ever. He made an effort not to cross the widow's path too often. It particularly hurt him, when she ignored him, because formerly she had been so friendly. She had been so warm and jovial in the old days. But what hurt him even more was to see his niece, little Kelele, blackened and shorn like her mother, crying whenever she saw him. The child would catch a glimpse of him and then run and hide behind the storage granary. Even his Seal Family uncle from Shalawa, blackened of face and worried as he was about his ailing daughter-in-law, treated him coolly. Chaki had been his only son, and now his daughter might die too.

Daily now, Alow walked away from the village and talked with his atishwin. He practiced his songs and danced his dance. He had never before been so serious about these things. But such things were private and he had to go out alone. Rarely did he think about his days on the islands. In many ways, the islands were still as much a mirage to him as they often seemed to mainland observers. However, he did bring back something valuable from his voyage: he now had a clear vision of the Timeless Time. He had truly experienced its permeation into everyday life. He was not sure how he would express that.

There was one immediate thing, though, that needed to be done. He had to sell some of the wares he had accumulated on the islands. So he received visitors at his father's house from time to time, people with an interest in buying his goods. Though the greatest part of his treasure consisted of shell money, newly minted, there was also a collection of digging weights and net sinkers, baskets and mortars, and steatite pots from distant Huya Island. He had also brought back harpoons of tough island ironwood and fur seal robes and woven otter blankets. He kept a fine huya pot and fur seal robe—for his future wife—and a Pelican robe for himself, but he tried to sell everything else.

One of his first customers was his friend Halashu. When he ducked into the open door of Mushu's house, Alow was not overly surprised to find Halashu alone inside, waiting. The fisherman knew he had been impolite in being late, but it seemed to him a minor failing when set beside his other faults. Halashu was cheerful and philosophical, full of shining words.

After greeting one another, Alow said, "What can I show you, ichantik?"

Halashu was comfortably situated on a mat by the fire. Cupped in his hands was a small treasure basket. It was beautifully wrapped and decorated in a spiraling pattern.

"Oh, if you don't mind, I'd like to see everything."

"Everything? Even the money?"

"Yes, I love the feel of new money, don't you? You must be quite wealthy now, you know. You could build a house for your wife."

"I thought it more worthwhile to save any money I make for buying my own tomol."

"Well, perhaps you are right. There's plenty of room in your father's house, anyway. Two families could live here easily."

"Yes," said Alow shortly. He did not want to talk about his impending marriage; it was still too indefinite. "Do you like the basket?" he said.

"Yes, very much," said Halashu. "The islanders do superior work. I should not say it, but this piece is finer than even my mother's best. It's so symmetrical, so well-composed. And pure. Did one of the wot's wives make it?"

"Actually, the wot at Nimitlala has only one wife. Do you remember his nephew? I spent some time with him over there. He sends you his greetings. Anyway, it was the wot's young daughter who made that basket."

"Really? Someone so young? She is certainly subtle—and skillful."

Alow smiled a weak smile. "Yes, she is, at that."

"My cousin Nacha is good at making baskets. But she could never match this." He held up the white, red, and black little globe and commended it: "Exquisite!" Then, softly, almost tenderly, he set it down and went ahead to examine the rest of Alow's collection. He admired and touched it all.

The two men relaxed as they looked over the acquisitions and commented on them. They began to talk freely. Halashu asked Alow about the tomol trip. It was the first time the trader spoke of it in detail to anyone. Alow shared a lot, though not of course his own involvement with the wot's daughter. Enlivened and relieved by the conversation, Alow in turn asked how things had gone in the village during his absence. Halashu told him about the ilepesh and hutash harvest, how it had been good and without loss of life. He described the Hutash Festival and the fight with the Yawelmani man.

"And Shuku?" Alow inquired cautiously.

"Nothing much happening," said the young wot. "No attacks. No threats. They even cooperate with us on some things. They seem to want only to impress us with this superior power, to lord it over us, but not to cause real harm. They are afraid to stir us up. It has been a good year for them, better than last; they are not hungry. We are confident, yet always vigilant."

Alow was relieved that no more secret ill had befallen his vulnerable little village. "Pichiquich's brother in Shuku?" inquired Alow.

"I hear your cousin is recovering," said Halashu.

"We can never expect real friendship with Shuku people," Alow glowered. "Whenever they need something they will get it from us somehow."

"Well I know it!" was the emphatic reply. And with that the political discussion ended.

Eventually, Halashu bought two expensive strands of fine huya beads and the elaborate little treasure basket with the delicate spirals.

Alow felt a certain relief in ridding his home of this basket. It was a reminder—however beautiful—of that little fox, Leqte. He felt stronger for having it gone.

Before he left, Halashu said, "I am going to visit Pichiquich. I want you to come with me."

Dutifully, Alow followed.

Pichiquich sat in the front work area of her mother's house, where she had moved. From where she sat, listlessly grinding seeds, she could see the wide blue channel and the backs of the islands humping up like spouting whales. The day was clear, blue, and breezy; not a cloud was to be seen. The young widow turned toward Halashu at the sound of his approach. She seemed pleased to see him. But when she became aware of Alow following some way behind, she began to cry and turned away.

"I told you I would come," the wot's nephew said to Pichiquich. "I told you I'd bring you something to make you feel better."

"No!" said Pichiquich. "Se, se! This one does not make me happy."

Alow hung his head silently. Then, trying to be brave, he said, "I know you do not like me anymore, cousin. You may have reason not to. But it was not I who decided to come here and bother you."

Pichiquich continued to cry, "Se, Se, Se!"

Alow felt like crying too. Halashu stepped back and away, almost like an atishwin when he retreats into the invisible.

Pichiquich looked at Alow sorrowfully. "You must not think I hate you," she said. "If I avoid you it is only because you remind me of so much. And of my own failings. Surely, you have done me no wrong. It was I who caused my own unhappiness."

Alow was startled by this pronouncement. "No, cousin. It was I who got seduced by the island. It was I who was late, and fatally impatient." He blurted it out, tactlessly. "I led us into doubtful weather. I thought…"

The widow was weeping once more, "No, no! Be quiet! It was not your doing. It was because of me! Don't you understand, I broke the proscription! I did it!"

At first Alow could not understand. Which proscription? There were so many. The woman had not been menstruating, he was certain. Then it hit like a bolt of liquid crystal. It had to have been the prohibition against sexual intercourse. His pity was aroused. So, Pichiquich felt as responsible as he did. She thought she killed her husband-and her brother as well. Did she, too, fear poison from the Shuku relatives?

"On the night that he left…" Pichiquich began her confession. But Halashu, from the obscuring shade of a green-leafed oak, stepped forward.

"Pichiquich," he said firmly. "It was your late husband, not you, who broke any proscription. You were only an instrument of necessity. He may have broken others besides. Perhaps the proscriptions were not strong enough to repair his violation of the sacred caves. Both you and your sister-in-law must understand that whatever happened to our former companion came originally from his own doing. It was inevitable."

"But my brother did nothing wrong. It's all because of me."

"There is much that we will never know. It was inevitable." Pichiquich and Alow were silent, she sitting, he standing. Both were trying to believe the young man's words. After a while they relented and began to soften, first toward themselves, then toward each other. They exchanged a few simple words and smiled faintly. Tears had cleansed the charcoal of death from Pichiquich's cheeks. Alow thought: "She is still beautiful. In a year or so, after the mourning period is over when her hair has grown out again, she will be able to remarry."

Just then, Kelele and her grandmother came out of the thatched house. Kelele smiled through her black paint. Halashu spoke to the taniw: "Look,

look. I brought your mother a pretty present. Alow brought these from the islands." And he took a beautiful huya bead necklace out of his carrying net and presented it to the widow.

The young widow commenced to cry again. As before, Alow could not interpret her tears. Did they spring from pleasure at the gift? Or from despondency over the thought of her husband's canoe sinking with all his valuable goods and money, as well as his own person? Or just the thought of the islands and the empty nights ahead.

Finally, Pichiquich looked up at Halashu and said, "You are very kind."

To her small daughter she said, "See, Halashu has brought two presents for us, taniw. Look." She showed Kelele the pretty necklace. Then she led the child over to the side of her cousin Alow and lifted her into his arms saying, "Your uncle is here."

The days, though warm still, grew shorter. And evening descended suddenly. Fires were tended through the black nights, and people going out after sunset wrapped in warm fur capes and robes. The clear skies and the leafy breezes announced, as resoundingly as a ksen might announce an upcoming festival, the imminent arrival of winter. Shup was dry now, and her creatures were thirsty. The first rain might fall any day. It was time to bring in the acorns.

For the last time that year the people went out to the hills with their baskets and gathering gear. Soon the bears and rattlesnakes would hibernate, and it would be safer to roam about. Now was the last time they were likely to encounter them. Later, wind, rain, and cold would drive the people into their own burrows. Or so the weather achana prayed.

When Alow came to say good-bye to Anihwoy and her children on the afternoon before their departure, he found the women stacking the coarse reed mats that had been spread all around the outdoor yard. For several weeks now, the women had been pulling tall basket reeds from the mud at the creek's mouth and from the adjacent salt marsh. They had been drying the reeds by weaving them into loose mats. Now, having made certain that the reeds were dry to their very hearts, they were bundling and wrapping them and storing them away from sunlight and moisture. There were enough reeds to supply the women with basket-making material for a whole year. Reeds were like acorns: they had to be plucked all at once, at the last minute, when thoroughly ripe. And it had to be done before the

rains began. Tilinawit must have been carefully observing the progress of
the reed drying, for he had announced the acorn harvest just when the reeds
were cured and ready to be put away.

Alow disliked parting from his friends so soon after his own return. He
was afraid of the bears and snakes that might attack them. He was afraid
that if he were left alone he would sink to the same abysmal state he had
fallen into after his arrival. He longed to go with the gatherers; he had
missed so many harvests. As a child, after his mother's death, he had to stay
in the village so that he could go out fishing with his father. The children of
wots and assistant wots and achanas could chase deer in the hills and fend
off bears, but his life had been, and had to be, in the ocean with the creatures
of the sea.

The young man and his future mother-in-law had come to a mutually
beneficial agreement concerning the exchange of fish and acorns. Now,
before the woman's departure, the two stopped to discuss some of the details
of the arrangement. When the business was settled, Alow shyly turned to
Ponoya. He told her he would miss her. He did not mention how afraid he
was for her. Now that she was so obviously pregnant she would be walking
bait for grizzly bears.

Ponoya answered his concern. "We are all strong now. Even Anakawin.
And we will come back soon, before you have time to notice our absence.
We have something to look forward to. When we get home the wot of Qoloq
will be celebrating his birthday; he has invited everyone to attend. The ksen
has just announced it. There will be music and dances and lots of food. He
is making it a farewell party for our summer visitors, as well. We can all go
to it together."

Alow smiled. He had not heard this news. He watched as Aleqwel and
Anakawin argued about where the picking poles were stored. The older
brother gave detailed instructions as to where they might be found. And
the younger went off enthusiastically, ignoring the instructions altogether.
Anakawin was not an ideal child, thought Alow, who realized he might
soon be sharing his home with him. But at least the boy was trying to help.
And it had to be admitted: it was the boy who eventually located the long
wooden tree-beaters in a highly unlikely place.

Alow set down the basket of tuna that he had brought for the family.
"The sky is bright and clear," he said. "Be careful!"

"Yes. Yes," they answered. "We will."

Nene spoke: "The days are dry, and the ground is covered with acorns.
It's better to have much work than none at all. It's better to have competition
for seeds than no seeds at all."

Alow agreed with these simple words and their unexpressed reference to rain and bears. He then turned and went back to his father's house.

Mushu and his son had never talked much. For one thing, the cold ocean water had begun to turn the older man deaf. For another, they were seldom home at the same time. And then his father had been apart in sadness. Alow had been afraid, when he returned from the islands, that the canoe disaster would make his father ill again. But, surprisingly, it did not. The fisherman had cried and wailed with the rest; he was obviously sad, yet the deaths did not seem to choke his heart. Perhaps it was because of the news his son gave him of Wenla and her happy arrival at her home village. He continued to work. He even assisted his more severely grieving relatives, those whose faces were blackened and whose heads were closely cropped.

The trip to the hills to gather acorns was probably the most important migration of the year. Most of the village, almost all of the women, had gone. The place was lonely. Alow and Mushu were forced to spend time together as they sat around the hearth fire, doing their own cooking, accompanied only by their dog.

The two men talked more than they ever had before.

"Father, will you look at me?" asked Alow one night. He was asking to be checked for fleas, lice, and ticks, which were particularly abundant at this dry time of year.

Mushu silently obliged. He picked the pests off his son and flicked them into the fire.

Alow felt a sense of well-being. He always did under this treatment.

It was a night during Grandmother Moon's absence. For the first time since his return, Alow wanted to talk about Wima Island. He felt like whispering his words, but his father's poor hearing required him to shout. Fish were roasting on the coals and, as he spoke, Alow had to tend them. He had to struggle with the boiling stones in the mush basket. Sparks flew up from the fire. They disappeared like souls in the night. Alow said, "Tell me about when you were at Wima."

Mushu did his best to oblige. Simply, he recounted the tale of the disaster that had befallen him at sea. One day, while fishing far into the channel, he and his mates had been caught by a strong wind. They lost control of the tomol. They thought they would all die.

Alow listened eagerly. He had heard this story before. He had heard it from all three men involved. He knew what had happened, how they had called on their atishwins and how, amazingly, they had managed to keep the tomol upright. "Just like Coyote and Duck Hawk," said Alow referring to the famous history.

"In some ways. In some ways," agreed Mushu. "But we landed on Wima, not Michumash. And we did not revive as easily as Coyote does."

"But you found an enhweq there to care for you—my late mother—who did the extraordinary thing of leaving her home with you for your own village."

Mushu did not indicate whether he had heard or not. "Tell me, how are your grandparents?" he asked. "Are they still alive?"

"Yes," said Alow. "They are old, but well. They were kind, kind to me even though I'm not sure they believed I was their grandson."

"Yes," said Mushu. "I was a stranger when they took me in. They cared for me. They were of the tomol guild, though they owned no boat; they made driftwood into planks."

"It is still the same," said Alow, "although it is my uncle who does that work now. Grandfather spends his days making nets."

"When I stayed in their home long ago," said Mushu, "I was very weak. My rib bones were broken. Our tomol was damaged. I remember their son and daughter, both so kind to me, giving me food and medicine. They taught me the names for things. They loved each other, too. It was their son who first called me 'Mushu.'"

"Tata recognized me. But he did not feel kind toward my companions. He thinks our relatives killed his sister."

"I suppose he dislikes me, too," said Mushu, sadly. "I did not want to leave. I could have lived the rest of my life in that little village. It was like being in the Timeless Time. It wasn't as civilized as here, but it was pure. You probably can't understand."

But Alow could.

Mushu continued: "I wanted to stay. Your grandparents wanted me to stay. I had no children then, of course. But my iwu, my cousins, were family men. As soon as they were well and the boat was repaired they wanted to return to their wives. I had my parents to think of, too. It is not good to make people worry too much. They light bonfires and wail and beat their chests in grief. In any case, I was not the captain. We had to cross the channel again."

"And my late mother?"

"I convinced her to come across with me. To marry me. I didn't ask anyone in my family. Her family thought it was ill advised. She should not leave her home village. But I had to bring something back with me from that place. She was the best."

There was silence as Alow threw brittle oak branches on the fire.

"Did she like it here?" he shouted finally, thinking of Wenla... and then, for some reason, of Leqte.

"I think she was content, especially after she had you children. But her parents were sad, I imagine. They never saw her again. And her brother... he was very angry when we left." Mushu broke off abruptly and returned to the present. "I'm glad your uncle was kind to you." He spoke a few phrases in Wiman.

Alow pleased him by replying in the same tongue.

The older man reached for his tobacco powder. He always used it to make himself drowsy at night. Alow rose stiffly and cleared away the dishes. Then he sat down again by the warming fire.

The two, and the snoring dog, were immobile for a long time. Alow could hear the breeze ruffling against the house thatching. The star crystals shone fiercely in the black night sky above their smoke hole. It was getting cold.

"Father," said Alow, at last. "Thank you for telling me. It was the same for me there, too. I never wanted to leave. Were you afraid for me? You seem so calm."

Mushu waited a long time before saying anything. His son was not sure that the man had heard.

Eventually, the older man spit out his wad of tobacco.   He was relaxed, intoxicated. He spoke slowly. "I never worried for you. I don't know why. When you left, I could see that your power was strong. But, for the others..."

Alow waited.

"I knew the moment your cousin—your late cousin—was dead. I saw his ghost, right here, by the fire. And the others, too. Their spirits had already left them. It was the night after Ponoya came here and took your necklace for the diviner. She didn't ask for it, but I knew what she was doing. Even before you returned, before you left the island, I knew my nephew was dead. It was a terrible thing to know, but I told no one. And, these same dreadful things made me believe you were still alive."

"Father," said Alow, "everything is strange to me these days. Things are not as they were. Your power has grown so strong."

Mushu replied, "Don't underestimate anyone just because they are in a weak time. Especially don't underestimate the Coyote Family."

CHAPTER 11

MONTH OF SULUPIAUSET, THE FIRST CANOE MAKER

hesiq momoy quwue sulupiauset

To honor the great inventor of the first tomol, Sulupiauset, the fishermen were abstaining in this season from going out on the ocean in their boats. It was a time of broken seas, of rough swells and changeable weather. Migrant tuna had already begun to leave the channel. The men had worked hard to bring in the mountains of fish that were dried and stored up for winter. The last of the big ones still hung on drying racks, like ornaments on a sacred tree. The days had grown cool and breezy, and streamside trees—sycamore, cottonwood, alder, and willow—were beginning to relax their grasp on leaves. Acorns were being hastily gathered and heaped in household granaries. The people knew that any day the first cold rainstorm could sweep down from the northern mountains.

Alow had been stimulated by his hearthside conversations with his father. He felt little regret when he had to haul in Silkiset's tomol for the duration of the month. He secured it under a roof of tall sycamores, away from high tides and sudden floods. Hawks on the highest treetops shrieked at him while he worked. He tried his best to hear what they were saying.

On the first day of Grandmother Moon's rebirth Alow left his father behind and ran up into the hills. In the cool shadowy autumn and unencumbered he was able to run nearly the whole distance to the hillside camp of his friends. He paused only at the tall shrine sycamore to tie a knot of squirrel skin on a sparsely leafed branch. He hurried on. The tree, like several other nearby places, was encircled by grizzly bear footprints. The rest of his way was clear. The blackened fields opened blackly before him. The sky covered him like a hard pale-gray shell. Shup was growing more ungenerous and, at the same time, weakening. Nonetheless, Alow felt in the deep breaths of cool air he took in as he ran the rising of a contrasting strength. In spite of everything that had happened he had managed to save the tomol. He had made money on his travels. He had even been able to bring in a good supply of fish for winter. Soon there would be rain and the Earth World would begin to be renewed.

Alow was relieved and delighted to find his friends all together. Ponoya was round and radiant, thoroughly alive beside her shy aunt, Kanit. Her younger brother and mother and her remarkable old grandmother were working nearby, packing things into carrying baskets. Various others of her kinsmen were there, too, even the powerful alchuklash and his wife. Alow admired the number of large baskets heaped full with brown acorns. The seeds were still wearing their little brown epsu caps. They clattered like shell money when he ran his hands through them. He praised Shup for her generosity: "It is because of the Earth Team winning last year in the Sky games. But how will it go this year, I wonder?" Everyone muttered something appropriate, expressions compounded of confidence and doubt. Then Alow remembered he had come to help.

Ponoya's family seemed grateful—even happy—to see him. "I suppose you have come to hurry us so we won't miss the birthday festival," Anihwoy said in friendly accusation. "We were just preparing to depart for the village. As soon as my elder son arrives. Oh, did you know, the rattlesnakes have finally gone into Shup's belly for the season."

Alow had been so relieved at the sight of his intended wife that he failed to notice the absence of Aleqwel. Where was Anihwoy's elder son? There had been so many bear tracks crossing the trail. Alow was certain his friend carried his talip bow, but in his true heart he did not have great confidence in his friend's marksmanship. Besides, what are mere arrows to a grizzly bear, or a bear achana? The beast could brush them away like cactus thorns.

It was shady under the dark oaken canopy where they stood. Alow began to shiver from his cooling sweat. He told himself, "How can I doubt my friend's power when we know that he and his sister can stand up to the bear. They outwitted him. Aleqwel's power is surely out of the ordinary— and growing. Someday, even I may be in awe of him. But the unrelenting poison, as much as a violated taboo, can break even the strong." Alow checked himself before unwanted memories of his late cousin took hold. He hopped around trying to keep warm, looking as if he were practicing his atishwin's dance. His bright-cheeked enhweq laughed openly at him while her aunt smiled discreetly. At that moment, the missing man appeared in the shady grove. A heavy acorn-filled basket was slung on his back.

Alow ran to his friend. While they were still apart from the others he said, "I tremble for you all. I saw the tracks. Have there been any sightings? Anyone attacked?"

"Se, Se," reassured Aleqwel. "The beasts are afraid of us. They wouldn't dare after the Bear Ceremony."

Alow wondered if the paint maker was serious about the Bear Ceremony. And, if not, was it right to joke? Certainly, Anakawin had not been protected. He said, "I saw many fresh tracks just outside the village—not far from the shrine tree—and beyond. And tracks don't appear without feet and claws, legs and bellies and teeth attached. You know how bears love pregnant women."

"How well I know it," said Aleqwel, bending to release his burden basket. With an air of greater seriousness he added, "I have seen many tracks here, too. But I am convinced that it is just one cowardly bear going around and around in circles. Alishtahan! Cheer up, ichantik! Soon old broadfoot will be taking a long nap and we will be safe in our own land again."

The wot of Qoloq's birthday party lasted a day and a night. The people of Mishopshno were invited along with the Yawelmani, who would be leaving the following morning for their Great Valley home; the people of Shalawa, neighbors on the north coast; and the inhabitants of Shuku to the south. The party commemorated the last of the acorn harvest and the end of the autumn fishing as well as the wot's birth. Rattlesnakes had gone to sleep and stories could be told. The next large celebration would be the Winter Solstice Festival. Because of this, the party was well attended. People flooded the small town like human driftwood. They were everywhere: talking, laughing, singing, gambling, playing sports, and eating. Wots and commoners jostled together in the narrow lanes of the little fishing village. At night there were dances.

Alow and Ponoya were the happiest they had been in a long time. They stood high on the crest of a sheer cliff above the village. They looked out over the black ocean. The night wrapped around them; it was dry and cold, the coldest yet of the declining season. They were dressed in their warm capes, Ponoya in the rabbit fur that sometimes made her look like a cottontail scurrying about in the fields and Alow in his expensive new robe of island pelican feathers. The sky over the mountains was obscured by clouds, but over the ocean in the west newborn Moon appeared as a crescent, more perfect than the finest pendant of shell or bone.

"Do you see those crystals?" asked Alow, pointing out two bright lights shining near Grandmother Moon. "Those are important Sky People. I believe the lower one may be the wot of the Sky World, himself."

Ponoya was not one to dispute with her man and so spoil her happiness. But she was almost certain he was wrong about the lower sky crystal belonging to Eagle. Wasn't the upper one brighter? Later in the evening she would ask her elder brother which gods they were. He was sure to know, having studied it all with the antap. Looking up at Alow's handsome features she wondered if she minded that her future husband was not of that select class of initiates. Her late father.... Tears sprang up at the memory. She blinked them away. Her late father had not been of the antap, and he had been a brave and honest man. He had called the star crystals "Sun's sparks." A cold wind began to blow. "Maybe we ought to go back to the ceremonial ground. It must be time for the dances," Ponoya said while looking into Alow's dark eyes.

The wot, whose birthday was being honored, sat by the foremost fireplace in the elliptical enclosure. The fire before him leapt high into the black autumn sky. He was not a young man. When he was born, his alchuklash, now gone ahead to Shimilaqsha and his own crystal abode, had told his parents that as a child of the Month of Sulupiauset he was destined one day to possess a great quantity of new-minted bead money. And so it had turned out; he was the wealthiest man in the village, not only in beads but in boats and seeds and with two wives. But, then, what chief wot, nephew of another chief wot would not be wealthy?

The dance began with whistles and rattles and singing. Down skirts swirled. Painted bodies were topped with high-plumed headdresses while feathered hand-wands waved.

The fire and the music made the old man dream. He recalled another prediction that had been made at his birth. He would grow to have a love of travel; the world would always protect him in his roaming. To his people—especially the common people—this forecast must appear to have come true. The necessities of his office probably made the prediction accurate enough. As wot he had to travel regularly for gatherings at Syuhtun. He even went to the big town as far west as Mikiw. And as a brother of the tomol guild he had voyaged up and down the coast and even occasionally across the channel to the distant islands. But, inside himself, the old wot was not convinced of the accuracy of the late alchuklash's prediction. As a wot the biggest journey he made each year was on the Winter Solstice when on the wings of momoy tea he flew to the Sky World to meet with Eagle and to learn what he could of the fate of his people in the coming year. But, in truth, the aging wot believed that the prophecy most likely concerned travel in the Earth World. And in the Earth World there was one place he liked best: home. He liked to fish and hunt and to make speeches. He liked giving parties and arranging the affairs of his people. He never had a lust to roam distant lands, to meet with uncivilized people in remote countries. Outlanders like the Yawelmani were tolerable as guests, as long as they followed the proper rules of conduct. But, for himself, he had no inclination at all to undertake the long trek that would lead to the other side of the mountains and their valley home. Leave that to the ksen. Here was the center of the world—or so it seemed to him.

He noticed his Yawelmani guests now. They had little experience in the proprieties of civilized behavior in the sanctuary, not being people of antap, and were talking too loudly and moving roughly around their fireplace near the dancers' exit. It was annoying. The wot of Qoloq sent his dance manager to quiet the rowdy guests and impose a fine if necessary.

Before long, the manager was back, sputtering with distress. He had been unable to subdue the Yawelmani. They had a local girl with them at their fire. She was a commoner, of course. They had been trying to persuade her to leave with them when they went home in the morning. The girl had refused and had tried to move away from the Yawelmani fire. The girl's Yawelmani would-be suitor had restrained her. She had fought back, creating the noise that had attracted the wot. They were still fighting and arguing when the manager arrived. Haltingly, he asked the wot's permission to evict all of them from the sacred arena. The dance performance was in danger of being seriously disrupted.

The wot sighed. What a thing to happen on his birthday. He was confident that his manager could handle the eviction safely. But he, himself, would now have to leave the arena to try to settle the dispute. He would miss some dances. He hoped not the Fox Dance; it was his favorite. He rose gravely. It was fortunate that in general he enjoyed soothing tempers and arranging compromises even more than he liked music and dancing.

Outside the enclosure a crowd had already gathered. In the center of the clot stood the thirty Yawelmani and the commoner enhweq from Qoloq and her family. Spectators hovered around the rim of the enclosure. Some found the prospect of a fight more stimulating than the sacred dances going on inside the ceremonial ground. Although there was no longer any danger of a fight breaking out in the sacred place, there was now a danger of emptying the arena and leaving the spectacle a shambles. The wot arrived just in time to hear the impassioned young Yawelmani man shouting at the grass-skirted enhweq of contention. She had evidently been wrenched from his grip and was folded in the circle of her family. "You said you would come with me!" he cried. "You said you were going…" Her family all began to yell at him at once, though undoubtedly none had understood his foreign words. A cold wind blew over the crowd from the northwest. The aging wot wrapped his long bear-skin robe about himself and stood up as tall as he could. He began to address the crowd.

With all the shouting and pushing and exhorting going on outside the enclosure and the singing and high-pitched whistles filling the arena itself, there were few who noticed the breathless arrival of a newcomer at the wot of Shuku's fireplace.

Aleqwel's gaze, however, never strayed far from the enemy. At first, when the stealthy young man arrived, Aleqwel's eyes could not identify him. But when he observed the young hunter speaking privately and with obvious excitement to the wot of Shuku, something inside him began to tighten in readiness and he felt for his atishwin. He was like a talip bow being strung. He did not recognize the messenger, but he could guess the message.

Shuluwish, wot of Shuku, turned as swiftly as a snake strikes. He spoke to a wealthy man of fearsome appearance at his side, whom Aleqwel imagined was the wot's poisoner. The poisoner—or whoever he was— seemed to be encouraging the wot to action. Then, before the discussion concluded, Aleqwel observed the entrance of another newcomer into the sanctuary. Though neither of the two runners approached him, the young man sensed that whatever was happening ultimately would involve him. He watched as vigilantly as his protector Lizard watches goings-on. No gesture or movement escaped his assessment. This new messenger was easier to identify—he was one of Mishopshno's spies. Aleqwel followed the progress of the spy from whom he had often attempted to hide. He narrowed his eyes as if he were dreaming, but he watched the spy moving closer to Mishopshno's fire. Like Shuluwish, Tilinawit had remained at his hearth when his host had gone out to try to subdue the storm that divided his own people from some of his guests. Aleqwel's stomach tightened as the spy approached. The tautly strung bow was being drawn. He prepared to jump up in an instant.

While the Qoloq singers sang and black-feathered Holhol danced, slapping his magic sticks together between his thighs, Shuluwish rose and went to Tilinawit's fireplace. Aleqwel was too far away to hear what they said, but the leaders' expressions confirmed what he already knew. The two occasional friends, descendants of Eagle, stood up majestically in their bearskin robes and left the enclosure together.

Aleqwel felt ill from the strain of holding himself back. He rose to one knee as if he might follow the two descendants of Sun out into the mundane world. But an old man's arm checked him. His great-uncle had also witnessed the important events taking place by the two hearths. He had a peaceful, almost cheerful, look. "Soon," he said.

Tilinawit returned alone and went to Aleqwel. He told him that Shuku's spies had spotted the Wokoch sneaking out of Shuku in his bear disguise. It was something Shuluwish had entirely prohibited. Tilinawit added that his own spies had seen a bear—a suspicious bear—lurking near the houses of Aleqwel's family in Mishopshno. When the spy, with his torch, had investigated, the bear scrambled toward the hills. The wot told Aleqwel—yes, he said it!—that if they found proof now, Aleqwel was free to kill the Wokoch.

The moment toward which all his concentration had been bent had finally come. Aleqwel and the alchuklash rose quickly and followed the spy to the path that led home. The young man wondered if anyone noticed their departure. He suspected not; he hoped not. Even his sister and her lover seemed oblivious to their leaving. He moved as in a dream. The spy, taciturn as ever, added little new information. No one was even supposed to know he was a spy.

The night was cold and the run from Qoloq to Mishopshno was not overly long, but the men were sweating. Slender Moon had long since departed, and clouds had begun to cover most of the sky. The men's way was lighted only by the sparks of their torches. "Now," Aleqwel sang to himself as he ran. "Now. Now."

The three arrived first at the alchuklash's house. All was in shadow. The doors were not as the old man and his wife had left them. They were flung open both inside and out. The old man bowed bravely and entered his domain.

There was a terrible shriek. A large feathered object hurtled past the doctor out the door and into the night. Aleqwel stumbled backward from shock. He trembled. The shock might have driven his atishwins away. The cry of the great horned owl had that power; it was a harbinger of death. Then he felt warm tears welling up. They fell silently. He could not bear for his great-uncle, whose house the owl invaded, to die now. Not this way.

But the old man had continued steadfastly on into the house. His grandnephew was left alone with his tremors and the unpleasant spy. Then the old man returned. He stepped outside, still alive. He came for Aleqwel as he would for one of his senior apprentices. He led the young man to his own sleeping place and pointed to some tiny flecks on the mattress. "See," he indicated, as if giving a lesson to the antap youth, "poison."

Aleqwel, still shaking and chilled and uncomfortable in the dark, defiled room crowded close to the old man. Their combined torchlights shone comfortingly. "Is it ayip?" he whispered.

"No. No, an herb," said the old man tersely. "But it's poison just the same."

With utmost care, the two removed the mattress. They dragged it the short distance to the creek. They threw it into the lazy, but purifying dark waters of late autumn.

Near Aleqwel's house they saw bear tracks. But inside they could find no poison herb, no ayip. Holhol Woman had given the young man the ability to see into things and to see underground, as well. He could see no poison. They were convinced there was no substance of that sort. But in his own sleeping place Aleqwel discovered one object: an owl feather. A single feather. The home of the young paint maker, too, was contaminated by the threat of death. Violent malicious death.

"Well," Aleqwel said tensely, "there is no lack of proof now, is there?"

It was dark, densely dark. The crystal houses of the Sky People were shrouded by clouds that had rolled in over the mountains from the north. Aleqwel did not follow the main trail that led southeastward to Shuku village. His enemy would not be there in the village, among people. And he would not be socializing at Qoloq. He would be alone. Aleqwel's wood-fiber torch, held close to his chest, lit his way through the blackened stubble of hutash and ilepesh to the territorial border and the southern creek.

Before crossing the creek, they young man had to extinguish his light. He listened to his noisy heart, which rattled like split cane at a festival dance. Then he touched his Lizard atishwin and began to crawl through the low dark brush. His senses were heightened by the blackness. The pungent odor of coastal sage filled his nostrils. It was the fragrance of purity. He found his way through faith. After the dense brush he forced himself into a forest of willows and cottonwoods and across a crunching bed of fallen sycamore leaves. The sound made him pause. Nothing moved, not even his heart. Not even an owl called. There was only the pulse of the gurgling creek.

Cautiously, Aleqwel went forward. He ducked under low-hanging branches; his bare feet squished along the muddy creek bank. While his determined hatred urged him to hurry onward, his natural patience, his experience in tracking, restrained him. With no light and no guide, he had only himself, the down cord encircling his chest, and the strength that his atishwins gave him. His miniature basket, their special gift to him, hung at his waist in the carrying net. In the basket, which until now had been hidden away, lay a perfect arrow point of black obsidian and a lump of deadly black ayip. Armed with these and his rage and despair, the young paint maker crept forward confidently. Had not two wots and their poisoners and his own great-uncle alchuklash sanctioned this act? What he was doing was right.

The pungent smell of bay leaves covered him. He had difficulty finding rocks over which to cross the deep places in the creek, so he waded right through. The lapping water ran cold between his thighs. But it was little colder than the long night itself. He believed he must be coming close to the place where the Wokoch's house might be. He had become an intruder himself.

Someone who behaved like the Wokoch would need to be alatishwinich. Aleqwel did not know who all his atishwins were, could not name them. But one, without doubt, was Holhol. Holhol could see over far-reaching distances and inside of things. Holhol could foretell the future. Would the black bird warn the bear achana of the approach of one who would bring him harm? Or had the evil achana not yet returned to his lair after planting his own poison in the rival village?

What was it the man had been called as a child? "Choi," they had said, "small." Had the intruder at Syuhtun been small in stature? He had forgotten the monster's actual appearance. The child "Choi" had been driven from Mishopshno long ago. Aleqwel followed the stream on the other side, keeping under the sycamores and oaks along the bank. He looked for signs of the achana's solitary home. He wondered what the bear doctor's real name was. He wanted more than anything to call it out in a final curse.

Then he spied the little isolated hut glowing in the black wilderness. The thatched dome was well hidden and he nearly missed seeing it. It lay in a shabby heap at the base of the foothills, even farther from Shuku village than he had expected. Thin smoke streamed out the top. It had the melancholy look of a dead soul wandering along the trail.

Aleqwel felt all his strength gather together and rise up. At the same moment, he experienced tremendous fear. The ramshackle hut was filled with power, ferocious power. And it was channeled against him, against his entire family, even against the mighty alchuklash. Aleqwel trembled as he had when the great horned owl had flown out at him with its message of death. His atishwins did not seem so invincible anymore.

The strong part of the young man tried to think. He had to devise a plan to gain access to the Wokoch. Above all, he needed to determine if the achana was inside the glowing house. It was time to get out his tools, too. He wondered if he was really doing this thing, this imaginary act. He felt empty inside. He was a shell, an acorn husk. He unwrapped his carrying net. This activity, this act, seemed ludicrous now for someone as unimportant as he.

Aleqwel had possessed the ingredients to do this act for some time. But, because of their nature, he had never been able to practice the moves and the feelings, not the way one could practice archery or harpooning. His close friends had always scoffed at his marksmanship. And now he had but one chance to achieve his goal. Wildly, he wondered if people really did kill with ayip. No one ever discussed the technique with him; he had never seen it done. He had only his dreams to guide him. Perhaps ayip was nothing more than a threat, an intimidation. That was how it had seemed to him in his long-ago childhood. Maybe he was about to do something no one else had ever done.

Just then, the outer door of the little tule house pushed open and a bear came out. No, it was not a bear; it was half a bear with a firebrand. The doctor's bear costume was half undone: the headpiece was thrown back and the front was unfastened. Fur still covered the man's legs and feet. He seemed to be wearing the attire more for warmth than for power. Aleqwel shivered in the shadowy clump of oaks where he lay in wait. Had the Holhol reported his presence? Was the intruder coming out to confront him?

The bear-man disappeared into a stand of oaks on the opposite side of the house from Aleqwel.

The young stalker remained crouching. He was as still as those First People carved in the high mountains. And he might never have moved had he not reminded himself of his hatred. The beast had killed his father. He had uttered his father's true name, like a curse, in front of his sister. He had attacked both Ponoya and himself in the guise of a grizzly. And he had torn his younger brother's flesh and eaten it. The litany of these black offenses moved the young paint maker. Quickly, he began to assemble the poisoned arrow. He moved surreptitiously in the shade of dark oaks.

The bear-man, with the animal's head flung back, sharp white teeth biting at the sky, returned. His firebrand revealed that the work he had been about had been purely domestic. His arms were filled with downed oak logs. They were clearly for his fireplace.

Aleqwel's indrawn breath almost gave him away. He felt disbelief… and relief… and anger. The Wokoch had no right to be so ordinary. He was a monster, only a monster. Merely a monster. But Aleqwel had no time to waste in contemplation. This moment was his best chance; maybe it would be his only chance. Cautiously, from its hollow cane tube, he extracted the ball of black ayip.

The powerful doctor stooped to enter the low door of his house. As he maneuvered the firewood through the doorway he turned slightly toward Aleqwel, the trees, and the poison. His thin chest and shoulders were bare, the bear's head thrust back.

Hurriedly, Aleqwel set the opened gift basket on his bare knee. Carefully, he placed the envenomed arrow tooth inside the basket. He did not dare spill a speck of the deadly substance on himself. He aimed the basket and the arrow point. He stared at the evil man. The man did indeed seem small without his bearskin. He did not look mighty at all. Yet, he was ugly; his eyes were remarkably round and his face was flat. An owl screeched in the trees above Aleqwel. He shuddered and nearly touched the deadly ayip to his own skin. The Wokoch looked up toward the owl in the oak trees.

The paint maker made a hasty prayer. He used the magical basket to launch the arrow point. The black obsidian point shot through the air. The sharp shaftless tooth flew across the night. It struck the bear achana in the left shoulder.

Aleqwel felt sick. He shook violently, as he did when momoy drink overcame him. He fell backward and died.

It was not long before he revived. He checked himself and found that he seemed to be unharmed. He sat up and looked over toward the little house. The bear doctor was slumped against the glowing frame. His firebrand was smoldering on the ground beside the heap of fallen oak branches.

Aleqwel, unsteady though he felt, had no choice but to advance toward the crumpled man. When he reached the doorway he picked up the firebrand. The bear doctor did not move, though it was possible that he was still breathing. Aleqwel saw the bloody gash on the achana's left shoulder. Tears filled his eyes. He exulted, "You are covered with dirt now, infamous crackfoot!" But the insults died there. There was no response; the creature was powerless. In a moment, all hatred drained from the young poisoner. The dead body lying before him was only a man, a former man. In fact, the man was of small stature and feeble build. He had been an insignificant man. "Choi," said Aleqwel, uttering a prayer of disempowerment.

But there was more to be done. First, there were the atishwins. They would be in the house. He was still awed by a place filled with so much power. He was reluctant to enter the intruder's lair. Yet it had to be done.

Inside, he found many atishwins. All were worthless now without their master. There were elliptical charmstones. There were herbs and powders and small baskets holding unknown substances. There was momoy root wrapped in leaves. And there were large baskets of money. The bear doctor must have been well paid for his dances. And he had no family to spend his fortune on. But most prominent in the house were the birds: hawks, owls, a red-headed condor. The docile assortment of powerful birds stood and stared at Aleqwel. They looked as though they were waiting. Maybe they intended to follow him. But the idea was ridiculous: he was no sorcerer. Two powerful atishwins were clearly enough for him. He shooed the birds out the door with a broom. Away to their freedom they flew.

Aleqwel approached the body for the last time. The atishwins that the former person wore had to be destroyed. The bear's foot, the down cord, and the others, all their power had to be undone.

The atishwins on the corpse still terrified him. But the man himself had already begun to subside. He appeared more like a spindly baby bird than a ferocious grizzly. Aleqwel was surprised to feel little fear as he stepped closer to the former man. Instead, he experienced only a sensation of great distance between himself and his late enemy. He wanted to be done so that he could go home and go to sleep. To sleep. And sleep. And sleep. It was getting colder, he thought, as he drew the knife from his hair.

He began to slash the atishwins from the neck of his former adversary. When he severed the cord of eagle down he felt Shup quiver a little. He cut a string with a yellow bear's tooth and put it in his magic basket. He heard a distant roaring in the mountains. Then he cut through a necklace of twisted human hair. What talisman could it be, he wondered?

Just then, a loud crash of thunder shook the hills near the house. Everything shuddered. A blanket of rain came down. Aleqwel felt himself drowning under heavy ocean waves. Everything was falling: water, trees, boulders. Frogs and rattlesnakes began to fall from the sky. He turned from the corpse and began to run for home as fast as he could.

"So, Thunder was his atishwin, too," he realized, as he tore across the creek and through the trees. "If only I could have cut off the bear's paw. But I have done my duty."

"I am alive and we are saved," he sang to himself over and over. "Now everything will be once again as it was." He chanted it in a flood of relief. He sang deliriously even as he was being struck with falling amphibians from the Sky World.

Mishopshno was filled with joy and mourning, especially among the well-to-do. For the wealthy had the most to gain and lose in trade and war and in the successes and failures of their children. Nothing could revive the brave dead seamen. And many of the leading villagers still went about in black paint, their black hair cropped more or less severely. Yet the intense joy felt by the family of the alchuklash, particularly his grand-niece, the curing doctor, and her children, at their release from the poisoner, spread like a fire in the wind—or an official secret—throughout the whole community. Commoners caught the excitement too. They experienced fully the sensation of having been rescued from a great danger, though, in spite of all the gossip, they could not name the precise nature of the danger or the manner of their salvation. They did know that the late paint maker's elder son had somehow defeated the power of one from Shuku who wished to destroy them all. Just as they had given themselves to despair when the traders returned without their companions, now they gave themselves up to jubilation. The wot announced a village feast.

Alow delighted in the look of emancipation he saw on his friends' faces. Anihwoy seemed to have grown younger overnight. Kanit came out more; she even smiled at people who were not kinsmen. Anakawin dashed around the lanes and beaches like a dog in spring, while Aleqwel wandered about with an expression of dazed relief on his face. Alow thought his friend looked like a person just returning from a bad dream. He was half amused to see the villagers coming to stare at Aleqwel, coming to witness the presence of a person greatly charged with power. The young hero, meanwhile, seemed hardly to notice the awestruck admirers. He sat down in front of his house and picked up his mortar and pestle and began grinding colored rock for paint.

Alow, now abstaining from the sea, shared in all this exuberance. Despite the weight of his mourning, he felt as if a large boulder were being lifted off him. He delighted in being able to associate freely with the Coyote Family, to be near them without fear of what the contact might bring. Soon the prohibitions would be over and he could build a house for his wife. His impulses were as strong and insistent as ever. But now he considered the consequences of his behavior and went out alone to dance and sing and listen to his atishwin. Most of all he enjoyed watching Ponoya. She had a brightness in her smile and a lightness to her step, in spite of an appreciable belly, that he could only indefinitely recall from the years when she was still a child. Now, she looked almost like that child again.

It had rained three times since the death of the intruder. And the salt marsh, which Alow crossed in his dugout, was filled with water. Alone, he poled his way between the herons and egrets. Ducks and geese, arriving for winter, were becoming numerous. It occurred to him that he could invite his companions to go hunting with him. Then he remembered the painful injury his friend and future brother-in-law had received on their last foray. This memory made him consider anew his friend's status as a poisoner of bear doctors. He wondered how his marriage would be affected by Aleqwel's fame. He had always had a natural trust in Aleqwel's sense, his judgment, his restraint. But he had never envisioned him as a powerful doctor.

Alow steered the hollowed log that was his boat to the shoreside of the lagoon. The high white sand dunes lay heaped up like hills of ground seeds. He arrived at his special place and debarked. With a sober mixture of melancholy and irrepressible happiness, Alow addressed his atishwin and danced a little. He expressed his doubts as to his own ability to succeed with a family. He wanted to listen earnestly to the advice of Pelican.

Finally, he decided to do something unusual; he hoped it would not displease Ponoya's mother. As he had no mother himself, he should have gone to the older women of the Pelican Family with his request. Most of these women were on Wima. Kulaa's mother in Qoloq was of the Pelican Family but not closely related. Instead, he would go to Anihwoy himself with his declaration and his gifts.

On the auspicious day of Moon's fullness, Alow announced his intention to his father and set out for Anihwoy's house. The village lanes were muddy as he climbed the hill. The sky was half covered with clouds; seagulls screamed and circled over the town. The day was cold. He had an uncomfortable sensation in his stomach. Would Anihwoy reject him?

Alow spoke to Ponoya's mother discreetly. He addressed her indirectly. "Woman, I like your daughter," he said. "Please pardon my saying this myself, but I have no mother to speak for me."

Anihwoy surprised him with her kindness. She seemed good natured every day now. The dark, smoky house looked sunnier, too. It was almost as if it was not the dying season, the short days of Sun's decline. Southern sunlight poured through the open door.

And then, they were no longer alone. Anakawin and his friends came running in, looking for food. Nene suddenly appeared with kindling for the fire. "I will tell my daughter what you say about her," said Anihwoy to the departing suitor.

Alow fled in elation. He told his father. Then he packed a bundle of presents—a thick fur seal cape, some long earrings, the expensive huya pot, fine things he had bought on the islands—and carried them solemnly to Anihwoy's door.

Then he waited. A day passed. Two. He could not eat or sleep. He walked alone at night in his pelican robe. The cold continued. The intruder had gone, but other nunashish always remained—the haphap, the yowoyow, the great horned owl, coyotes. He stayed up watching the Sky People in their travels. But he did not know what their movements signified. "Perhaps if I were antap," he sighed. He went home.

In the cool afternoon of the third day, when the sea and sky were gray, when Sun was so low in the south that the village shivered in shadow, Alow saw her. She was walking toward the beach. She was not far from his house. She was wrapped in a luxurious brown fur seal cape. She was walking where he would be sure to see her.

Alow wondered if he could have acquired Hummingbird as an atishwin without noticing it. It seemed to him that he flew to Ponoya's side with remarkable speed.

She did have Hummingbird for her atishwin. She, who had this powerful protector, she, who wove fine baskets, who cooked well and cared for young and old with such devotion—she would be his wife. For she was wearing his soft dark cape that he brought from across the sea. And all Mishopshno, all the Earth World, and especially he, could see.

"Is your new fur cape warm?" he asked.

"Yes, it is warm, warm," she replied cheerfully. Then, asserting herself, she asked, "Will you come home with me now?"

And, so, they were married. He went home with her and hung up his carrying net. Her mother had enlarged the sleeping place. Ponoya cooked and served thick acorn soup out of a beautiful green huya pot.

Alow built a house next door to Anihwoy's for himself and Ponoya. Aleqwel felt the change. It was only a short walk to his sister's new home. He still shared many meals of porridge and dried fish with her and her husband, his oldest friend. But he missed Ponoya's private attention. There was still Aunt Kanit to look after him and tell him how to behave, but they weren't close. He was aware that he lacked credible reason for visiting his sister so frequently.

His mother's home was warm and secure, if smoky, these short chilly days. He did not care to wander far afield. Instead, he sat on his mat by the fire. He was still filled with wonder and elation that things had returned to normal. If only his father could be restored to life. Such an admirable man he had been, so competent, yet unambitious, and so kind. "Well, now," thought Aleqwel as he stretched out by the hearth, "now I can begin where I left off. I can try to earn a good living for us all." And he dreamed of springtime travels and purchases and new contacts.

When he woke he thought, "At least, my wise sister has already married a man with good prospects." He dimly realized how his own terrible action had been decisive in making such a marriage possible. But the idea of his own significance made him uncomfortable, and he dropped it as he would a useless rock. He liked to look around the fire at the faces of the people he loved. Kanit and Anakawin were making animal shapes with their hands and their cat's cradle string. Alow and Ponoya came often. He watched his mother stirring the coals with the hearth stick. He stared up at his grandmother as she softly, but certainly, recounted stories of ancient days, of the power-filled days when people and animals could still talk together. He saw on every face relaxation, even contentment. Once again, Aleqwel felt a kind of joy. Could it be true that he—only a young paint maker—had brought this change about? For many days he was very happy.

But something peculiar happened that altered things. The excitement became too strong. His practiced vigilance would not leave him, and he stayed awake all night. His thoughts would not stop. His schemes proliferated so that he could not remember them all. In the long cold nights he listened for portentous sounds, the calls of coyotes, the cry of an owl. He worried about his great-uncle. And then he began to forget how to think. Work became difficult. Something that had sustained him was missing. The hatred he had lived on for so long, hatred for the evil intruder, was gone. It had abandoned him; it died with the puny achana. What was there to direct him now? Should he work just to acquire wealth? Grind rocks and more rocks. Make paints and clever bargains? Wasn't this what he had wanted?

Some days Aleqwel still went to see his sister at her house or at Mushu's. But he had trouble sitting still. He tried to concentrate on watching her work. He could see that she was happy working for her new husband and was helpful to her father-in-law. She was growing larger. She was clearly proud of her older brother, of his strength and courage. She probably could not imagine that he might need her now.

Whenever Aleqwel ventured out into the sharp blue waning days with their biting breezes and their white-flecked seas or into the cool gray overcast days of slim light and the promise of rain, whenever he ventured out into the lanes of Mishopshno to bathe in the creek or just walk on the beach he would come across someone in the sleepy sedentary village who would stop and stare at him. The villager would give him that peculiar look of admiration mixed with fear. People passing by no longer called out a casual, "Haku, haku. How is it going, paint maker?" A few hailed him in terms of exalted respect. But children ran away. No one called him "Ichantik" or "Aleqwel" anymore. This change was hard to accept.

Sometimes, in frustration, Aleqwel went to the sweathouse to hide in the smoke. He lay on the floor in the dark greenwood heat. He was confused. He was happy, floating, yet everything was mixed-up. Even in the sweathouse he was treated differently. He was hailed—or avoided—by powerful men much older than himself. It was even worse than the time when he had frightened away the bear in the mountains. He lay full length on the sandy floor, turning his face to his sweatstick, and trying to think of a plan. But nothing came. There was nothing for him to do now but lie by the fire and listen. He would listen to the old stories and wait for the rebirth of Grandfather Sun and spring.

One day, the official bard came to the sweathouse. He came to tell about the long ago adventures of Coyote and his friends. He began the stories as they always began: "It happened one time…" but Aleqwel found the bard's affected speech and stuttering irritating. Where was Piyokol, their true-born bard? Were there no artists left in Mishopshno? Even a small village like Matilha had more men of talent than his hometown.

The storyteller droned on about Coyote and Lizard and their adventures together. Aleqwel thought of his own adventures with his atishwins as he lay on the floor with his hand by his face. They seemed much more exciting than the ones the bard related. He looked at his hand; it was calloused and cracked. Yet it was dexterous and beautiful; it had been created by Lizard from the model of his own hand. Once again, Aleqwel felt grateful that humans had escaped getting Coyote's rough paws for hands. Such mitts could never grind paint and wield fine brushes, or shoot with bows or with magic.

Suddenly, unprepared, Aleqwel was overcome by the irrevocableness of what he had done. No matter how much he wished it, he would never be able to put the deed aside. He had poisoned a man. It had been his duty. Necessary. But it would rest with him forever. And if he were ever to forget, people would soon remind him. Much as he had longed to return to things as they were, he would never be able to. Never again would he be "the paint maker's elder son." He would be "the poisoner" or one of the other new names people called him. He would always wonder if others really killed as he had done or whether poisoning was only a threat that he had carried too far. Either way, he was set apart.

In the cold time, the sweathouse was usually crowded. Some days, Alow came too. Instead of being comforted by his friend's presence, Aleqwel found himself irritated even further. "Do you find married life agreeable?" he managed to say, hoping to imply that his friend was a fool not to be at home with his wife.

"Oh, yes, it's very comfortable, all I had hoped," smiled Alow sincerely. He displayed no intention of leaving the warm masculine refuge that was the sweathouse. "Did you hear my good news? Silkiset has given me the new tomol as a wedding gift. Very generous, don't you think?"

It was indeed. Ponoya was fortunate. Yet the young man felt stifled by the close quarters. He scraped off and, risking the ogling and trembling of the commoners, climbed out into the cool breezy day before the storyteller had reached the conclusion where Lizard and Coyote hang up their carrying nets.

At the top of the hill, where the cemetery nearly meets the ceremonial ground, Aleqwel ran into Tilinawit. "We were just going to see you," the wot said. He looked warm and powerful in his ankle-length bearskin cloak. Together, they went to the house of the official poisoner and from there to the alchuklash's. Aleqwel was bewildered by the attention. He passively accepted anything now.

The three high officials treated him with kindness and respect. Yet they did not quite elevate him to their own ranks of highest prestige. The wot made a charming, somewhat formal speech expressing his gratitude on behalf of all the people for helping keep the community safe from harm. He extolled Aleqwel's personal courage and ability, as well as other—to Aleqwel—implausible attributes. Then the wot spoke in a more personal way. Was Aleqwel aware of the rumors going around?

Did the wot mean was he aware the commoners had learned he had killed the bear doctor?

"No," said Aleqwel's wot. "There is a new story being told, and we believe it may be true. The people have gotten a hold of it somehow. You know how gossip is. Soon they will be worrying it to death."

"What is it?" asked Aleqwel, only mildly curious. What could it matter now, now that the Wokoch was dead?

"They say you did not kill the achana, not entirely. They say you killed him as a man, as a doctor, yes. But his atishwin, his bear paw, was left behind."

"That's true," said Aleqwel simply. "Thunder and rain drove me away before I could touch it."

"Well, they say—and I heard it from officials at Shuku themselves—they say they never found a body, only some bear tracks leading into the hills."

"I've heard that's often the case," responded Aleqwel. "The bear doctor becomes a real bear when he dies. But there are many bears about. An evil man is much worse than a wild animal."

"That's true, true," soothed the wot. "I intend no criticism. Your contribution stands. But we must gather facts as accurately as we can. Without knowledge we are powerless."

"You are right, wot. What you say may well be true," said Aleqwel, the junior poisoner. "I can't tell you what became of the Wokoch, for the achana's body was still at his front door when I left."

"I see. I see," the wot said.

Aleqwel waited. After a dignified pause, the wot spoke again. This time it concerned another subject.

"It is not long until the solstice."

Aleqwel found no appropriate reply to make so he waited.

"Soon I will be going to Syuhtun. I will meet with the others, even with the high wot—yes, the paqwot—to make plans for the celebration."

Aleqwel thought: "Now maybe he will ask what contribution I can make. He may assign something. It's bound to be something larger than last year, but what could it be? All I know is rock grinding and body painting."

But the wot surprised him. "The alchuklash and I have been talking. Before I leave for the big town there is something we ought to settle. As you have undoubtedly noticed, the people regard you differently now, now that you are a poisoner full of power. Maybe you have also noticed that they call you differently, too. No longer do they think of you as just "the Artisan."

Aleqwel had, indeed, heard some new nicknames. But they had left little impression on him. He almost took them as insults. After all, he was still grinding their paints every day; he was still making what they needed.

"Well, we have heard the names, even if your ears have been closed. And we believe it is important for us all that you accept one of them as your new name. You must not develop a habit of ignoring people. The alchuklash has selected an appropriate name for your use."

"What is it?" asked Aleqwel, embarrassed. He was flattered, but reluctant.

His great-uncle, the old man with pendulous earlobes, spoke. "Your new name is Ahiwalich," he declared.

Shortly thereafter, the meeting came to an end. The older men seemed pleased with the youth. They seemed to sincerely want his help. When they had left the alchuklash's house, the wot addressed him by his new name.

Ahiwalich. Ahiwalich, the Seer. He felt numb, like he did when he stayed in the ocean too long. When they were alone, the young man glared at his great-uncle. He felt betrayed; he hated the new name. It was as bad as Junior Poisoner. He probably would have hated any new name. He was honored to be called by such an exalted word, of course. But the only honor he wanted was the privilege of being allowed to return to his former ways. Couldn't they make things be as they were before? Couldn't people stop staring at him and calling him by ridiculous new names? Ahiwalich. Ahiwalich. How could he be the Seer, Ahiwalich, when he was still the Artisan, Aleqwel?

One night, the young paint maker had a dream. He slept little these days as he was stimulated by all that had happened to him. He also felt pressure to plan for all that was to come. He had to help his family regain its former economic security. And he wanted to reestablish his own peaceful obscurity. He was tired from trying to push away the new name they had given him. The dream came to him in the early hours before dawn, when he must have dozed for a moment. Its meaning was unmistakable: Eagle, Coyote, and Owl invited him to a conference in Coyote's house. They offered to make him an achana, to give him the abilities of the most powerful doctor; they did it simply, almost casually. They advised him that if he did agree to receive their gift he would, naturally, be bound to use these powers for the benefit of all the people, not just for himself. It was a flattering offer, but a frustrating one. They told him that he need not feel obliged to accept. He felt an urge to run away. But his feet stuck to the sandy floor of Coyote's house as if it were a bed of soft woqo. So he remained with the three great doctors and gravely gave his promise to consider their proposal. He would return, soon, with an answer.

The young man rose in the dark wintry morning. He shivered through his daily cleansing in the shallow creek. The sweathouse looked so much like a gopher mound and he laughed thinking of himself and the other important people as no better than gophers gnawing away in the dark.

Later, Grandfather Sun was just lifting his torch above the pass over the eastern mountains when Aleqwel-Ahiwalich presented himself at the door of the alchuklash's house. His great-aunt offered him a tempting array of dried fish and fruit and bulbs. She stirred fresh porridge in a dark huya pot set on three stones over the coals.

The young man wanted the alchuklash to tell him how to reply to Eagle, Coyote, and Owl. He knew that his great-uncle had always hoped he would follow his own way, instead of his father's. Nevertheless, he trusted the old man's fairness in the matter; he would adhere to the guidance of the Sky People.

The alchuklash thought for a moment. He did not seem startled by the question posed in the dream. Finally, he said, "Ahiwalich, besides dedication and even enthusiasm, a doctor must possess an inborn talent to do his work. I know you have questioned whether you have that gift. But, consider: the First People must have seen your ability if they decided to give such an invitation. We can trust them. "However, we are not certain of your other attributes. Could you be dedicated to a difficult service? Above all, are you capable of enthusiasm for this calling? The requirements of any healing practice are more severe than those of craftsmanship alone. I cannot give an answer for you."

The young man looked as if he might cry from disappointment or frustration, or maybe fatigue. He pleaded, "I am confused. The village stands as it always has, and we are here. Yet everything is different. I can't understand it. Won't you help me?" He looked beseechingly at the old man, who was decorated with his impressive atishwins. He felt more like an awestruck child than like the courageous hero he was acclaimed to be.

The alchuklash considered his words carefully: "I am not in a position to give you an answer. I only know your abilities. You must consider you own desires, your own leanings. It is growing close to the winter solstice now, and my thoughts must be bent beyond my own family to the healing of all the people. I must assist the wot and reconcile with the Sky People. But I do believe that now, even in this dark and cold time, if you went out by yourself into the hills you might find the One who could help you."

The young man made a movement toward the door. The old man held up a restraining arm: "Wait a few days. See if the great doctors come again with their offer. If they do, you will know the depth of their sincerity. And if they visit and you still don't know your heart, then go!"

The young man was disappointed at not being given an answer. He would have liked some advice, or hints, at the least. He did not want to go into the hills alone, not in the cold and dark time; up there it might rain or hail or even snow at any moment. He wanted to be in the village, free, at last, of fear. As he walked home he saw two people in one of the lower lanes. It was the carpenter and the carpenter's brother. They looked up at him and then resumed their conversation. He was certain he heard the name "Ahiwalich" floating on the wind.

The young man was gloomy all afternoon. Though the rattlesnakes, and even the bears, were hibernating now, he still would not be safe if he went into the hills. Fall and winter was the weak time for Sun and Earth. And for their human children. Nunashish were everywhere. And, if he managed to escape the nunashish, he still might freeze before he met the One who could answer his question. Who was the One, anyway? How could he find him?

He pondered this last question the rest of the day. Finally, he knew where he had to go. He would go east to Matilha and find its ancient alchuklash, Chnaway. The simple man had the spark of Grandfather Coyote, the first alchuklash, glowing in him still. He must be the One. Aleqwel would face the winter hills alone. He began to fast and to wait for a dream.

A few nights later, Aleqwel had the same dream as he had before. He was offered advanced power, the ability to see into things, to foretell the future, and to travel rapidly through time and space. He was offered all these skills to use for soul healing.

The next day the young man prepared to leave Mishopshno. He wrapped his chest in his down cord and made sure of his other atishwin, too. His mother prepared a few neatly tied packages of light food. His great-uncle gave him a small bundle of tobacco-shell powder for endurance. White frost covered all the damp puddles and the leaves in his mother's herb garden. It was the coldest morning of the season.

The youthful traveler picked up his toyon staff and walked out in the direction of Sun as he arrived near the eastern pass. The day, though cold, was clear and blue. It was good not having to be on the lookout for snakes or bears. And he had his otter cloak for warmth and his tobacco for stamina. His three-holed flute gave him companionship. He sang some traveling songs, invented for the occasion. And he trotted up through the valley and hills and then, beyond Shuku's creek, along the east-running mountain ridge. In fact, it was good to be alone again, not to have to listen to people whispering about him as they stepped aside in awe. Here, in the chaparral, he would not be called a poisoner or some new name. He could be Aleqwel still. He basked in this solitude like a lizard on a rock. No one talked about him. No one asked him to choose. He went forward without resting; he was neither tired nor hungry. He subsisted on tobacco powder. Many new songs came to him.

It was not long, however, before the wintry day began to draw to an end. Sun was low when he came to the top of the first pass. Aleqwel looked backward toward the ocean and forward to the streams and villages of the long valley in the east. The traveler considered the little smoke-wreathed settlement of Koyo below him. He remembered its old woman wot and its hunger for gossip. He did not crave their nighttime companionship; he wanted to avoid them, their questions, their stares. Even these mild isolated people would be able to sense his difference and might shun him. Or their fear might lead them to poison him. If those simple people down below knew who he was and what he had done they would certainly try to kill him. They could brush past him—so casually—with their ayip. Or they could plant it in his food or among the belongings in his carrying net.

Aleqwel decided to descend into the valley, skirting little Koyo village and instead head up the creek on which it was situated to some favorable-looking campsite. He knew it would be dangerous, alone at night and in the cold of winter. And if the villagers spotted him.... But he knew the art of concealment. His atishwins were strong; they would keep him safe from monsters. He would extinguish his fire before even the first flicker of dawn. He must see no one but the one man who could help him answer his question.

Aleqwel set down his staff and made his solitary camp by the side of the creek under yellow-leafed sycamores. It was a cold and uncomfortable night and he slept little. But in the morning he felt full of energy. He had the idea that he might be able to reach Matilha before noon that very day. He had never made the journey that quickly. But wasn't he stronger now and courageous and enduring? Hadn't he survived the night alone? He felt he could do anything.

Cutting across the fire-blackened soil of the oak-wooded valley he came once more to the principal trail where it ran beneath the sacred mountains. He stared up at the high white-rocked peaks with the forms of First People embedded in them. Aleqwel stopped to say a prayer to the tallest mountain, which reached upward to the Sky World. He addressed the petrified remains of the First People, those who had not survived the Great Flood. He felt drenched with holiness. He looked out over the fire-scarred oaks that shared the deserted field with him. How strong and enduring they were, how immortal their ever-renewing leaves. Aleqwel approached them as if they were shrine trees, though their stature was shorter than any sycamore. He made prayers to the oaks. He tied little strips of rabbit fur to their fire-yellowed leaves. Then he noticed other trees, more humble still, but beautiful in their endurance. He began to speak to them as if they, too, were capable of stretching to the roof of the Sky World. Why had the great doctors failed to realize that all trees were equal to the great shrine trees? Any tree could be a ladder to the sky. Or was it one of the secrets withheld from the less initiated? Ought he to tell them? Then his attention shifted to the sacredness of everything around him. He experienced it not as he always had, with the knowledge that all things live and have power, but immediately, intensely. He could feel the feelings of even the plainest chunk of sandstone rock. For a while he felt heavy, lethargic and mindless. Then he shifted his attention and began to address each humble plant and twig and pebble in turn. He listened carefully to their replies and offered them his prayers and even his tears. In this way he wandered through the fields—and some distance from the main path. He was startled when he heard human voices in the distance. They were well below him on the trail, a group of about thirty men, women, and children. They walked slowly with heads bowed; heavy baskets hung on their backs. The transition from attending to humble pebbles with all their power locked in rigid immobility to these noisy purposeful humans was alarming. Instead of hurrying to the trail and going forward to greet his fellow wayfarers, Aleqwel ran, dragging his staff, toward the hills, farther away from the main path.

When he had covered some distance he climbed a small knoll with an oak tree on top. He hid himself behind the tree and was still. Finally, the travelers passed beneath where he could see them. Some of their carrying baskets were filled with pine nuts. "Of course," laughed Aleqwel to himself. "They're pine nut gatherers. They've been to the highest mountain, Iwihinmu, the Center of the Earth World. Who but pine nut gatherers would be out camping at this time of year?" Still, he did not rush down the hillside to meet them. He thought he had seen one or two of these people at the Bear Ceremony at Shuku. What might they do to him if they saw his evident power?

Like a ground squirrel scurrying to its hole in a rock pile, Aleqwel darted farther into the hills. If he could stay far enough away from people he'd be safe from poisoning. He longed to recapture the sense of holiness and beauty he had begun to experience among the plants and trees—before the arrival of the pine nut gatherers. He could always regain the path later on.

Aleqwel climbed higher into the hills. Before long he came to a narrow creek that ran parallel—he was certain it ran parallel—to the now-distant trail. He thought he would follow it in the direction of Matilha. He could bypass the trail for a short distance. It was more pleasant here by the stream. He would not have to worry about water. And he loved the tall trees. There were no people.

But the pathless going was very slow and about midday Aleqwel decided to regain the trail. He struck out away from the creek toward where the trail should be. There was nothing there. He could not understand it. There was no meadow or valley or anything recognizable, only rough chaparral: sage and sumac and poison oak. Things didn't make sense. The creek had not changed course. It was unthinkable that he could be lost. He was experienced... and powerful. If he really got into trouble his atishwins would come.

He sat down on a rock and shook some tobacco from his nose plug. It ought to clear his mind. He thought maybe he should eat. But he still was not hungry. He wanted to be light so he could travel swiftly. He took out the elderberry wood flute from his carrying net and began to play. Then he put it down. He talked a little to the hummingbirds buzzing by the stream. He felt a little better. He followed the creek again, hoping he would find his direction when he came to its source.

When evening fell—especially early it seemed—Aleqwel was still tracing the little stream. He was still following the narrow banks where he could and leaping from stone to stone and boulder to boulder when the trees on the banks grew too thickly. He still had not found the source. He had to give up. He made a sleeping place under a crisp canopy of autumnal sycamores. Dying yellow sunlight filtered in as he drilled a small fire with his firesticks. Everything was damp. Walking upstream he had begun to feel a little like Coyote, searching impatiently for gratification and lapsing into self-pity on not getting it. And an annoying rattling sound had begun to disturb his ears. Even now, when he rested and shook his head, it would not leave him alone. Aleqwel sat by his smoky fire as the night deepened. Thin dry leaves, curled like fists, fell gently on him. Though he did not know it, he was beginning to grow afraid. His sleeping place was beside a mottled sycamore trunk, but he dared not sleep. He had the sense that he might die here, though what the danger was he did not know. He wished from the center of his heart that he were at home. Why, he asked, was he lost out here in the chaparral instead of being with Chnaway, his guide at Matilha? He should have gotten there in a day. Who had led him to make this error? Were there new enemies?

The night wore on and still Aleqwel did not sleep. A great Holhol bird, like a condor only more monstrous, landed on the tall sycamore that sheltered him. A shower of leaves fell on him when it settled. And then the massive black form addressed him: "Ichantik."

"I am not your friend!" cried Aleqwel. "You do sorcery and poisoning. You worked for the Wokoch. I must respect your power, but I do not like you. Why are you here? Fly away! Go west!"

"You may curse me and wish me dead, but I am your friend," squawked the ominous creature. "Remember your atishwins!"

Aleqwel hid beneath his fur blanket. His felt a sharp pain in his gut. Much later, when he looked up, the Holhol was gone. Aleqwel wondered why he had not heard the noisy thing taking off.

Later, in the black night, Aleqwel saw something else. It was a little white light glowing just upstream from where he lay staring into nothingness. He got up and stumbled toward it. Up close, he saw that it was a kind of nunashish, though not a terribly fierce one. It was like a tiny bird made of only one glowing piece of down. He had never seen such a creature before. But he had often heard of them, especially from his grandmother. He whispered the name "Pelepel."

At that moment he was distracted by something more surprising even than the glowing feather. By the dim light of the feather he saw a spreading pool of water and a sheer rock wall with water flowing out of it. It was a spring, a spring with pine trees growing above it. The source had been only a short distance beyond where he had made his bed. Why hadn't he heard it dripping, he wondered? But when he listened he heard only the rattling sound in his ears.

The shining Pelepel began to fly all around. It flew not only around the pool and the rock wall but entered a tiny crack in the wall. The wall was the base of a huge mountain. It seemed to the traveler it must be Mount Iwihinmu, though he wondered how he had traveled such a great distance so quickly. Things were too strange for someone who had not drunk momoy recently. He cried, "Please, Pelepel, I am ill. I need to go home."

But the shining light ignored him.

Recklessly, he grabbed the downy creature and cried out, "I will not let you go until you promise to take me away from here. I know you can do it."

But the little nunashish replied, "How can I? I am too small to go anywhere."

He answered, "I have seen you go into that little hole in the rock. Take me in there!"

They argued for some minutes. The traveler insisted he was not afraid of going into a cave. At last the shining creature relented and agreed to take the lost man with him into the hole in the sandstone wall.

T he fissure in the mountainside was tiny. And the long narrow tunnel inside was cramped; Aleqwel's traveling gear barely fit. The walls squeezed his ribs so that he could hardly breathe. He gasped and was afraid. He had no idea where he was going. Probably to his death. But the shining bright light of the Pelepel was always before him.

After a long, long time the tunnel expanded. It opened into a large room. It was a house more spacious than any Aleqwel had seen before. It was warm inside. There were many people there. Some of them were lying by the fire, others were walking around. The traveler felt exhausted from his journey. He tried to straighten up. The people there looked different from ordinary people, but somehow the place seemed familiar. It reminded him of stories he had heard describing Sun's house in the east: that dwelling was enormous, bigger than the paqwot's ceremonial house. It was crowded with First People. But the traveler was too hungry and weary to appreciate the wonder of the place. He staggered to the inviting fire.

One of the people came up to him; it was Lizard. Lizard asked, "How did you get here, ichantik?"

"I lost the path," sighed Aleqwel. "I was heading for Matilha village, but I took a wrong turn." Then he added despondently, "I think I am dying. Last night, while I slept, Holhol came and fed on my insides and then I entered a dark passage."

Lizard drew a warm blanket over Aleqwel. Without saying a word he scrambled away. Aleqwel slept.

Some time later Lizard returned with Coyote at his side. Coyote, who was an alchuklash and sometimes a curing doctor as well, examined the patient's belly and listened to his breathing. He said gravely, "You are sick, sick indeed. But Condor is not your enemy. You suffer from something else."

Aleqwel was not listening very well. He was watching the embers in the fire and trying to remember the purpose of his journey. It wasn't clear. But he knew that Coyote was diagnosing him and that he was the best doctor in the world. Maybe there was hope.

"I will bring out the harmful thing that is inside you," said Coyote confidently.

Falling back to sleep Aleqwel thought he remembered why he had come. He had gone out to discover if he should accept the powers of an achana... yes, that was it. He was tired, tired, and he slept on. This time there were dreams.

He awoke with a scream. Coyote was there. At his side were two assistants, one small and busy, the other large, dark, and beady eyed. This one's hair, in a high topknot, had a ruddy sheen. This assistant frightened Aleqwel. He sat up and insisted that the man go away.

"This man is your friend and helper," said Coyote, but he sent the assistant away. Then Coyote demanded, just as the alchuklash always did after giving momoy, "Tell me your dream."

Aleqwel's dream was horrible. It was about a bear, a real grizzly bear, killing and eating people: women, children, a whole family. The beast left nothing but the heads and intestines. Aleqwel was sweating and his heart was pounding hard.

Coyote asked questions. At what time of year was this happening? Where? Who were the victims?

Aleqwel recalled it all clearly. It was at the acorn harvest. The killings occurred in several places. He described the various places in detail. The victims—yes, he saw them. Yes, there were some he recognized. They weren't his family, at least.

Coyote patted his hand and told him he would be well soon. He said he must learn to appreciate the value of his dreams. Did he understand how the people might benefit from them? "Not everyone can foresee the future," the gray old doctor said. "But without foresight, how can the future be rearranged—just a little bit?"

Then he told Aleqwel to lie still and rest while he gave him a bath. Everyone in the house, Owl and Deer and Duck Hawk and all the others, came and assisted the old achana in the curative bathing. Aleqwel felt a deep wave of comfort. He gave himself up to the ecstasy of renewal. When at last the cleansing was completed, Lizard announced in his languid way, "The party we have been preparing in honor of your visit is ready."

All of them ate together. The food was the most delicious Aleqwel had ever tasted. It never ran out. They danced for one another. When Coyote accompanied some of the dancers by shaking his split-stick rattles, Aleqwel realized that the noise in his ears had finally gone. He felt exceptionally well now, relaxed. He was still a little bewildered by what was happening, but he felt the happiest he had been in a long time. He joined the others and improvised for them on his flute. The songs that came to him were the best he had ever played. That night he learned many new songs from his timeless friends.

In the morning, he still felt well. His purpose was being restored. His dreams that night had been of a pleasing and auspicious nature. He told Coyote, "I think I understand now what has been happening to me. I must accept what I am. I can see that it is not beneficial to keep my gift from the people. I am ready to resume my journey."

Coyote told him he was not really cured. "You soon will be, though," he promised.

Because Aleqwel was impatient to be on his way, the doctor agreed to allow him to leave. He said, "Here is your guide. Go where he leads you." It was the gangly bright-eyed assistant who came forward.

Aleqwel objected. "This man is a poisoner; he would like to devour me. I won't go with him!"

"Idiot rock crusher," said Coyote with his customary rudeness, "who are you to look down on poisoners? I have been around the Earth World a long time, my young friend. This fellow is far-seeing; he can lead you. So what if he knows the art of poison? Don't you think it might be useful to learn a little more about it? Because you have squashed one pest, do you think you know everything? Ha! You yourself have let Holhol loose."

Aleqwel did not like the sound of these words. He almost wished his ears would close up again. Was Coyote trying to trick him? Was he teasing? He made an effort to trust and believe his fickle helper. He tried to accept that an evil achana like Holhol could be his friend.

With a pout, Coyote said, "Have you no faith that my down cord will protect you from harm? Should I take it back?"

This was too much. "No," cried Aleqwel. "Se. Se. Se." He did not want to lose an atishwin. He clutched his chest, shuddering at the memory of the doomed fishermen.

The young man said to his new friends, "I am going now, Deer, Owl, Duck Hawk, Hummingbird, all of you. You have saved my life. I will always remember. Kiwanan, kiwanan!"

"Alishtahan, friend," they replied. "Have courage, Ahiwalich! Alishtahan!"

Great hulking Holhol—or was it Condor—led the way out of the cavern. They followed a different route than the tight little tunnel that had been the entrance. This time the voyager found himself rising up a long shaft at great speed.

P ew! Who farted? Coyote, are you still there?"
There was silence.

"What is this place, anyway?" exclaimed Ahiwalich as he surfaced out of the deep pool of water. "It stinks like rotten eggs! Am I back home? Is this the salt marsh?" He looked around for his great bird guide. But the man had disappeared. Coyote was not there either. He was alone.

Ahiwalich was standing in a pool of yellow-green water in a grove of oak and sycamore and cottonwood beside a pretty creek. The early morning air was cold against his damp beard and face. But his lower half was delightfully warm. He laughed. Suddenly he knew where he was. Instead of hurrying to climb out, he lay back and bathed in the warm, foul-smelling hot spring. He felt revitalized, remade even. He saw the world with fresh eyes. Everything was clear. He relaxed and looked up into the sky. The yellow morning light was just beginning to filter into the shadowy high-walled valley. The open sky glowed a pale blue. High, high above a large black bird circled—a buzzard, or a condor.

Ahiwalich lay long in the warm bath. He watched the bird circle. He sensed he was being watched in return. But he did not feel preyed upon. He began to accept the possibility that the poisoner, man or woman, buzzard, condor, or Holhol, might be his colleague after all. Such an assistant could help him understand what was solitary and wrong in the world, and in his own heart. In what way was he different than the most vicious sorcerer? Only through such self-acceptance would he be able to cure poison and unbalance in the world.

The black bird flew off to the north over the tree tops and beyond the creek. It flew in the direction of Matilha village.

Leaning on the toyon staff that had stayed beside him through all his travels, Ahiwalich pulled himself out of the warm, murky pool. He and his clothing and gear came out completely dry. He was no longer bothered by the sulfurous odor.

The wot of Matilha was standing at the outskirts of the village. He had come out to meet him. The leader told him, "We heard that you were coming."

The girls of the village also came around to take a look at the guest. They did not recognize him from the previous spring when they had found him so ridiculous. They thought this man looked wild and handsome. The guest stared hard at all the enhweq.

With the wot's permission he left them behind and went straight up the creek and into the mountains to the caves where their alchuklash had been fasting and drinking momoy root tea. Ahiwalich looked around him. The hills were bare because the tok had been gathered. In the most inaccessible cave he found the old man. The doctor said, "I have been traveling far into the sky." He was learning what he could of the year to come. He was thinking of Sun and the Sky World and the winter solstice. Little of him remained with the Earth World.

"Wot told me to expect a visitor, an initiate," he said. "Have you come to help? Let me look at you. Yes, I know you now. You were a paint grinder, from Mishopshno. Forgive me, I forget what they called you."

"They call me Ahiwalich now."

"I don't recall your being so powerful, young man."

"I was called differently last spring. My great-uncle, the alchuklash, sent me here to help you. And to seek your help."

"How thoughtful of him. I suppose that down on the coast where you say you come from there is no shortage of clever antap assistants. But here we are always short, especially of those who know how to paint."

"It appears that I have been chosen for the life of a healer, an achana. I have had an insight into the future that should be addressed."

"Does your vision include the hand game between Eagle and Two Thunders?" prompted the old man eagerly. "At this time of year such information is vital for understanding the rain and crops."

"I am sorry, alchuklash, it does not," said Ahiwalich. "I only saw the bears."

"Bears. Keti! Was it your first dream for the people?"

Ahiwalich said it was.

"It is no small thing," said the aged alchuklash. "Come, did you bring your paints? Here on the floor are the mortars. You can help me. You are good with a brush, as I recall. As you know, my eyes are not so good anymore, nor my hands, either. I have had an important dream myself. You will be my translator. Then I will show you how you can use your own dream."

"Tell me," he said, changing his thought's direction, "did you have a difficult journey here? Did you come alone? You were courageous to come alone in winter." He rambled on like a child who was happy to find an iwu, a companion, even a young and ignorant one.

Ahiwalich stayed at the caves with the alchuklash and with the other doctors. They were there many days. Each day he mixed colors—red, white, black—and helped the old men paint their dreams, their encounters with nunashish and spirit helpers, with the hand game players. When he was intent on his work, especially the new art of painting, the short, gray days passed as rapidly as hummingbirds' flight.

His teacher gradually learned of his apprentice's adventures and misadventures on the trail between Mishopshno and Matilha. He expanded for him on the interpretations that Coyote had given of his dream and of his experience. He told Ahiwalich that the balance between positive power coming from solitude and the dangerous power of isolation is precarious and must always be corrected. Didn't the Wokoch have power in his estrangement? He explained the difficulty of avoiding both notoriety and obscurity, of the need for, and impossibility of, perfect equilibrium. Ahiwalich heard the old sayings with new ears.

Then his teacher slowly began to impart the most important technical skills Ahiwalich would need as a healer: how to paint his visions so as to alter—just slightly—forecast events. How to pull the balance toward life. In this instance, how to salvage a few innocent gatherers from the jaws of the bear. Such manipulations required great power and were full of danger. Ahiwalich could only attempt to do what he could with his novice abilities; he had no certainty of success. He worked hard. He worked with enthusiasm. No one would be able to judge his success until the following season's acorn harvest.

Meanwhile, the other doctors worked on the rainfall and crops for the coming year. One of them built a shrine pole for Kaspat, Matilha's sacred mountain. Once again, the young man was chosen to prepare red pigment for decoration. While he was working on this, the wot arrived. He quickly withdrew to consider the tallies of the year's hand game, which team had won most often in Matilha in the previous year. He was preparing to visit the wot of the Sky, so he could appraise, in person, the victors of the celestial hand game. Like the alchuklash, he would have to assess the relative powers of the Sky Team and the Earth Team of Eagle and Thunder and Fog. Could people expect favorable rain and crops as they had enjoyed this year, or would the coming year be a hard one of drought and austerity? If the friends of mortals did not win, the wot would have to exert all his force to improve things as much as possible.

Throughout all these preparations, Ahiwalich was completely lost to himself, working with intense concentration and passion. Every day he learned new and powerful things. He renounced any remaining thought of returning to his old life. Pride and regret over the killing of the intruder began to leave him as well. Before he knew it, several weeks had passed. The winter solstice was at hand. More vividly than the red ticking on the cave wall, which counted out the days and the movements of Sun and stars, the red berries growing on the toyon trees at the mouth of the cave told him that the rebirth of Sun was near. "Go home now and be of use to your own people," said the old alchuklash at last.

Ahiwalich would have liked to remain at Matilha with his teacher and his work. He felt he belonged with these people. At the same time, he felt ready to go home. His family would be worrying about him.

When he left the caves, the old alchuklash walked into the village with him. The sky was gray with clouds that might hold rain. The sycamores by the trail were half bare. Sun traveled in a low arc beyond the southern mountains. It was cool and shady on the creek path where the two men walked. They followed the trail beside mottled gray sycamores and green willows and red poison oak. The alchuklash made conversation: "I seem to remember that when you were with us before you were having trouble with visits from a lewd and destructive woman, a nunashish, I believe."

"You remember correctly," Ahiwalich answered his now-beloved teacher.

"Is your trouble any better now?"

"I have subdued her power."

"And have you destroyed her entirely?" asked the old man with sly simplicity.

"Yes… and no," responded the apprentice, thoughtfully. "We have become friends," he elaborated. "Allies. And I've accepted the man holhol, too."

"I am relieved to hear it," his teacher said. "This outcome shows you are on the right path. Your calling will benefit."

"It's strange," remarked Ahiwalich, "I once considered trying to understand women. But I gave it up as too difficult. Then, in spite of myself, I kept learning more and more about the female half. How strange it is that the nunashish bird, who was my enemy—and may still be sometimes— should also become my atishwin."

The alchuklash may have smiled; a few of the wrinkles near his eyes moved upward. And, indicating that maybe he did not find the young man's experience quite so strange, he said, "A healer benefits from every encounter he has. Whatever he needs to know will come to him. Never be afraid of experience. Knowledge is the source of power." Then he added, as if Ahiwalich had never heard the injunction before, "But remember: always use your knowledge, your power, well. Use it for the benefit of the people. All the people."

On the young artist's departure from the village the old man showered him with still more advice. Anything less would have been a lapse of duty. He told his apprentice: "Go home now and assist your great-uncle and your people. But come back soon. With every sunset I am a day older. You have so much more to learn. There are few caves or great painters down by the coast where your people live. You must come here if you want to know what is important."

Ahiwalich saw that the old man's eyes were brimming with tears. But whether they arose from emotion or from age and dimming eyesight he could not tell. Through all the speech the raw-boned old man maintained his composure.

"But in the meantime, nephew, listen to your kinsman, ask him to teach you the movements of the star crystals and their significance. Remember your dreams. Keep your balance. Improve your skills of prognostication. Despite all the teachings, you are the One who knows. When you return, bring your best paints and fiber brushes. Then we will drink momoy together and I will show you all that I know. You have the possibility of becoming a true seer and benefactor of the people."

This speech was especially moving because of the commitment the young man had made to his new calling over the past few weeks. Joy filled him when his teacher said he needed him. In his first steps, he could not see his destination clearly, but he had been able to fix his attention on his guide. By now he loved the frail old man who had led him to paint his terrifying vision of the bears.

When Ahiwalich came out of the canyon valley and picked his way down through the river gorge to the wider valley below, he did not feel the pain of loneliness or the fear of his own power. This time he was accompanied by the clarity of his new atishwins who would show him the way.

In the sky above, with its gray clouds and its blue openings, he could make out a black speck circling high, high above. It nearly brushed the Sky World with its black wings. It was his fearsome friend and ally: the enormous condor. Ahiwalich felt safe in his journey knowing this mighty carrion eater was soaring overhead. It surprised him to think that even the cry of the great horned owl might no longer fill him with dread. All the terrible creatures that had once belonged to his father's killer were now free. They were free to belong to him, Ahiwalich. They were free to save him and serve him and to help him heal. All the way home Ahiwalich held firmly to his staff and never deviated from the path.

CHAPTER 12

MONTH WHEN RAIN KEEPS PEOPLE INDOORS

hesiq momoy an tuhui pimaam

Young Anakawin had to fight heavy rain on his way to the sweathouse. His uncle Alow would be there; he was sure of it. Though the month when fishing was forbidden had come to an end some weeks ago, the fisherman was unlikely to be at sea on such a day. All the men were listening to the old-time stories in the sweathouse these days.

As he sloshed the short distance to the smoky mound by the creek, Anakawin could not help but think of his absent brother. His older brother was now called Ahiwalich. The new name was impressive but hard to digest. Anakawin could not help imagining his dear brother out on the trail in the miserable rain. He consoled himself that it was the first such rain in many weeks. He hoped it would not last long.

Anakawin went to the sweathouse for companionship and comfort. He felt lonely in his own home. It was usually full of women. They were loving but alien. There were no men or children around most of the time. At the dark of Moon the place had become practically deserted. And now, the number of days that Aleqwel—the boy did not want to use that lofty name—had been gone was getting worrisome. Anakawin, though usually confident, knew he was not old enough to take up the work of a paint maker if his brother did not return. How could he support so many people, when he still used only a toy bow? Here, on the roof of the sunken sweathouse, in the drenching rain, he vowed that in spring he would insist on having a real bow made; Uncle Alow would teach him to hunt deer. But, truly, what would the family do if Aleqwel were lost? Could his mother and the old alchuklash support them all? Could Alow? Anakawin decided, consciously, for the first time, that the best thing for him to do was to move in with his sister and brother-in-law. He would learn the high-paying skills of a fisherman. Somehow, he would make his way into the tomol guild. It was what he wanted anyway, he told himself as he slipped through the grassy roof entrance of the men's refuge.

Climbing down the pole ladder he heard Piyokal's beloved voice beginning a new story as all timeless stories began: "It happened one time…" Anakawin thought, "My brother has not been gone terribly long. The people at Matilha are friendly to us, I believe; we have a trading uncle there. Most likely, he is being distracted by too much hospitality. Maybe he will stay with them for the Winter Solstice Festival. Maybe he has met a girl. Maybe he's even married already." His thoughts jumped faster and more erratically than fleas on a dog. By the time he landed on the hard-packed floor of the underground burrow, he was admitting to himself how much he missed his older brother. The next day, everyone would leave for the big town and the Winter Solstice Festival. How could they go without Aleqwel? It was bad enough last year without his father.

Anakawin crawled on all fours through the thick smoke until, by some invisible instinct, he came to the side of his new relative, Alow. He lay close beside him. It had been a comfort in the past few weeks to be near him and the other men, to lie in the dark and listen to the old—and sometimes new—stories.

The people had been filled with joy when their own storyteller, Piyokol, finally returned to his home village. He had appeared only days after Aleqwel had walked out toward the winter mountains. Since that day the sweathouse had been packed tighter than an ant's nest with people longing to hear once again the old tales, well told, as could only happen in the winter months. They eagerly awaited word of their entertainer's own exploits in the far-off lands.

Cheerful Piyokol did not disappoint his admirers. He had enjoyed his adventures in Teqepsh town and beyond. Storytelling was his joy and his acclaim; he could do it anywhere. The tales flowed easily. Though some recitations of the old histories went on for two or even three days, the man never seemed to tire. Nearly every day he came to the sweathouse at Mishopshno and satisfied the people.

At first, the official bard had been polite to Piyokol, the returned artist. The two of them had taken turns relating their narratives. But it always seemed to happen that people would take the time when the official bard spoke as their opportunity to go out. Anakawin was not sure why they left, but he did know that the sweathouse would become nearly empty whenever the bard spoke. The high-born bard was being humbled before his colleague, who was, himself, born a humble man. Anakawin did not mind when the official bard stopped coming. As a child who craved tales, he found the man's affected delivery boring. And he did consider it a family insult when the bard went straight to the alchuklash, without first consulting Anakawin's mother, who was an outstanding curing doctor, to complain about the pains he was having in his stomach. Now, on his last day at home before the big expedition to the festival at Syuhtun, Anakawin wanted nothing more than to lie quietly by the fire and let himself be bathed in Piyokol's healing words. He opened his ears.

The storyteller was saying, "I turned to the wot of Syuhtun and to Syuhtun's bard, who was walking along with us by the shore, and said, 'Well, I'd be happy to follow those strange tracks to see where they lead.' And, naturally, the wot and the bard came to a complete halt. They stared at me with horror. 'Don't you know what those tracks are?' sputtered the bard. 'They belong to the sea monster, a snake, a powerful nunashish. Haven't you heard of that creature down where you come from?' And I answered—so coolly and casually, you know, 'Ah, yes, I think I have heard some mention of the creature, but I have never seen one. If I am to keep up my reputation as an entertainer, I had better investigate. I need new stories.' And I pretended to ready myself to run after the scaly tracks, which led off toward a nearby finger of land. I said, 'I'm sure there will be no danger to one as clever as I.' And both stopped still." Piyokol paused to look at the faces of his friends. He waited until one cried, "What did you do?"

He answered solemnly, "It was at this point that the esteemed wot stretched out one of his noble arms and physically prevented me from going ahead." Piyokol laughed. It might have been the end of the story—many people were smiling contentedly—but the storyteller was only pausing to catch his breath. He continued, "Then, the two of them forced me to turn around and go back to the big town with them. While we walked they related a shocking story, one that I promised myself I would share with you. It's about a boy from Syuhtun who accidentally did bump into the giant sea snake." Piyokol laughed again, "You know, I think I really had those two wise men believing I was about to go chasing after that terrible nunashish." Then, before plunging into the story of the frightful sea snake, he added, as he looked quizzically from face to face in the smoky chamber, appearing to inquire of each man personally, "I wonder if they ever would have shared with me this appalling tale if I had behaved differently on the beach at Syuhtun?"

Anakawin was lost to himself and everything around him. He was wondering how he would react if he accidentally came across a dreadful beast like the sea monster. Would he be calm; would he have the sense to propitiate the creature? Would he have the power to survive? He felt powerful. Hadn't he survived the bite of Grizzly Bear at Shuku? And the sight of Holhol in the trees last winter at Syuhtun? At Syuhtun. He would soon be going there. He wondered if there were really such sea monsters as Piyokol described? When he got there he might try to find out. He would look for their tracks. Of course, he wouldn't seek out a meeting with one of those serpents.

He heard Piyokol begin a new personal story. It was about his visit to the big town in the land to the west, Mikiw. He heard him describe the mounds of mussel shells and the piles of shimmering abalones heaped along the lanes. He listened intently as Piyokol launched into a history of the bloody conflict between Mikiw and its neighbor across the creek, Kuyamu. Anakawin looked over at Alow. He was lying on his stomach with his face in his hands. The boy sighed and closed his eyes.

T here were many red tomols spotting the shore at the big town of Syuhtun. Although they looked like so many mounds of kelp tossed up in a storm, they had been drawn up deliberately. They belonged not only to the many fishermen of Syuhtun village but to visitors from all along the Middle Coast. Once again people from villages that spoke the Syuhtun tongue and visitors from far-off lands as well had come together to greet newborn winter Sun, Kakunupmawa. The paqwot had extended personal invitations to many guests. Mishopshno village had landed several boats. Among them was Alow the fisherman's somewhat battered new possession. Besides his pregnant wife and his father it had carried the curing doctor and her mother and sister and his wife's younger brother.

The foreigner visitors were guests, not intruders. Two of the tomols from farthest away bore the abalone-inlaid insignia of Michumash Island on their ears. They belonged to the wot of Nimitlala, the most important wot of all the islands, and to a wealthy fisherman and fur trader, also from Nimitlala. There had been quite a discussion within the families about making this trip.

The soft-eyed adolescent Qupe, who had family connections with the wot as well as being the daughter of the tomol-owning fur trader, had quietly insisted since summer's end on going to the mainland. There, she said she would marry the wealthy fisherman from Qoloq village who had shown such interest in her. Throughout the autumn she had reminded her parents of past promises.

Her mother's opinion was finally decisive. She disliked nothing more than ocean travel, especially in winter, yet she could not resist the opportunity of making a good match for her daughter. The mainlander did appear to be well-to-do, and they had already traded with him. He seemed a bit young to marry, though. But Qupe favored him; that was good. They might make a lasting marriage. Qupe said he told her he was willing to move to the islands. Though Qupe's mother might even consider allowing her daughter to move to Qoloq. She had dreams about moving to the mainland when she and her husband got older. No, they were only dreams. As long as her husband lived he would have duties in his business. But, maybe—if there were grandchildren, and of course there would be—her thoughts turned like changing Moon. At last, Qupe's mother and uncle agreed to let her go on her first trip to the mainland. They would participate in the Winter Solstice Ceremony at Syuhtun, and incidentally old acquaintances could be renewed; they could do some direct trading with their trading partners. If things did not work out for Qupe there would be no shame or loss in having gone. And Qupe was related to the wot, and he and his nephew and daughter Leqte were going.

Qupe's cousin and friend, the bright-eyed Leqte, had insisted on going to the mainland. It was her idea in the first place. In spite of her mainland lover's inconsistent response to her and his sudden silent departure she was ever optimistic. When they married she would definitely move there. This trip would lead to her marrying well and staying to see the great world, rattlesnakes and bears and mountain lions and all. Any difficulties would be overcome. As soon as her Alapapa apologized for leaving her so precipitously she would forgive him and they would be married. She told her parents she must go to Syuhtun. Leqte's parents usually ended up doing whatever she wanted, even though her father was a very important wot. Her cousin, of course, supported her in all this.

So the two prominent families decided to paddle their sea-worn but sturdy tomols to the other side of the channel. As soon as the month-long prohibition on seafaring ended they set out for Wenemu, the port of arrival. Because it was nearly winter, they experienced a thrilling swell; there was froth on the dark sea. But there were no clouds in the sky, and the only wind was a steady landward breeze. Their transit was safe, if cold and tiring.

Now, somewhere among the crowded lanes and campsites of Syuhtun these remote islanders wandered wearing their capes of island fox fur or fur seal. They traded, gambled, gossiped with distant relatives and, most important, discreetly searched for two young fishermen and their parents who were from the villages of Mishopshno and Qoloq in the region southeast of Syuhtun.

While the wots of the twelve villages met to settle old debts and to determine the fate of those who had behaved inharmoniously toward the community, those celebrants who were not involved in judicial matters socialized and played. Though the season of the year was dim and gloomy and people's moods were hesitant and reverential, the gathering was festive. Human beings experienced their weakness; they acknowledged their dependence on stronger powers; they rejoiced in their surrender to them. They trembled thinking of Solstice Night.

Leqte and Qupe, the young island girls were jubilant at the sight of so many people crowded together in one place. The possibilities were endless. The so many new faces, strange animals, varieties of baskets and jewelry. They could not grasp it all. The enhweq in their island seagrass skirts admired the beautifully painted women—and women who had been born men—of the province. They coveted their soft-fringed buckskin aprons. Secretly, Qupe hoped for one of these skirts as part of her wedding gift. She could then, at once, distinguish herself from the commoners and be more quickly accepted by Kulaa's mother—whoever, wherever, she might be.

But while Qupe thought anxiously about her future in-laws and about finding her lover in the congested throng, her carefree cousin threw herself wholeheartedly—even recklessly—into gambling and playing games. Leqte particularly loved to go to the playing field where the hockey games were fought. She appeared to give little thought to finding her lover, as if she were certain that he would come to her. Certainly she had not forgotten him. And while she waited for him she played hard on the field at Syuhtun just as she loved to do at home. She joined the team of any village that could use her. Her cousin, Qupe, when she saw her on the field, cringed with disapproval—and jealousy. Leqte was meeting—and becoming familiar with—many young male athletes. But Leqte could see no danger in it.

So, while the wots of the twelve villages met and dealt with the practical concerns affecting the region and measured out their agreed on contributions and suggested new ones, the people, the island girls Leqte and Qupe among them, awaited the later days when the big ceremonies would be held. They prayed for the rebirth of Sun and for rain. They played sports and games and made new arrangements in their own personal affairs.

A little ironically, it was at the field hockey games that Kulaa eventually discovered Qupe. It was a cool gray day. As he and his Qoloq teammates charged the length of the field in pursuit of the tiny wooden ball, he brushed past a young girl player, nearly knocking her over. She smiled at him. It was a chipped tooth smile. The grin was triumphant. Recognizing Leqte as she sped past, Kulaa began to scan the sidelines for her family, losing interest in the game that Qolog was on the brink of loosing. Surely her cousin had come, too. She had promised. Why hadn't he been able to find her before? He had looked everywhere. In the last moments of the game he finally picked her out in the crowd. Her wide otter's eyes were on him.

Kulaa leapt off the field. In another instant, he and Qupe were together. They walked away from the village toward the upstream creek. It did not take the couple long to ascertain that their interests were still the same. "Come! Come with me, my poppy flower. Come meet my mother," he cried at last. "She has been wanting to know you."

When Leqte observed that her cousin had been reunited with her lover she forgot about the handsome athletes. Not only was she happy for her cousin's sake but she began chattering with anticipation at her own impending happiness. Kulaa would certainly know where his cousin Alapapa was. She completely disregarded the need for circumspection that the winter solstice period demanded. When Qupe returned from her excursion with her lover, Leqte demanded to know about hers. Qupe's insistence that Kulaa had not once mentioned his cousin did not daunt her. Leqte demanded, "When you go to meet his parents, take me with you. Surely, my Alapapa and his father can't be far from them. Maybe he is feeling a little awkward because he has no mother to ask for me. I must be sure to make him apologize for leaving so suddenly. What a kilamu man he sometimes is. He gets the strangest ideas. Sometimes he has a funny look, don't you think? Do you think he is gifted with power?" Her words rambled as she ran to brush her hair and touch up her paint.

Leqte's impetuousness prevented Kulaa from reaching Alow before she herself did. Kulaa ran to his parents' temporary shelter to prepare them for a visit from their potential daughter-in-law. At the same time the impetuous Leqte quickly found someone in the Qoloq area who could direct her to Alow's temporary home, which was not far away. She entered the Mishopshno camp area while Kulaa as still listening to his mother. A tall—very handsome, she noted—young man was strolling through the camp. He seemed to be making sure that all was well with the people. She recognized at once by the crystal hairpin in his topknot that he must be some sort of wot. For a moment she was dazzled. This man looked nothing like her cousin, nor even her father, wot of Nimitlala. This young man was not only handsome, beautiful even, but he was clearly, from his manner of adornment, vastly wealthy—at least by any standards she had ever known. None of this knowledge made her afraid to address him. Was she not of noble birth herself?

Halashu responded to her query in perfect island speech. Having no idea who she was he simply directed her to the fisherman's tule shelter. The doors of the temporary home were open. Without invitation, she ducked right inside. Alow was calmly sharing some acorn porridge with his pregnant wife, his father, and his young brother-in-law.

It took Alow a long instant to place the small grass-skirted girl. But Ponoya knew who she was right away. She had an instinct; she had seen her in the egg. But she also had an instinct that told her to maintain her manners. She realized that whatever danger this girl might bring, she herself had the upper hand. She offered the intruder a bowl of porridge.

Leqte had the grace to accept. She sat on their mat and made a comment on the fine patterns on the nearby baskets. Now that her eyes had adjusted to the darkness she could see that her gracious hostess was large with child. "Alapapa, why did you never tell me you had a sister?" she exclaimed.

Silence fell all around as Leqte slowly came to realize her error. She felt weak. It was as if someone had run into her headfirst on the playing field. She wondered if it would be impolite to run out so suddenly after making her entrance. Could she even stand up? She hardly dared look in the direction of her Alapapa. Was he the same man she had known on the island? Was she even in the right house? It had been so dark when she came in.

"Ponoya is my sister," spoke the youngest one there. His tone was protective. "And if my older brother doesn't return soon I'm going to go live with her and her husband. Isn't that right, uncle? I'm going to apprentice as a fisherman."

Alow took cover under Anakawin's chatter to try to regain his composure. He had wilted with embarrassment.

Ponoya watched his deep distress with invisible sideways eyes. She seemed in no hurry to rescue him from it. Instead, she addressed the young visitor sweetly, "I'm curious, my dear, what is it they call you at home? Is it 'Little Fox'? It seems so apt. Tell us, did you come over with your parents for the Festival of Kakunupmawa? What a long way to come for... I won't say for so little, because it is a fine, fine ceremony, certainly. But you understand what I mean: it must be more than a little disappointing to risk your life at sea for…" She made a vague gesture.

Mushu, reclining impassively in the dark, almost grinned. His respect for his daughter-in-law was rising. He had always appreciated her. She displayed such unimpeachable virtues—he would never deny the worthiness of a steadfast fire tender and cook, not to mention a fine basket maker. But now he saw the hardness in her and he was pleased. He wondered with a detached curiosity what would happen next. He himself would like to get a report on Wenla, if this island girl knew about her. But tension and embarrassment were thickening like greenwood smoke in a crowded sweathouse.

Just when Leqte looked as if she might try to rise and possibly say something, a head peeked into the open doorway.

"Haku, haku Halashu, ichantik," called Alow in an unnaturally mouse-like voice. "Have you met our guest? She was one of our hosts on the islands this summer, the daughter of the esteemed wot of Nimitlala. "Please," and he sounded entreating, "please come in and join us for awhile. Leqte is the artist who made that lovely basket that you so admired. Here she is, the maker, herself."

Halashu, still standing in the entrance, looked genuinely pleased. "You are so young to be such an accomplished artist," he began.

But Leqte was already on her feet. "Please excuse me, but I must be going now. My parents must be worried. Kiwanan," she sang out rapidly to Alow's family.

"Kiwanan!" the others echoed as she ran to the exit.

She fell headlong, crying, into the arms of the wot's son. He did not mind. He was used to helping people in trouble.

The gray winter day did not even promise rain. It was thickly foggy, as foggy as the island home Leqte had left behind her. Until now she had succeeded in fooling herself about her marriage prospects. But she was balanced enough to be able to see now that her dream was hopeless. Her scheme for happiness was shattered. The wot's nephew held her upright and restrained her when she tried to strike herself in her sudden outburst of grief and rage.

He made her walk. They walked toward the beach. Halashu always found that the endlessly pounding surf had a good effect on the dispirited. They walked far, around a point of land. The girl gradually began to lose the impulse for violence. She found herself talking to this stranger. She told him everything that had happened. She surprised herself by confessing her connivance in trying to win Alow. She even confided about the love potion. Her companion was so easy to talk to. He did not condemn her for her schemes. He looked at her intently and supported her. Gently he told her that Alow was one of the Earth Team, as he understood she was also. She began to cry less.

That day was a long one with no special ceremonies to mark it. When the damp shadowless evening began to grow insistent, Halashu escorted the young island visitor to her parents' shelter on the far side of Syuhtun. Courteously, he went inside to meet the wot of the islands and his wife. The girl he left behind with them in the winter dusk was cheerful and smiling. She flashed a hopeful, slightly chipped grin at him as he disappeared behind the reed shelters of her temporary neighbors. If she felt humiliated or disappointed no one near her could tell.

Still later that night, with no star crystals and without Grandmother Moon for guidance, Halashu went to call on his dearest friend, the woman who had been born a man. Konoyo was staying at Syuhtun with her natural family, who were related by marriage to Tilinawit, something she rarely did at home. At the last moment, the senior caretaker of the dead had had to attend to an unexpected funeral back home. Aquyuhut, the lame man, had suddenly died where he lay in his sleeping place. The ceremony would be small. Konoyo, the assistant, had not been needed.

Halashu paid his respects to his friend's parents, who were his distant relatives. They responded with equal courtesy. They were in awe of him, of his power. But in their hearts, they secretly feared he was wasting their daughter's time, since they knew he would have to marry someone who could produce heirs. Still, a person never knows. They had no objection to his taking her out for a little walk—if he wanted. Long ago, when the alchuklash had first spoken to them about their child, they had accepted that she would become a free individual, bound only to the service of the sacred. She was professional now, accustomed to living on her own.

Halashu and Konoyo went out to walk on dark sands under a starless sky. Halashu seemed agitated, distracted even, as he presented his lover with a present. The gift was a length of expensive deep-blue huya beads. "I wanted to give you these before," he said absentmindedly, "but there was never an occasion."

"And now?" Konoyo asked, caressing the stones, her questioning look lost to the night. "Is it to commemorate the end of the old year?" There was something he had to tell her. She waited for him to find the words. It was cold near the sea; they had not brought their heavier robes. They could not stay out indefinitely. They walked in darkness. The new beads hung heavily, if obscurely, at Konoyo's neck. The night covered all appearances. They could only touch.

Finally, Halashu spoke. "I've met a girl!" he burst out. "An enhweq."

A stiff soggy silence crept round the pair.

Konoyo said, "So you gave me some beads!"

Halashu stopped still in his tracks, "Oh, no! Se, se. It's not like that! Forgive me. I mean, I have met a suitable girl, one who meets our requirements. Or, at least, I think she might."

"Yes?"

"Yes, she is the right age and of the right station. She is the daughter of Matipuyaut, the wot of the big town on Michumash Island. She is here looking for a husband. It seems she is enamored of our life of culture and refinement. She would like to move here."

Konoyo laughed. "Is she lazy, then?"

"Oh, no, no, I don't think so. Islanders are hard-working people. She makes baskets, fine ones. And she's not even bad to look at."

Again, silence descended.

"Are you truly enthusiastic?"

"You know, of course, I have no interest in her personally… nor she in me, but…"

"But?"

"We had a long talk today. I think she might find me acceptable."

"From what you say, it sounds like she might find any well-to-do mainlander acceptable."

"No doubt you are right. But you understand my meaning: I think she'd do for us. I mean… she's independent."

"Well?"

"Tell me what you think," he implored. I need to know your view of course." It was a style of request to which he was unaccustomed in his daily routine, though not with her. "It is for you that I go through all this! It was your idea! Tell me, does she sound like the right woman for me?"

The young caretaker stood still in quiet thought. At last she said, "This little enhweq sounds like an improvement on the Dog Girl from Mistumukun. Perhaps I should meet her."

Halashu smiled. "She's no Dog Girl, more of an Island Fox, which is what she is called."

"It's just possible," Konoyo admitted judiciously, "that she may be the best one for you. And I'm sure you are the best man she could ever get."

In the cold dark they embraced.

To Saqtele, Mishopshno's master tomol builder, watching the arrival of the official messengers to Syuhtun was like witnessing the descent of a flock of real mud hens. The ksen, like their mud hen namesakes, arrived swiftly, without any noisy warning. They looked homely yet important in their black-and-white paint and their feathers. Like most temporary inhabitants of the swollen town, Saqtele was careful to speak softly and infrequently as befitted the dark season. He, too, was encased in expectancy over the turning of the year. He, too, was fearful of causing any offense to Sun in his weak and angry time. But although he joined quietly with the others in observing the arrival of the forerunners, he was also filled with his own tension. One thing kept him balanced: he was not alone in his worries. The perennial questions, though not always spoken, were in the air. Would the doctors be able to draw Sun back on his course? Which team had won the celestial games? Would the new year bring rain and crops or drought and hunger? At the same time as he brooded on these questions Saqtele also felt excited. The Winter Solstice Festival brought such a mix of emotions; the dread combined with joy. He felt joy at the prospect of the festivities to come: the dance of the paqwot and his solar rays, the feasting, and even the fertilizing of Shup. Saqtele was not too old to appreciate the thrill of Grandfather Kakunupmawa.

The crowd of spectators understood precisely why the messengers were returning from their chiefs' place of retirement in the hills. Every year, after arranging secular affairs, the paqwot and his lesser associates, the other wots and achanas, retreated to hillside caves to await the sign that Sun's rebirth was at hand. When the sign came the ksen would precede their leaders to Syuhtun to announce their imminent arrival.

In a day's time the great doctors would be installed in the ceremonial enclosure, performing their secret ceremonies. These ceremonies were for the initiates only, mostly the higher antap. In private they would prepare the hole for the sacred Sunstick. Then, the next day, in front of everyone, the paqwot would exert all his strength to pull Sun back on course. Saqtele knew that the day of the doctors' return would be a day of shrinking back. The uninitiated would experience the lowest level of human insignificance, powerlessness. He, like others, would spend the rest of the day indoors, fasting and hiding from Sun, reflecting on the old stories and the people's hopes.

The ksen of Mishopshno came to their village's camping area and made his official announcement of the high priest's return. Then he went to relax in the company of his uncle. He found Saqtele where he expected to find him—in a large house near the sweathouse mound with his brothers from the tomol guild. The messenger and the canoe builder went to the smaller place where Saqtele was camping to share some moments' comfort that can be found in long acquaintance. Mirroring the passion of the Sky People they threw themselves on the floor and into a game of shell dice.

Occasionally, during the play, the two kinsmen of the Duck Hawk Family spoke. It was a terse conversation at first. Each man was acquainted with the innermost thoughts of their wot—one with the official secrets, the other with those personal ones that are even more powerful. Both remained in the wot's trust because of their exceptional discretion. Gossip, though rife, did not emanate from either of them. So, when they socialized, neither one would introduce information that they both knew. There were other spies than the ksen to hear.

This day, in the cold blue sky of the time of turning, the ksen's initial remark was, "The wot would like you to donate more prepared boards for the ceremonial grounds."

"Yes, of course," Saqtele agreed. It no longer stung him that as a noninitiate he could not oversee the building to which he contributed so much material and advice. Even so, at his age he was still curious—and frustrated. Long ago he had decided that the gatherings of the tomol guild were sufficiently important to keep him occupied. The esoteric rituals of the antap did not attract him. He had devoted his life to mundane calculations and measurements. The celestial reckonings were probably beyond his grasp and, certainly, beyond his experience. No question that the responsibilities of the antap were immense, especially in regard to hunting and seed gathering. He liked to say he was content to deal with simple things such as making certain his canoes were seaworthy. But he believed without bragging about it that for Mishopshno his own work was of paramount importance. He smiled. "How does it look?" he asked.

The ksen understood his meaning. "Even though I'm up there with them I can never tell. But I think the paqwot knows. Such early rain as we've had this year is not a good sign. But there are other signs, more subtle, I'm sure."

The altomolich sighed in resignation. He was not going to get any advance information. "Perhaps it's too late for our dice contest to make any difference," he said and moved to put away the walnut shells and the gambling tray into his carrying net. He said, "Tell me, is there any news of that young man, the one who poisoned the Wokoch? I saw him passing through Syuhtun when we first arrived. But he went on so swiftly. He was going toward the place of the doctors somewhere up north in the hills. And to think we believed him dead. You never know whether a person has power. But tell me, have you talked with him? He's more of your generation. Would you say he is… sound?"

The ksen did not have a chance to formulate a reply. Saqtele rambled, rather uncharacteristically, but safely with such a close relative. "The late paint maker's son has always seemed a pleasant boy to me. He's respectful, hard working, reserved—a little too modest, perhaps, like his late father. But who knows what happens when they go to the hills. It's easy to become unbalanced. I only know him as a painter, anyway. I could tell you more about the fishermen, the new generation. We lost some of our finest this summer. You never know. . ." Saqtele paused, sensing he was talking too much—especially under the circumstances.

The ksen sat back. He had retreated to his customary silence. He might have smiled faintly. Surprisingly, he decided to speak. "Ahiwalich, that's what they call the paint maker now. He looks strong, strong. I saw him up there in the hills. He went up in the cave with the wot and painted with his own brush. That's what I heard. Of course, I didn't witness it. I am only a lesser antap. But the young man was initiated with the higher."

"He seems to have risen terribly quickly," said the canoe builder. "That can be worrisome." Through the door he could see the white-capped ocean with its careening gulls. High above the shore a bald eagle began a dive.

"Many will surely say so," replied the ksen. "But the wot is convinced that it is he who saved us from certain destruction. I think he sees in him an achana in the great line. A spark of the Sun. But despite all his assistance and dedication I believe they are not certain that the young man will accept the invitation. There is a residue of restraint in him. Of course he has every right to decline. Things could turn out fortunately for our little village if…"

"Just think, two prodigies of renown in one village," interrupted the altomolich, a little irritably. "A bard from the common people and a craftsman-doctor." He believed that there was no craftsmanship greater than canoe building.

"Don't be alarmed, ichantik. Ahiwalich is an initiate. The balance won't be upset. This sort of confusion from below can bring benefit to the people." The feathered messenger spoke in the charitable manner of one born to secure high status.

"But in moderation," conceded the canoe builder. He, too, had nothing to fear from the common people or the poorer antap. Again, he shifted the subject slightly, "Is it true, then, that the danger from Shuku is past?" He had come to the meat of the conversation.

"Our wot seems particularly optimistic about it. He and Shuku's wot were able to work together in solving the recent… problem."

"As long as there is rain and plenty of seeds, I suppose such a friendship will last."

Ksen made a disapproving noise.

"Sounds just like a mud hen," Saqtele thought. But, in truth, he was very fond of the younger man. "Well," he groaned, "kiwanan, nephew. I must be going. I dare not waste my energy. Not if I am to be a worthy participant in the upcoming ceremonies and not a drooping old seabird. I'm not such a fresh sprout as you."

The unmarried ksen stretched his sinewy, painted legs out in front and began warming them in preparation for standing. The clear-eyed messenger said to his uncle, "Alishtahan! Have courage!" He would keep his eyes open to spot a perfect little mud hen woman for the evening's ceremony.

After the Solstice Ceremony and the Festival of Kakunupmawa and Solstice Night everyone was exhausted. The people had not gone indoors until dawn. When they did, they slept deeply. The achanas had expended all their strength on their work. And the people, too, had happily done what was required of them.

In the evening, after a deep day's sleep, Ahiwalich emerged from his mother's house. He was groomed and well outfitted. It was only a short walk to the place of his great-uncle, the alchuklash. He did not want to disturb the doctor in case he was still sleeping, yet the achana had told him to come on the evening after the celebration.

As he lingered outside the door, Ahiwalich recalled with satisfaction the previous day's activities. The ceremony had been a joyous occasion.

The paqwot's report had been encouraging. His own level of involvement had increased markedly over the previous year. At that time, he had been flattered to be chosen to help in the construction of the shrine pole. This year he had been invited to paint in the sacred caves with the eminent achanas. Last year, he had been troubled with doubt and uncertainty and a terrible dread concerning the well-being of his family. Now, he felt the strength of his own power, his own atishwins. He had eliminated the terrible danger to his family and the village. He knew now that he could make a contribution, a difference. This year even the cold night's erotic mandate had not intimidated him. There had been no exceptional aversion or compulsion, no woman like an apparition; only one ordinary one who seemed to find him just as he found her. Ahiwalich, the man who, in the fading light of this first evening of the new year, waited in front of the healer's house was certainly tired from the festivities. But he did not feel depleted this year. He felt confident. He was prepared to speak with his powerful great-uncle. If only the alchuklash would open his door.

At that moment the door opened. Ahiwalich's awkward standing around came to an end. The doctor stooped in the doorway. Like his nephew, he was fully attired, adorned in his most impressive jewelry and atishwins and well painted. But his personal colors had faded; his hair was thin and gray, his skin, dry.

At that instant, in the ebbing light of reborn Sun, Ahiwalich felt blinded by the old man's vulnerability; he was certain the old doctor would not see another winter solstice. He wished he had not seen it, yet he had. When he saw into such things he could not help becoming acutely aware of the fragility of life and the shortness of one generation. And above all that he saw the relentless decline of power throughout the Earth World, of increasing fragmentation. Even the strong break apart. Rocks fall and crumble. The power of the great decline. Doctors inevitably grow weaker. And those that would come after—would they have enough force in them to maintain the balance? Would they be able to keep up the vital communion with the First People of the timeless realm?

"Ahiwalich," the old man said, waking the seer from his reverie. "You know why I asked you to come to me, don't you?" As the alchuklash said it he drew himself up to his full height. Even in the dim twilight the old man was clearly not as tall as he once was.

"Yes, I think so."

"Good. Good. It is easier, then. When you came to the caves to help you were late. There was no time to talk at length about your trip to the hills, your search for the One with the answer. All our focus was on the Sky People and the imminent needs of our own."

"Yes, forgive me, I returned later than I should have."

"It couldn't be helped. We were doing fine as always, though what you brought was important. It was useful. But I must know now what you found on your journey. I know you got to Matilha. I know you helped in the caves. But did you get an answer to your dream choice? Did you find someone? Finally, can you tell me now what you have decided?"

The two powerful men stood close together in the thickening shadows of a stand of green-leafed coastal oaks in the big town, not in their accustomed home. Their feet rested in pale brown dust, the skin of Shup. They stood there, virtually alone, while others slept off their burden of gluttony and sex or crept about inside their shelters with slow, slow movements. The shelters, thatched tule reeds, look frail. Yet these winter burrows constantly proved their endurance. They were the portable rinds of their home village, Mishopshno. And they heaped round the wakeful two in peaceful dozing mounds.

Ahiwalich, who had consulted his heart deeply during his journey back from Matilha, told the alchuklash his decision.

"It is as it meant to be," replied the old man, betraying no excess of emotion. If the old alchuklash was weary from the labors in devotion to Grandfather Sun, he did not let it prevent him from initiating a long conversation with his youthful kinsman. His advice, both studied and extemporaneous, was plentiful. At one point he surprised his young companion by asking bluntly, "What did you think of the paqwot's prognosis?"

When Ahiwalich took a deep breath and bravely told the doctor what he thought, the alchuklash listened attentively.

The two talked until it was fully night. A mature Moon pulled herself over the eastern mountains. Later on there would be songs and dances in the ceremonial grounds. Most of these would be danced and sung purely for the enjoyment they gave. One special song, though, would be presented in honor of reborn Sun, Kakunupmawa, the companion of fertile Shup, Hutash. With regret, the alchuklash informed his new apprentice that he would have to leave soon to prepare for his part in the performance.

After the old man's departure, Ahiwalich thought of the ceremonies still to come. Suddenly, he became aware that the past days' and night's activities had left him more tired than he had realized. Seeing his beloved great-uncle in decline and having made a lifetime decision and given it, he could think of nothing more significant than to get a little more sleep in order to be refreshed for the evening's festivities.

He walked back to his mother's little tule shelter, in its temporary site at the village of Syuhtun. Bending low, he passed through the inner door and went inside where the three women were still asleep. Before falling on his own sleeping place he stopped a moment to unwrap his carrying net. Carefully, he hung it up on a peg near the door.

GLOSSARY

All terms are Barbareño/Shmuwich unless otherwise noted. Note that diacritical signs including glottal stops are not included.

achana
shaman

alatishwinich
a person with many dream helpers (atishwins): a shaman

alchuklash
a soul healer, namer, astronomer: a type of shaman (Ventureño)

aleqwel
maker, craftsman, artisan

alishtahan
Have courage! Frequently used expression of encouragement (Ventureño)

altomolich
planked canoe maker (Ventureño)

antap
initiates of ceremonial organization representing the shamanic-priestly leadership and intelligentsia of the community. Each village has twenty members. (Ventureño)

atishwin
an animal-god who may protect an individual, sometimes called the "dream helper" (since they present themselves during a vision); the talisman given by a protector/dream helper

ayip
a medicine or a deadly poison, made perhaps of putrefied rattlesnake meat and ground shells. It has supernatural qualities. (Ventureño)

enhweq
young woman who is single

epsu
a brimless woman's basketry hat, also use for measuring seeds

haku or haku, haku
a greeting

haphap
a malevolent supernatural being (one of the nunashish), a giant who inhales everything in his path (Ventureño)

holhol
a supernatural being inhabiting the Sky World; identified with the condor, condor impersonator (Ventureño)

hutash
n., tiny black red maids seeds and cereal made from them, delicious and expensive; adj., beautiful (Ventureño)

Hutash
the personified Earth (ceremonial name for Shup)

huya
steatite; the island where steatite comes from (Huya Island, now Santa Catalina) (Ventureño)

i
yes

ichantik
friend

ilepesh
chia sage and its golden seeds in a cake (bread) or drink (gruel)

iwu
companion

Iyi!
Go on! All right!

Kakunupmawa

Sun personified as a god (ceremonial name); literally, "radiance of the child born on the Winter Solstice" (Ventureño)

Keti!

My! How!

kilamu

crazy, stupid

kiwanan

good-bye; literally, "I'm going for awhile"

ksen

a messenger; a mud hen (Ventureño)

malak

type of soft tar found on the beach or in the ocean: not useful as an adhesive

mekhmey

juncus grass, rushes used for making baskets

momoy

datura or jimsonweed, "toloache" in Spanish; momoy tea, a drink made from momoy plant

Momoy

datura plant as Grandmother Moon, goddess who is protective and health giving

nunashish

a dangerous beast; an animal such as a rattlesnake or bear or a malevolent supernatural creature (of which there are a great many)

paqwot

the leader or head of a group of villages

pelepel

heron or egret; also a supernatural being (Ventureño)

pohoh

Pacific bonito tuna

poyok

fish that lives at the offshore rock at Shuku (Rincon Point) (Ventureño)

pulakak
woodpecker

se
no

Shimiliqsha
name of the village in the Sky World where the dead reside; also called the Land of the Dead

show
mixture of tobacco and ground shells that is chewed for strength or to kill pain

shup
earth, dirt, soil

Shup
Mother Earth as goddess

sihon (shikhon)
blue dicks plant (brodiaea): either the plant or bulb

talip
a sinew-backed recurved bow

taniw
child; little

taqtaq
quail

tata
uncle, often used for an older man who is not kin

tok
red milkweed; string made of milkweed (Ventureño)

tomol
a frameless canoe built of driftwood planks and caulked with tar

Woi!
an exclamation of disagreement

wokoch
an intruder (Ventureño)

woqo
> type of hard tar found near the beach and used as an adhesive (as in the tomol or basketry)

wot
> the head of a family (clan); a wealthy person; especially the leader of a village

yop
> adhesive mixture of pine pitch and woqo (hard tar) (Ventureño)

yowoyow
> one of the malevolent supernatural beings (Ventureño)

WORKS CONSULTED

I list here only works I consulted when writing *Mishopshno* in 1980–85. Manuscripts were located at the Santa Barbara Museum of Natural History. Since the time of writing there have been several worthwhile publications on Chumash ethnography. An outstanding one is Jan Timbrook's 2007 *Chumash Ethnobotany: Plant Knowledge among the Chumash People of Southern California*, Santa Barbara Museum of Natural History and Heyday Books.

Anderson, Eugene, Jr. 1978. *Revised, Annotated Bibliography of the Chumash and Their Predecessors*. Socorro, NM: Ballena Press.

Aginsky, Burt and Ethel. 1967. *Deep Valley.* New York: Stein and Day.

Applegate, Richard. 1974. "Chumash Placenames." *Journal of Calif. Anthropology* 1, no. 2: 187–205.

———.1975 "Chumash Narrative Folklore as Sociolinguistic Data." *Journal of Calif. Anthropology* 2, no. 2: 188–97.

———. 1975. "Datura Cult among the Chumash." *Journal of Calif. Anthropology* 2, no. 1: 7–17.

———. 1975. "Index of Chumash Placenames" with map. *San Luis Obispo County Archaeological Society Occasional Paper* 9:19–46.

———. 1978. *'Atishwin: The Dream Helper in South–Central California*. Ballena Press Anthropological Papers 13. Socorro, NM: Ballena Press.

———. n.d. "Notes for Chumash Speech Ethnography." manuscript.

Balls, Edward K. 1962. *Early Uses of California Plants.* Berkeley: University of California Press.

Bandelier, Adolph. 1971 (1890). *The Delight Makers.* NY: Harcourt Brace Jovanovich.

Bean, Lowell J. 1975. "Power and Its Applications." *Journal of Calif. Anthropology* 2, no. 1: 25–33.

Bean, Lowell, and Thomas Blackburn, eds. 1976. *Native Californians: A Theoretical Retrospective.* Ramona, CA: Ballena Press.

Bean, Lowell and Chester King, eds. 1974. *'Antap: California Indian Political and Economic Organization.* Ramona, CA: Ballena Press.

Beebe, Burdetta Faye, and James Ralph Johnson. 1965. *American Bears.* NY: D. McKay.

Beeler, Madison. n.d. (1980?). *Topics in Barbareño Chumash Grammar.* manuscript.

Blackburn, Thomas C. 1962–63. "A Manuscript Account of the Ventureño Chumash." *UCLA Archeological Survey Annual Reports,* 135–60.

————. 1975. *December's Child: A Book of Chumash Oral Narratives.* Berkeley: University of California Press.

————. 1977. "Biopsychological Aspects of Chumash Rock Art." *Journal of Calif. Anthropology* 4, no. 1: 88–94.

————, ed. 1977. *Flowers of the Wind: Papers on Ritual, Myth, and Symbolism in California and the Southwest. Socorro,* NM: Ballena Press.

Bolton, Herbert Eugene. 1916. *Spanish Expeditions in the Southwest, 1542–1706.* (Cabrillo and Viscaino). NY: Charles Scribner's Sons.

————. 1926. *Historical Memoirs of New California.* (Palou). Berkeley: University of California Press.

————. 1927. *Fray Juan Crespi, Missionary Explorer on the Pacific Coast.* Berkeley: University of California Press.

————. 1930. *Anza's California Expeditions,* vols. 1 and 4. Berkeley: University of California Press.

————. 1931. *Font's Complete Diary: A Chronicle of the Founding of San Francisco.* Berkeley: University of California Press.

Cook, D. I. 1940. "Indian Trails." *Santa Barbara Museum of Natural History Leaflet* 15:5–7.

Dawson, Lawrence, and James Deetz. 1964. *Chumash Indian Art.* Exhibition Catalogue. University of California, Santa Barbara. UCSB, Department of Anthropology. Noel Young.

de Angulo, Jaime. 1926. "Background of Religious Feeling in a Primitive Tribe." *American Anthropologist* 28, no. 2: 352–60.

————. 1974. *Don Bartolomeo.* Berkeley, CA: Turtle Island.

————. 1974. *The Lariat.* Berkeley, CA: Turtle Island.

Eliade, Mircea. 1964. *Shamanism: Archaic Technique of Ecstasy.* NY: Bollingen Foundation.

Fages, Pedro. 1937. *Historical, Political and Natural Description of California,* edited by H. I. Priestly. Berkeley: University of California Press.

Gayton, Anna. 1930. "Yokuts and Mono Chiefs and Shamans." *UC Publications in American Archeology and Ethnology* 24:361–420.

————. 1948. "Yokuts Ethnography." *UC Anthropological Records* 10, 2: 143–301.

Gayton, Anna, and Stanley Newman. 1940. "Yokuts and Western Mono Myths." *UC Anthropological Records* 5:1–110.

Geiger, Rev. Maynard, and Clement Meighan. 1976. *As the Padres Saw Them: California Indian Life and Customs as Reported by the Franciscan Missionaries, 1813–1815.* Santa Barbara Bicentennial Historical Series no. 1.

Goldschmidt, Walter. "Social Organization of Native California and Origin of Clans." *American Anthropologist* 50, no. 3: 444–56.

Grant, Campbell. 1965. *The Rock Paintings of the Chumash.* Berkeley: University of California Press.

Greenwood, Roberta. 1961. "Excavations at Goleta." *UCLA Archeological Survey Annual Reports* 1960.

———. 1969. "Coastal Chumash Village: Excavation of Shisholop, Ventura County." *Southern Calif. Academy of Sciences Memoir.*

Guggisberg, C. A. W. 1975. *Wild Cats of the World.* NY: Taplinger.

Harner, Michael. 1980. *The Way of the Shaman: A Guide to Power and Healing.* San Francisco: Harper and Row.

Harrington, John Peabody. 1928. "Exploration of the Burton Mound." *Bureau of American Ethnology Annual Report* 44:25–168. Washington, DC: Smithsonian Institution.

Heizer, Robert. 1960. "Notes on Excavations Made in Indian Burial Places in Carpinteria 1887 by H.C. Ford." *UC Archaeological Survey Report* no. 50. Berkeley.

———. 1978 *Handbook of North American Indians,* v. 8, California. Washington, DC: Smithsonian Institution Press.

Hoffman, Eleanor. 1981. *The Charmstone.* Santa Barbara, CA: McNally and Loftin.

Howorth, Peter. 1976. "The Voyage of the Helek." *Santa Barbara Magazine* 2, no. 4 (Winter): 17–21.

———. 1977. "Light into the Past: Condor Cave." *Santa Barbara Magazine.*

Hudson, Travis. "Wind Sycamore: Some J. P. Harrington Notes on a Ventureño Chumash Shrine." Ventura County Historical Society Quarterly 24, no. 1: 1–15.

———. 1975. "Photographic Anthology of Chumash People." *Pacific Coast Archaeological Society Quarterly* 11, no. 2: 1–12.

——. 1977. "Marine Archeology along the Southern California Coast." *San Diego Museum of Man Paper* no. 9, 2nd ed.

——. 1977. "Patterns of Chumash Names." *Journal of Calif. Anthropology* 4, no. 2: 259–72.

——. 1977. "Rebirth of the Sun: Kakunupmawa." *Santa Barbara Magazine* 3, no. 4: 20–21.

——. 1980. *Breath of the Sun: Life in Early California as Told by a Chumash Indian, Fernando Librado, to John. P. Harrington.* Banning, CA: Malki Museum Press.

Hudson, Travis, and Thomas C. Blackburn. 1978. "Integration of Myth and Ritual in South–Central California: The Northern Complex." *Journal of Calif. Anthropology* 5, no. 2: 225–50.

——. 1979. *Material Culture of the Chumash Interaction Sphere,* vol. 1, Food Procurement and Transportation. Ballena Press Anthropological Papers no. 25. Los Altos, CA: Ballena Press and SB Museum of Natural History.

——. 1983. *Material Culture of the Chumash Interaction Sphere,* vol. 2, Food Preparation and Shelter. Ballena Press Anthropological Papers no. 27. Los Altos, CA: Ballena Press and SB Museum of Natural History.

——. 1985. *Material Culture of the Chumash Interaction Sphere,* vol. 3, Clothing, Ornamentation, and Grooming. Ballena Press Anthropological Papers no. 28. Menlo Park, CA: Ballena Press and SB Museum of Natural History.

——. 1986. *Material Culture of the Chumash Interaction Sphere,* vol. 4, Ceremonial Paraphenalia, Games, and Amusements. Ballena Press Anthropological Papers no. 30. Menlo Park, CA: Ballena Press and SB Museum of Natural History.

——. 1986. *Material Culture of the Chumash Interaction Sphere,* vol. 5, Manufacturing Process, Metrology, and Trade. Ballena Press Anthropological Papers no. 31. Menlo Park, CA: Ballena Press and SB Museum of Natural History.

Hudson, Travis, Thomas Blackburn, Rosario Curletti, Janice Timbrook, eds. 1977. *The Eye of the Flute. (Fernando Librado).* Santa Barbara Museum of Natural History.

Hudson, Travis, and Janice Timbrook. 1980. "Chumash Indian Games." *Santa Barbara Museum of Natural History.*

Hudson, Travis, Janice Timbrook, and Melissa Rempe. 1978. *Tomol: Chumash Watercraft as Described in the Ethnographic Notes of John P. Harrington (Fernando Librado).* Ballena Press Anthropological Papers no. 9.

Hudson, Dee Travis, and Ernest Underhay. 1978. *Crystals in the Sky: An Intellectual Odyssey Involving Chumash Astronomy,* Cosmology, and Rock Art. Ballena Press Anthropological Papers no. 10.

King, Chester. 1975. "Names and Locations of Historic Chumash Villages." (with map). *Journal of Calif. Anthropology* 2, no. 2: 171–79.

Kroeber, Alfred. 1904. "Languages of the Coast of California South of San Francisco." *UC Publications in American Anthropology and Ethnology,* 29–80.

Laird, Carobeth. 1975. *Encounter with an Angry God: Recollections of My Life with John Peabody Harrington.* Banning, CA: Malki Museum Press.

Landberg, Leif. 1965. *Chumash Indians of Southern California.* Highland Park, CA: Southwest Museum.

————. 1975. "Fishing Effort in the Aboriginal Fisheries of the Santa Barbara Region: An Ethnohistoric Appraisal," in *Maritime Adaptation of the Pacific,* ed. Richard W. Casteel and Jean–Claude Passeron, 145–69. The Hague: De Gruyter.

Eastwood, Alice, ed. 1924. "Archibald Menzies' Journal of the Vancouver Expedition Extracts Covering the Visit to California." *Quarterly of the California Historical Society* 2.

Minton, Sherman, and Madge R. Minton. 1969. *Venomous Reptiles.* NY: Scribner.

Mohr, Albert, and L. L. Sample. 1955. "The Religious Importance of the Swordfish in the Santa Barbara Area." *Southwest Museum Masterkey* 29, no. 2: 62–68.

O'Dell, Scott. 1960. *Island of the Blue Dolphins.* Boston: Houghton Mifflin.

———. 1970. *Sing Down the Moon.* Boston: Houghton Mifflin.

Olson, Ronald. 1930. "Chumash Prehistory." *UC Publications in American Archaeology and Ethnology* 28: 1–21.

Orr, Phil. 1943. "Archeology of Mescaltitlan Island and Customs of the Canaliño." *Santa Barbara Museum of Natural History Occasional Paper* 5.

———. 1952. "Review of Santa Barbara Channel Archeology." *Southwestern Journal of Anthropology* 8: 211–26.

Patterson, Charles. 1978. "An Opportunity in the Channel Islands." *Fremontia* 6, no. 1: 3–5.

Radin, Paul. 1963. *The Autobiography of a Winnebago Indian.* NY: Dover.

Robinson, Alfred. 1848. *Life in California and Chinigchinich* (Boscana). NY: Wiley and Putnam.

Rogers. David Banks. 1929. *Prehistoric Man of the Santa Barbara Coast.* Santa Barbara Museum of Natural History.

Schumacher, Paul. 1878. "Method of Manufacture of Several Articles by the Former Indians of Southern California." *Peabody Museum of Archaeology and Ethnology, 11tn Annual Report.* Cambridge, MA.

Simpson, L. B. 1961. *Journal of Jose Longinos Martinez.* Santa Barbara Historical Society.

Smith, Clifton. 1976. *Flora of the Santa Barbara Region.* Santa Barbara Museum of Natural History.

Stickel, E. Gary. 1967–68. "Status Differentiation at the Rincon Site." *UCLA Archeological Survey Annual Reports.*

Sweet, Muriel. 1976. *Common Edible and Useful Plants of the West.* Healdsburg, CA: Naturegraph.

Timbrook, Jan, John R. Johnson, David D. Earle. 1982. "Vegetation Burning by the Chumash." *Journal of Calif. Anthropology* 4, no. 2: 163–86.

Viemeister, Peter. 1972. *The Lightning Book.* Cambridge: MIT.

Walker, Phillip, and Hudson, Dee Travis. n.d. *Chumash Healing.* manuscript.

Whistler, Kenneth. n.d. *Interim Barbareño Chumash Dictionary.* manuscript.

Woodward, Arthur. 1934. "An Early Account of the Chumash [Daniel Hill]." *Southwest Museum Masterkey* 8: 119–23.

———. 1959. *Sea Diary of Fr. Juan Vizcaino to Alta California, 1769.* Los Angeles: Glen Dawson.

For Katy, who has read all of this and shares so much in the pleasure of working with it. Good Luck on your book! Travis

THE AUTHOR

Mishopshno/Carpinteria tar mounds
Photo credit: A. Friend, 1985

Katy Meigs is a native of Carpinteria, California. She studied English and history at Stanford University and UCLA. For several years she was the proprietor of Mishopshnow Books in Carpinteria and later worked as a writer and editor for the *Santa Barbara Independent*. Currently, she is a social science editor for academic presses and writes and lives in Ojai, California. *Mishopshno*, completed in 1985, is her first novel.

19845310R00234

Made in the USA
Charleston, SC
14 June 2013